GW00456004

Before

"Bring your torch. It's a dirty night."

It was advice, given to Howie Dearlove in the last eighteen minutes of his life, he would come to regret having taken.

The human mind holds fast to its surroundings when death is near. Clings to quick snatches of experience as a drowning man clings to wood. *The wind whipping about him, rain sheeting across the tarmac and cutting into his skin, the father holding his dead baby son hard against his cheek, the half-naked blonde woman screaming at the moon, the boy spitting at his feet with a look in his eyes that meant more than murder.* The tangled chaos of these moments raced and repeated across Howie Dearlove's brain as if played and replayed at double speed.

'I'll bring my torch. Mind if I use it to smash your clumsy face in?'

He'd been frantically copying numbers from a spreadsheet on the Company's computer onto the underside of a beermat, his markings barely holding shape, the ink spreading like oil through the mat's rough fibrous underside when fellow Company security guard, Alan Watson, snatched back the cloudy wet tarpaulin that separated the loading bay office from the outside world to peer in at him with a shady stare.

1

Five minutes on and they were battling the wind, Company issued oilskins clutched tightly under their chins, trudging their way, torches in hand, across the loading bay's bumpy blacktop towards the spot where the three great lorries were sounding their reverse alarms and backing into place.

The first lorry had opened with atypical routine, revealing nothing but a dense rectangle of black to face them in the night. Watson lifted the same industrial hook he had used to heave open the lorry's sliding back doors and bashed it against the inner walls. The cargo emerged cautiously from between the crates, as if the reverberating clang of the hook's metal was some impossible to ignore dinner bell. They revealed themselves in the murky light and clambered down on weakened legs, falling into the arms of relatives in the waiting crowd where they would be gathered up like luggage, carried to cars to cross the final leg of their hellish journey into a stranger's cruel world.

The opening of the second lorry carried with it a sense of the horror that was to come. The cargo poured from it as soon as the doors were released like an unstoppable wall of water, wailing, sobbing, vomiting violently and collapsing as the damp air hit their parched throats.

"You people look alive in there!"

It was Watson bashing that obscene metal hook against the third lorry's dense walls. But the only answer returned to him from its abyss-like black mouth was silence.

"Move" Howie willed them in the quiet of his mind. "*Move*".

With a strengthless arm he lifted his torch to the side of Watson's head and saw, carved into the inner metal door, a succession of claw marks and pummelled fist indentations as dreadful and inevitable as the scratched walls of Auschwitz.

2

The realisation burst open in Howie's heart like a bloom of black roses.

Watson, was first to react; doubling over, reeling against the thick, gassy gagging smell of high-speed decay with a revolted groan "Oh my fucking Christ!"

It was enough to sweep panic through the crowd like a fever.

They had been waiting as patiently as relatives at an airport arrivals lounge. Now they surged forward in a stampeding mass to peer in at the carnage of fathers, sons, daughters, wives, brothers, friends; all of whom had met a wretched suffocating end. They lay together; a tangled mass of cadavers. Amid the twist of black shadows, arms emerged, frozen by death's permanence, still clawing for escape, or clutching at ruined throats, nails digging savagely into their own skin or that of others. Blind dead eyes bulged madly. Pale skin repainted crimson by the network of blood vessels, distended and erupted under its surface.

"Dearlove! Dearlove!!"

Over the roar of bedlam Howie could faintly hear his co-worker screaming his name. As if he could do anything more than join at his side and await the same abysmal fate. Fate in the shape of the once calm crowd rapidly turned to a lynching mob, closing in on the two beleaguered men, their Company issued uniforms, their places within the organisation, their mere presence there that night, making them instantly guilty, responsible, receptacles for the swelling tide of hate.

Howie shut his eyes hard and turned away as they closed in, pressing one side of his face deeply into the lorry's cold metal door; a man groping back for his god.

Lightening split the sky to glass and the storm crashed through the night's ceiling, exploding above them like a bomb, hurling rain and thunder down onto the hate torn crowd below. The crowd below, where the final shards of sanity also split, and one man rained murder down upon another.

'I'm sorry Luke.'

He slipped away.

PART ONE

'What if I'm far from home?'

'Brother I will hear you call.'

Avicii

One

One Year Later

Luke Dearlove squinted against the light and struggled to see up to the precipice of the chalky ragged bluff. At its ridge stood the shell of a half completed, long abandoned luxury housing complex, looking more like a crumbled ancient ruin, rotted with decay, than a multi-million pound project, now discarded and ignored. Huge wreaths of protective plastic, once wrapped around the building's metal skeleton had torn loose with time and floated in the high wind like the caught hems of ghosts that passed through its gaping firmaments.

And down in the world below the people of Skidaway Island seemed to be fleeing the structure as though it were an angry god. A volcano, waking and readying to burst. At the bluff's feet they gathered their belongings, grouped their families and packed out the ferry, leaving behind the only lives they'd ever known.

Luke knew these nameless strangers. He'd met them on other continents, countless countries around the world. The types who never travelled more than fifteen miles away from their own homes. They for whom progress was a hindrance, expansion; an interference to life's routine. Their roots belonged in farmhouses built two or three hundred years ago by trampling mud and straw, whittle and daub, ragged flint. They would have gladly stuck to televisions with three channels, phones that were anchored by cables and wires to houses, transport via horse and cart. And yet in their droves they lined up to leave their land for places where the world moved fast and forgave no one.

The fading posters of all that the housing complex could have been still adorned the brick walls and fences of the harbour. A perfect nuclear family standing outside an illustrated version of a castle in gleaming white, as gleaming white as the teeth of the widely smiling blonde haired mother waving joyously in the foreground; in all but one of the posters.

The placard that faced the line of passengers queuing up for the ferry had been desecrated long ago. Her right front tooth coloured over black to emulate a gaping hole and a cartoon bubble drawn from her mouth encapsulated with the words 'Bye Bitches!' making her huge smile and emphatic wave more of a mocking insult, adding the final touch of degradation to the original islanders as they trudged their one way journeys up the ferry's ramp.

Click.

It was strange – the things that fished the embedded deep-hidden memories that remained lodged within the fleshy folds of a soldier's mind back above surface.

For former Combat Army Medic, Lance Corporal Luke Dearlove, it was the simple click and snap of a shutter within the aged mechanisms of an old Polaroid camera as the twelve-year-old boy with the darkest of eyes, eyes darker than any twelve-year-old's should ever live to be, stepped up behind him, uninvited and unannounced to take his picture.

The memory unraveled like a filament. Not the recalls of bullets and death but of a boy, probably only a year or two younger than the one who had taken his picture, running along behind the back of their

7

Warthog. He and fifteen other boys had taken to chasing their vehicle every time they crossed that stretch of sand where desert gave way to civilization six miles northwest of Lashkar Gah along the route to Camp Shorabak. He and his squad had theorized that soldiers from a previous tour had thrown sweets and soda out to the boys on similar crossings, their concept enforced by the boys' continuous shouts and jeers ranging from 'WHATTSUP MISTER CHOCOLATE' to 'FUCK YOU SHADDUP'. One afternoon Private Harvey Jackson, while on top-cover, had decided to wait till the kids were racing after them, right behind the Warthog, then signaled for the driver to slam on the breaks. It was the sound of the boy's face hitting metal, his bottom jaw broken apart that came back to Luke then, the rip and crunch of tearing flesh and splitting bone, the blood, the sand, the befuddled look in his eyes, just before he crossed them to try to stare down at the two halves of his jaw, opening up like a stag beetle's front feelers and allowing his tongue to flop out like a bloodhound's.

Luke's brothers, Howie and Tyler, both laughed when he'd told them about it. Apparently, they found Private Jackson as funny as the other soldiers on the Warthog had that day. They would have found him even funnier if they'd been back on the same route with him for the next three months where he progressed to throwing bottles of piss out to the boys, and, in time, homemade brownies, 'home made' in the truest of senses. "Sorry kid," Tyler, his oldest brother, had said, trying to stifle a smirk, "I would have laughed too." Quickly adding when he sensed Luke's scorn. "That being said, what a dick".

"What a hilarious dick." Luke had agreed, making a mental note never to share the memories of his war with Tyler again. . . . Postcards from Afghanistan. Just one from his collective set.

From the assortment of memories war had stamped across his brain, there was always one monstrosity to top the last. They had all heard stories about those they were there to protect having their eyes plucked out while their families were tortured in front of them, the idea being that the last thing you saw was your wife and children being raped with white hot pokers so that singular image would be ingrained on your memory forever.

But damn if they didn't make the best chicken, pita and chickpea suppers.

"I give you good price. Five pounds. You pay me now." It was the boy again, thrusting the developing Polaroid picture into Luke's hand and demanding a fair wage for the service.

Luke wondered if the boy had noticed his flinch at the sound of the shutter clicking. Judging by the small smile sat on those roughly chapped darkly purple lips he guessed that he had. "You pay me now!" the boy repeated his demands in an English heavily pregnant with the accent of his Albanian homeland.

"Get out of here you filthy rodent!" They were Luke's thoughts but not his words. He looked to his right to see one of the only English traders still clinging to the ways of his forefathers; selling postcards, buckets and spades, inflatable rafts and seashells in a shop fronting the harbour, the remainder of the stores either standing empty or having been replaced by the foods and trades of east European and north African ethnicity.

The trader was bellowing at two scruffily dressed boys wearing rubber animal masks that encased their entire heads, a lamb and a fox, grabbing items from his shop front. The boys scampered, seizing bigger prizes as they bolted passed the line of islanders queuing up to board the ferry. They each grabbed a suitcase and fled.

"Steve, they're taking everything!" It was the wife of the last family in the queue for the ferry, her scream strangled with despair.

Steve, the husband, and a few neighbouring passengers, grabbed the fox boy's purloined case, their efforts evolving into a one-sided tug of war that the men easily won, prizing the case out of the boy's meager grip, sending him to fall clumsily to his backside where one of the men slapped him heavily round the face. Several men of Eastern European extraction immediately forced their way in front of the boy, defying the islanders to swipe at them, as the fox and the lamb made their escape.

The thieves passed Luke. He grabbed the lamb boy with one hand, twisting his forearm until he dropped the bag and wailed his lament. Luke let go his hold and he tumbled to the ground, rubbing his arm, his mask falling from place and revealing a face hot and stained with tears.

Tin-Tin, Luke's young photographer, and the fox boy scooped him up. The fox boy howling insults from behind his mask "Pink-arse! Cracker barrel! Fish belly!" Luke stared at them blankly as they disappeared into the crowd. He picked up the suitcase and handed it to the man who had made his way towards him. The man nodded quick thanks, too wound up with angst to extend any meaningful gratitude, he took the suitcase and marched angrily back towards his wife. He stopped suddenly, turned and came back to Luke, leaning in, speaking quietly. "There's an infestation on this island. A cancer here. Stay at your own risk."

The man stepped away and returned to his sobbing wife, leaving Luke to come face to face with a tall man in a maroon suit flanked by two younger men wearing camouflage clothing and carrying hunting gear, watching him intently from an opened top jeep.

Finally, the tall man raised his head and threw a question in Luke's direction. "You on your own here son?"

Luke looked down at the Polaroid picture the boy had thrust into his hand, its square of white now developed into an image of him standing alone on Skidaway's shores. Luke opened his jacket. Within his inner pocket was a brown envelope, stuffed with beermats, napkins and various other folded or crumpled papers. Luke tucked the Polaroid picture inside to join them.

"For now." He answered and turned to walk towards a nearby café with a car rental sign in the window. He felt their suspicious stares follow his every step, watching him like snakes, snakes watching a bird, a silly little bird that didn't know the danger it was in. The tall man pulled out a mobile phone to make an urgent call.

Luke smiled.

It was beginning.

Two

The wolf baby sat in the first-floor window above the café, languidly fanning herself with that month's copy of the Company's news brochure and playing with a strand of her long blond hair while watching the little slice of beautiful who'd just landed on Skidaway's shores.

He'd already created quite the fuss. Defying Tin-Tin and his grotty little pals. Playing the hero for the self-pitying pink-arses. And now catching the attention of Skidaway hierarchy; Mason Hare and his two gormless sons. Mason Hare, in the same gaudy maroon suit he wore with peacock-esque pride, seemingly unaware of the fact it made him look like he'd just been clothes shopping on Idiot Street. Hare had quickly made an '*oh so important*' call on his mobile as the young man had turned away and begun walking towards her café, snapping his fingers and pointing at his youngest son in a demand for him to shut up while he spoke. Now, with the call complete, the three of them were swaying in unison like a trio of cobras, lifting their heads above the crowd as snakes would above grass, keeping wary eyes on their prey.

'*I know you.*' The thought tugged at the back of her mind as the young man weaved towards her through the crowd in the harbour below and his features became more easily examinable.

One of her strong smooth legs was bent up in the window frame in front of her, the other lolled casually outside for the entire world to see. *Look but don't touch you worms!* She kicked her stilettoed heel against their sign, SKANDERBERG CAFÉ, in a subconscious attempt to attract his attention. Eva Skanderberg attracted all men's attention, and most women's, and she did not like being ignored, especially not by someone as delectable as this.

In truth The Skanderberg Café was more than a café; it was a coffee shop, bar, car rental, pawn shop, unofficial money lender, and, when the rest of the island slept, drug emporium for the migrant community, and any of the island's other denizens who liked their nightlife on the dangerous side of darkness.

The Skanderberg Café sign was crudely nailed over the sign for the fish and chip shop which had preceded it; the oh so wittily named, *The Codfather,* by the family who had run it for ten years. Clearly, they'd done their best to keep up with the tradition of the neighbouring shops along that row with plays on names they'd assumed to be somewhere in the realms of clever and charming. She never could get her head round British humour, especially in the form of their silly puns. The Codfather, for instance, had been set among the various establishments; *Curl Up and Dye*, the hair dressing salon, *Sellfridges*, suppliers of refrigerators and kitchen appliances, the *Woofs-a-Daisy*, pet groomers, *Back to the Fuchsia*, the florist, *Spruce Springsteen,* the cleaners and the low brow removals company; *Jean Claude Van Man . . . oh you guys*.

They'd been the first, *but by no means the last,* of the drifters to have had one of the harbour fronted establishments practically given to them as a gift. The middle-aged couple that had run the Codfather were a meek and mild pair. Their breath, seemingly unbeknown to them, had become so permanently infused with the smell of plaice, rock, haddock and crab that you had to lean back from the waist when speaking to them. But they were as polite and dignified as gentry when Mason Hare and his sons had come to evict them. So much so that even her normally robust and hard-boiled cousin Luan had been soft as a kitten with them, helping them out with their belongings until it formed a tower of cardboard boxes on the cobbled street.

Mrs Codfather had handed the key over to Mason Hare with a sad smile and held back tears long enough to politely ask Luan what he and his family were going to call their new coffee shop when it opened, and whether they would keep up the tradition and name it with a wordplay witticism.

"Yeah," Eva had answered for him, sloping in the doorway. "We're calling it Fuckoffee." She looked at them without the trace of a smile and bit deeply into a dark red apple.

With that Mrs Codfather's face collapsed in tears and Mr Codfather had no choice but to drag his eyes from Eva's endless legs and help his wife back home where they would pack their things and leave the island the next morning.

She wanted to whistle as the young man got closer. The sight of her was normally enough for a man to fix his eyes upon her as if glued. But this little minx kept his affixed straight ahead, focusing on the café door as he strode towards it.

What mission you here on gorgeous?

She thought about repeating one of the obscene catcalls the labourers had thrown her way when the housing complex was still under construction, looking down lasciviously from the lofty heights of scaffolding as she passed. Unfazed by them, she'd relished in the power, treating them to an overwhelming eyeful of arse cleavage courtesy of her low-slung shorts as she strolled on by.

She back kicked the sign again, harder this time, small crumbs of plaster breaking free from behind the sign and raining down in a little mini cement waterfall, but still it wasn't enough to snatch his stare. For a moment she thought of raising her arms, tapping her long fingernails on the upper part of the window frame. If the sight of her plentiful breasts gliding upwards like two large round moons wasn't enough to snare his attention, then the thick dark tufts of body hair growing wildly from her armpits would be. They'd shocked many a man of Skidaway into stiff silence. The first, a lithe and darkly tanned outdoorsy type who unpacked crates at the port, until that job went to Dalmat Xhoi who'd come over on a lorry the same night as her, but not her lorry, *not her womb and tomb*.

He'd gawped at her with such open-mouthed shock and wonder that for a second, she thought it was the first time he'd seen a pair. Soon enough she realised it was her curly brushes of pit hair making him gawp like a bug-eyed fish out of water. "Fuck me!" he'd exclaimed as he peered closer at them. She pushed him backwards onto her bed and did so.

The talk of her unshaved body made her something of a legend on the island from there on in. She liked that. What she didn't like was the island's new arrival making it all the way inside the Skanderberg Café without noticing the wolf baby up on the first-floor window above, watching him intently and calmly smacking her chops.

Where the fuck do I know you from beautiful?

Then it came to her, like a suddenly escaping pocket of trapped gas. She flipped open the Company's newsletter to its centre spread. His face was there, handsome and refined, wearing full military dress and staring unemotionally into the camera.

Above him a headline in block capitals proclaimed. WAR HERO TO BE HONOURED IN THIS YEAR'S 'CHAMPIONS OF BRITAIN' AWARDS. She snapped the brochure shut with a sense of victory.

Now something else in the harbour below would take her attention. Jed Burke, the sly old fox, he never stepped out into the light unless life, *or death*, would beckon it. Yet here he now was, out among the minions. Suddenly it made sense. It was Jed Burke, who Mason, his brother-in-law, had called with a message of such urgency and importance that the bat had left the cave, the lion his den, the sly old fox his hole. And now he and the Hares were making their way through the jostling crowd towards the café.

She slid off the window frame. This was something she needed to see.

"Pyesni atë se sa njerëz është vrarë. Pyesni atë se sa njerëz është vrarë. Pyesni atë se sa njerëz është vrarë."

The six-year-old boy in the plastic cowboy outfit rocked back and forth on his heels repeating the same nagging demand to cousins Tariq Skanderberg and Luan Palaciki. Clearly gun obsessed, the boy had been pointing a silver plastic pistol at various objects and people around the café, shooting at them and emanating irritating little 'pow' noises. A large bunch of brightly coloured balloons were tied to the same board which sat on the café's counter inscribed with rudimentary and misspelt English 'YOU RENT CAR – TOO I.D.s – FIFY POUND DEPOSITS'. The balloons had attracted the boy, easy targets, and more compliant than the people he'd been mock shooting at, they swayed and bobbed for him as if struck. But the boy's attention soon turned to Luke. The whole café's attention had turned to him in fact; such was the rarity of white skinned English strangers on the island. The patrons' eyes followed his every move as if attached to him by invisible threads; all the while they nodded and glanced, whispering to each other about him in their native tongues.

It was when the boy had got wind of Luke's military background that his inquisition had begun. Luke had handed over the obligatory two I.D.s to Tariq. Luan, sweating and grease stained from a recent oil change to one of the cars, had leant over his cousin's shoulder and together their scrutiny had gone from Luke to the I.D.s and back to Luke, as wary and suspicious as passport controllers of a country operating under an oppressive regime studying the entry papers of an investigative journalist.

They kept their discussion about Luke to clandestine Albanian. Luan, nodding at Luke's first I.D.; "Ai është një njeri i kompanisë. (He's a Company man.)"

Tariq, switching to the second; "Ai është një ushtar (He's a soldier).

Luan ran a greasy finger under the expiration date of Luke Military I.D. "Ai ishte një ushtar, që është skaduar. (He was a soldier, that's expired.)"

With that the boy's excitement picked up and he began his repetitive jabbering demand. Luke spoke no Albanian but had a strong idea what it translated to. It was also when the blond woman emerged from the back stairs of the café's 'staff only' area.

Tariq handed Luke's rental agreement form and his I.D.s to her. She sauntered over to an outdated photocopier in skyscraper high heels, the slide of light from the copier illuminating her shape. Luke found himself staring.

Noticing the stranger's eyes skating over his sister's body, Tariq pierced his pen nib into one of the balloons beside Luke. Luke jumped at the resulting explosion and the eyes of the café crashed in on him again, studying his reaction.

Eva came back from the photocopier, put the copies and originals down onto the counter and slid into Tariq's lap, slinging one arm around his neck. Tariq swayed his sister lightly back and forth on his knee, she smiled a small sultry smile and pressed her nearest breast into his chest.

The boy turned his plastic gun up to Luke now and began his mock battle fire and the accompanying 'pow' noises, punctuating his actions with the same insisting plea to Tariq. "Pyesni atë se sa njerëz është vrarë."

Finally, Tariq translated, nodding at the military I.D. as he slid it and the Company I.D. back to Luke. "The boy's asking how many people you've killed."

Luke let out a thin sigh. "How long on the car?"

Tariq looked back at Luan who shrugged and mumbled. "Pesë."

"Five minutes." Tariq translated.

"You have three." Luke responded coldly.

Luan, who needed no translation, glared indignantly at Luke, threw his oil-stained rag down on the counter, grabbed a set of keys from a hook on the wall and walked out to the back.

By the time Luke turned away from the counter the four men were waiting for him. Mason Hare in his maroon suit. Calum and Damien Hare, hovering at their father's side, feral grins stretched over their toothy mouths. And the fourth man. The one that commanded the most attention. This man was Jed Burke.

He was a rough-edged man of powerful physique, deep voice and grave manner, with sun cracked skin and weather ruined hands. The uncompromising stare from his cold eyes was heavy enough to punch through another man's guts, sharp enough to sever an artery. The kind of man who left the taste of himself in one's mouth, hours after he'd left the room.

All four had entered the café unnoticed. Luke wondered how they'd managed it. His training wasn't that far behind him, his skills not that rusty. He still knew how to sense the smallest of movements, danger coming from any direction. Maybe it was the blond woman consuming his attention as few things ever did who brought about the momentary weakness.

They had grouped into a formation around him. He could have barged through them quite easily. Not that there should be any need to. There was no crime in him coming to their island. Any more than there was any crime in four men coming into a café to form a loose semicircle that blocked your exit path. But Luke knew, in the turn of his guts he knew, they were here for a reason. They were here for him.

It was Jed Burke who spoke first, sitting at one of the café's tables and staring at its dirty plastic surface so intently Luke glanced at it to see if he was reading something. A bucket of dead rabbits sat on the floor beside his boots, boots caked with thick mud. One of the rabbits within the jumble appeared to be clinging to life and twitching feebly, despite its cut throat, a throng of flies danced around them, diving for an easy meal. Dried blood and earth was incrusted under Jed's nails and he scraped at it continuously with a gut hook knife, but made no real progression towards getting them clean. His hunting cap was pulled down so low that his eyes were set in shadow, and when he turned them towards Luke they were nothing but tiny robotic dots of light, making them seem like eyes that weren't living, weren't real.

"A man could get killed, groping around a place he don't know." Jed Burke's voice was as thick with dirt as the ridge between his skin and fingernails.

"I guess that's the danger." Luke answered calmly, as if nothing about the man's imposing presence bothered him at all.

Mason Hare chipped in, more ebullient and direct than his counterpart. He straightened his spotted tie and smoothed down the lapels of his maroon suit as he spoke. "No more cheap deals on land, if that's what you said you were doing here."

Luke, "I didn't since you ask."

Damien, the oldest of the Hare boys butted in. "We had a bunch of out of towners here two years ago thinking they could build that." He pointed with his eyes to a copy of the Company's poster of the Housing Complex pinned up on the café's wall. From the many tiny holes in the blond mother's skin, like a smattering of acne scars, it was evident the poster was used many times as an impromptu dartboard. "Left us with that." He nodded his head back to the half-finished rusting skeletal version of the build the Company had started and abandoned, just visible through the café's steamy windows.

"And a bunch of other ugly eyesores!" Calum, the youngest and most inarticulate of the Burke-Hare family added, smiling at his own wit, and nodding towards a group from the migrant community sitting nearby.

Two men from the group got angrily up, coffee cups spinning on the table with the sudden movement, they puffed their chests and retorted heatedly in Albanian, moved to confront Calum, their wives and girlfriends grabbing their arms and pulling them back.

Calum offered them a smug smile which still carried traces of his breakfast, strings of bacon fat stuck out obscenely from the gaps between his teeth; teeth, which were hopelessly crooked and jutting, like a row of dried corn.

Jed scraped the gut hook knife round the tender skin surrounding the half-moon of his thumbnail. "Could have saved themselves some trouble if they'd asked us before diggin'. We could o' told them the ground here's rotten." He stopped his barbaric manicure and looked up at Luke. "You want to save yourself some trouble boy?"

The café's front doors rattled open and Luan entered, holding a key on his index finger towards Luke.

Luke straightened up, ready to leave. He nodded down at Jed. "Sometimes you just gotta let a man dig."

Jed shoved the bucket of rabbits out in front of him and put his foot defiantly up on the rim, cutting off Luke's path and trapping him on the spot. The cloud of flies turned in crazy squares in the air till they caught scent of the rabbits again and moved over to them in one buzzing black cloud.

"What do you want here?" Calum called out in the in whiniest of voices.

It seemed not only the Burkes and Hares, but also Tariq and Eva Skanderberg, their cousin Luan and all the remaining patrons of the café wanted an answer to this question for a low whispering hush fell about the place and all eyes anchored in aggressively on Luke, awaiting his response.

Luke stood quietly in his imprisoned spot.

Mason cleared his throat, glaring at his youngest boy before turning to Luke. "*What my son means is*, can we help you with something?"

Luke surveyed the many eyes that peered at him like wildlife in woodland at night. He came back to Jed's dead eyes. Dead eyes in the most expressionless of faces. He decided to give them what they wanted and take Mason up on his offer.

"Can you tell me where Howie Dearlove is?"

What was a low whispering hush immediately became a sharp cold silence, as if someone had pressed a TV's remote control's mute button on the place.

Luke waited within the silence and only spoke when, as expected, slow seconds passed, and no answer came. "Then you can't help me." He stepped over Jed's leg and headed towards Luan at the door.

He reached for the key on Luan's fleshy index finger. Luan snatched it back from his grip in mid-air and loomed above him, all six feet seven inches of machine-like muscle daunting and impenetrable as a reinforced wall.

Finally, Luan spoke, keeping cold eyes on Luke. "Jini të huaj të kujdesshëm në këto brigje. Demoni pret në qoshet e errëta."

Eva's voice called out from behind the counter. "A little saying from our homeland sir." Luke turned to look at her and her mesmerizingly fierce beauty. "Be careful stranger on these shores." she translated "The demon waits in dark corners."

Tariq began swaying her on his lap again as the silent patrons slowly restarted their chatter. She gave Luke the strangest and most indecipherable of looks, then smiled, adding. "That one's for free."

As Luke left and the door rattled shut behind him she got up from Tariq's lap and the strange smile fell from her face leaving behind the cold hard stare of a murderess.

Three

Luke Dearlove was no stranger to death. He knew its shocking suddenness, its permanence, its irreversibility, its sights and sounds, its slices and cuts.

And he knew its smell.

With the windows of his rental car open, that most recognizable of odours surrounded him now. The whole of Skidaway Island stank of it.

It was as though a giant rat, the size of an elephant, had lumbered into some looming hiding hole and laid down and died; its demise leaving the scent of festering decay to seep through the granite rock of mountains, the tangled limbs of dense woodlands, the soup-thick waters of swamps. To permeate an entire island with the stench of ruin.

Luke turned the rental car onto the rutted rock-strewn road that carved a pathway of hairpin turns through the marshes. The entire island could be circumnavigated in two hours, around the encircling coastal road; serene and picturesque on the south side where waters of lagoon-like blue encircled the shores, fierce and unforgiving on the north; all hard-edged savagery, blind corners and deadly falls where the cliffs suddenly gave way to nothingness, nothingness that was, until you hit the razor-edged rocks and cruel waters of a cold sea two hundred feet below.

Taking the road through the marshes, which twisted like intestines through the island's midst, would shave his journey time in half. It wasn't pretty, in fact the scenery was grim. But picture postcards and charming sights were not the reason he had come. He had come to face whatever truth the island presented to him, and he knew before he'd arrived that that was no doubt going to be ugly.

He had two options to try. Two thin hopes. He could have gone straight to the fisherman's shack on the north side shores. It was more accessible, also more exposed.

So instead he'd opted for the lockups Howie had mentioned in passing the last Christmas he'd been home. They, along with a never completed hotel, penny dreadful style museum amusements and small restaurant, were the discarded legacy of a rich nineteenth century industrialist. Legend had it he had been first attracted to Skidaway's spectacular shores, then, seemingly seduced by her dark heart. He'd opted to build an empire there in her slimy midst on the other side of the swamps at the spot where the rocks that began the great white bluff met the waters of Lake Woebegone. But he, like the Company over a hundred years later, would be thwarted, by nature, or by the island's mystical intent, and ultimately forced to abandon what he had begun.

As Luke stepped out of the rental car and looked up at the Victorian brick buildings he knew he'd been right to try this place first.

Above the buildings the sky was pregnant with gloom, seemingly permanent sagging rainclouds hung directly overhead as though they'd taken up residence, waiting, watching. A heap of rotting trees, branches and deadwood had been blown over the rocks' edges in some long ago storm and created a daunting maze which required guts as much as navigational skills if you really wanted to try for a pathway and gain entry.

If Howie had hidden his secrets anywhere, it would have been here.

Luke shut the rental car door but didn't bother locking it. No need. There was no other soul but himself in this baleful place. He checked that the thick brown envelope was safe inside his inner jacket pocket and began traversing the dead branches.

One of the problems with having suffered a considerable psychological injury was that, even when '*cured*' its symptoms remained, intermittently manifesting, occasionally revealing themselves, but always lurking along the corridors of a man's interiors, forever '*there*'. A wounded animal that simply will not die.

Another major problem being that the mind could no longer trust everything the eyes presented to it.

Luke had no need to mistrust what his eyes had shown his mind within the lockup so far, even with the dubious lighting; quickly flickering shafts from a naked bulb on a worn and faulty overhanging cable, accompanied by the glow from his mobile phone. Together they set the building's interior in an ethereal pulsating silver-blue.

Once through the maze of deadwood he'd only been able to push the iron doors to the building open a small gap. The two stone he'd lost since leaving the army came in handy for once and he was able to squeeze through, even if he did carve up his back on its rough steel edges in the process.

Once inside, he'd headed straight to the small kitchenette; the cups, the kettle, the paper towel dispenser and the toaster were modern, probably all less than three years old, even if they were covered in a sheath of cobwebs and dust so thick Luke could peel it back in one entwined piece like a lace tablecloth with tattered fraying edges.

No matter how hungry he may have been for toast, how in need of a caffeine injection, it was the paper towel dispenser he made the avid beeline for, pulling off a sheet and examining it. He then emptied the contents of the brown envelope from within his jacket onto the counter. Those contents were made up of various other envelopes of smaller sizes, menus, bus tickets, receipts, several beermats and one paper towel; along with the most recent addition; the Polaroid photograph 'Tin-Tin' the boy with the dark eyes, the purple lips and the thick greasy black hair had taken of him at the harbour. Each of these items, other than the picture, contained hand scribbled notes and several lists of numbers. Luke placed the newly acquired paper towel and the one from his envelope buff up against each other in the flickering light. The perforated edge of the new towel was made of large round curves, bulging at one side, like a row of waves in a child's crayon drawing. The paper towel from his envelope, with Howie's handwriting all over it, by contrast, displayed an edging of sharp triangles which were prominent, like a row of shark's teeth. Luke ran a finger across them, just to be sure he could trust what his eyes were showing his mind.

As he returned the paper towel and other transcripts to the envelope, re-deposited it in his jacket pocket and turned away, he saw the figure waiting, silently watching him from the inky blackness of the far side of the building's interior.

He closed his eyes hard, opening them again, hoping the figure would disappear in the blackness, as a sleepwalker who's crossed to the other side of town in his pyjamas might close his own eyes, hoping to open them and find he's back in bed and able to write the somnambulistic excursion off as a dream. But for Luke it was no dream, the figure's undeniable silhouette remained.

"Who's that?" Luke demanded, accidently taking in too much air thick with dust, and coughing sharply.

The figure only waited, inspecting him like a silent black panther. When the broken light flickered on, Luke could pick out more details, the outline of unkempt hair, the hunched shoulders, the hands with fingernails like claws. "Who are you?" Luke called out, trying to sound in control, as he slowly began crossing ground towards it.

Two feet away Luke lifted his phone and turned the full bright torchlight onto it. The figure, in Victorian dress, looked blankly at him with lifeless eyes, a doll's eyes. Luke reached out and rapped his knuckles on the figure's hard cheek.

He looked down at the floor beside it and saw a succession of limbs, torsos and disembodied heads. He had seen such things before, on roadsides, the handiwork of machete wielding guerrillas and fanatics out to make themselves a name. The disembodied heads on those occasions trailed with thick tatters of flesh and severed spinal cords; the grim legacy of hastily hacked beheadings, the eyes bulging, staring aghast at nothing as if still outraged by their own murders.

But the heads on the floor beside him were calm and the limbs and torsos bloodless, the lines of their severed joints perfectly neat and sterile.

Luke wiped his hand through an inch-thick layer of dark grey dust on a crate to his left and read across the top of it a sign in fading colours; SKIDAWAY ISLAND WAXWORK IMPORIUM EST. 1898.

Luke looked again at the figure, one of the only waxworks intact; the representation of some infamous nineteenth century murderer.

As he turned back, readying to search the remainder of the building's interior he came upon the reflected faces of two of his cohorts from his years in service, Corporal William Castlebridge and Sergeant Jim Harper. He stared at them in the dull mirror. It was thick in patches with dirt as dark as dried paint, but the faces of his two buddies were there without question.

Castlebridge was the first to speak, shouting out his nickname, "Oi-oi Little Sexy!"

Luke spoke back to their reflections. "What are you two doing here?"

Harper replied, "What are we doing here? Dawson, what are you doing here? Thought you'd still be home sucking on mum's chebs."

Luke hadn't noticed Private Tim Dawson till now; he was squat on the floor beside them, crouched in a pose with his rifle rested on one knee. "S-Screw you Harper, screw you C-Castlebridge." He stuttered. In service there was always one in the squad who suffered the worst of the banter and a side helping of bullying, always someone who couldn't run as fast, didn't want to go out drinking, didn't know how to talk to girls, couldn't get the simplest things such as polishing their boots quite right. For them it had been Private Dawson.

"Go home and tell it to the RSM." Castlebridge barked.

"After you make him a brew and laugh at his jokes while he gives you a good shoeing." Harper added.

"Screw you." Dawson piped up with uncharacteristic gusto, which only served to encourage Castlebridge and Harper.

"And if that don't work tell it to your daddy." Castlebridge retorted. "Wait a minute. Harper's your daddy."

"I would have been. If the crack smoking wannabe gangster boy who cleans the toilets at Kandahar Airport hadn't beaten me up the stairs."

Luke turned around to them, "Shut your cock-holsters you three, I'm . . . "

Luke's face dropped.

In the spots where his three friends should have stood were another three waxworks, soldiers, dressed in uniforms from the Crimean War, pinched plastic features and tidy moustaches that were typical of that era.

". . . thinking." Luke finished his sentence sadly when he realized he was alone.

He'd had enough of the place now. Some inner sense told him that whatever secrets it may have held none were Howie's. Nothing here needed his attention. The whole placed served only as a tomb to remind him of all he'd lost. He wanted out. Immediately.

Taking a pathway through the darkness at speed had been a mistake. He tripped over something, probably one of the disembodied limbs of the waxwork figures, and landed heavily on the cement floor, sending up a cloud of dust. That was when he saw it.

He knew it didn't make sense. Somehow, he also knew, it was real. A tumbledown mind may play tricks on the last few shards of a man's sanity. But still those brittle shards manage to come together and form something, something with substance, something real.

Luke crawled towards it for a closer look in the sooty light.

The pair of shoes were in a row with several others. They sat between the scuffed boots on the waxwork legs of a farmer, representative of those known from photographs of agriculturalists at the turn of the penultimate century, and the outsized red huge-toed boots of a clown.

The shoes which had caught Luke's attention were seated on a figure between the farmer and the clown. They belonged to no exhibit from the 1800s. Luke knew this as he owned a pair just like them. Their style and shape, if not the same, were like shoes popular not more than a year or two ago. But what was more recognizable, and more disturbing, was the red stripe that ran up the side of the trouser, trousers worn only by the Company's fleet of security guards.

Howie's voice came to him in the darkness. "Brother, my brother. How selfish was I? While you seemed to struggle I sat idly by."

Luke looked in the direction of the voice, but knew he would find nothing but the twist of swirling shadows in the spot from which it came.

He rose slowly, keeping cautious eyes on the figure wearing the security guard trousers and modern shoes. It was covered in a cotton sheet; a shroud. Luke summoned his strength and whipped it back in one swift movement.

The figure seated before him was no waxwork. It had once been real. He had no need to distrust the tricks his eyes played on his mind to know that. Luke Dearlove had seen his share of death. Enough to easily recognize when he was in the malodourous presence of fetid corpses.

The cause of the man's death didn't require Luke's medical training for identification. There was a hole in his skull the likes of which occurs when a stone is thrown from some distance through a window. The smashed open dent in his cranium was large enough to put your first through.

The creeping smell of a year's decay wafted towards Luke and he stumbled back, forcing a hand under his nose. He turned the torch light from his phone onto the cadaver and skated it about, examining its features. The bloodless shrivelled lips were wrinkled back from the teeth. Its eyes, like deep gorges, seemed suddenly alive in the glow of the phone's electric light. A cockroach, disturbed by the unexpected fuss, scurried out of the mouth, breaking free the last shred of skin that held the lower jaw in place. It broke, dropping the mouth into a sickly gaping grin. Luke turned away and made a frantic stumble for the door.

"You want to be sure, don't you?"

"We all . . . want to be sure."

Luke sighed. The two policemen had been questioning him for half an hour. The decrepit body from the lockup was now sprawled on a table in the Company's island headquarters; an impromptu mortuary slab, a tablecloth serving as a second shroud.

Exhausted from repeating himself Luke told them for what felt like the thousandth time. "That man was in his sixties, at least. My brother is thirty-seven."

"We just want to be sure." The policeman with the ginger beard repeated. The wiry layers of his curly red facial hair, Luke knew, were masking a grin.

The second policeman, with, for some reason, only one eyebrow, from, Luke guessed, the drunken handiwork of mates who thought it hysterical to shave it from their sleeping friend's forehead the night before he reported for duty.

'One Eyebrow' and 'Ginger Beard' gave each other knowing looks and picked up the corner of the tablecloth, beckoning with their eyes for Luke to make an identification.

"I keep telling you. I don't know who that man is, but he is definitely not . . . " Luke's firm voice gave way to a brittle whisper "my brother."

Ginger Beard had whipped the tablecloth back, leaving Luke to face the waxwork figure of the Victorian murderer, which they'd placed on the table-top slab.

One Eyebrow had no thick brush of red fuzz to hide his smirk and crammed his hand to his face, barely holding the bubble of juvenile laughter in.

Ginger Beard nodded, and they stood in front of the table, arms folded, the weight of their stares bearing down on Luke.

Ginger Beard began it. "Is it true you served out in Afghanistan sir?"

31

One Eyebrow took over with what Luke knew only too well would follow. "Did you . . . kill a lot of people while you were out there?"

Luke closed his eyes.

Ginger Beard again, "Had to spend some time in Belleview when you came back didn't you sir?"

"All got a bit much for you did it sir?" One Eyebrow threw in for good measure.

"Alright you two that's quite enough." The voice, full of command, demanding respect, had come from Detective Ackerly Standing.

Luke opened his eyes to see him scowling at his two subordinates. He was a handsome black man in his early fifties; a non-uniformed officer with a certain grace and elegance, combined with a powerful physique, smooth voice and earnest disposition. Something about his eyes let Luke know he didn't like to see anyone being bullied and would take his stand for the underdog. Luke had met his type many times before in service. They quickly rose through the ranks, became majors, progressed to the SAS and other elite organisations. Luke suddenly felt awash with great comfort.

"This way Mr Dearlove shall we please?" The detective said to Luke while holding the door open for him, but still glaring at his underlings.

As Luke got up to move One Eyebrow chipped in, "Aren't you going to tell him?" Both Luke and Detective Ackerly Standing turned to him with a questioning stare.

It was ginger beard who explained for his foil, nodding at Luke. "They found his brother after all."

Luke kept to the slow measured pace of a funeral director as he walked the winding corridors of the Company's long deserted headquarters.

Ackerly Standing and the two police officers kept a similar stride behind him at a respectful distance. Luke stopped, bringing them to a sudden halt.

Around the next bend a man was waiting, sitting on a hard bench and playing with his hands as if wound up in some considerable tension. But what brought Luke to the standstill was his attire. The trousers. They were the same. Black and made from stiff polyester. *Well it was cheap and didn't need ironing.* And down one side the distinct tell-tale mark of a Company security guard's uniform, the thick red style-less stripe.

Luke held his breath, barely able to believe it. Surely it wasn't going to be this easy. Or this perfect.

It wasn't.

Tyler Dearlove, Luke and Howie's eldest brother got up and slowly crossed the corridor towards him. He had a vehement non-negotiable look in his eye, like a man coming at you for a bar fight.

"You stupid prick."

The words formed a kinder greeting than the one Luke had been anticipating from him.

"Lance Corporal Dearlove I presume!"

These words, in the flowery clipped accent, had not come from his still scowling eldest brother. Luke knew the owner of them immediately and felt every muscle in his body constrict.

Francis Grayson flounced by him, swivelling like a ballet dancer executing a demi-point pirouette and eyed Luke sardonically.

"Two days into your annual leave and here we have you, causing quite the commotion on the banks of Lake Woebegone. Tedious, tedious, predictable at best."

Francis Grayson, the Company's CEO opened the door to the former boardroom, its rusting hinges emanating a grating groan. He held it wide open for the Dearlove brothers and invited them to enter in an icy tone, "Shall we?"

Luke and Tyler remained, facing each other in tense silence.

Grayson entered the boardroom without them, calling back to Luke. "And none of your flim-flam. As we both know I am more than capable of sniffing out the fartish waft of a lie."

The policemen passed them, entering behind Grayson.

After a painfully long minute Tyler nodded at his youngest brother and ordered him into the boardroom with his eyes.

Four

"With the rest of the trash why don't we?"

Francis Grayson looked down at the architect's scale model of the Company's prized luxury housing complex like it was a fresh turd being held under his chin.

The ginger bearded policeman had picked it up and offered it to him, with a questioning stare as to what should be done with it. Upon Grayson's response the policeman shrugged. Seemed like something that someone much cleverer than him had spent many painstaking hours assembling. But the grey-haired man from the Company in the fancy suit clearly hadn't gotten to his position in life without making the hard decisions. And he'd made that one with the quickest of efficiency and unfeeling decisiveness. The policeman obliged and crushed the model with his hands as an industrial digger could well have done if the actual thing had ever been built. When compressed into a misshapen foam-core ball he laid it on top of the plethora of posters and brochures with the smiling mother, *she of the pearly teeth and perfect family*, filling a nearby bin and crammed the whole pile deep into the bin's innards with his foot.

Detective Ackerly Standing and the one eye-browed policeman were still pulling dust sheets back from tables and removing polystyrene coffee cups, left behind long ago by unknown colleagues, when the bookends of the Dearlove brothers; Tyler the eldest and Luke the youngest, joined them in the Company's former onsite boardroom.

"Ah messers Dearlove." Grayson looked at them over the rim of his glasses with the overconfidence and haughtiness of a Dickensian judge

35

watching a pickpocket enter his courtroom. He gave a grand sweeping gesture to the five men in the room. "Gentlemen have seats."

Ackerly took his place at Grayson's side. The two policemen perched on stools against the back wall and Tyler found a seat behind one of the long boardroom tables. Only Luke remained defiantly on his feet, looking up at Francis with an unflinching stare.

"Luke. Sit down." Tyler ordered under his breath.

"Oh leave him Tyler dear boy." Grayson purred. "We all know your brother likes to go left when they say go right." Francis Grayson's eyes were grey-blue and looked permanently startled. He turned them onto Luke and the irises seemed to be widening across the strange washed-out mix of colours by the second, like an owl that has just caught sight of a mouse. "How you managed to 'follow an order' in the realm of your former profession is beyond my comprehension."

"I respected my superiors." Luke told him bluntly.

"Ooh, touché." Grayson muttered, feigning mock insult.

He turned to address the room; looking as much like a headmaster as he did a judge. "Now, though it pains me to find myself back on this . . . *crumbling carbuncle* . . . of an island. Certain questions much be answered. Certain issues have been raised."

Luke was immediately sickened by the man's arrogance and his pompous words as they tumbled out of the thin-lipped mouth. He opened his own mouth to try to override them. Grayson cut him off before he had the chance.

"No, young man. Our issues. Our questions." Grayson nodded to Ackerly and his two uniformed policemen. "Namely why Skidaway's finest were called away from their matters this a.m. to investigate the unfortunate demise of what amounted to being nothing but a waxwork dolly."

"There's an entire network of catacombs that run under this island." Luke told him, referring to the web of tunnels built three hundred years ago to consolidate the old stone mines, deceptive and complex as an Egyptian tomb, but able to provide escape routes and a myriad of places for a person to hide themselves or their secrets, should they be brave enough to enter their dank guts.

"Anyone could have moved that body in the time it took me to get back to signal range and call them." Luke added.

"And whom are we accusing of such duplicity and cover-up? Detective Standing and the rest of his constabularies perhaps? Your dear brother and my good self while we were helicoptering it over? A passing sheep rapist with a sudden taste in necrophilia? Perhaps the Board and the whole of the Company's Executive Committee?"

"Perhaps." Luke said it with so much defiance that Tyler let out a small groan.

Ackerly cleared his throat in a clear indication that he wanted to speak. "Mr Dearlove, I was the first investigating officer that responded to your call. In that light, with all that dust. I damn near thought one of them was real."

"I know what I saw. I'm sure of what I saw." Luke had said it with such utter conviction that if he hadn't been so acutely aware of his youngest brother's medical history Tyler would have had no choice other than to believe him.

Ackerly sighed, knowing he was going to have a tough job convincing the young man standing stubbornly (in what was feeling more and more like a dock) in front of him to see reason.

"Your Company have always done what's right and fair." Ackerly said.

Luke shot a hot look up at him. "Including carting human beings across the world like cattle only to treat them like dogs?"

Grayson let out an insultingly put on laugh and lifted his glasses to look at Luke. "Pause while I raise glasses." He pushed his glasses back up the bridge of his nose, gave Ackerly a look of contrived frustration and turned back to Luke. "The sad business of human despair is that if these people cannot get in the front door they will come in the back door. And if they cannot get in the back door they climb in the window. It happens whether-"

Luke cut into his words. "Whether good men do nothing or not."

"I was about to say 'whether we like it or not'." Francis retorted.

Ackerly added to the debate once more. "Mr Dearlove, I'm not only the most senior police officer on this island. I'm also studying to become a human rights activist. And I can unequivocally state that your Company has managed the situation here with the utmost integrity."

Luke sighed, his eyes roaming round the room, like a teenager being lectured.

Unfazed Ackerly went on. "When we were alerted to the unorthodox practices being carried out here by a renegade few your Company worked with us long and hard to root out that sedition."

"Heads rolled," Francis quipped with a silly little shake of his own head, "they rolled."

Ackerly continued his tub-thumping. "They've since set up an initiative to repatriate the migrant population brought illicitly over into the wider island community. Many now have the best jobs, homes, businesses."

"Where are the rest?" Luke asked scornfully. "Huffing paint thinner and shivering under a sheet of cardboard?"

Ackerly let out a riled sigh. "They could have walked away from that particular problem."

Grayson nodded in enthused, over the top, agreement. "As we had to walk away from a twenty million pound investment when we discovered the land here to be made of sawdust."

Ackerly continued. "Instead they've worked with us, again, *long and hard*, to help create a symbiosis that runs on harmony."

"How's that working out?" Luke asked, his voice thick with irony. "Half the island want to leave. The other half want to kill each other."

Finally Ackerly's calm tone gave way to a trace of anger. "Don't start a war here Mr Dearlove, please, not here. You may never be able to end it."

Tyler shifted uncomfortably in his seat. His irritation with Luke for causing all this was disappearing fast and being rapidly replaced with a need to protect him from what was feeling more and more like a group of corporate bullies doing their worst. He was on the verge of getting up and standing next to him when a merciful knock from outside the door broke the tension.

One of the policemen perched nearby opened the door to reveal a man who wore a sweatshirt, the hood pulled so far down over his face that you could see no part of it other than the faintest trace of a chin and nose among the shadows. When he spoke his voice was muffled, as if a large undigested bite from an apple had become permanently lodged in his throat. "Mr Francis Grayson?" he questioned to the room.

"That's me baby." Grayson responded.

With his head kept shyly down he crossed the room and handed a large package the size of an old-fashioned photo album to Grayson. As he scribbled his signature on the delivery form the man seemed to be turning his obscured face to look intentionally over at Luke.

Grayson thrust the signed form back to the man and, on this cue, he crossed the room for the door. Luke couldn't be sure but the man appeared to pause halfway to glance at him again from under the darkness of his hood, sending out a signal that let Luke know there paths would cross once more.

Luke shrugged the thought off as the man left and turned his attention back to Francis Grayson and the package he seemed so delighted to have received and was now carefully opening, as if savouring every moment like a child unwrapping their final present from under the tree at Christmas.

It was a large hardbound leather book, again, very much like an old-fashioned photo album. Grayson ran a bony hand over it, pursing his lips and almost cooing with delight.

With sickening dread, and a better vantage point than Luke, Tyler had an idea as to what the book might be. The thought of it left him with the sensation of having something chewing on the threads of his nervous system, like a mouse chewing on cables. The only thing he could do under the circumstances was hope to god the Company wouldn't stoop so low.

"Now," Grayson said, playing with the book cover's corner and demanding the attention of the room once more. "Before I must be forced to '*bring out the big guns*'. How about one last chance little Luke? How would you like to rethink what it was you thought you saw?"

"I know what I saw." Luke said without a second thought. "I'm sure of what I saw."

Grayson smiled an unctuous thin smile that seemed to say 'so be it' and opened the cover of the large book with the whip of his index finger. He ran the same scrawny finger down the centre of a page, looking for the spot he wanted to come to, muttering "*Just . . . give me . . . five.*"

"You have three." Luke fired up at him coldly, causing the two policemen to laugh.

"Oooh," Grayson countered. "At ease soldier."

The policemen laughed again. Louder this time before being silenced by Ackerly's unassailable stare.

Luke heard Tyler let out a long sigh, clearly wanting to get Luke's attention. He looked over at him, expecting his eldest brother to give him a look of angry contempt. Instead he found Tyler giving him the smallest of smiles. Nodding his head. Letting him know he was there.

Grayson pushed his glasses up the brim of his nose again and began reading from the book. "Belleview Hospital March 16th . . . "

Luke gasped.

Grayson went on ". . . Dr Whelan; How are you today Luke? L.C. Dearlove." He pointed at Luke with splayed fingers. "That's you. 'I'm fine Dr but we have to do something about Nurse Barker, she's been fraternising with the enemy. I saw her last night with some chogie. He's giving her ammo, she's hiding it in her blanket-stack."

Tyler closed his eyes.

Grayson skipped a few pages ahead. "April 8th Dr Whelan; Are you any better Luke?"

"Shut up." Luke said weakly.

Tyler opened his eyes and looked over at Luke. Willing his brother not to break.

Grayson ignored Luke's demand and went on with the conscienceless soul of an assassin. "L.C. Dearlove, that's you."

Luke, "Shut your mouth."

Grayson, "My bed went out the window again last night Doctor, you told me they'd bolt it down, when are they going to bolt it down, it does the same thing every night. November 18th; 'Can't you see them doctor, Taliban, dancing, dancing all around. Look at them, they're line dancing and turning into frogs just before their heads explode. It's hysterical."

Tyler shifted in his seat, so overcome with clammy necked anxiety it felt like a python had constricted his entire body. He opened his mouth to shout up to Grayson, but Luke said the words his mind was forming before he got the chance:

"Shut your bitch mouth."

Grayson went on remorselessly, the barest trace of a viper-like smile dusting his thin-lipped mouth. "Dr Whelan; 'Are you sure Luke?' 'Yes, I'm sure doctor. I know what I saw. I'm <u>sure</u> of what I saw."

He snapped the book shut triumphantly, raised a thinning grey eyebrow above one of the blanched grey-blue perma-startled eyes and gave Luke a self-satisfied glare, revelling in his savagely brilliant annihilation.

As Tyler feared, it was enough to make Luke break apart. His brother lunged across the table, screaming at Grayson. "You slimy abortion! I'll kill you, you nasty glob of spit!"

"I dare say. I dare say." Grayson muttered, leaning casually back.

The two policemen moved before Tyler had made it round to the other side of the table. They grabbed Luke before he touched Grayson, forcing him face down onto the boardroom table and twisting his arms behind his back.

Two years ago, when he was still in service, Luke could have broken free from the men in seconds, but he was two stone lighter now, and weight wasn't the only thing he had lost. He fought and wriggled and struggled but they held him fast. One more humiliation. A soldier overpowered by two civies.

"Alright, let him go." Tyler ordered, reaching their side.

But the more Luke fought the harder they manhandled him. Twisting his skin until it looked ready to break open.

"I said get your fucking hands off him!!" Tyler barked at them like a Rottweiler.

Ackerly nodded and his two subordinates released their hold. Luke was immediately up, scrabbling to get at Grayson. Tyler grabbed him round the waist and slid him backwards across the table-top, gripping him in a bear hug, pinning his arms down at his sides and hoisting him two inches off the ground. Two years ago he wouldn't have been able to do this either. Luke kicked and struggled as his brother heaved him out of the room.

Grayson called out after them. "Careful out there Dearlove. There may just be a great white shark waiting to pursue you down the hall, yes there will."

Tyler back-kicked the door shut. Luke's enraged shouts could still be heard in the boardroom, receding down the corridor as Tyler carried his struggling brother away.

Francis Grayson repositioned his glasses on his razor-thin bone of a nose and wiped an invisible fleck of dust away from the table-top. "Lunch I think."

Five

Tyler kept his arms hard around Luke as they tumbled into the men's bathrooms.

They always seemed to end up like this. From the moment Luke had been born it had been Tyler's arms he had either fallen or been forced into in the great pivotal moments of life. From the day he was born quite literally.

That December the local electric company had decided to strike over some long-forgotten dispute and periodically would turn off all power in the area for thirty minutes, sometimes an hour, at a time. Tyler and Howie had loved being at their grandparents when the blackouts occurred to hear whatever moans of indignation and disdain they'd come out with next while bumping into the furniture and each other in the dark. Their expletives, *swearing while not swearing*, because their grandsons were visiting, included such profane blasphemes as; 'Fopdoodle!' or 'Those gillie wet foots!" sometimes the unpardonable 'Damn those saddle-goose strewed prunes.'

It was also the year of the heaviest snowfall London had known that decade. On the particularly bleak night of 11th December, with a drift of snow piled up so high on the access road to their house that it kept their father stuck at work until it could be cleared, their mother, eight and a half months pregnant and barely able to bend down, had charged her two sons, eleven-year-old Howie and thirteen-year-old Tyler with putting up the Christmas decorations.

With wild excitement, and feeling more like men than ever, they'd prized open the hatch into the loft and elbowed each other for pole position as they clambered up the ladder, ignoring their mother's irritating bleats to 'be careful'.

But being boys the fun of decorating the house soon turned to a far more interesting 'cops and robbers' game and when Mary Dearlove came in to check on her sons' progress she found Tyler pointing an angel at Howie as though it were a gun and Howie, bound and gagged with tinsel, being forced into an impromptu noose, also made of tinsel, hanging from the plastic hook on the ceiling from which they normally suspended their cherished Christmas Star.

Upon sight of the chaos Mary balled her hands into fists and crammed them into her face, pulling her cheeks down until her mouth formed an ugly grimace. That was when the electric company decided an hour-long power cut was due.

"Fuck those saddle-goose strewed prunes!" Mary had hollered out from the darkness and let out a groan, sending the boys into peals of laughter. But this was quickly followed by the soggy splash of water hitting the carpet, letting them all know it was also the night Luke Dearlove had decided to be born.

He picked his moments. *Stubborn little sod.* When he made up his mind to do something that was it.

Couldn't have waited a few more hours, could you?

The thought crowded Tyler's mind now as he hoisted his still squirming and wriggling brother up onto the edge of the sinks.

Couldn't have waited till dad was home and the lights were on.

Wilful little prick. Right from the start.

By candlelight and the beams of shaking torches they'd helped their mother into the kitchen and turned on the battery-powered lamp their father had bought three days earlier.

Howie began shrieking hysterically when the lamp lit the kitchen up in bright blue. Tyler wasn't sure whether it was hysteria over the fact a baby was about to be born among the pots and pans and their leftover dinner or that he'd just got an eyeful of their mother's vagina.

Tyler had seen his first a year earlier and had to stifle a similar reaction. He and four other boys in his year had offered the classroom slut, Jennifer McKenny (she was known as a slut for being the first girl in their peer group to have a kissed a boy with her tongue you see) fifty pounds to put hers on display for them.

'Fifty pounds,' she'd mused a long while, thinking the deal through with deep deliberation and serious intellect. Tyler heard later that little Jenny Mac had gone on to become an investment banker earning 250K a year and the same again as a bonus at Christmas. 'And no touching?' They nodded their agreement like a group of the bobbing headed dogs people stick in the backs of cars, not quite believing she'd agreed to it, less sure they had actually wanted her to.

But for any one of them to pull out now would be a major loss of bravado in front of the other three, so they grouped whatever money they had, went without lunch for a week and that Friday followed Jenny to the clandestine spot where kids normally went to smoke, or make out; an old unused port-o-cabin in the junior department's playground, each 'man' secretly feeling slightly sick about what they were asking a girl they'd grown up with to do.

After the private viewing and little Jenny had hoisted back up her pants and tights, pocketed her cash and headed off to Home Economics, they put on a major communal pretence of lustful satisfaction, laughing and howling like cartoon wolves, each pre-bragging about the furious wank they'd be bound to enjoy that evening.

Tyler wasn't quite sure how his cohorts felt but he walked home in a traumatised daze.

That was it? That was the thing that drove men wild with desire? That was supposed to make his cock hard? That weird looking alien flower? He was meant to put his most sacred parts in that? It looked like a gummy misshapen mouth, something that probably had a retractable hidden layer of teeth and would have bitten it right off for him.

Women, marriage, children. None of those things were going to be for him if that fleshy multi folded monster was what he had to face in the process.

And here poor Howie was not only experiencing his first viewing but had the double whammy of it being his own mother's he'd had to come eye to eye with. Tyler remembered digging him hard in the ribs with his elbow to make him shut up.

His mother was half standing, half squatting and with shocking suddenness Luke Dearlove came streaking into the world. With athlete quick reflexes and remarkable alacrity Tyler had lunged across the floor, hands outstretched, and caught the baby like a goalie saving the day at Wembley.

'What the fuck!!!' Howie had shrieked, wondering if this day could get any more surreal. Mother and baby both began wailing. In his primal instincts Tyler knew this was a good sound. He slipped gently onto his backside and leant against the cabinets, cradling the new born infant into his chest, slippery wet with amniotic fluid and huge eyes staring blindly at the battery-blue hue of his strange new world.

Tyler kissed his new little brother's forehead and wrapped his arms tight around him like he would never let him go.

Both boys overcame their fear of vaginas.

47

With one hand flat on Luke's chest, holding him against the large mirrors behind the sinks, Tyler turned on the cold tap and began splashing water in Luke's overwrought reddened face.

Luke was looking right at Tyler, but also looking through him. Staring at nothingness like a blind man. Tyler had seen this look before, dreaded it, knew what was coming next. And then it began. Luke started fighting Tyler, fighting an invisible enemy.

"Luke!" Tyler threw all the command he had into his voice. Luke momentarily calmed, and then the battling erupted again.

"Hey! Hey!!" Tyler shouted as if trying to wake him from a dream. "Alright breathe, breathe." He held on to him hard, steering Luke's erratic breathing with his own calm breaths, clinging onto him until they were breathing as one, and the need to fight left Luke's soul and he felt his muscles sag.

Tyler leant back and pushed Luke gently against the mirror, taking more water and spreading it over his face, tidying his hair. Luke stared at him, befuddled and disbelieving, the new born child again, once more his eldest brother being the first person his bewildered eyes would come find in the world.

Minutes passed until Tyler knew it was the right time for him to speak. "They want me to bring you back with us."

Luke's voice was brittle and weak, as though he was suffering laryngitis. "I'm sure they do."

"Are you going to come?"

"Are you going to make me?"

"It's a free world."

"Is it?"

Tyler stepped back from Luke, angrily drying his hands on a towel. "You shouldn't have come here looking for trouble."

"You know *exactly* what it is I've come here looking for."

Tyler let out what was a cross between a prolonged sigh and an angry laugh. "I can guarantee you, the most that's happened to our brother is he's run up twenty grand of credit card debt."

"Did they buzz you through like someone who mattered?" Luke threw in as if from nowhere.

"Or got some local girl up the spout." Tyler added, trying vehemently to keep his own side of the argument on track.

"Ask you to have a seat?" Luke's resentment of the Company they worked for began itching under his skin.

"Or more likely done the same thing he did when I got him a job in the high street butchers when he was seventeen." Tyler added, regardless of the fact the two of them were now on paradoxical trajectories with their points.

"Make you a cappuccino? Call you 'Mr Dearlove' sir'?" Luke took the mocking inflection in his voice up a degree.

"And jacked his job in without word to anyone. Bored of earning an honest man's wage." Tyler hit back with.

"When they told you to go and get your annoying little brother?" Luke threw in sensing victory.

"Either way he'll turn up like he always does, without so much as a scratch." Tyler spat at him, knowing he'd won the final round when Luke slumped slightly, stung by the inescapable plausibility of the final comment.

An admin assistant who'd flown over in the helicopter with Tyler and Francis Grayson knocked lightly at the door before opening it and leaning through the doorway. He looked to Tyler; "Mr Grayson's ready to leave for the heliport."

Tyler nodded, signalling for the man to give him a minute. He duly left, setting the bathrooms in awkward tension.

After an endless moment Luke spoke again. "Do you remember the day they took me into Belleview?"

Something dark, something sad, passed across Tyler's eyes, like the shadow of a pain briefly remembered. He looked at him but didn't answer.

"Uncle David told me Howie carried me for nearly half a mile back home through those woods. Wouldn't let anyone else so much as touch me. Nearly dislocated his shoulder through the strain."

Luke clambered off the sinks and looked up at Tyler.

"Are you really asking me to believe that the brother who loved me enough to carry home, even with near broken arms, would suddenly abandon me because he didn't like his job anymore?"

Tyler kept his eyes on Luke for a long moment, finally answered in an emotionless voice. "I don't know. I don't remember anything much about that day."

Luke recoiled slightly, as if he'd been slapped.

The assistant came back through the door, this time without knocking. "Are you with us? Mr Dearlove, sir?"

Luke looked up at his brother; his eyes asking the exact same question.

Eva, Before

Screams were let off in all directions like fireworks on the 4th of July that night.

Her brother, Tariq, had begun it, the first in the crowd to articulate the horror that the opening of the third lorry had thrown at them.

"Motra ime është atje!!" (My sister's on there!!) With that he bolted onto the back of the truck and began frantically picking through the tangle of the dead like they were knockdown goods at a jumble sale until he found his twin.

Their six-foot seven inch man mountain of a cousin Luan watched with eyes awash with fear. The lumbering giant suddenly reduced to a colossal great baby, cramming his fists in his mouth, whining thinly in the wind and doing a little dance of terror.

Luan could only gawp, useless and ridiculous, as Tariq emerged with Eva lifeless in his arms like a giant rag doll and laid her down on the tarmac. Tariq screamed again, but this time his bawling would not be heard above the mass shrieks of hysteria from a crowd rapidly turning mad with rage.

He grabbed the great slabs of roast beef Luan called arms and pulled him down to the tarmac alongside her. There they yelled a violent prayer to their god, ripped open her shirt, pounded on her chest as though it were a drum and took turns laying down their mouths over her mouth in the most savage of kisses, forcing their air into her lungs, their life into her cold veins.

Even half-dressed and sprawled out on asphalt Eva Skanderberg was a sight to see, her long limbs gleamed like chiselled marble under the moon's bony light, her golden hair spread out in a circle around her head like a halo.

She only rocked against their attempts to drag her back to the world of the living, her blind eyes staring upward into the dark sky and the slow dance of the infinite stars; the call and languor of death beckoning her spirit evermore to leave its earthly bonds and come its way like smoke.

The more powerfully death called her, the more vehemently her brother held her back. To have a sibling ripped from your side, from your world, was as obscene and unnatural as losing a child, or a limb, he simply would not allow it.

Finally, either god, or the devil himself, gave in to Tariq's demands. Eva opened her mouth in three quick successions, puffing for the air like a fish, half dead from flopping, begging for oxygen in the choking world.

Tariq and Luan froze at her sides, petrified that if they should touch her now she'd slip away, forever out of their reach.

She let out a low moan and twisted and writhed then violently arched her back as if suddenly set on fire. Her voice cracked and rose and whined into a shrill, senile treble. "I've seen death!! I've seen death!!" She screamed out to oblivion.

Luan and Tariq sagged like two men whose endoskeletons had collapsed inside them. They flopped upon her in tears. The one saved life from the cargo of crumpled ruin.

Eva Skanderberg, stolen back from the jaws of death, fixed her strange manic stare to the moon, a wolf baby, suddenly ripped from the womb, new-born and howling.

Six

The Martyr sat in the pose of a Buddha without a lotus flower. His oil rubbed skin set the deeply penetrated tan off with a subtle glow and his thick dark hair was greased and the top half of it tied in a ponytail at the back of his head.

"Makes you look more like a champion's league footballer than any man's religious saviour or a high priest warrior." Eva had told him the first time she'd seen him wear it that way.

"Ana last min tilk al'ashya." He'd replied, which loosely translated from Arabic, (which he'd chosen to speak in for a month as part of a *process of purification*) to "I'm neither of those things."

"You don't say." She'd said with a smile more mocking than she'd intended it to be and walked her right foot up his bare back. That was the first time he'd ever pushed her away.

She watched him now, through the window of his quarters, in the small garden oasis he'd created with the help of his believers.

She dug her fingertips deep into the flesh of her arms and ran them down their length, murmuring slightly, always a lover of that strange illicit periphery between pleasure and pain.

The monks, *his believers*, were circumnavigating him as usual, their silly shaved heads bobbing about the grass like buoys on the water as they bowed and entreated to his greatness.

Oh please.

Like any dutiful woman who likes to gratify her man, she'd gone to great lengths to find him a book on the history of spiritualism when he'd first started to ramble on about what he wanted to create. There wasn't much to choose from in The Turkey Cage.

The Turkey Cage was what they'd come to call it. Officially it was listed by the Company as Area 36. A former set of 1960's summer chalets set around a sparse grassland. They'd been built as affordable holiday accommodation on the island but failed to attract mainlanders and had fallen into a state of neglect. Several decades later they would come to provide an easy solution for the Company as to where to accommodate the construction workers and project managers employed on the build of the luxury housing complex. Later, when their project ran aground, it became the ideal place to stick the overspill of vagabonds, drifters and emigrants that washed up like jetsam on Skidaway's shores.

Renaming the complex, *The Turkey Cage*, had come via an on-point joke made by her usually humourless and unsubtle cousin Luan. Six families had been in the compound with them for a month before being spirited away to run a succession of businesses at the harbour, a month later another four would be plucked from the compound's grim obscurity and speed-tracked into entrepreneurialism. When, finally, it was their turn, and they were handed the keys to The Codfather, Luan, Tariq and she packed up and as a parting gesture Luan turned to the accumulated faces of the miserable tenants left behind in the filth and, with a cheeky smile, had broadcast his message 'We're off, they've fattened us up for Christmas. See you turkeys later!'

In truth none of her family left. They could have easily taken up residence in the apartment above the newly renamed 'Skanderberg Café' but their friends were here, Tin-Tin was here and she'd promised she'd never leave him. But mostly, yes mostly, he was here.

She never really knew why he'd come. To most he was just another wanderer, one of the world's rejects, destined to roam its waters until he could find some ragged crook or stone where he wasn't hated enough to be thrown out. For others there was talk of legendary status over his background; he'd supposedly slain two security guards the very night she was brought over in an act of almost supernatural justice, or perhaps, of pure red-blooded vengeance.

It took some time for her head to acclimatize from the insanity of her arrival on the island. And then she found him. He was wondering around like a dazed lamb who'd survived a culling almost as much as she was.

From there, lingering looks gave way to small snatches of conversation. No one would normally intimidate this wolf baby, but there was something about him. *He did.*

Finally, when the sexual tension for all other inhabitants of the Turkey Cage had become stifling as summer, Luan had thrown down his cards in a game of poker and bellowed at him, 'Will you just fuck my cousin and be done with it!' With that a permission was given out. And well, it would have been rude not to. Tariq refused to speak to either of them for the following week.

Three months on and the Martyr was born. He'd been teaching a few of the teenagers Tae-Kwon-Do for several weeks and supposedly it was 'divine calling' but she knew he just liked being a rock star.

But aiming to please she'd set out to find something to enhance his studies. Something to make him smile. She'd had to pickpocket the paperback 'Lessons from a Higher God' from the harbour bookstore, 'The Moby Dickens'. *Oh, you crazy Brits.*

He'd sat up the whole night reading it. Pouring over every detail the way men from her country poured over car parts when they got their first Trans Am. She soon began to regret the stolen contribution to his mystic journey.

The chapter on Chudakarana Samskara in the religion of Hinduism was of note. Both Hindu boys and girls undergo a ritual at about four years old in which they have their heads shaved. Hair is an adornment so by shaving the head, the child confronts his or her bare ego. It teaches humbleness and devotion. Children with shaved heads are innocent and holy and are treated with great respect. Shaving the head can also be an act of humility for adults. For example, at the Kumbha Mela the first ritual observed by most pilgrims is the mundana ceremony, the shaving of the head. Hair is considered the symbol of vanity, and to receive the full benefits of a pilgrimage to a holy place, one must first give up vanity. Thus, the pilgrims believe that the hair should be shaven from the head in a gesture of surrender.

"All very nice," she'd said as he recited the passage to her. "But don't be shaving yours." She ran her hand through it and gripped a firm fistful, giving it a powerful tug and biting his ear. "Gives me something to hang on to."

She could tell he'd wanted to push her away then. She knew the way a woman knows. But he'd resisted. That first and most wounding of rejections would come a few weeks later when she'd pushed him that one inch too far.

By that point all his believers were bald headed and entranced. And she'd decided to start a religion of her own. That night at dinner after exercise and prayers, the Martyr joined them to find Luan and several of the most machine-like, brutal and savage of the men in the Turkey Cage sporting bare skinned scalps.

He barged into her room and confronted her viciously. Pushing her angrily up against the wall, demanding she explain why the need to make a mockery of all he stood for.

She'd murmured in what felt like ecstasy at his fierce words, his hands around her throat, stretching forward to breathe in the scent of him.

'I want to see you, one last time, kiss your smile, smell your handsome.' He banged her heavily into the wall, so hard she moaned. *'I'll slip a poison in both our cups. Till we choke and spit. I'd rather die alongside you. Than ever let you go.'*

Finally, he turned for the door only to find she'd locked it and hidden the key. When he turned around to her she was leant back in a chair, its two front legs off the floor. With both hands under the rim of her skirt, and the way she was sinking her teeth so hard down on her bottom lip that blood arose, he'd first thought she was pleasuring herself.

But when blood also arose in dots on her skirt's white cotton he'd snatched back the layers to find Luan's straight razor in her hand and her pubic hair being hacked unceremoniously from the tender skin of her labia majora.

He prized the razor out of her hands, but her femininity was already stripped bare, other than a few stray tufts and criss-crosses of unsightly gashes.

She looked up at him with the innocence of a child. "I want us both to be clean when we descend into heaven."

Whether it was shock, or the fact that there just was no other woman on earth like her, he did not know. But the Martyr allowed her to control him that night. She guided him onto the bed like a thing with no being, no will of his own, no conscious thought.

She straddled him and walked up the outside of his body on her knees until she was hovering over his neck and from there bent her pelvis forward so he could kiss all the bloody places she had just desecrated.

She snapped back from the memory of that night as the Martyr got up on the grass outside. As he allowed each of his believers to kiss his outstretched hand she pulled back her shirt to expose her bare tanned shoulders and leant her long lean legs up against his wall.

He entered the room as if he did not see her. He undressed from his golden satin robe and kissed the eternal sun symbol on the long sash that formed its belt. Finally, he spoke, without looking round at her. "What do you want Eva?"

"What do you want Eva? What do you want Eva?" she mocked. "Do I always have to want something? Can't I just come over?" She took her legs from the wall, got up and sauntered over to him in her impossibly high heels. Ignoring her as best he could he kissed the eternal sun symbol on the breast of his robes and folded them on the bed.

"Still worshipping that patch of cotton on your tit? Once was a time you were worshipping me?" She walked her index and middle finger over his bare shoulder, his skin was smooth and still burnt bronze from last summer's sun. He immediately shrugged her away.

Like a footballer making a dive she allowed the gentle shrug to seemingly knock her onto his bed. She flicked back the tumble of hair that had fallen across her face, her voice turning suddenly serious. "Looks like we've got a hero in our midst."

He turned back to see her lying beside that month's copy of the Company newsletter, its centre spread open to reveal the picture of Luke in full military dress under the headline:

WAR HERO TO BE HONOURED IN THIS YEAR'S CHAMPIONS OF BRITAIN AWARDS

"Who needs a medal from the queen when the Company want to make you their poster boy for the daring do." She purred.

Below the main titles was a subheading:

"Here looking for a missing brother." She informed him.

Without comment he turned away and began hanging his religious
clothing in the appropriate parts of his storage unit. She got up and
stood behind him. "I was thinking. Wouldn't it be funny if we sent
them a little award of our own on their special day, with the eyes of the
world a-watching?" She stretched up on her already frighteningly high
heels to whisper into his ear. "His – pretty – head."

The Martyr sprang round like a scalded cat, gripping her by the forearms
and throwing her against the wall, holding her in place there with his
own body. She smiled, a thick dirty smile, liking this reaction, liking it
very much.

"Let him look around the island." The Martyr told her unemotionally.
"Let him leave. Don't ever speak of this again." He stood back, letting
her fall clumsily from the wall.

Unable to bear to look at her sickly face he left her alone in his room.
She slid back down onto his bed, searching for the smell of him in his
sheets. Above her on the windowsill was an old memento of a beach
holiday, the possession of some former holidaymaker from a time in the
sun many years ago. A snow globe, but rather than depicting a festive
scene, the landscape enclosed within the plastic dome was of a beach
with ragged cliffs, overbearing dunes and a small tumbledown shack at
one side.

Eva chewed on a piece of her hair and shook the globe violently,
whipping up a frenzied storm of sand and stones that rushed over the
plastic painted landscape with frightening speed and canonical
proportions.

Seven

"Shit's getting biblical."

Tyler's statement was a caustic response to the fork of lightening, speared, as if by some mythical temptress, into a sea already churning with a brewing storm.

Luke indulged his brother with a sideways glance. Tyler hovered at Luke's side, clutching his collar tight around his neck like a man afraid of everything. Luke turned back to his task at hand and sent a kick that would knock a bison from this world into the next into the centre of the boarded door to the ramshackle hut at the side of the expansive beach.

Tyler forgot his concern with the tempest along the horizon and grabbed Luke's arm.

"And what if whoever lives here comes back and finds you kicking the door down?"

Luke pulled his arm out of Tyler's grip, readying himself for the next attempt to boot the door off its hinges. "He won't."

"What if he's got a big angry dog inside?"

"He hasn't."

"What if he thinks I'm the out of towner who impregnated his virgin daughter nine months ago?"

"We'll show him the size of your gonads. He'll know you're a jaffa immediately."

Tyler tightened his collar around his neck again.

"And what if the locals decide to sacrifice me to their pagan sun god?"

Luke turned to look up at Tyler, something over his shoulder making his face fall slightly – on a ridge of the bluff that faced them he'd seen the double-quick flare of light that can only be made by the sun bouncing off the lens of something – usually the spying eyes of a pair of binoculars.

Luke hid whatever he might be feeling and looked earnestly back at Tyler. "Then I'll protect you."

With that he sent an almighty kick into the door's centre. Old wood creaked and groaned with an aching strain and finally gave up its fight and bounced dramatically open.

"Christ!" Tyler snapped after they'd taken their first few tentative steps inside. "Does everything on this island smell like two cats fucking in a bucket of piss?"

The stale air inside the shack was grainy and so thick with the odours of filth that both brothers knew it would be hours before the taste of it left their mouths. Tyler pulled the neckline of his sweater up over his nose and mouth, leaving only his eyes free to scowl at both Luke and the shack's dank interiors.

Long moulded food, festering with flies, sat on paper plates, tin cans, heavily dented in the middle, a pierced hole in the depth of their valleys and crusted with the ash of marijuana were accompanied by a litter of hypodermic needles. The whole place was the mass aftermath of some grand junkie picnic, boarded up to be dealt with later by whoever was given the disagreeable task of having to do so. The wooden laths of the ceiling were thick with cobwebs but otherwise exposed, revealing a large bat hanging upside down with its wings wrapped ardently over its face as if it too could no longer stand to look at the chaos of its surroundings.

Ignoring the stench, Luke pulled out the brown envelope from inside his jacket pocket, sat it atop a relatively clean table and began rooting through the bedlam of the hut's disarray.

Tyler watched in silent bemusement as Luke searched rubbish bins, drawers, the backs of the threadbare couches. Finally blowing a year's worth of dust from a paper-towel dispenser and tearing off a sheet.

"Here have mine." Tyler said numbly, more baffled than ever by Luke's actions, and held a clean tissue from his pocket out to him.

Not in the mood to have to explain, Luke only offered his brother a quick scowl and spread out the contents of the envelope until he found the paper towel bearing Howie's writing. He held the two together by their perforated edges. No match.

"What are you looking for anyway?" Tyler asked, curiosity catching up with him.

"Howie's next letter." Luke replied, still picking his way through the filth and litter. "He'd been writing to me on napkins, menus, the backs of old beermats. Anything he could leave lying around unnoticed because his emails were being intercepted and his room was being searched."

Tyler emanated a huge belly laugh, to which Luke served back another unimpressed scowl.

"*Really?*" Tyler asked sardonically.

"A little over a year ago he sent me six lists of numbers and was one letter away from explaining what they meant. I haven't heard from him since."

Luke's face fell.

Tyler followed his train of vision to a wall mounted cabinet, conspicuous among the grimy run down shack for being about a year old and still gleaming white.

Tyler followed his brother over to it. Luke opened its doors and a family of beetles that had made the place their home scuttled away in a hundred different directions.

Tyler, stifling the urge to let out a girly scream of revulsion, turned to Luke with a 'Can we get out of here now please.' look on his face.

Luke was not ready to. Not just yet. He wrapped his knuckles on the wall inside the cabinet. Initially the dense flat thud of concrete met his knock, then the distinct sound of a hollow.

Without pausing for thought Luke pulled at the cabinet, gently at first, then with a mighty yank, and heaved the whole thing right off the wall.

"Are you mad?" Tyler cried out with alarm.

Luke thumped the wall with his fist. Crumbs of lose powder spilled away from a small hole. He gave Tyler a quick smile, knowing he was on the right track and poked his finger into the hole pulling away small clumps of plaster until he revealed a secret crevice.

Shaking his head like a befuddled cartoon character Tyler watched as Luke fished inside the crevice with his hand, soon retrieving an envelope.

They bent over the kitchen table together, pulling out the contents with the nervous excitement of two boys who had found the first major clue in a paper chase.

Howie's name was on a second envelope inside, and within that, a report;

'LAND MASS SURVEY - SKIDAWAY ISLAND SOUTH SHORE BEACH AND MARSHLANDS'

"T'sh t'sh little Howie. Stealing company files." Was Tyler's helpful remark.

Luke shook his head. "It's from the Department of Agriculture. It's public information."

Tyler nodded to the hole in the wall. "Then why the hullaballoo?"

"Why indeed?" Luke whispered.

Luke sat at an old rickety chair behind the table and began leafing through the report muttering to himself. "Forty-eight."

Tyler shook his head, still utterly bemused "Thirty nine." He contributed.

Luke looked begrudgingly up at Tyler. "The shoreline has a land mass density of forty-eight. On Herrick 2 a bunch of Wedge Heads worked out the foundations for a school after Terry blew up the old one. And that had an LMD of only forty-one."

Tyler stared slack-jawed at Luke. "Do you actually think I know what you just said to me?"

Luke spun the report round to face Tyler. "There's nothing wrong with the land here. There's no reason why the company couldn't build."

"Hey! Little doggy with your big juicy bone. Don't start getting ahead of yourself. We're not trying to solve a puzzle here."

Luke held the report up to Tyler like a prize. "Aren't we?" he said with a hard earned sense of triumph. "Because I'd say we just found a big piece."

PART TWO

'Must you carry the bloody horror of combat in your heart forever?'

The Odyssey, Homer

Eight

Churning waves vomited small bits of driftwood and thick sea foam onto the sand by Tyler's feet as he marched angrily up the beach.

Luke followed, keeping a few paces behind to allow space for his brother's equally churning mood.

"Tyler . . . Tyler. . ." Luke would call out his brother's name occasionally only for Tyler to ignore him and continue to storm away like a disgruntled lover.

"I can drive you to the harbour." Luke offered.

"I'll walk thank you!" Tyler snapped, continuing his angry march to nowhere. He came to an abrupt stop, causing Luke to near rear-end him like a car. He turned and pointed an irate finger in Luke's face. "You know I had to lie through my teeth when I got Howie the job there?"

A fierce wind whipping off the water blasted their faces. Luke pulled the hair out of his eyes and readied himself for the remainder of his brother's torrent of rage.

"But with you it was easy. I could be honest. He's a good kid. A good boy. You can trust him."

"You can." Luke responded.

"Yet here you stand, on a beach, eighteen months later, having your period and trying to bring down their empire!"

Knowing a smirk would likely make his brother want to throttle him, Luke bit his lip hard to keep any humour from his face and let his eyes wander over Tyler's shoulder up to the ridges of the sloping cliff face that bordered the beach. It was then he saw the hunting jeep, close enough for him to make out the figures of the four men inside and to see that two were carrying rifles. Seemingly as soon as they realized Luke had spotted them, they turned on the jeep's engine and began traversing down the cliff's pathway and turned onto the flat sands of the beach.

"I'm an ordinary man," Tyler went on, forcing Luke to look reluctantly back at him. "I like women, I like my mates, I like beer. And I happen to like my job thank you very much. "

"I think we'd better go Tyler." Luke said in a flat voice that barely masked his concern.

"I'll say!" Tyler retorted. "I did not ask to be involved in anybody else's war!" He turned back to continue his disgruntled trek.

This time Luke reached for him and grabbed a fistful of his shirt at the shoulder, pulling it out from under the belt of his trousers.

Tyler looked incredulously back at Luke then, seeing the harrowed look on his face, followed his train of vision and spotted the jeep with the two men in the front, a driver and a passenger, and two standing in the back seats, holding rifles aloft. The jeep picked a strangely sluggish winding pathway across the sand towards them.

Luke nodded slowly, and Tyler understood exactly what that meant. They turned and began quick-stepping together, retracing their own indented footsteps in the sand.

A shot rang out in the air above them like the overhead crack of a whip. Tyler and Luke ducked in unison and a hundred sea birds screamed and took to the air as one. Luke grabbed Tyler's arm and forced him to up the pace on his stride.

"What do we do?" Tyler asked urgently.

Luke glanced over his shoulder to see the jeep almost upon them, only slowed from reaching them by the strange zigzagging pathway it chose to take in pursuit.

"How do we handle this?" Tyler nagged at him again.

"Just keep walking." Luke ordered and pushed his brother down toward a swiftly flowing current of water in a channel across a receded section of the beach, which, if crossed, would provide a shortcut back to the car.

Tyler stared uneasily at the stream of water he was being ushered towards; the alluvium carried by its rapids appeared to be a slurry of decaying food and animal, *(also perhaps human)*, waste. He dug his heals into the sand and resisted Luke's attempt to push him into the ravine like a stubborn goat.

"Get in there!" Luke demanded.

Tyler kept wary eyes on the water, shaking his head like a two-year-old afraid to get in a swimming pool for the first time. "It's cold!" Tyler protested. "There's sewage in it. It smells."

"It's cover dog tits! Now move your arse!" Luke yelled and pushed him unceremoniously down into the gorge.

A second gunshot pierced the air. Closer this time. Feet away. The recently resettled sea birds squawked as one, this time their combined noise seemed more a shriek of antagonised resentment than startled fear as they made the obligatory climb into the air once more.

The Dearlove brothers had no choice but to turn and face the men behind them; Tyler, knee-deep in the fjord and shivering, Luke tottering on its banks.

The four men remained in the jeep, watching. Calum and Damien in the back, still standing, small smug smiles on their toothy faces, the recently fired rifles in their hands. Mason Hare in the passenger seat with the foot of his right leg resting on the knee of his left, looking decidedly bored with it all. He soon took his eyes from the Dearloves and began examining the content on his mobile phone.

It was Jed Burke who'd been driving. And he was also the first to move.

He climbed out of the jeep and trod a strange pathway towards the brothers, like an expert traversing a minefield, knowing exactly where the hidden zones of danger lay.

Every muscle in Luke's body tensed, his eyes darting to the corners of their environment, quickly scanning for anything he could do, anything he could use to defend the two of them.

Jed Burke's eyes were also scanning the surroundings. He bent down and picked up a large piece of driftwood. Luke's hands balled into fists and he bent his arms at the elbows slightly.

Jed tossed the driftwood passed them. It landed far over on the other side of the gorge in a direct line between them and the rental car.

Tyler's eyes danced wildly from his youngest brother, to the men in the car, to Jed, to the hurled plank of wood, confusion mounting with each passing second. Finally, the reason behind the man's strange action became clear. The mudflat, where the plank lay, where Luke and Tyler were sure to have crossed, bubbled like thick soup and dragged the wood down deep into its murderous depths.

The emotions of relief and uncertainty were a strange mix.

Tyler and Luke looked from the spot where the plank had been devoured by the earth, to each other and up to their . . . *saviour.*

Tyler let out a slight laugh, half tension release, half embarrassment, with a small touch of bravado forced in to overcome the fact that he was a grown man shivering in a stream of shit and piss in front of a group of hulking great outdoorsy types who'd had to come and pluck him and his brother from danger like a pair of kittens in a tree.

He looked to Luke expecting to see a mirrored reaction but only found him and the man who'd come to them regarding each other in cold sterile silence.

Distrust had stolen back into Luke's face.

A distrust as obdurate and as bottomless as the treacherous grounds of Skidaway Island had also proved themselves to be.

Nine

"You coming for me? You coming for me? Yeah you are. You come here."

To a stranger, if they were stood side-by-side, Luke Dearlove and Kai Burke, Jed Burke's only son, would easily be mistaken as brothers.

They were the same age, twenty-four, the same height, five feet eight, the same weight, now that Luke had let his muscles fall to waste, and the same Adonis-like features, as if they'd been chipped from marble by the same sculptor, the same thick dark hair and Caribbean Sea blue eyes; their looks seemingly gifts from the gods.

But there the similarities began and ended.

"Yeah, you come here." Kai Burke ordered into his mobile phone while sitting on a stool in the bar of his parent's hotel. "It's going to be wall to wall birds I'm telling ya. We'll get pissed here first for free then go down there. Yeah you are, you're coming." He lowered the phone then returned it quickly to the side of his head to add. "You prick." And finally ended the call.

Luke's actual, but less physically similar, brother, Tyler, was sitting in his changed clothing two stools away from Kai Burke, laughing hysterically with his cousins Damien and Calum and their father Mason as if he'd known them all for years. Several empty beer glasses had accumulated in front of them.

As soon as Kai tapped the 'end' button on the call a hand swiped at him and he received an eye-watering bitch-slap courtesy of his twenty-two-year-old girlfriend Shelley Morgan, a glass full of vodka and coke upending on the bar and soaking his white shirt.

Tyler, Mason and the Hare brothers all winced in unison. Calum being the first to laugh before exclaiming. "Ruthless!!"

"What the fuck was that for?" Kai demanded, holding his reddening cheek and pulling his sodden shirt out from his chest.

Shelley wobbled drunkenly on high heels, glaring at him with cut glass hate in her eyes.

"Fucking 'ell cous'," Damien remarked, opening two beers and handing one to Tyler. "Wouldn't have taken that when she was my bird."

"Your bird!!" Shelley half screamed. "I went out with you for two weeks when I was eighteen and you never even touched my minge!"

Mason laughed, his eyes half closed in whisky laden sleepy content. "Nice work stud."

Calum sniggered heartily, it wasn't often he had a break from being the object of his father's ridicule.

It was enough for Shelley to strike her venomous rage at him. "Don't know what you're laughing at. Whosever gonna fancy you? You look like a foot."

Mason nodded, still in his blissfully contented mood. "Fair dos son, you do look a bit like a foot."

Janice Burke, Kai's mother, hurried into the bar from the back room to investigate the commotion. She lifted up the heavy wooden hatch that allowed exit and entrance to the back of the bar and examined the red mark on her son's face. Pushing her hand away Kai pulled off his stained shirt and demanded his mother iron him a new one. Ignoring him Janice turned to his girl. "Shelley what's this all about please?"

Shelley wobbled more violently this time, Tyler darted out a hand to stop her falling right over. Besides Eva, Shelley was the rare beauty of the island. The one they all wanted. The only one she wanted however, was

73

Kai Burke, the only one she'd have. Not that he appreciated that. He'd thrown her away so many times like garbage that that was how she'd come to think of herself at all times; when, bored of his mates, and he picked her up, when cataclysmically bored of her, and he dropped her, it no longer mattered which. Still she clung to him as clouds clung to a mountain, circling him, unable to drift anywhere other than near to him, smothering him entirely if she could.

She was all fierce dark hair and rosebud features. Right now those features were covered in thick colours where the makeup had streamed with her tears, making her look like a set of crayons which had melted in nearness to a flame. Normally, she would lead the set of the young and the beautiful on Skidaway. They learned life, not from the farmers and local business owners who'd sired them, but from the rich and the glamorous of reality TV, emulating their hair, their accents, their clothes, and made desperate attempts at pale imitations of their lifestyles. They were fledging pursuers of fame. For them mediocrity was a crime. Unattractiveness a sin. And they would leave the leaden listless shores of Skidaway as soon as time, money or opportunity would allow. They were the natural expatriates, they went, and their parents stayed. That was the order of things. Until recent times.

Kai was routing through a pile of clean washing, searching for a shirt, discarding other items and letting them drop carelessly down to the beer and dirt covered floor. "Mum, find me a shirt!" he hollered.

Janice, for once, ignored her son and kept her attention on Shelley. "Shelley what is this about? We're going to have customers through the door any minute."

"Why don't you ask him?!" Shelley yelled, flicking a hand contemptuously at Kai. "Or better still your husband."

She'd said it just as Jed Burke made his way to the back of the bar and took hold of his son's face, examining the large red patch that practically covered his whole left cheek.

"Fifty years my family have had the only cleaning contract on this island." Fresh angry tears filled Shelley's eyes and she nodded her head towards Jed while shrieking at Kai. "You said you were going to talk to him."

As if on cue three young Albanian women who'd been cleaning the seating area, rattled into the bar with their mops. They felt the thickness of the tension in the room immediately, and observed Shelley in her distressed state, whispering about her to each other behind cupped hands.

"Yeah!" she spat at them. "It's you I'm talking about you scruffy little slags."

Janice snapped her fingers and ordered the three girls back to work. They begrudgingly set to it with their mops, still talking about Shelley, small smiles on their faces.

Janice took Shelley's elbow and turned her away before trouble ensued. She wet the corner of a hanky with her tongue and began daubing at the mess of colour on Shelley's face.

"Now look, you know, us, your family, the McGregors. We've all got to do our bit."

Mason Hare drunkenly chipped in to support his sister. "We take care of the fuzzy wuzzies, the fuzzy wuzzies take care of us."

Ignoring them Shelley fought to glower back at the three girls, "Keep staring bitches!"

They laughed and muttered about her in Albanian to each other.

Shelley leant forward, her voice going up several decibels as Kai came back from behind the bar holding a crumpled shirt. "You can come round after you finished scrubbing the toilets and stare through the window and watch him fingering me all night. There's no one else left at my house now it's up for rent and my dad and brothers are on the next ferry out of here."

Kai held out the shirt to his mother, "You going to iron me a shirt or what?"

Janice grabbed the shirt from Kai and tossed it aside. She gripped Shelley's arms and shook her slightly. "Rent? Shelley, we told your dad to sell if he wanted off the island." She turned to Mason. "The McGregors got what? One over prime."

"One over prime." Mason confirmed, and shot back another whisky.

She began ushering Shelley towards the door. "Now you get down that harbour and tell your dad to come back and talk it through with us. Where's your little coat? This your little bag?" She threw her head back to her son. "Kai, take her down that harbour."

"I'm going out." Kai fired back indignantly as if someone had just asked for his kidneys.

The three cleaners' chatter about Shelley, still kept to their own language, rose higher and was intermingled with spiteful laughter.

Shelley tore herself free from Janice's arms and darted up to the bar, gripping hold of the wooden edge and blabbering nonsensically, making a cruel mimicry of them and their native tongue. "Blah blah-blah blah blah blah-blah."

The three women all fired back fierce insults in Albanian.

Shelley turned to her now seemingly forgiven boyfriend. "I swear Kai, I will go ham on those gooks."

76

At her wits end Janice implored her husband who was leaning quietly against the bar in quiet observation of the melee. "Are you going to do something about this?"

Jed gave the red handprint on his son's face one last look and followed up with a small nod for his wife. He straightened up and, barely touching it with his hip, managed to nudge the bar in such a way that the entry hatch crashed down onto the opening with the speed, force and sheer ferocity of a heavily swung axe.

It smashed into place, sending splinters flying from its edge and making the beer glasses along the wooden bar top jump.

Shelley screamed.

As intended, the hatch had slammed towards her finger, which was still wrapped round the lipped edge of the opening. She saved herself with less than a fraction of a second to spare, snatching her hand away and stuffing it into the safety of the plunging cleavage created by her push up bra.

The act shocked the whole bar into silence. Even the three Albanian girls gave Shelley looks of sympathy.

Jed's voice cut through the silence like a second wielding axe. "You should be careful where you put your hands."

The next wave of tears crowded Shelley's eyes. She began wobbling backwards towards the door. "Know what this island's going to miss now my dad and brothers are gone?" She asked the assembled group in a choked voice. "A real fucking man."

She turned hastily round and nearly crashed right into Luke. He'd returned from showering and changing his own clothes in the room Jed and Janice Burke had insisted on them taking and was standing in front of her, clean and impossibly handsome.

She wobbled again in her ridiculously high heels. He quickly reached out a tender hand and steadied her. The small act of kindness was enough to make her emotions spill over. Sobbing hysterically, she bolted out through the door.

Kai looked up from the bar, studying the young man who resembled him in every way other than character. Not particularly concerned about any competition, he picked the crumpled shirt back up and yelled at his mother. "I'll iron it myself shall I?"

With Kai gone and the fracas over, Janice Burke began an agitated one sided conversation into her brother Mason's ear punctuated with emphatic shakes of her head and wild gesticulations, the Albanian girls returned to their duties and the men swivelled back on their barstools, turning their attention to each other and their drinks. Tyler nodded for Luke to join them at the bar, tapping on the side of a beer bottle.

Luke shook his head in an unemotional decline and left them, heading into the empty seating area where he thought he'd be alone.

Jed Burke's voice seeped out from the darkness and wrapped around Luke like a pair of great gnarled hands suddenly squeezing his throat. "Sorry about the smell."

He didn't know the man. He'd encountered him. That's all. Twice in one day. Once to warn him with a thinly veiled threat. The second time to come to his and his brother's rescue. And that, for a reason he couldn't justify, was an act that felt more like murder.

And now, from the shadowy depths of a booth in the restaurant seating area of his own hotel he was apologising for the odour that seemed to invade every street, every beach, every building, every crevice of Skidaway Island's hundred and forty square miles. Luke didn't know the man, but the one thing he did know was that Jed Burke wasn't the type to apologise for anything.

"We got a mad dog problem you see." Mason Hare had joined them. He was standing in a doorway slapped with blue paint that separated the seating area from the bar. He leant up against its frame, eating an apple, in a hopelessly transparent attempt at showing Luke how irrelevant his presence on the island was to him. "Got loose on Trencher's farm, been after the lambs and the chickens. They fall into the catacombs if it don't get 'em first. Break their legs, or their necks, lay there till they rot."

The sudden interest of the two older men felt like guns pointed his way. "That explains it." Luke said it calmly, daring himself, and adding, "I've been smelling death all over this island."

The two men exchanged looks, Luke's small audacity something they would soon need to discuss.

As he turned away Luke saw the man again. The same man who'd delivered a copy of his medical log from his treatment at Belleview to Francis Grayson earlier that day. Again, the hood of his sweatshirt was pulled fiercely down as if he was prepared to show his face to no man or woman that walked the earth.

As soon as Luke spotted him the man gathered his things and headed out the hotel's back doors which lead to a veranda overlooking the beach.

Luke moved to follow the man.

Jed Burke had no bucket of rabbits there with which to block Luke's path. He needed something else to stop him leaving, something else to hold him fast so he could make his final point.

Before Luke reached the door, Jed Burke was upon him, whipping him round and forcing him up against the hotel's alcohol and cigarette stinking walls. His fingers wrapped around Luke's face and for the briefest of moments Luke remembered his time in Belleview; the doctors who pinned him down to jab needles into his arms, electrodes into his head in their desperately valiant attempt to cure him of his mind.

Mason gave a quick look over his shoulder, checking no one was approaching, nodded a 'go ahead' back to Jed.

But Jed needed no man's permission, least of all his brother in law's in his fuck-awful maroon suit. Jed Burke did as he wished. And if it had been his will to pull out his gut hook knife and slice it through the boy's jugular, that's exactly what he would have done. Mason Hare didn't need to check he was safe and clear to go about his business. He knew only too well how to go about his business. If he'd made it his business there and then to sever his head from his neck and stroll casually back to the bar and drop it into his brother's lap then that's what would have followed.

In his infinite mercy, he decided to give the boy one last chance. His breath, no doubt, was as stale and foul stinking as the hotel's paint chipped walls. He bent into him like a lover going in for a long hard kiss and let him smell it before speaking. "This island is nothing but a mile long strip of dirt and mud. It hasn't the depth for holding building or burying anything."

Luke stretched his mouth free of Jed's fingers, long enough to speak;

"Except perhaps the truth?"

The countenance carried a strength Jed Burke had not been expecting. The gut hook knife in his pocket seemed to glow warm like hot metal against his chest, aching for Jed to reach for it, bring its viciously sharp point up and press it into the fleshy bulge of cheek that he currently had squeezed within his hand, nick him just enough for a drop of blood to run down his cheek, strip that superior look from his face, make him wince, show him just who was running this show.

Luke showed the man no fear. In truth he felt none. He was able to withstand the stench of the man's breath that spread over his face like gas from a dentist's mask. The hate in his eyes. He'd known and seen worse in his young life.

Jed Burke better have something bigger in his arsenal if he wanted to see him twitch. He prized himself out of his vice like grip and looked him defiantly up and down.

With that he turned and followed the path the man in the hooded sweatshirt had taken out through the back doors.

Jed Burke stared hard at that back door, long after Luke had exited. That boy's last chance was gone.

Ten

Luke leant on the railing of the veranda that overlooked the sea with a cold sharp wind coming at him, tearing his hair back savagely from his head and bringing the blood to his cheeks. He stared down at the mile long strip of dirt and mud Jed Burke had been referring to. If Skidaway Island was a cell, then this was its nucleus. This finger-like stretch of beach, narrow enough at some parts for a man to spit across it. It was where the residents of Skidaway island had settled over the centuries; the hub of its life. The spot the Company had picked to set its castle, the castle which, for reasons known only to them, never was.

Jed Burke had been conspicuously keen to reinforce the official story, and more besides. *'It hasn't the depth for holding building or burying anything'.*

Luke smiled at the idea of following up the statement by squirrelling out of the man's grip, hot footing it up to his and Tyler's rented room and returning with the official report from the Department of Agriculture and reading verbatim the four-hundred-word passage on the south beach's land mass density, then turning to Jed and Mason's befuddled stares with a smug smile and the words 'Your thoughts?' His smile deepened. Intelligent upper handedness always hurt the brutish more than a barstool across the nose, just as dogged determination and a moral compass always hurt the avaricious and the corrupt. The smile left Luke's face as he pondered this last point and his eyes skated over to the skeletal shell of the housing complex, still the great grey ghost, rusting in its rooted spot, an enduring reminder to all of what could have been.

An intuit of hope swept through Luke's body. Something instinctive, something primal, was telling him that he might just be here trying to solve a murder mystery, the crime of which, hadn't been committed yet.

If Howie had stumbled on something maybe they still had him here, handcuffed, blindfolded, chained to a wall. Cowering in a corner. Clinging to life after a year shitting into a disease ridden chamber pot infected with maggots and flies.

But how the fuck was he ever going to find him?

His eyes left the castle's skeleton and searched the land beyond; fields, woods, grasslands, peat bogs and marshes . . . then he saw it and his body tensed. He knew of it but hadn't noticed it till now. The octagonal structure set around a large gardened area. About a mile and three quarters due east, set equidistant from the coastal road and the little used, barely travelable pathway that cut through the island's centre. A 1960's holiday complex of chalets, bungalows and one central house. It had been procured by the Company from the original owners six years ago. It was shabby and in disrepair, but that was nothing a lick of paint and a rewiring overhaul couldn't fix to ready it for the hordes of construction workers, architects and project managers required for the build. Those construction workers, architects and project managers who'd left along with the Company's supposedly ruined dream.

But life was there now, not only dwelling but growing. Luke squinted and struggled to see in the day's failing light. Sure enough there it was; a village of tents grown around the complex. The darkness was gradually encroaching on the messy organic shapes, but still, Luke knew a shanty town when he saw one; the haphazard layout of an unplanned, thrown together, sprouting settlement. The smoke from fires, the stench from raw sewage, the chaos of wasted rotting human life.

The relative luxury of the chalets and bungalows had obviously filled to bursting long ago and the overspill, or the unwanted, were making do, clinging to the fringes of an existence in their own filth and squalor. *'Many now have the best jobs, businesses, houses.'* Francis Grayson and

Detective Ackerly Standing had told him that day. *'Where are the rest?'* he'd asked. *'Huffing paint thinner and shivering under a sheet of cardboard.'* Here were the rest. Just as he'd predicted they would be.

He would go there. Now. The sky was turning gunmetal grey. Night would give him cover. He would leave the rental car on the coastal road and cross the remainder of the land by foot. That would allow him the advantage of a surprise arrival. He'd kick down every door, rifle through every room, tear down every damn tent till he found his brother, or someone who would tell him where his brother was.

Suddenly a sound, metallic and discordant, coming through the gentle rush of the tide, stole into his thoughts. Luke put his plans on hold and stretched over the veranda's railing to see the great grated opening to the catacomb on the beach being pushed open by a tiny foot. A boy tumbled out from within its depths, then another, finally a third. It was Tin-Tin, his dark haired, purple lipped photographer first encountered on his arrival on the island, along with his two thieving cohorts. Luke looked from them to the hilly ground between the beach and the holiday complex and its surrounding shanty town. *'An entire network of catacombs run under this island'.* The boys had made what would have been a twenty-minute journey by land in probably five mins by scrabbling through the tunnels underneath it.

He knew boys like this. Had crossed paths with them in numerous countries around the world. They were the natives of shanty towns and slums. The street children of war. They were as deadly as bombs. Thieves and liars with nowhere to go. All fuck you attitude and ragged torn clothes. Permanently high on their own ride of religion and sin. They'd trade cigarettes for secrets from the soldiers and blow jobs for small change from anyone else. Sad, sick, hungry, lonely, exploited.

Haters. Hateful. Products of hatred in wars they'd had the misfortune of simply being born to.

They knew the secrets soldiers could capitalise on. And they'd just presented Luke with one he'd spend the rest of his life thanking them for. A foot arrival would work, but still leave him exposed. If he followed their route back, he'd be able to burrow under and climb up smack into the middle of the shanty town before any of them knew what they were about to fuck with.

Luke pushed through the metal gate on the veranda and hurried down the worn stone steps onto the beach.

At the bottom he took a breathless look around. Night was drawing down the last colours of its day, painting the whole beach in a melancholic dusky crimson.

He looked to his left and saw the grated opening into the catacombs, still ajar, and took a slow step towards it.

The demon waits in dark corners.

The crossed metal of its frontage, covered with cancerous patches of rust was as menacing as a portcullis. From within something seemed to be breathing, and on that breath was the coarse and putrid stench of death. At first it was only an aroma, feint and stale. Then suddenly death seemed everywhere, skulking in the air, in the water, through the trees.

Is this where the giant rat came to die?

The optimism and fragments of hope he'd known a few moments earlier were fading now, replaced by another deeper, and more primal instinct, a savage, unignorably intense, sense of dread.

As water slapped in and out between his feet, entering and receding from the tunnel's yawning mouth he fought to see through the murky depths and down into her bowels, her beating heart.

Luke Dearlove had seen his share of death.

'Oh god,' he whispered, '*oh god.*'

He begged his brain not to pick this moment to start showing his eyes something that wasn't real. For there, among the twisting shadows and stagnant air lay a hand, flopped down, palm upwards, its long dead skin shrunken around it like an overtight wrinkled leather glove. Luke took in the air in three short gasps, air heavy with the sourness of old corpses. 'Oh god,' he whispered again, '. . . Howie.'

Luke closed his eyes hard and rubbed them savagely. He opened them wide, peering intently at the same spot. What once seemed unequivocally, undeniably to be the shape of a mummified hand now seemed more like a tangle of deadwood covered in wet leaves and moss.

Seemingly answering his silent thoughts, and refusing to relinquish her secrets that easily, the catacombs breathed out with an ugly, foul stinking wind that bellowed through its innards and threw itself into Luke's face.

Luke coughed violently, reeling, and stumbled down to the water's edge, his hand clamped over his face.

That was when he saw him again.

He coughed and struggled to recover, calling out to the stranger. "Are you looking for me? Hey! Hey!! Are you looking for me?!"

Luke knew the man had heard him. There was always the possibility he was deaf, when he'd spoken before in the boardroom, while delivering the package to Francis Grayson, his voice had had the same muffled tone of a man who may have been without the ability to hear. Or he had earphones on under that hood, bobbing his head to some banging rap tune, that or his favourite 80s classics mixed tape. But Luke didn't think so.

Soon he was close enough to grab the back of the man's loose hooded sweatshirt and spin him around. Luke did so demanding the man tell him, "Why do you keep following me around?"

The action was enough to pull the man's hood from his face. Luke gasped and immediately forgot the question he'd just ordered an answer to.

He'd seen people afflicted with Neurofibromatosis twice in his life before. As a child, a girl at his school had become stricken with the condition at the age of six. His classmates had watched as her face had changed slowly over the years, the first of the non-cancerous tumours growing upon her, making her forehead look unnaturally pronounced, and a patch of skin on her cheek overlaid with a narrow ridge of pebble-like bumps.

The second case was more extreme. And more tragic, if you could describe anyone's challenges in life according to scale.

It was on deployment his first month in service in Iraq. He'd been warned by others of how the mentally ill and the facially disfigured were treated in the region; basically, *if not worse than,* animals. One time they'd intervened when the police had handcuffed a mentally ill woman to a light pole simply because she'd been 'bugging them'. And because they thought it funny.

It wasn't unusual to see homes with small locked stone shed dwellings next to the main house. The infantry battalions he'd been attached to had had to search such places and more than once came upon someone with a mental affliction, chained up inside, or simply sitting there. The families would bring food and water, and clean them up as often as was necessary.

That July he was with a troop searching for IEDs. It was in one of the more precarious parts of the region and at least one Combat Medic had to be in tow. Sgt Everly had led the search into the small shack at the side of a farmhouse. That was when they found him.

They'd called for Luke immediately, hustled him up from the rear to front. As he weaved his way through the tangle of men their revolted laughs, cruel jokes and gasps of disbelief grew louder.

He couldn't tell how old the man was, no part of his face was visible; it being masked by such a crowding of small tumours, each one fighting the other for space. No feature was visible, just a thick nodule coating that gave the appearance of a mask made of tree bark. From the man's body, lithe and smooth, blissfully free of any of the offending growths, other than a small patch on his shoulder, Luke guessed he was a young man, younger than him, most likely a teenager.

"What the hell is it?" Sgt Everly had demanded to know.

Luke wanted to turn and tell him to keep his insensitive voice down, but a Private, as he then was, could do no such a thing to a Sergeant. English was the one saving grace. The young man couldn't have understood what was being said about him. However, what Luke also knew, with a sadness that threatened to corrode his soul, was that this young man was not mentally ill, any more than he was an animal, despite the chain round his ankle keeping him shackled to a large cement block. And even without an understanding of their language he would have known the laughs, the jeers, the cruel smirks, the questions in the foreign tongue were in response to him, the '*thing*' on the ground before them.

'If you're not mad now, go there soon.' The thought was something that rose up within Luke, as he knelt in front of the tethered teenager, searching through the tragedy of his face for a mouth, a nostril and eye. 'No one would blame you.'

Sometimes the only possible answer to life's cruelties was to go completely insane.

Luke stood on the beach staring at the third person he'd now encountered in life with the condition and hated himself with impunity.

"I'm sorry," he told him with a sincerity that was palpable. "I'm really sorry."

The man, Rory Benson, nodded slightly. The progression of his condition was nowhere near as advanced as the poor chained teenager Luke had encountered on deployment. Perhaps worse than the girl at his school. His features were still visible and succinct. Only his right eye was changed dramatically; crowded with lumps and puckered, nearly closed. 'Probably blind in that one', Luke surmised. His left cheek bulging out at one side as if swollen after taking a right hook. A large cluster of tumours hung from his neck like a bunch of grapes. Luke understood why he kept the hood permanently pulled down. *The world picked its jokes with impunity.*

But today Rory left the hood to hang freely and flap in the sea breeze. He wasn't sure why. But he did so. As though he was meant to. As though something ordained it. *You show me your scars. I'll show you mine.*

"Is there something you want to say to me?" Luke asked him.

Rory studied him without answering. He knew the young man's name was Luke. Luke Dearlove. Lance Corporal Luke Dearlove to be precise. He'd passed the first few tests. He'd defied Francis Grayson, Mason Hare, Jed Burke with a courage and a dignity that was uncommon in most men.

Could you be the unmet friend?

"Is there?" Lance Corporal Luke Dearlove was asking him again.

Rory swallowed hard. One large internal tumour was bulging in his neck, it pushed his vocal cords forward slightly and restricted his airway. He always had to perform this little ritual before speaking. The recipients of his conversations normally assuming it to be through nerves rather than mechanics. But not this man. This young man quietly waited rather than giving him the usual looks of either desperate pity or slack-jawed curiosity.

"Have you ever heard of a mineral called palladium?" Rory asked.

The name was familiar. Luke squinted, scanning his memories. Finally he seized hold of how he knew it. "Yes, it's a rare earth element. They use it in mobile phones." He answered, pulling his own phone out of his pocket and holding it up to Rory.

"Phones, laptops, gaming. Almost any device requiring an electronic touch screen. Last assessment listed it as being more valuable than platinum. Thanks to its scarcity on the planet, and the bloody conflicts behind its mining and export."

"I know." Luke countered, wondering where this was heading. "I was attached to an infantry battalion protecting a hospital build on the Somalia borders when they uncovered a pocket. When the financiers found out what they'd stumbled upon they made them down tools and stop. . ."

Luke froze, the internal wiring of his body firing small electrodes within him, little jolts of realisation, nudging him on . . . *yes, little man, you're going the right way.*

He looked slowly up at the half finished build of the housing complex, perched atop the cliff further along the beach and gazing out to sea like an Egyptian Sphinx.

". . . stop the dig immediately." Luke finished the sentence, realisation set in his face like a sickness.

"Does it strike you as strange," Rory asked him, "that when the Company where building that thing about fifteen migrants a month were being trafficked over for cheap manual labour, but, when they found out something was . . . *'wrong with the land'* . . . and stopped their work that number went up to fifty a week?"

Luke's eyes fell over to the lines of houses, shops and restaurants on Skidaway's mile long strip of dirt and mud running from the harbour to where they now stood. The nucleus of the island's life. Lights were coming on from within, flickering like stars in the midst of an encircling night, seemingly blinking out signals for Luke as he struggled to order the muddy thoughts in his brain.

Rory smiled, knowing Luke nearly had it. He nodded at the phone in Luke's hand. Luke looked at it, drawing his finger across the screen, its elements leaving a feint trail like a dying star. "Twenty first century oil." Rory said with a wry smile.

Rory nodded back to the narrow stretching mile of homes and businesses across the beach, loading his voice with sarcasm as he spoke. "If they could just do something about the few hundred pesky people sitting directly atop the goldmine." He took a step towards Luke, his voice resuming a serious tone. "The rightful owners of that land. And everything under it."

Rory looked out to the darkening horizon, now a blurred smudge of dark red light where sky met sea. "A few hundred years ago on the other side of an ocean the US military were ordered to hand out smallpox infected blankets to Native Americans."

As if on cue Tin-Tin, and his two cohorts, Isni and Sokol, ran passed them and raced down to the water's edge, laughing and shrieking.

Rory nodded at the tear-away little ragamuffin boys. "These days you have to be even more inventive if you want to displace a generation."

91

Suddenly it all made perfect, sickening sense. Luke took an urgent step towards Rory. "Did my brother know about this?"

"Yes." Rory told him truthfully.

"Is he still alive?" Luke asked desperately. "Is he?"

"I don't know." Rory answered, equally truthfully.

Luke sighed and looked back out at the water. The sun had finally gone, its last lingering traces distorting sky and sea together in a wash of red. A few low-lying stars began to blink, mirroring the lights from the houses and restaurants along the seafront, sending out their own message to earth.

Luke looked down at the ground beneath his feet. "Our reasons for being barbarians never change." He whispered.

He turned but Rory had gone.

Message delivered. Roger that. Over and out.

First part of his message at least. Luke sensed more would come. *We'll cross paths again, you and I.*

A clanging boom from the water's edge demanded Luke's attention. He turned to see the boys had started three-barrel fires and were lighting firecrackers and hurling them at each other like grenades. The sparks from the barrel fires rushed upwards and fizzled out in the dying light. Luke moved to trot down to the boys, admonish them, take the firecrackers away. But he stopped himself. *Let them kill each other if they want to.*

The boys pulled on their animal masks, Isni the Lamb, Sokol the Fox, Tin-Tin the Pig. They picked up large bits of driftwood and embarked on a swordfight with them. Three tear-away ragamuffin boys, the street children of war, who roamed the earth looking for a home. They were knights of old now, warriors battling, as warriors do. Boys laughing, as boys do.

Tin-Tin lanced his 'sword' into the space between Sokol's arm and chest. Sokol let out an exaggerated howl of pain and suffering and fell to ground, his torso hitting sand, his stiff legs following.

Tin-Tin held the sword aloft in a stance of victory.

Men dying, as men do.

Behind them the fires in the barrels grew wilder, embers from them spat and hissed and rose in crazy twists up to the darkening sky.

"Brother, my brother. Forgive me my sins. I was not at your side when hell came closing in."

Luke turned in the direction of Howie's voice.

The silhouetted shape high above, was standing on the veranda outside the hotel, like a Captain at the prow of a ship. He was gripping the iron railing and watching. Watching Luke.

Luke took a cautious step towards the man.

"Brother my brother. Yes try as I might. I now realise it was also my fight."

Luke squinted and, as a firework display marking the beginning of the autumn festival began raging its warfare of light and noise in the sky behind him, he could see in its flashing colours, that the shadowy figure was Jed Burke.

Tin-Tin let off another firecracker and threw it hard in Luke's direction.

Luke jumped as it exploded harmlessly at his side and, for a second, he wanted to scuttle like a crab to the safety of the rocks, doss down in the sand until the night was over.

'*I'm sorry,*' he said to the centre of his own being. '*But sometimes going mad is simply the only thing a man can do.*'

He put his head down and walked slowly back to the foot of the steep stone steps feeling Jed's relentless gaze crawling over his skin.

Moses, Before

He had had no premonition.

He had waited patiently in the rain. Neither it, nor the biting wind, could knock the smile from his face.

Two of the Albanians, standing miserably around a barrel fire, resenting the ebullience that would not be knocked from him, turned scornful eyes his way. Tossing their questions at each other, loud enough to ensure he heard. "What's he got to be so happy about?"

Moses caught the question over the howl of the wind and was more than happy to answer, "He's got a big surprise coming to him in the belly of one of those big steel birds."

He had said it to Tariq Skanderberg just as the three lorries began sounding their reverse alarms and backing into place.

He hadn't felt any fear at first. Not when the first lorry opened and the passengers came cautiously out into the night, coughing the clogging hell of their journey out of their lungs. Not even at the opening of the second lorry when they poured from its depths like rats from a sinking ship.

But the silence. The silence that they were presented with as the third lorry's door was heaved upwards, that was what sent the first minnowy flutters of disquiet to the tender space around his heart.

He whispered her name in a terrible cold voice inside his own head.

The silence was soon replaced by screams. The crowd, surging forward as one, carried him with them. The tsunami of panicked beings, thrusting him heavily against the lorry's opened platform. He used his frantic neighbours as props to scramble on board; sheer terror quick to make even the most mannered of men uncivilized.

There in the chaos, among the twisted limbs of the suffocated passengers, frozen, still clutching at their collapsed throats, frozen, still clawing at impermeable walls, sat a young woman in a long black coat. She lay against the lorry's inner wall as calm and serene as the virgin mother herself, a sleeping angel who may, at any minute, wake with a gentle stretch and a hazy look around. Moses had found her. Found his wife.

With the acceptance of a saint he kissed her cold cheek and pulled back her coat. Resting in her arms lay his infant son, his face pressed deeply into his mother's belly, as if, in their final moments, she had tried to draw the child back into her womb and spare him his fate. Moses lifted the boy as reverently as any priest has ever handled the Eucharist, meeting him for the first time, kissing his cold forehead, cradling him to his chest, 'my heart, my heart'.

Moses clambered from the lorry with his child. One of the security guards, the younger one, helped him with a guiding hand. Moses, manners returned, paused to nod the young man his thanks.

He then turned and raised his child to the moon and blessed his small dead body with a name 'Amani' which, when translated from Swahili, means 'Peace'.

Eleven

Nothing was harder for Moses Bogdani than to see a father neglecting his child.

Neglect, for him, was not the brutal hand of abuse but the squandering of moments.

He collected the glasses from the table of the young family in the booth at the hotel's bar and tried valiantly not to stare at the three-year-old boy reaching desperately with clawing hands for the nearness of his father.

'Pick him up,' he thought in the privacy of his mind. 'Drown him in warm smacking wet kisses. Know what's yours. Become one with it.'

Devoid of mental telepathy, the only connection the young father made was one to his mobile phone, begrudgingly, for the briefest of moments, acknowledging his son's chocolate and tear stained face, before nodding to his wife as an instruction to settle him down.

Moses could look no longer and left without the tip the man was fishing with one hand into the side pocket of his jeans for.

At the next booth he saw the young man sitting alone. No family, seemingly. He too was engrossed in his mobile phone. Scrolling through information on it and rubbing his temples intently.

Moses stole a quick glance at the information this young man was so absorbed in, quickly reading a few of the titles as he swiped through them; 'Rare-earth Mineral Substitutes could Defeat Chinese Stranglehold', 'Minerals for Tomorrow's Needs', 'Europium; Chemical Properties, Health and Environmental Effects.'

As he excused the interruption and began wiping the booth table in front of the young man he wondered if he might be a student, doing his masters in geology, picking the fierce sands of Skidaway for a field trip of some sort.

"It must have been a really hard time for them."

Moses did a small double take, it being such a rare occurrence for any patrons in the hotel's bar to take up conversation with him. At first, he wasn't sure what it was the young man was referring to. Until that was, he followed his train of vision through the window onto the veranda that overlooked the sea and spotted the group of shaven headed monks in solemn prayer. They often picked that spot at dusk to chant and meditate as the sun's final rays departed the earth.

'It takes one fractured soul to recognize another.' Moses thought, again in the quiet recesses of his own mind and wondered who this sorrowful young man was who so easily recognized the pain of others.

At the neighbouring booth the father finally gave in to the needs of his child and scooped him up, shaking him gently until he induced the boy's laughter then met his son's face with a peppering of kisses.

"The crossings." Luke added, so the tall waiter with the kind face would know what he was referring to. "They must have been really hard times for them."

Moses smiled, sensing the young family get up and leave, seeing the boy clutching his father's hand in his peripheral vision. "They were really hard times for a lot of us." He said to Luke with a sad smile.

Moses turned away and nearly collided with Tyler who was barreling towards the booth, clearly suffering the effects of the first few lagers of the evening. Luke hated him like this. "Watch it." He snapped at Moses.

Luke sighed deeply, trying to give the tall waiter an apology with his eyes. Moses smiled reassuringly at Luke and went about his business.

"Dr Enid Foster's Quarterly Report on Elemental Variations in Trace Earth Elements." Tyler had snatched up Luke's phone as he lumbered into the booth seat opposite him and recited the title of the article open on the screen with the reading skills of a four year old. "Bet they're queuing in the streets for that one." He tossed the phone back across the booth table to Luke. "Come and have a beer with us." Tyler ordered, nodding back to Calum and Damien and a few of their other assembled friends getting steadily drunker by the minute at the bar.

"No thanks." Luke turned down the offer with intentional bluntness.

Ignoring his brother's demeanour Tyler beat out a mock drumbeat on the tabletop, readying Luke to listen to some major news. "Mark Neville from HR called. They're getting us both tuxedos made for the awards ceremony in July."

"I won't be there in July." Luke countered flatly.

"We're booked in for our first fitting Saturday." Tyler said as if deaf or oblivious.

"I won't be there Saturday."

"What you talking about Luke?" Tyler's irritation surfaced.

Luke picked his phone back up and returned to studying its contents.

Tyler shook his head, trying valiantly to pretend Luke's mood away. He pulled the phone back out of his hands and put it face down on the tabletop. "You're not sitting here sulking all night. Now come and have a beer with us. Do as you're told."

"You do as you're told Tyler." Luke snapped. "You're good at it."

Tyler glared at Luke, itching to slap him.

Luke leaned forward, returning the glare. "I don't want a beer, I don't want a tuxedo and I don't want to be part of their pathetic PR stunt. I just want . . . " pain rose in Luke's throat. "I just want to know what happened to our brother."

Tyler could feel the anxiety, the sickness, creeping up on his brother and his irritation quickly left him. He leant forward, trying to crowd out the rest of the bar. "What do you want me to do Luke?" He whispered.

He laid his hand over Luke's on the tabletop.

Luke looked fiercely up at him, pulling his hand away. "What you always do Tyler." He answered coldly. "Nothing."

Tyler got up from the table with the hollow haunted look of a man whose partner has

just left him. He turned blindly back from Luke and crashed heavily into Moses, now carrying a tray full of drinks which wobbled precariously then crashed into each other and came down like bowling skittles, forming one mass intermingled cocktail which blasted Tyler in the chest like a tidal wave.

"Fuck sake!" Tyler's frustration was more at the world than at the waiter.

Damien and Calum goaded the moment with cruel laughter at the bar.

"I'm sorry sir," Moses offered with saint-like dignity.

"Sorry's not going to dry my shirt." Tyler spat back.

Luke closed his eyes. He could hear Calum and Damien egging Tyler on. Their catcalls from the other side of the bar thrown Moses and Tyler's way:

Calum, "Oh . . . oh . . . be nice to the wetbacks now Dearlove."

Damien, "Sorry Jesus. He's fresh off the boat too."

Calum, "His name's Moses you dumb shit."

Tyler brushed himself angrily down and threw Moses a dark look. "Open your fucking eyes will ya?" He yelled pointing at his own forehead before glaring Moses indignantly up and down and turning back to Calum and Damien.

"Are your parents proud of your manners sir?" Moses had said it and Luke didn't blame him, but in the gassy depths of his stomach he knew this would now plunge from awkwardness to perdition.

Tyler turned slowly back, the colour of hate rising in his face. "I don't know. They died in a car crash ten years ago." He looked cruelly to the dripping tray in Moses's hand, the apron tied around his waist. "Are your children proud you're a waitress?"

Laughter erupted from the bar as though Tyler were the main act at a comedy store, subsiding just enough for Calum to chip in, "Ooh . . . ooh . . . you won. You won that one Dearlove."

But the jeering crowd may as well have disappeared. Tyler and Moses faced each other like warriors, something primeval and unspoken between them, as if each knew that if they fought now it would have to be to the death.

Luke was about to clamber up and stand between them when Moses spoke in a strange soft tone, keeping his eyes fixed firmly Tyler's way. "Uishi katika nyakati za kubadilisha."

Speaking no Swahili, Tyler had no idea that the words Moses had just delivered to him were; 'May you live in changing times'. He grunted like an old bull, turned and rejoined his new friends at the bar. They slapped him mightily on the back, rewarded him with freshly pulled pints. Calum and Damien determined to throw in a few last punchlines with cruelly raised voices;

Calum, "I think that's a gook curse he just put on you."

Damien, "We'll see your head on a stick in the centre of some wetback wank mag before long Dearlove."

Luke lowered his head a few inches, rubbing his temples. The environment around him began to soften and blur. 'Not now', he begged his brain, 'Just let me stay with the world a little bit longer. I've got so much work to do.'

But as an epileptic could not control his seizures, so the recipient of a fractured mind could not control his torments. He held his breath as the man with the thick dark hair slid into the booth behind him and rested his arm out on the back of his seat.

"Howie," Luke whispered.

The man with the dark hair turned his head the merest inch towards him.

"Brother, my brother now look at your leg. There's so much left missing yet not once did you beg."

Luke gasped slightly and turned slowly to look at the back of his head.

"Brother, my brother, though I lost more in mass. It is you far more haunted by our mistakes in the past."

Like a nervous butterfly, fearful to land, Luke's hand reached out and, gentle as a warm summer wind, lightly touched the thick brush of dark hair. "Please," he breathed. "Tell me what to do."

The man turned around and glowered at Luke.

The whole world rushed back to normalcy. Luke broke back to reality like a drowning man suddenly breaking the surface of water.

The frowning man in the booth behind him was Kai Burke, so taken aback by Luke's action he'd swallowed his drink erroneously and was struggling to speak. When he finally did recover his vocal cords the first words he would declare were, "What the absolute fuck?!"

He let out a strange half laugh, half gasp and turned to the three friends sitting with him. "Did you see that?"

They nodded, as bemused as he was, and got up to gawp at Luke.

"You're stroking my hair?!" Kai fired at Luke in something that seemed to be a question and a statement at the same time. He began relaying the incident to his friends, despite the fact they'd been there to see it. "He says 'tell me what to do' and strokes my fucking hair." He shook his head, laughing. "I don't know what to tell you to do bruv." Kai said to Luke and with the same breath turned to bellow at his parents behind the bar. "What sort of fucking weirdos you letting in here now?"

Tyler broke through the small crowd that were forming round the booth, sobered up considerably and holding out an apologetic hand as he protested for calm.

Janice Burke signaled with her eyes for Kai to come away from the situation.

Kai and his friend clambered out of the booth, muttering and laughing as they went, one pausing to throw back an insult which would cut Luke and wound him in more ways than he, or anyone else at the bar, could ever understand.

"Freak!"

Tin-Tin, Before

The young boy Tin-Tin had surprised them all. He strode out onto the first lorry's jutted metal lip, lit a cigarette and breathed in the night air, surveying the new land he'd been brought to as if he owned it

Tariq nudged Luan in the crowd. "Look who it is."

Luan called up to the boy. "Tin-Tin! Why aren't you with your family?"

Tin-Tin's eyes found Luan in the crowd. He thumped himself on the chest and drew another deep drag on his cigarette. "They needed more men on this ship." With that he jumped assuredly form the lorry's platform and strutted around the loading bay with the confidence of a young god.

Tariq laughed, shaking his head. "Still nothing dents him."

But the opening of the third lorry would do more than dent the eleven year old. Tin-Tin edged forward, all bravado robbed from his harrowed young face. As his dark eyes scanned the grim secrets the third lorry now revealed, he mouthed the word "mama".

And soon those dark unsolvable young eyes grew darker still. As dark as death.

And the light would not return to them that night, nor any night that was to come. They remained hollow and black as a moonless night.

Even one year on when the twelve-year-old Tin-Tin Berisha stood at a spot most men fear to tread, the protruding rock sticking out from the side of the cliff like a broken tooth, with the plastic face of a pig on his head and a tin cup full of hot urine in his hand, wondering who in the hell it was that had just gotten off the ferry and dared to come to his island.

104

It was a position he and the two other members of his tiny gang occupied often, the only thing that marked their morning ritual out as different on this occasion were the recently procured set of animal masks they wore, Tin-Tin; the pig, Isni; the fox, Sokol; the lamb. Tin-Tin the pig, he liked that.

Sokol and Isni hung back at the strength of the overhanging rock's ridge, lying on their bellies to lean over the edge, while Tin-Tin the Pig stood defiantly out on its precipice, daring god to fuck with him.

The masks and the Polaroid camera which Tin-Tin now had slung round his neck on a multicoloured strap were recent procurements from the hastily grabbed theft of a pink-arse's suitcase outside a cab rank just after dawn.

They'd made their getaway through the giant mouth of the north side catacomb that cut its way through the granite like a vein. Isni had the job of carrying the case, bringing up the rear as he and Sokol had bombed it through the tunnel's watery depths on their bikes. Isni, always carried the case. Isni, always, brought up the rear. And, as expected, Isni would not get through the tunnel with his breath held all the way, tripping under the weight of his load, he fell short at the central point, right next to the covered recess of Hell's Mouth Curve. He stumbled onto his knees and seized in a great gulp of air just as the wind that found its way through the tunnel lifted the great white plastic sheeting that enclosed the Curve and threw the odious stench of death at his beleaguered face.

As expected, this led to the inevitable vomiting. Isni had managed to make it down to the water's edge before spilling his guts. Crying and whimpering for his mother between bouts of revisited breakfast that were projected onto the surf.

Sokol and Tin-Tin watched from their bikes at the mouth of the catacomb, in front of its huge metal entrance grate. Sokol, with a small ugly smirk, Tin-Tin, drawing deeply on a cigarette and watching his suffering subordinate with cold unforgiving eyes, showing nothing more than a slight trace of distaste as seagulls flapped and fought for bile and chunks of regurgitated food now spreading out on the tide.

Sparing Isni little time for recovery they'd made their way up to the clifftops at the sound of the arriving ferry's horn.

As always, they filled their tin cups to the brim. As always, Isni stumbled and spilled half of his back down his arm as they took their position at the cliff's overhanging rock. As always, a hoard of pink-arses twenty feet below them were lining up in another exodus, traipsing a sorry path up the ramp towards the ferry, leaving their lives behind.

As always, Isni and Sokol emptied their piss directly onto them, howling with delight as the pink-arses realised what they'd been subjected to and glared up with curses of violence. Most of the women and often the men crumbling as rage gave way to sobs, this final indignation too much to take.

But today, Tin-Tin the pig faltered, the tin cup in his hand growing lukewarm from its contents and letting off a light steam like a recently brewed cappuccino. He pulled the pig mask from his face. He needed to see this more clearly than the narrow slits of view that the rubber encasing his head would allow. Isni and Sokol looked up at him, nodding at his tin cup, smiling their encouragement.

Who did they think they were? It was he who'd had to encourage them six months ago when he first thought up this game.

'Wetbacks is you men or is you little girls? I forget. Ah go strum the pink-arses a banjo. Go get you on a table for them and dance.'

Did he need their encouragement now? Did he fuck. This was his sport. He'd play when he chose to and when he chose to only. Yes. He was right. He had seen it. The cold sobering common sense of morning hadn't played any trick on those black and unknowable young eyes.

Down below, in the merciless crowd. Down there where the worms crawl and the spiders spin their webs. There in that melting pot of sorrow and sin the unprecedented was happening. Someone was walking the other way. Pushing through the departing crowd. A fish against the stream. Someone had dared to come to his island.

What you looking for down there pink-arse? You looking for hell?

You found her.

Twelve

Luke would quite happily have sat in a world of his own listening to the local folk-rock band that were playing up at the bar's small stage area. Still, try as he might, he had no choice but to endure the sparkling intellect, charm and wit of the small group that now surrounded him.

Kai Burke was busily texting on his mobile phone, ignoring his returned and stunningly put back together girlfriend Shelley who sat beside him. Still sulking, she stared moodily at the tabletop and continually rubbed at her finger, lest anyone forget the injury she had nearly suffered earlier that day.

Beside Kai was his cousin Calum with a cartridge belt wrapped around his head like a baby's bonnet, his face twisted into the ugliest of gurns as he smacked his head repeatedly down on the table for the group's amusement.

Damien paused from cleaning their hunting kit in readiness for the next morning to dig his brother in the ribs with his elbow, embarrassed by his antics, and knowing people laughed at him rather than with him, he pulled the belt roughly from his head. Unfazed, Calum grinned over at Shelley.

"You should come with us tomorrow Shelley." Calum said, nodding at the hunting kit. "Ain't nothing like making a kill when a woman's watching."

Shelley, still pouting and rubbing her hand replied sullenly. "No thank you."

Calum turned to Kai, "Cuz?"

"Fuck off." Was Kai's polite decline without so much as looking up from the text he was writing.

Damien looked over at Tyler.

"What about you Dearlove? Ever handled a gun?"

"Leave all that to my brother." Tyler had said it without thinking, just before draining the last of the beer from a pint glass, then froze, sickness rising up from the gassy pit of his stomach as he felt the tables' attention hone in on Luke.

Luke tried to keep his own attention on the band's sorrowfully melodic tune, remain lost in the singer's mellifluous voice as he sung about the human condition and man's many failings as a thinking animal. Luke knew what was coming next but wasn't ready to be dragged into it just yet.

He knew Tyler hadn't meant for it to happen. He'd watched his oldest brother from the same booth an hour earlier, gesticulating wildly and explaining emphatically at the bar, making a valiant attempt at clarifying to Kai Burke and other members of his kith and kin that Luke had a few 'problems' which he'd be so grateful if they'd be kind enough to overlook.

Following his mother's perfuse insistence Kai had traipsed begrudgingly back to Luke and offered an outstretched hand, which, equally begrudgingly, Luke shook. And all was well in the world. Let the beer pour freely and the good times ensue.

"Oh yeah." It was Damien Hare who'd honed in on the words the Dearloves were trying so desperately to forget. He turned squarely round to Luke. "Your brother told us you were in the army."

"Did he?" Luke sighed.

"You were in the army?" Calum chipped in, clearly absent during that previous conversation, mentally if not physically at least. "Did you meet any Taliban?"

"Only the second most annoying question anyone ever asks." Was Luke's only response.

"What's the first?" Damien enquired.

Kai looked up from his phone. "Have you ever killed anyone?"

Luke let out a longer sigh. "Not yet." He said under his breath.

Unperturbed Kai fired back with a follow up question. "What's the worst thing you ever saw?" Shelley leant against Kai. He elbowed her roughly. "Sit round properly."

Luke nodded at Shelley, "There are ladies present."

Kai smirked. "There are?"

Shelley fought to keep tears at bay and got up.

Calum gawped up at her beauty in bug-eyed wonder. "I'll go to the bar for you Shell-Shell."

"That's ok." Shelley answered. "I want to order some food."

"Tell my mum to make me a chicken dinner." Kai ordered. "And not fake mash. I want real potato."

Even Calum and Damien stared aghast at Kai's lack of sensitivity. Shelley made it to the bar before breaking down in Janice's arms.

Kai grumbled under his breath and got up, heading reluctantly over to the bar to placate his mother and his girl.

During the respite Rory entered the hotel. He took a place quietly at a neighbouring booth and buried his face in a menu.

Moments later the bar doors rattled open again. This time Tin-Tin, Sokol and Isni came barreling in with a gust of wind, their faces burning red from the cold and their animal masks tied to their belts and bouncing about their hips like trophies from a hunt.

The boys took the booth intentionally close to Rory and began steeling prolonged looks at his face, laughing and throwing out deliberate comments in Albanian. Both Rory and Luke's discomfiture intensified by the second.

Damien drew Luke's attention back to the booth. "Did you like it? Being in the army?"

"I liked sharing my life with my brothers." Luke answered.

Damien and Calum gave Luke confused glances.

"Men who would have, in a second, died for me. As I would have died for them." Luke stated in answer to their ignorance. "It was love, really."

"Is it true they line your beds up close together like that so you boys can choke each other's turkeys at night?" Calum asked with a thick greasy smile.

"Not on your first tour." Luke responded evenly.

"And don't the drill sergeants come in and make you drop to your knees and give 'em the old moustache mouthful if your cells aren't tidy?" Damien asked, grinning.

"We weren't in prison. Or the US Marine Corp."

Damien chipped in again. "Come on. Tell us. How many people did you kill?"

"I was a Combat Medic in the forces." Luke said, not bothering to mask his contempt. "Always amazes me no one ever asks how many men I might have saved."

Damien looked under his brow at his brother. "Well. It's fun learning about life in the army."

The Hare brothers rewarded each other with smirks and a bubble of juvenille laughter.

Luke sat suddenly upright, commanding their attention. "What do you do when your supply of would be suicide bombers dries up? The preferred method for Taliban in the central provinces was the systematic use of gang rape as a friendly form of persuasion. After subjecting young, eager to please, teenage recruits to several rounds of stank downing they'd strap 4kgs of explosives to their chests and tell them to go into town and 'wash off their sins'. What we could never work out was what their cohorts in the outer regions had in mind, reports in the area detailing a sudden increase in the raping of goats. Half way through my first tour we were on a patrol in Helmand Province clearing a dust track of explosives, only for our Senior Warrant Officer, the most experienced bomb disposal expert we had on the squad, to head into the brush for a slash and step on a double stacked land mine. Only him and his right arm made it out in the dust off. Me and a mate came back an hour later, couldn't find his legs. Found his boots though. That always happens. Told him we never did find his left arm. Truth was we saw a large goat playing with it in a nearby field and didn't have the heart to deprive her of her favourite new toy, we were guests in her country after all. And what with all the noise we were making and fuss we were causing. Not to mention the recent spate of arse raping she'd had to endure."

The men sat in shocked silence as if waiting for the dust to settle after an explosion. They stared slack jawed at Luke who sipped calmly from a bottle of beer. Only Tyler's face carried a different expression, concern, mixed with a tiny glint of pride.

At the next booth Tin-Tin screwed a napkin into a ball and threw it behind him at Rory, laughing hysterically when Rory leant round to tell them to stop.

Kai came back to the table and sat down, immediately going to his mobile phone, oblivious to the surreally awkward mood at the table.

Damien broke the silence first. "You missed all the best stories cuz."

"We've had one about suicide bombers." Calum told him.

"One about goats." Damien added.

"One about a bomb disposal expert that blew both legs and an arm off." Calum said with a spreading grin.

Kai shrugged with grand indifference. "Yeah? Couldn't have been much of an expert."

At that moment Tin-Tin and his friends got up and passed Rory. Rory breathed an audible sigh of relief that the boys were about to be out of his hair. Tin-Tin suddenly darted back, pointed his Polaroid camera at Rory and took his picture.

Still glaring at Kai Luke moved with lightning speed, bolted up, grabbed Tin-Tin by the back of the neck with one hand and slammed his head down onto the table in front of him.

"Apologise." Luke demanded.

Kai looked at Damien as if for protection, not knowing if Luke was ordering an apology from him or the boy in his stranglehold.

"Apologise." Luke repeated in a voice as cold and hard as stone.

Tin-Tin began wailing in pain. "I'm sorry mister!"

"Not to me." Luke corrected him. "To him." He twisted Tin-Tin's face towards Rory.

Tyler clambered up and climbed over people and coats to get to Luke.

"I just wanted to take a picture of his face. Show my girl." Tin-Tin bemoaned, wriggling and writhing in Luke's relentless grip.

Luke twisted Tin-Tin's arm savagely, tears flooded his face and urine spilled hotly down his leg, initially as warm and comforting as bathwater, as a mother's touch, before staining his tatty trousers and forming a puddle on the floor by his feet and eliciting the smirks and whispers of the crowd who'd formed around them.

Tyler fought his way to Luke's side. "Luke look at his face. You're breaking his arm."

Ignoring Tyler, Luke glared hatefully at Kai, "Why don't you go get daddy to buy you an alcopop princling?" He snarled, keeping his stare fixed firmly Kai's way. "That ought to soothe that aching throb. And stop worrying your little head about what real men do in the trenches. You'll never go to war."

The rage was set in Luke's face, coursing through his system as tough and immovable as steel.

Tyler gently laid a hand cautiously on his shoulder, then touched the side of his face with the back of his finger and whispered. "Comrade . . . comrade."

Luke returned, as if from a trance. Finally, he let go of Tin-Tin who spilled clumsily to the floor.

Tin-Tin scrambled up, hot and humiliated, he looked at his urine stained trousers and saw Isni and Sokol, his two subordinates, as well as most of the assembled bar staring at him.

He spat hatefully on the floor at Luke's feet. "You soldier! You dog!"

Tyler grabbed Tin-Tin by the neck and pushed him towards the door. "Go home to your mother. If you've even got one."

If Luke's actions had scratched Tin-Tin's soul, then Tyler's words had cut its throat. He turned back to the Dearlove brothers, a suffering in his eyes so extreme that for once their utter blackness seemed to lift and they burned with a light which made them look madly, dangerously alive. "I'm going to kill you both." He told them calmly.

"Yeah-yeah. Off you fuck." Tyler spat unthinkingly back.

Sokol tried to touch Tin-Tin sympathetically. Tin-Tin pushed him angrily away and tore out through the doors.

Kai looked over at Jed at the bar. His father had caught the tail end of the situation and was now having the full story regaled to him by Damien.

Kai turned back to Luke. "You're brother's right. You are mad."

Thirteen

It reminded her of the first time she had seen a penis.

That was Eva's overriding thought as she sat hunched in front of the laptop screen, hands rammed to the sides of her face, trying to block out Tariq, Luan and her other cousins and their incessant laughing jabber as they cut drugs, drank beer and whisky, and played poker.

Shrugging off their invitations to join them with stiff shouldered irritation Eva kept her face pressed as close as possible to the buzzing computer screen re-watching the two minute video clip of a young insurgent's blood-spattered slaying. Barely twenty, the young man blinked at the camera pointed towards him, his hands tied behind his back and a numb look of disbelief on his face. The big man next to him caught him by the shoulder with one hand and with the other executed a swift backhand stroke with an insanely large rusting machete. The beheaded rebel performed a crazy and somewhat comical little dance before falling down next to his head and twitching grotesquely.

As with the first time she'd ever come face to face with a man's private regions, her initial viewing left her pale and weakened; a being with no center. But such feebleness is easily overcome. At age fourteen, the pulsating thing with the head of purple thrust her way was that of her cousin, Rakin. He roughly grabbed a handful of hair and demanded she 'lick it' as the two engaged in a vehement battle of reluctance and want. A battle that she, the fourteen-year-old girl, would win. Not by disobeying but by obliging. Not by licking but by biting. Her teeth had sunk easily into that strange raw sausage. The veiny roll of muscly flesh had squelched satisfactorily between her clamped teeth. In later, stronger years she'd regretted not biting all the way through, lifting her head with the thing torn off in her mouth like an animal, blood streaming down her jowls, showing it defiantly to her grease smeared, sweat stinking cousin while he howled and screamed for his dark time.

After that they'd become something of an interest, a preoccupation. She overcame their ugly curiosity by studying them incessantly. First in pictures, then in flesh, many a boy of the Velipoja neighbourhood succumbed to her sultry demands and let their pants drop to the dusty ground of back alleys, waiting with toothy acne crusted smiles for what was coming next. Few expected the quizzical examinations Eva would deliver, not touching, just looking, the occasional prod with the tip of her index finger like a nurse performing a prostrate exam.

On one occasion, when an eighteen-year-old, back from a four week stint working as a lackey, fishing for red porgy and scomber scombrus on the far reaches of the Adriatic, with no one for company but six burly middle aged men, expected more than mere scrutiny, things had taken an ugly turn. He'd pushed her up against a wall, shaving skin from her shoulders in great chunks, and rammed his hand up her skirt, breathing hard into her face as he stole for her insides. What many would have thought of as rape, Eva channeled into experience. It was another great lesson in the understanding of the slutty art form she would come to make her own. She endured it, stiff and silent, as he pounded away, wondering if this was all there was to it. From there her studies progressed to pornography; a multitude of magazines, films where possible, hungrily learning more and more about what men liked and what women performed. The crazy dance in all its sticky glory.

By the first time a man had ignited her, it was she who was the master manipulator, little more than a stolen virgin, the girl of seventeen grabbed the hair of the twenty five year old, pulling him towards her as she knelt upright on the edge of his bed. Giving him only seconds to tear open her shirt and kiss and suck at those magnificent breasts, bend down to her crotch and breathe in her scent. She soon threw him onto the bed like a wrestler, climbing on board him like he were nothing but a thing she now owned and forcing his head violently back, tasting the exposed bulge of his neck. By the time she moved down to put into practice all she'd been learning these past few years, scratching her nails up the insides of his thighs hard enough to leave thin traces of blood and opening her mouth to inaugurate her 'art' the man was already jerking and spasming to a thunderous climax.

She leant back from him on the bed, wiping her mouth on the back of her hand and eyeing him coldly. He recovered, shaking his head in self-satisfied disbelief and reaching for her, a gauche smile on his face.

She bent down to him. He closed his eyes expecting a kiss. Instead she spat hatefully onto his eyelids, sprang from the bed like a cat, snatched up her discarded clothing and ran from the room to his groans of repulsed frustration.

And so it was with the internet's clips of savage barbarity.

At first she'd stolen quick glances, then longer looks through the orange glowing gaps in her latticed fingers. Pictures of disembodied heads, lined up on the sides of dusty roads for maximum propaganda. Videos now. Mass shootings, men bound and knelt at the sides of pits, waiting calmly as the row of the living became the tumble of the dead, cascading down into an earthy cavern to join a mass jumble of cadavers. Children, as young as two, dead in their fathers' arms. A woman in her twenties, naked and silky smooth, trussed like a turkey and hoisted into the air, over a large dank barrel, her throat sliced open into an ugly gash, her blood spilling furiously into the barrel's depths with the force of a suddenly burst pipe.

It became easier and easier the more she went on. Tolerance increased and became an irrelevance. This too could be overcome and mastered.

She sat squat across the chair feasting on the images like a man watching a boxing match. She could become the fine artist, the master manipulator of this crazy dance too. She smiled.

It was only the cold drop of water, filtered through the ceiling from the floor above, splashing onto her face, that stole Eva back from her schemes. She touched her nose, examining her fingertips, finding them wet and looked up to see the greying plaster spreading with an upside-down puddle that seemed to defy gravity.

She'd heard Tin-Tin come rattling in ten minutes earlier, his small feet pounding up the stairs in furious stomps. She'd heard the bath being filled at full pelt, but lost interest at that point, her engrossment in a new dark world leaving little room for thought of anything else.

Reluctantly she set the buzzing laptop to sleep and followed Tin-Tin's path up the rickety stairs. She pushed the bathroom door lightly with her fingertip and let it come quietly open a few inches, peering inside.

Tin-Tin was in a bath, full to the brim, the tap still gushing water into it. Great sheaves of it tipping over the rim like wads of material and adding to the growing pool on the floor.

Eva shut the bathroom door behind her, stepped over the pool, turned off the effusive tap and sat on the toilet, crossing her strong legs and looking at Tin-Tin, pointing a swaying stilettoed heel his way.

He had Luan's straight razor in his hand and had been hacking at his greasy long hair, trying, and failing to emulate the closely shaved heads of the men of the community, those men who, like warriors, took no shit from anyone. Instead of a successful emulation, Tin-Tin had sliced into his scalp in a mishmash of unsightly gashes, and left his hair hacked and ruined like a fire ravaged crop of corn.

Blood ran down his neck and slid into the bathwater at the same rate tears ran from his angry eyes and slid down his flushed cheeks.

Eva sighed knowingly. She picked up the pig mask from within his crumpled clothing on the floor beside the bath, pulled it on and snorted whimsically for Tin-Tin's amusement. For a moment it worked. Tin-Tin's haunted, deeply cut sorrow lifted and his face broke into a chuckling grin. But this would not last and the grin gave way to a collapse of tears that betrayed the young boy's wounded pride.

She pulled off the mask, and to his surprise, followed this by pulling off her shirt and the remainder of her clothing, underwear included, and slipping into the bath in front of him.

Tin-Tin trembled slightly, as any boy, however proud, however broken, would the first time he experienced a woman naked and near to him. Especially a woman such as this.

Eva took the razor from his quivering fingers and examined the tattered remnants of his hair like a stylist being asked to fix an 'at home' perm that had gone horribly wrong.

With great tenderness Eva skated the razor over the remainder of the stubborn clumps of thick black hair, left like desert Mormon Tea Bushes on the round of Tin-Tin's scalp. The final tufts twirling down like leaves in the wind and landing on the bathwater's surface to float like feathers. When finished she turned Luan's shaving mirror towards the boy to feast on his own reflection.

Tin-Tin took in a gleeful gasp like a child at Christmas laying eyes on the bicycle his parents had told him he couldn't have in the sweetest of deceptions.

Tin-Tin smiled his thanks to Eva and his eyes glassed over with fresh tears. She took his face in her hands with an uncommon gentleness and laid him against her bare breast, resting her cheek on the top of his head and swaying him slightly.

They remained like that a long time. The childless mother and the motherless child, wrapped up in a unison of slippery wet skin and dark promises.

Outside a dog howled at the moon and the night gave way to a grimy air, thick with smoke and grit from the shanty town surrounding the Turkey Cage and flies from the marshes. When the wind spoke, its voice was brittle, full of filth. 'Soon' it said.

Fourteen

Luke plunged his head into the sink full of water in the men's toilets of the hotel bar. He kept his entire face below the surface, tiny bubbles escaping from his nostrils and winding their way to the surface in little explosions besides his ears. He wondered if he had the will to stay this way until he drowned.

Of course he did. 'Willful boy' 'Stubborn little prick'. They were his brothers' pet names for him from practically the first moment he learned to walk. Such were the reserves of tenacity and commitment he deployed to whichever mission was currently at hand. He knew as well as anyone that the day he took it into his head to take his final breath would be his last. Such was Luke.

But for now that needed to wait. He lifted his head free of the water. He still had a mission to complete on this shit-fest of an island. He still had a brother to find. Perhaps a brother who was dead, a stiffened corpse, lying beyond the first turn in the catacombs that lead off the south beach, no doubt with a bullet from Jed Burke's hunting rifle bounced around the inside of his skull.

Perhaps kidnapped, starved and petrified, tethered to a radiator in the holiday complex or a tree in the shanty town that surrounded it, his security guard uniform having marked him out as a hate symbol; made him a focal point for the swelling resentment towards the Company that raged through the migrant community, a target for their vengeance, beaten and abused, barely alive after a year of sufferings.

Either way there was a brother lost among the ragged bluffs, the raging seas and the rancid swamps. A brother who needed him. Who needed rescue. Even if it was only so his story could be closed. He would not leave the field of battle, not while there was blood in his veins and hell in his heart. Luke knew that of himself, knew it to be true.

A truth he was not quite so certain of was the flickering image of the figure, entering the bathroom behind him and leaning up against the wall. He could sense its slow movement, hear the sudden blast of noise, music and laughter from the bar, as the toilet doors opened and quietened to a muffled din as they closed. He could just make out one image of its form in his peripheral vision and another of its cloudy reflection in the dirty mirror that bordered the sinks.

'Brother, dear brother. Listen when I say. I will stick by your side. Until this goes away.'

'You go now Howie.' He thought privately and rubbed his temples hard. For he knew that the shadowy figure was not his brother, just a longed for ghost of him. The ache in his mind and the shape it formed behind him on the wall remained. He turned to face it and found Tyler standing there as angry and unmovable as a steel girder.

They faced each other in stony silence. As if neither knew quite what to say, or had no courage with which to say it.

But finally Tyler was the one to find the courage and the words.

"Why can't you just be normal?"

The question seemed to be cathartic for Tyler. His pent up frustration, embarrassment and despair, releasing like steam with the outflow of each irate word.

But for Luke every word was a bullet spat at him as if from a pumping machine gun. And just as merciless, just as deadly.

He looked down to his heart, half expecting to see it burst forth from his chest, explode and shower the toilet walls in blood. That would knock the superior scowl off his brother's face. He wondered if Tyler would rush forward to catch him as he collapsed to his end, the ruin of his exposed heart beating valiantly a few final times, pumping blood chaotically into Tyler's eyes and all around the room.

But his heart remained lodged safely inside his ribcage and the irreversibility of death did not come. He turned away from Tyler and pressed his head against the wall.

'Brother, dear brother. Listen when I say. I will stick by your side. Until our final day.' This time there were no ghosts. It was Luke, saying it, barely above a whisper, too soft and mumbled for Tyler to hear what his words had been. They were words for the walls, for the cracked cold tiles and the grimy black grouting that kept them permanently separate from one another.

Luke spun suddenly back, his eyes alive with hope like a child daring to believe it might get all it had wished for. He called out to him, called his name as he turned. "Tyler." And the hope laden in that one word alone said everything. It said 'Will you sit with me, with my pain, will you let it spill to the floor in its entirety in front of us without turning away, without moving to mop it up from sight. Will you hear me without closing your ears, without shutting yourself off from the story I have to tell you? Will you pick me up with broken arms? Will you carry me home?'

But Tyler was gone.

Luke slumped back against the sinks, holding his damp face in his hand. After moments passed he stood tall, sniffing back his pride. He whipped a paper towel from the box on the wall and pressed it onto his face, screwed it up and tossed it in the nearest bin.

Luke stopped cold.

What he had seen had passed so quickly before his eyes that his mind hadn't registered it at first.

Slowly, he bent down and retrieved the screwed-up paper towel from the bin, opened it and laid it out on the top of the sink.

His trembling hands reached into the envelope, still in his inner jacket pocket, and fished for the paper towel bearing Howie's scribbled writing and laid it down on top of the damp towel plastered to the edge of the sink.

The prominent triangular shark's tooth like shapes met flush as a matching partner to the damp sheet below.

Luke snatched both towels up together and tore from the room.

Luke, Before

"Have you done any work today Dearlove?" Sergeant Major Glen Hughes asked with a nonchalant glance at Luke who was standing by the coffee machine in the Troop Office. He let the huge stack of files he was carrying tumble to the office's main desktop, tidied them into a well-ordered pile, hung his overcoat on his designated hook and shook the light covering of snow from his hair as he rubbed his hands together to get the blood flowing after his walk through the bitingly cold wind, and strode briskly towards Luke at the coffee machine.

His brisk stride slowed when he neared his subordinate. He examined Luke's posture with concerned eyes. Luke's right hand was on the coffee decanter, his left on the 'Little Sexy' mug with his picture printed on the side that William Castlebridge had had made for him as a gift last Christmas, his jacket half pulled off and hanging free from one shoulder. It was near enough the exact same stance Hughes had left him in when he made his way out at 9.00 a.m. that morning.

Luke remained in his posture with waxwork-like stillness, staring at the steamed-up window.

Hughes made effort to mask the alarm in his voice as he reached Luke's side and asked the same question. "Have you done any work today Dearlove?"

Luke took time to answer, when he did his voice was flat, robotic in tone, his fixed gaze never leaving the window. "No sir, I've only just got in."

Hughes glanced at the clock on the wall beside them and noted the time; 11.07 a.m. He nodded and cautiously took the coffee jug and mug from

Luke's hands and pulled the disheveled jacket back up over his shoulder. Luke barely seemed to notice or move his position.

With the care of a sculpture repositioning a piece of art, Hughes turned Luke towards him. He pulled his jacket tighter around him, fastened the top few buttons and walked him to the door.

"I want you to do something for me Dearlove." He told him. "I want you to go back to your room and get some sleep for the rest of the day, and that's an order."

Luke nodded slightly, not really understanding his superior's reasoning, but an order was an order and he followed it as he would any other, stopping first at the Spar shop as he always did on his way back to his room when his shift was over, to buy enough food to see him through until he returned to work again.

He hadn't eaten at the cook house in weeks, probably only once or twice since returning from Afghanistan. Instead he stockpiled supplies and barricaded himself in the place he felt most safe, and the most alone; the darkness of his room, his little world. There he ate simply, drank only water and milk, and absorbed himself in endless marathons of film watching.

It was easier that way, especially with everyone around him acting so weirdly. They would drink and fuck the pain away and laugh as though the world still meant something. Then have the nerve to question him about his conduct. At least he had a handle on what was going on. It was easier now just to shut them out, just as he could shut out the light with the blackout curtains he'd improvised from material he'd procured from the Quarter Master. Just as he could shut off or ignore the phone when his brothers called. This is what he wanted now; a tomb of sterile darkness.

He lay enveloped in that darkness on an otherwise bright and snowy afternoon and endeavored to follow Sergeant Major Hughes' command.

But sleep was an elusive mistress these days. In total he guessed he'd been having around two hours of it a night for the past three weeks.

And so began his ritual. 1. Carry on Camping, 2. Carry on Cleo, 3. Carry on Screaming, 4. Carry on Henry, 5. Carry on Jack, 6 . . . . 6 . . . he could never get passed 6 with the Carry On Films. They were his mother's favourites. That's why he'd seen so many. But he could never remember them all, same with his father's favourites, the James Bond franchise. 1. The Spy Who Loved Me, 2. Moonraker, 3. Thunderball, 4. Doctor No. He rarely made it beyond those four. He needed a count of at least fifty, sometimes a hundred before his mind numbed and spared itself and the haven of sleep set in.

There was only one thing for it, one audit he could take that would subdue his psyche and sedate him.

1. The bullet smashed into the head of the nineteen-year-old ANA soldier I was talking to, bursting it like a cantaloupe, making me half chow-down on a mouthful of blood, bone, brain matter and skin. 2. Not recognizing the terp who'd been translating for us on Tuesday when I saw him again in the field hospital on Thursday with his entire face missing 3. That father gone mad with grief, gawping at the Tactical Recognition Flash on my arm, holding out the decapitated body of his twenty one month old daughter to me with one hand and her disembodied head with the other, her black hair still tied up in that bright blue bow.

Luke paused on that one, his mind tumbling back to the memory of it. The father's besieged eyes had gestured helplessly, speaking to Luke with a terrible silence. A silence that became an undiscovered language, a language only they could understand, a language separated from the voices of the human world.

The reliving of it made his heart race and his throat close up. Abruptly he fought to push it down, like a large piece of meat stuck in your throat that might pass safely into your gullet or might choke you.

With the thought of it deeply buried he went on counting his particular brand of sheep.

4. The two mid-level Taliban leaders who got shredded by the 30mm cannon of an A-10. Their body parts scattered everywhere. Then ten minutes later when the pack of wild dogs showed up and ate what was left of them. 5. The gunner riding turret on the Mastiff when the mortar hit, turning him into mist, leaving the inside of the vehicle coated with him. 6. That night on patrol with some crap-hat American Jarheads who thought it'd be a laugh to bust open a truck they'd seen rocking, thought they were gonna find a local couple at it inside, found two men raping a ten year old. 6. The woman in Kabul who'd hollowed out her dead baby, stuck a bomb inside and gave it to a couple of fresh out of training Crows to hold, blowing up the three of them and a couple of old men playing chess on the roadside, ending the war for the two Crows after less than a week in Helmand.

By number seventeen Luke realized he was making repeats. But it didn't matter he supposed, he felt sleep encroaching. The quick firing cylinders of his brain were switching to the neutral position that made the world go away. He gave up the audit and took effort to continue to roll in that direction. This worked. He would try it more often. And it would only be a few more weeks before his deployment in Iraq.

Lucky, really, he could stockpile his reserves.

Fifteen

Room 11 on the first floor of the Burke's hotel was like any other room in any other average hotel around the country. Loose net curtains, infused with the smoke, stains and smells of the accumulation of guests who'd stayed and slept and screwed and shit about the place. A hard bed, with thin foam pillows, a brown blanket that would itch more than it would keep you warm. Sheets as stiff as cardboard. Cheap ugly artwork clashing glaringly with the garish overly patterned wallpaper.

Luke scanned the interiors quickly as he switched on the overhead light and turned the key in the door to lock himself in.

The key, and his certainty that this was the room where his brother had stayed, were both easy enough to procure. Janice Burke was the only person in the part of the bar that doubled as their Reception. She was heavily involved in a long drawn out lecture to one of her patrons as to how to make the perfect roast potato. Each step of her oral instructions repeated at least three times as she made an exuberant physically mimed demonstration of what she was describing as if the poor man, who'd probably been making roast potatoes all his life, simply couldn't understand the sophistication of her methods with the mere use of the English language alone.

Luke had been able to keep himself pressed flat against the wall outside and reach in with a grasping hand to steal the guest registration book from near enough under her nose. He absconded with it to the downstairs toilets and whipped back the pages until he found the guests entries of a year previous. He knew he'd spot Howie's handwriting, but if he needed further validation, the pseudonym Howie had used was 'Tyler Lucas'.

His method for obtaining the key was somewhat more audacious. He simply walked into the reception area behind the bar and took it. A simple trick he once learned from a Sapper pal of his, Matt Weston, was that if you go about a task, even a covert operation, or a crime, with such confidence and entitlement, such certainty and decisiveness in your actions, the average man will not even question what he sees as being abnormal. So much so that a man could walk into a restaurant and take a pork chop right from a stranger's plate and walk away chewing it, if he did it self-assuredly enough, and neither the man nor the restaurateurs would register this as strange until you were half way down the street, belly full of pig-meat.

'There's an art to stealing Little Sexy.' Weston had told him. 'Think of it as permanently borrowing. That's all. We all intend on returning this shit. We just never do.' Post military the Sapper had transitioned into a successful career in banking, no doubt putting his theories and expertise to good use.

Luke had the physical resemblance to Kai Burke on his side. If any of the patrons, or even Janice or her family spotted him, they'd surely pass it off as their son looking for a clean shirt, or taking money from the till, or whatever else he may be in the habit of doing.

By that point adrenaline had kicked in and Luke wasn't prepared to wait any longer. He felt answers getting closer, the truth drawing in. A thirst and excitement for those answers and that truth was building in him like a child on the run up to his birthday. He strode purposefully into the bar through the back entrance, set the register book back down from where he'd taken it, picked Room 11's door key from the hook on the wall and strode back out like a man with every right to have done so.

As Luke began his hunt, picking through Room 11's litter bins, searching through drawers, under the bed, under the mattress, in, on top of and behind the wardrobe, he wondered if Mason Hare had caught sight of him grabbing the key. He couldn't be sure but he thought he saw the man lift his head up from a pint and give Luke a bemused double take. But if Mason had seen him surely he and Jed Burke would be here by now, the full weight of Burke's stare pinning him to the wall as he closed in with that gut hook knife he loved so much.

Luke put the scenario aside and scanned the now ransacked room with his eyes. He knew Howie's trick of leaving his most clandestine of secrets out in plain view – the best place to hide anything. And yet Luke could find nothing. From the entry date in the register book this was certainly the last place Howie had stayed. What had once seemed the answer, the golden ticket, now felt moot. Hope felt futile. All seemed lost.

Exasperated, he went to the window and slammed it down shut, the damn stink from the beach was near burning his sinuses and churning up his guts. With the accompanying blast of air the tissue thin pages of a bible, open on the bedside table flipped over in ghostlike fashion. Something within the bible caught Luke's eye.

He'd held it upside down when he'd searched that part of the room. Shaken it to see if any note could have been tucked inside. Then tossed it aside, where it had fallen, open on its back on the bedside tabletop.

Luke crossed the room towards it, flipped cautiously back through the pages and saw it; Howie's writing. The words were scrawled by a thick black maker, standing significantly out over the tiny feint print of the Holy Scripture underneath.

The only sounds now were the continuous dull thump of the music from the bar below, matched by the deeper thump of Luke's heart. He cradled the bible into his chest and slid down the wall with it and read. As he did, the dark shadowy shape of his brother Howie appeared sitting on the bed beside him, narrating the words as they ran across Luke's brain.

My Luke,

The war on this island wasn't started on the streets. It was started by gentlemen, in a boardroom, wearing suits, with a very specific agenda in mind.

Your instincts about them were right. They deal only in bastardized versions of the truth. Half-truths, and twisted truths. All the while gobbling up everything in sight, like one great big corporate greedy child.

The reason they stopped their build was not down to this land's substance fragility, but to the substance of what lies underneath it.

They make promises to the frightened, the misplaced and the vulnerable from the most savage corners of this Earth. Dish out just enough hope for them to let us pack them up like colour TVs and bring them across continents, never knowing that they're only ever to be used as cannon fodder, in the most unjust of ways. When their presence on this island has pushed the last native out of the Company's way they'll be left here to rot.

The numbers I have been sending you are employee IDs of those who thought it up, those who are making it happen, those who stand to benefit from it. And those who've done nothing to make it stop. The first of which is my own.

Luke let out a slight gasp and stopped reading. Howie's shady figure paused with him. Waiting for him to continue.

Giving evidence now, against the Company, is the only way I know how to pay back the thirty pieces of silver I have earned for my part in it. My biggest fear is that I will not be able to stop it before something goes very, very wrong one of these nights and those thirty pieces of silver in my pocket becomes a weight that drowns me.

I stand in the shadows of Judas, who had virtue enough to hang himself. Sadly, I am not that strong.

Well, for now I must leave off for if I write more my thoughts will turn to the days of our youth and tears no doubt will follow. Those days are gone now.

If by chance you get this letter and I haven't returned take it, and the employee numbers I have sent you, to Kier O'Bannan, Head of the Human Trafficking Department at New Scotland Yard.

Whatever you do don't come here yourself.

Everyone is involved.

Always, H

Luke closed the bible and held it tightly against his chest. What he'd hoped would be a great bursting of light, exploding from the darkness, was nothing more than the grimy shameful drops of man's sin, one by one breaking out like beads of sweat on his forehead.

He looked over to the empty bed where a few seconds earlier the imagined shape of his brother had sat. Howie, who hadn't been a hero, just a man who'd succumbed to greed, to corruption, and had reached out to him not for help or for rescue, but to buy him a ticket out of turpitude. But such things as turpitude, corruption and greed could not be mopped up so easily. They oozed forth and stained anything and anyone they touched, leaving everything in their path sluggish, foul stinking and fifthly.

Luke clutched the bible more tightly, his eyes still glued to the empty bed.

"Oh Howie," he said to the silence. "What have you done?"

Sixteen

The Skanderberg Café was crowded with people, smoke from cigarettes and marijuana and the fumes of tequila and absinthe when Eva came in with Tin-Tin.

Most of the patrons were either drunk or high, or both. If not by their own intake then unwittingly through the second hand consumption of the cloud of intoxicating fumes that filled the place like a fog.

Moses and his friends seldom joined this crowd or frequented this place. But on occasions even he needed a drink, a release. And tonight was one of those occasions.

Just when he thought his day couldn't get any more skin-crawlingly irritating Eva Skanderberg entered with the boy.

In a drastically out of character turn, she stood back and let someone else have centre stage. Tin-Tin proudly pulled back his hat and exposed his newly shaved scalp. The crowd let out a communal gasp and then burst into applause. This was quickly followed by men pulling the boy from one to the other, rubbing the round of his head, slapping his back, hugging him, pouring him shots of tequila, offering him cigarettes. Tin-Tin beamed an enthused grin that stretched from ear to ear and lapped up every second of the revelry and their admiration.

All the while Eva smiled proudly from the door like a mother watching her child play Joseph in the school's nativity play.

When she eventually moved to the bar Moses grabbed her roughly by the arm, pulled her taut against his chest, glaring at her vehemently.

"What is that you want?" He demanded to know, nodding at Tin-Tin's shaven head.

Eva tore her arm defiantly away from him, held his eye with the strength of a lioness as she gave him her answer in a flatly brutal tone; "War."

Seventeen

Luke dropped the bible down on the bed in his and Tyler's room and began rooting through his bag. In the adjoining bathroom a shower was running at full pelt, so hot and heavy steam was escaping from under the connecting door.

A pair of hands, with fingernails encrusted with dried blood and dirt picked up the bible and began flipping through it.

"Oh brother Christian, with your high and mighty errand. Your actions speak so loud I can't hear a word you say."

Luke dropped his bag and turned to see Jed Burke laying at full stretch across his bed, slowly fanning himself with the bible, his head up against the wall and his chin near rested down on his chest.

Mason Hare was in his obliging pose, maroon suit and shit eating grin in place, standing in the doorway, biting down on an apple and blocking Luke's exit.

Jed held the Bible open at its inner cover, showing Mason the 'Room 11' label written inside.

"You've been looking in the wrong room." Mason mumbled to Luke through a mouthful of apple.

Luke dared himself. "Digging in the wrong spot?"

Jed and Mason exchanged glances, their practiced faces giving nothing away.

Jed got up slowly from the bed and sauntered the few paces over to Luke, swaggering like a cowboy who'd been riding all day.

Luke tensed, rigid and prepped with a fighter's awareness of the possibility of violence. And with good reason to be. Without warning

Jed slammed a thunderous right hook into his face, knocking him violently onto the bed.

Jed stood back, quietly observing Luke reeling as he struggled to make a recovery.

Mason checked behind him in the corridor to make sure they were alone, then leant in from the doorway. "Sorry about that son. But you shouldn't have downgraded his kid. Man loves that boy like a wolf loves meat."

As if on cue a dog began to howl on the beach outside their room.

Mason joined it with a spontaneous impersonation, contorting his face into that of a cartoon wolf and howling with mischievous delight.

Luke staggered off the bed and fought to stand tall and defiant in front of the men. He straightened himself valiantly and looked Jed squarely in his near yellow, reptilian eyes, struggling to stay focused through his swimming head and the pain tearing across his face.

Other than the pelt of the shower in the adjoining bathroom the room sat in dead silence. Jed Burke took a step towards him. Luke tensed once more. He wondered if Tyler would hear if the two men began to beat him to death. And if he did hear whether he would even come.

Jed Burke scrutinized Luke's face, as if looking for a crack through which he could see his weakness. In return, Luke studied Jed Burke's own septic aspect.

Finally, Burke spoke. "What does it take to break you?"

Luke sniffed back the blood that was climbing its way down his nasal passage like a slowly crawling insect. "More than you." He told him. Then nodded at Mason. "Or your stupid little man pet."

Jed let out a cold chilling near silent laugh, almost seeming to admire Luke his audacity.

He spoke to Mason but kept his stony face directed at Luke. "Tell your boys to quit their drinking now. I want them up with a steady aim at dawn. Time we did something about that hound."

"Time to shoot the mad dog." Mason interjected.

"You gotta shoot the mad dog." Jed acquiesced. "Before he gets the chance to bite ya."

He tossed the bible to Mason.

"Sorry to deprive you of this." Mason said to Luke, holding the bible aloft. "You wouldn't like it anyway." His face turned brutal, full of a threat that could have given Jed's best intimidating stare a run for its money. "Doesn't have a happy ending."

With that they left him.

Luke stood motionless for thirty seconds at least. The air in the room was still thick with them. When finally he was sure they wouldn't return he half fell, half collapsed on the bed, the force of Jed's punch overcoming him again. He slowly recovered and rolled to the side, pulling the brown paper envelope back out of his bag, and opening it to check inside. Howie's letter scrawled across the bible pages which Luke had already torn free remained safely tucked inside.

Eighteen

The pain screamed through his esophagus as though he'd swallowed a sword. The pounding of his heart so violent in his chest it throbbed up towards his head, making the glands in his neck feel as though they were about to explode. But still something drove him forward. Adrenaline perhaps. Maybe just pure old-fashioned fear. His former sports teacher would have been proud. He hadn't run like this since he was at school. 'That's it Dearlove. Keep those knees up.' The air in the woods they ran through that Friday evening was heavy with moisture, autumn giving way to the promise of spring. 'Woods' was something of a misnomer. It was one of those typical dense patches of ground that ran along the backs of rows of long gardens in suburban London streets, thickly populated with trees and overgrown conifer plants. They could see quick glimpses of family life through the portals of sliding patio door windows; families arguing, eating, watching the early evening news. It was the kind of grounds burglars would find so convenient for staking out the suburbanites and planning early morning thefts. The kind of grounds that the neighbourhood boys in their prepubescent years reveled in for adventurous excursions, accessing it through clandestine holes in the backs of their garden's fences. That was probably how Luke had entered it at some point after they'd left him. Howie stopped first. Quite suddenly, leaning on his bent knees and panting. Tyler, just behind him, couldn't hit his own breaks in time and came to a colliding stop, nearly ending up on top of him in a cack-handed version of a piggyback. It was a moment of god sent serendipity. When they turned breathlessly towards each other Howie saw Luke and his face collapsed in a heady mix of heartbreak and shock.

"Can you knock?"

Luke had yanked back the shower curtain on Tyler, seizing him pugnaciously back from the memory he was in the middle of replaying in his mind, staring near comatose at the shower wall, as though a moving image of the event were being projected upon it.

"I need to talk to you." Luke's voice sounded both demanding and desperate.

Tyler pulled the shower curtain back over him a few inches and began aggressively soaping himself.

Luke stood there defiantly, watching him, as if angered that Tyler hadn't immediately leapt from the shower, half washed and soaking wet to give Luke his undivided attention.

"Alright just give me five will ya?" Tyler grunted at Luke.

"You have three!" Luke snapped and stormed out of the bathroom.

Tyler sat at the edge of his bed, still wet from the shower, only a towel tied loosely round his waist; such was Luke's irritating insistence that he turn his immediate attention to the crudely scrawled note on the tissue thin bible page. As he read he let out quick knowing sighs and small near silent laughs.

Luke watched him from the opposite bed, holding his breath like a fledgling author who'd just given the first draft of a novel to a master to read. His eyes skated over Tyler's bare broad chest, dotted with beads of water, and his mind travelled back to one of the sparse memories of his father. Weekday mornings, before anyone else arose, he, the baby, and him, the patriarch, would hit the kitchen while the others slept, furtive predawn breakfasts, his father fresh from the bath and smelling as clean and hopeful as spring. Luke still rubbing the sleep from his eyes as his dad made him pancakes and let him watch the cartoons his mother wouldn't allow. This was their time. Clandestine and golden.

For a crazy moment Luke wondered if Tyler smelled the way he remembered his father had on those crisp mornings and felt the urge to sidle into his lap, press his face against his chest, wrap his arms around him like a blanket, breathe him in. The thought of Tyler's befuddled reaction to such an act brought a smile to the corner of Luke's mouth. A smile that would be quickly knocked from place as Tyler finished reading and tossed the Bible pages nonchalantly aside with the sudden retort. "Told you he was an asshole."

Luke shook his head, watching Tyler get up and dry himself with the towel. "Am I conscious?"

Tyler grunted back at him. "Caught with his hand in the cookie jar. What did I tell ya? He'll hide his sorry arse long enough for people to forget then show up like we should all break open the beer and throw him a party."

Tyler suddenly noticed the welt slowly coming to prominence under Luke's left eye from where Jed Burke had struck him, and, only too pleased to change the subject, grabbed his chin to examine it. "What's wrong with your face? You been scrapping?"

Tearing his face away from Tyler's grip, Luke fished through the tenants of the brown envelope to find something to write on; the Polaroid picture the boy from the bar had taken of him when he first arrived on the island. He tapped his phone and wrote the most recently used number down on the back of the photo along with the name Kier O'Bannon, wrapped Howie's letter on the Bible page around it, grabbed Tyler's wallet from the top of the chest and pushed it deeply inside.

"I spoke to the detective at New Scotland Yard tonight, that's his personal number." Luke told Tyler, nodding to the wallet.

143

Tyler pulled on boxer shorts and a white T-Shirt, opened his small travel bag and began throwing clothes inside, seemingly ignoring Luke's every word.

Luke tossed the brown envelope containing Howie's many scribblings into Tyler's travel bag with his crumpled clothing. "When you get back to London I want you to take Howie's letter and the rest of this stuff to him."

Tyler turned back to look at him. "Something wrong with your legs? I'm not doing your dirty work for you?"

"No? Just theirs then?"

Tyler slammed the travel bag angrily shut and glared at Luke. Somewhere on the distance of the beach a dog began to bark, the slow defiant call of the animal taking the edge off the rising tension in the room. Luke wondered if it was the mad dog the Burkes and Hares had promised to kill; defying them, rising to their threat, calling on the thunder at the edge of the giant sea.

Tyler broke through Luke's thoughts. "I think before we leave tomorrow you should apologise to him. And his son."

"I'd sooner stir your shit with a stick and eat it." Luke replied.

"You don't look a man like that in the eye and call him a mug."

"I call him a monster and I call his idiot son a sniveling little prick."

"You don't look a man like that in the eye at all."

"I'd rather look him in the eye than look at him from my knees like you do."

Venom glowed in Tyler's eyes. Brother or not he wanted to grab hold of Luke, throw him up against the wall, growl in his face like a wild thing.

A light knocking came from outside their door. It opened before either had answered and Janice Burke bustled in, nodding at the two single beds, uncoupled from their original formation as one double.

She smiled at them, oblivious of the animosity between them. "You managed to separate the bed?"

Tyler, "First thing we did."

Her smile became a laugh, "Not in love then?"

It was Luke who would answer, keeping angry eyes on Tyler. "Clearly."

Janice straightened visitor pamphlets, hotel information and other literature on the chest, instinctively picked up Tyler's wet towel and began folding it, their dourness failing to drizzle on her jubilant mood. "I won't do a full breakfast in the morning. You're the only guests and the men are all heading off for a hunt first thing. Except my little cherub who'll be sleeping it off somewhere no doubt. So I thought I'd just make you some of those little sausagey, mushroomy things."

Tyler and Luke forced smiles through their tension and nodded their agreeing thanks.

"Or I could do you some nice local haddock if you'd prefer that Tyler?"

Luke answered for him. "Don't worry about my brother Mrs Burke." He said dryly. "He'll swallow whatever he's fed."

Janice returned a confused smile and left them alone.

Seconds of awkward silence passed. Tyler slowly reopened his travel bag and continued his packing, his back to Luke, knowing his eyes were burrowed into him.

Finally, when Luke did speak, all anger was gone and there was placidity to his tone.

"Some people think brothers are just friends life's put on the earth beside you. But Howie was the air that I breathed, my everything. I know he never left this island. And now I know why. I think I know where they . . . where they put him. And tomorrow, after I find him, I'm going to cut a hole in my wrist so deep even god won't be able to stop me from bleeding, then I'm going to lay down in the cold earth with him, forever at his side."

Tyler kept his back to his brother, closed his case with a gentle click. Finally, he turned. "Go to sleep Luke."

Almost obligingly Luke switched off the bedside light, slid under the cool cotton sheets and wool blanket, turned his face to the window and was sleeping as quickly as that. As though his confession of aforethought sin had cleansed and calmed his being, lifted the heavy pressing thing that had laid against his heart for so long, keeping him from sleep, and when he did sleep, ravaged his dreams.

Tyler ran a hand through his still damp hair, turned off his own light, and climbed into his bed, two feet from Luke's. But sleep would not come to him so easily. Above him a fly darted crazily against a plastic coating, pounding and fighting for the dim beam of an emergency light like an addict. Outside on the beach, the dog continued its chorus, barking and howling, growling for the sense of an ending.

It was only Luke and the sea that remained calm. Tyler leant up, pushed back his covers and sat on the edge of the bed watching his brother sleeping, his chest rising and falling as softly as a whisper, in time with the roll of the tide outside. Tyler held his breath as Luke stirred, but it was only to lift a lazy leg and kick back the blanket on top of him.

The air had mercy on them that night, carrying the smell of death and decay that permeated Skidaway Island away from their window and sending it out to sea where great waves and a heavy sky could make it

146

their own. Tyler was glad of the purity, the kindest of breezes that found its way in through the window and swept over his brother's face.

He sat, and watched that face for what may have been minutes, but felt like hours, like an endless night, like eternity.

Nineteen

Howie and Tyler gripped each other for support as they neared Luke's prone naked body. He was lying like a heap of crumpled rags in the undergrowth of the dense wooded area at the back of theirs and their neighbours' gardens. One of the homeowners had spotted men roaming around in the wasteland and was now scrutinizing their activity while demanding her husband phone the police. That was a good thing. The emergency services were needed here fast and it would save one of the two of them from having to run back to the house to call them. They'd both bolted from the house without thinking of their mobile phones when they came back home and found Luke gone.

As they neared him Tyler silently blamed Howie. Luke had only been back from Belleview a week, he hadn't eaten in all that time and mostly remained silently in his room. Either sleeping, or pretending to sleep, or, when Tyler crept in quietly enough, staring blankly at the ceiling like a dying man looking up to heaven before he passed. Howie had convinced him it wouldn't do any harm to go out to pick up the new TV. It would only take twenty minutes and the sixty-inch whopper that had just arrived in the store was too big for one of them to collect alone. Howie being Howie had maxed out his credit card to get it, offering up the explanation to Tyler that it would 'help Luke'. While livid at his middle brother for adding to his mounting debt a small part of him did agree. Boys like their toys, no matter their age, and maybe the kick-arse TV with wrap around sound and a plasma screen would be enough to coax him out of his bed to join them in the living room. Howie, also being Howie, had spent two grand on it but opted out of the fifty pounds charge it would have cost to have it delivered. That blazing row would be put on hold for another time. For now they had to think of Luke, laying naked among the shrubs and quivering and twitching violently like a not-dead-yet deer who'd succumbed to the bullets of hunters. Tyler looked at him, blinking his eyes hard, as though trying to wake from a nightmare. He didn't move. He couldn't. Howie pushed passed him, bending down to Luke, prizing the pair of scissors he had in his hand out of his trembling fingers. He'd already used them to hack off half his hair and, when they spotted him, was carving out great lumps from his skin. Wounds, weeping with fresh blood, were dotted about his body, his arms, his belly, his genitals, his bare buttocks and thighs. Howie laid his hand on the side of Luke's beleaguered face and let out a long, pained sigh that shared in his suffering. He skated his eyes over his trembling form and the patchwork of lacerations, without a clue how to begin to put his brother's broken being back together again. Luke made a strange gargling sound, as if trying to speak, there were words he was trying to form, but his poor body only convulsed more ferociously from his inability to articulate them. Howie glared hatefully up at Tyler, still standing uselessly on the same mossy spot and screamed; 'Do something!!'

'Do something!!'

The words echoed in Tyler's head so violently they punched him out of his dream. He opened his eyes wide to see dawn's bright light streaming through the windows. From outside were the sounds of seagulls fighting for food, delivery vans opening doors and unloading crates, and the island's native gannets, kittiwakes, razorbills and choughs, busy with birdcalls to one another; effusively chattering about the business of breakfast. In all regular and recognized ways, the world was waking for its day.

Tyler came bolt upright in bed, breathless and wet with sweat, for a few sickly seconds not knowing where he was or how he'd come to be there. As he calmed, he heard it; a different vehicle opening its doors. Not a truck, arriving with barrels of beer, boxes of crisps, crates of milk. This was a vehicle whose doors he'd heard being opened and closed a few times before in his time on the island.

He turned towards Luke's bed, already knowing what he would see. It was empty of his brother and neatly made, leveled off like a table, precise and exacting, a bed made the way only a soldier could do so.

149

Tyler fought back the tangle of covers and stumbled for the window. Knowing what he'd see there too. Sure enough, the hunting jeep was being filled with men; Jed Burke, Mason Hare and his two lanky sons to be precise. This time even Mason Hare had relinquished that god-awful red suit in favour of a hunter's camouflaged gear.

Each man had a gun.

'Do something!!' Howie's voice bounced off the walls of his head.

Tyler tore away from the window, hastily grabbing his keys and clothes, still half dressing as he left.

The sea was shining with purest gold by the time Luke had made his way down to the beach. The early morning sun caught the ridges of gentle waves and set it off in sparks like diamonds in a jewellery shop window. It was a vista smooth and becoming enough to make a man forget his life.

With only the gentle roll of the tide for company, Luke set about his business and began prizing open the grated mouth of the catacomb. He'd prepared himself mentally. The sea wind was blowing east which helped carry the stench away from him and back through the tunnel to the other side of the island. Still, the lurking tainted odor permeated his senses like a fear that won't leave you. But he fought on. Nothing would stop him. Not now.

He couldn't see the hand that had lain flopped out in front of him the night before. But other things were coming to light today. What was buried was about to be brought up. The last hook clasp holding the grating in place came open with a satisfying rasp and the whole great thing swung discordantly open like the front of a medieval washing machine.

Fate, and the wind, chose a great unkindness for Luke at that moment. The backdraft whipped towards him like cruel laughter, churning up the goods currently stashed in the curve's depths and threw its gassy stench into Luke's face.

It hit him like a car, forcing him to part fall, part roll, part stagger down on to the velvet smooth carpet of sand where the sea lolled casually in and out with the tide. He remained there a while, doubled over, resisting the urge to vomit.

That was when he saw the two hands sticking out of the sand about ten feet from him; their fingers outstretched as if still clawing for life.

Luke shook his head disbelievingly and then crawled slowly towards them. He touched one. The darkly tanned skin was icy. They sat there as firm and stubbornly defiant as two thick shrubs that had grown in that spot, or the root remnants of felled trees.

Luke ran his hand across the smooth sand where the owner of the hands' head was most likely to be. He took a deep breath in, drawing strength from the sea, and began to frantically dig.

Five inches down he uncovered a face. It was that of a young Afghan national who'd escorted them through a village, sharing his knowledge of local IED placements. He'd been shot by the Taliban three weeks later, the price he paid for raising his head above the precipice and playing a part in someone else's war. Not much older than Luke, his eyelids were half closed and from under them the eyes were fallen slightly apart from each other in death's cruel joke. They were staring, staring at Luke, but, at the same time, staring through him.

"What happened to the body I was promised?" the young dead man asked Luke without moving a single dead muscle in his face, his disembodied voice gentle, angelic, still accented heavily in Pashtu. "Where is my wondering heart?"

Luke shook his head, but before he had the chance to answer the dead man, Corporal Sam Martins was calling him from the other side of the beach. "Oi Elsie! Hey Little Sexy! Tell that farmerbarma to get back on his jingly truck and get up here."

Luke hadn't seen Corporal Martins for two years. The last time he'd seen him his face was the colour of deep purple and swollen to three times its normal size, courtesy of the bolt that had been driven into his skull to alleviate the pressure that was building in his brain. Despite being in the pitiless depths of a coma and undoubtedly completely brain dead by that point his body had twitched and bucked continuously in a mocking parody of life.

Luke staggered towards him. Martins was sitting in the same position he had been in when Luke first reached him after the ambush, propped up against a tree, his hands clasped together below the plate of his body armour, trying, but failing, to stem the thickly spreading gush of black blood that seeped out from where bullets had shredded his liver.

"What are you doing here?" Luke asked breathlessly.

"Couldn't resist seeing you kick up a grade A cluster fuck here on civi beach." Martins replied, his deamour as chirpy and ebullient as it had been in life.

Luke struggled to fight back tears. "I'm sorry I didn't save you. I'm sorry I told you I could."

"Shine on Little Sexy. It's just another day." Martin's gave him the warmest of smiles but soon his face fell suddenly calm and serious.

Luke summoned his strength and asked "Is my brother with you?"

"No son," Martins replied softly. "He's with you. He's standing right behind you. Just like he always does."

Luke turned slowly towards the shore.

Howie was there, down at the edge of that beautiful blue water. Gazing out upon it. His hands resting gently in his pockets. He didn't turn around but knew Luke was watching him. Finally, he took one hand out and reached back with it towards Luke, beckoning him into his embrace.

Heart racing, Luke rushed to the water's edge and flung himself against Howie's chest, burying his face into his warmth, his emotions rising and raging against his shirt '*my blood, my blood*'.

Two great arms closed around him.

It was only when Luke noticed that the fingers on the hands of those arms were weather beaten and gnarled and that the skin under their nails were crusted with dirt, mud and dried blood that he realized he had fallen into Jed Burke's wet stinking embrace.

He slowly stepped back and looked up at him, almost immediately hypnotized by the cold eyes and the cruel stare. Mason Hare and his sons were around Luke, the men forming another circle, as they had in the café on the occasion of their first meeting, this time it was a circle from which, Luke knew, they would never allow him to pass. Each man held his own rifle.

Luke looked back to Jed Burke and spoke to him, with the quiet ease of a man resigned to his fate; "After you kill me. Put me where you put him. . . please. I just want to lay by my brother."

The men exchanged looks over the top of Luke's head. Jed released the safety on his rifle with a soft click.

"Hey! Hey!!" It was Tyler, stumbling across the uneven sand towards them like a drunk.

Jed lowered his gun.

Tyler reached them, gripping Luke's shoulder, and babbling breathlessly. "Good job I found you. Come on, ferry master just called. They've brought the time of our boat forward. We've got twenty minutes to get there."

"Brought the time of the boat forward?" Mason questioned, forcing as much sarcastic inflection as he could into his tone.

Tyler was already walking Luke back up the beach, he turned his head only to call back briefly. "Yeah, something about . . . . a turning tide."

Luke let Tyler lead him back up to the spot where he'd parked the rental car and fish the keys out of his back pocket. Tyler was fumbling with them at the car door, as if he'd forgotten how keys work.

"I'm going back to-" Luke started before being violently cut off by Tyler's bark.

"Get in the fucking car!"

Luke looked down and saw that Tyler's hands were shaking violently.

Luke knew he'd have to comply. For a while at least and obeyed, allowing Tyler to push him into the passenger seat. He waited patiently as Tyler went to the other side of the car and got in beside him, his still violently shaking hands fighting to get the keys into the ignition before they sped away.

Twenty

Tyler knew it had been a mistake to relax.

He leant on the edge of the booth where the clerk was selling tickets for the ferry and let out a long sigh. What he really wanted to do was scream.

He could see the hunting jeep pull up alongside the ticket booth from the right peripheral of his vision. Mason and Jed were the only two to get out. Damien had moved to follow them and been ordered to wait behind. Obviously, this was going to be a 'men only' piece of business and Tyler felt a sad resignation of ill-fated laughter bubble up from his midst.

Thankfully he and Luke had parted ways. After ten minutes of arguing at full bore with the passion of lovers Luke had traipsed down onto the beach like a sulky teenager and was now a lone figure, standing at the edge of the tide. This might make things harder for them, depending on what it was they were here for. If they'd followed them down to the harbor just to make sure they got their tickets and went 'safely' on their way, then things should run efficiently.

If they'd decided, however, that the most appropriate course of action was to grab the two of them, abscond with them to some piteous warehouse, hands tied behind their backs, blindfolds over their eyes, fire a slaying bullet into the backs of each of their heads, then proceedings might prove a little trickier to . . . execute . . . if you pardon the pun.

Luke was far enough away to run, to hide. They couldn't get hold of the two of them at once. But Luke would never run. Never hide. Never abandon him any more than he had abandoned Howie. He'd stand in front of Tyler like armour if it came to it, let them slam a bullet into his

155

chest before they got near his kin. Such was Luke. Tyler's fear was overtaken by shame and abruptly he sagged.

Jed and Mason were suddenly next to him, watching him with hawk-like intensity as he reached the front of the queue.

"Two one way for the mainland." He whispered it, like a man about to collapse.

"Forty-eight pounds sir." The clerk said chirpily with an irritating grin stretched across his characterless face.

"Everything alright here Minty?" Mason Hare leant over Tyler's shoulder to ask, deliberately pushing him forward a few inches with his chest.

"Running like clockwork Mr Hare. Running like clockwork." Minty informed him.

Mason turned his smug stare down on Tyler. Tyler felt sick to his stomach, as though he'd drunk too much beer, far too fast and wolfed down a chicken madras. Sometime soon something was going to come up.

He threw down a twenty and three tens and tore off the tickets as they slid out of the clunky little machine. Without looking at Jed or Mason, or bothering to wait for his change, he pushed back through the queue and went over to the habour wall.

They'd followed him of course. Hard eyes on him like a pair of perverts trailing after a schoolgirl. Now they were flanking him at either side.

Jed Burke opened his hand and revealed two pound coins; Tyler's discarded change. He spat a small accumulation of saliva onto the ground by Tyler's feet. "That all the change you're getting out of a fifty these days? Don't know how they justify that." He dropped the coins into Tyler's clammy hand. "Some people get away with murder they do."

Jed Burke's eyes crossed the beach as calmly and steadily as if they were the lenses of a hunter's binoculars scanning for prey. Those cold eyes settled on Luke, the solitary figure down at the water's edge.

Tyler Dearlove was not a brave man, he was an ordinary man, a man who wanted no part in this war or any other, but he also wanted that man's eyes nowhere on his brother's body. He dared himself; "I'm sure it's easier to commit murder than it ever is to justify it."

Jed Burke's lifeless, somehow inhuman eyes, darted quickly back from Luke to Tyler.

Burke sniffed back the sea air and chewed on something, which may have been nothing, as if about to suddenly spit again.

But this time he didn't spit. This time he spoke. "Don't come round here no more." He ordered Tyler; his words as hard and cutting as an uppercut punch.

With that he left Tyler, Mason closely following. They pushed unceremoniously through the line of islanders queuing up for their tickets to exile, got back in the hunting jeep and rattled away.

Tyler was pale and fragile by the time he reached Luke at the water's edge. He carried the demeanour of a man who'd just received the most devastating news of his life but still had to continue with his day.

"Ferry's here." He told Luke numbly.

Luke kept his back to his brother and continued to stare out to the horizon.

Tyler was about to dispense with pleasantries and manhandle Luke back across the beach when he suddenly turned and asked him. "Why did you never come to see me in the hospital Tyler?"

The question seized Tyler's breath as if suddenly sucked out of him. He shook his head, they did not have time for this. Not here. Not now. He glanced over his shoulder to check Jed and Mason hadn't returned with a change of heart and their hunting rifles, and weren't now crossing the beach towards them with decisively murderous intent.

"Luke you're the mayor of shark city." Tyler told him, struggling to keep his stress under control. "These people think you want the beaches open. Now can we please just end this?"

Luke finally turned around. "Uncle David was there every day. Cousin Paul, Mark, Fiona. But not you. Not once."

Tyler sighed heavily. "It was because I-"

"Couldn't get the time off work."

"No, because I couldn't-"

"Couldn't be bothered."

"Because I couldn't stand to!!" Tyler bellowed furiously at Luke.

Tyler calmed himself, full of regret. "I couldn't bear to see you like that."

After a moment's awkward silence Tyler nodded out to the sea. "Over there is your life Luke. The other side of that water. It may not be what you want. It may be tragic. But it's real. And it's yours. Can't you feel it? It's waiting for you." He shook his head sadly. "But there's nothing I can do if all you want is to stay here and cling to the earth."

"I'd rather cling to the earth than crawl on it."

The words hit Tyler like a punch in the guts. And Luke knew it. Taking advantage of the chink he'd found in his armour he ran on. "Go to our island Dearlove. Get off our island Dearlove. Stand, sit, run, jump. What are you going to do when they tell you to kneel?"

Tyler took an angry step forward and drove the flat of his thumb to Luke's forehead as if trying to push through it and dig around in his skull. "I think we'd better get the doctor to up the dosage on those pills of yours. Either that or you start taking them rather than flushing them down the toilet. Anything to iron out that addled little brain."

Luke's face drained of all colour, he felt the heat of fury rise up in him with a mix of angry tears. Soldiers were defined by their physicality. By their strength. Since he'd been in this hateful place three different civies had got the better of him physically and now one of the fuckers was about to make him cry. Fuck that!

He pushed Tyler's hand furiously away from his head. "Did you actually just say that to me? You're my brother."

Tyler gave him a goading grin. "Yeah, plonked on the earth by life beside you. My condolences."

It was the grin that made Luke snap. He lunged at Tyler, the fury now coursing through his system like a drug. Tyler couldn't quite believe it was happening. He put his hands up to half protect himself and half protect Luke. From there they fell into clumsy wrestle. The kind of raging wrestling battle only brothers can partake of, wanting to kill and hug each other within one crazy spiralling movement.

Tyler broke it off first, shoving Luke away from him.

Both stumbled on the sand and steadied themselves, glaring at each other like warriors. They looked at each other across a separation so deep and profound the space between them no longer seemed crossable. They wanted to speak but could not. Tears glassed over both their eyes.

The tide surged towards them, seemingly wanting a closer look, only to be pulled immediately back by the might of the sea.

Neither knew quite what to do from here. Tyler turned and began walking away, not sure if Luke would follow, begging him to believe he hadn't meant what he said. Or whether he might remain, so rigidly embalmed with wounded anger that when that surging tide did reach him it would carry him out to sea, and he'd lose him forever.

Luke watched Tyler as he stormed away. Finally, he took one defiant step forward on the sand and his words came tearing up and out of his throat like sobs.

"The first doctor I saw told me I needed to get my eyesight checked. Said there must be a reason I was looking too deeply for the meaning of things. Forget what the next three said."

Tyler only turned his head very slightly and continued up the beach. Luke stumbled after him.

"The psychiatrist said for forty-five pounds an hour she'd help me combat all the trauma I'd endured. I gave her fifty and said go home and cuddle your boyfriend sweetheart. You'll never have a man die in your arms."

Tyler quickened his pace.

Luke threw his words after him, fighting for them to be heard over the roar of the waves and the pound of his heart. "The pharmacist said clozapine, onalzapine, risperidone."

Luke stopped, his face so vulnerable, so forlorn, and with a sea wind thrown so violently against it that if Tyler had turned and seen it, he would have sunk to his knees in the sand and wept.

Luke struggled to keep composed. "Then my brother said, 'Why can't you just be normal?' And my heart said 'Don't answer him. No one wants to hear about a soldier, with grief inside his bones', but my bones said, 'soldier on.'"

Luke stood watching his brother trudging purposefully up the beach, deaf to the way he had exposed his soul, leaving him far behind. His heart began to break, tearing apart at the strain of the lives they were not living.

A further set of tears prickled in the corners of his eyes. He blinked them savagely back. He would not cry on this island again.

This place would not break him.

Not today.

PART THREE

'All wars are civil wars, because all men are brothers'

Francois Fenelon

Twenty One

Tyler hadn't been sure what to expect when they'd brought Luke back from his first weeklong stint at Belleview.

"So, you're cured now?" had been his opening line. Prompting Howie to dig him violently in the ribs in an action that demanded he 'shut his stupid mouth'.

'Shame no one was this protective of me.' He'd wanted to scream out in response but managed to keep his 'stupid' mouth shut. He'd been shaped by trauma too after all. All the elements were in place for him to have a total all-out collapse. Become a babbling idiot. 'That's right buddy! I'm the monkey in the ball gown. Bring me the chum old timer, let's grab two spoons and sick down!'

What business did Luke have losing it?

He'd managed to stay sane. Afloat.

Howie had been deemed 'too fragile' despite being only two years younger than him. So, it was he who'd been summoned, as a twenty eight year old, to Queen Mary's Hospital to make the formal identification of his parents' stiffening corpses. Still fresh and gooey from his father's prized Saab Turbo 4000 convertible's recent headbutt with a gas tanker.

Out of the three brothers, it was Tyler left with the image of their mother's half decapitated head hardwired into his brain.

Their parents were devoted, to each other and to them. Everything in their world that needed doing Howard Snr and Mary Dearlove had done. Tyler had never had to make an appointment with a GP, open a utility account, bank a cheque. And suddenly those great arms that had enfolded him were gone. Stripped away, forever.

Who was he now? What was he?

He was suddenly father to a twenty five year old and a thirteen year old. A role he hadn't asked for and didn't want.

'All life's great plan.' His grandfather had told him, as if he should somehow consent to the most ruinous thing that ever smashed into their world as a masterstroke of strategic design to be acknowledged and accepted with grace.

"We'll both always be here to help you." His grandmother added. She died six months later of cancer. He followed two months after with a stroke.

All life's great plan. All god's great work. Smile and say thank you Tyler. 'Thank you boss. Thank you.'

What had they done to him in Belleview anyway? Chatted it all through over tea and sympathy? Or lit him up like a tree at Christmas, shot him with electricity until they'd wiped the hard drive clean of its corruptive memories. 'Here he is Mr Dearlove, good as new.'

Luke slept for nearly three days straight when they brought him home after the first week he spent there, lost still in that same miasma of soul-sick tiredness. He ate nothing other than one boiled egg on the Tuesday.

That Friday Tyler and Howie had broached him with a suggestion of watching the match the following day. It'd been something they'd done religiously with their father and after he died all three boys decided to keep up the tradition no matter how painful.

Luke had solemnly agreed and gone back to bed, in Howie's room of course, he'd slept with Howie ever since he returned, almost unable to stand being parted from him.

Tyler had made plans to head out for the usual barrage of beer and junk food before Howie had stopped him with a troubled look. 'Should we let him have alcohol?' They compromised by agreeing to buy it and keep it out of sight, only drink it if he did. Tyler, it was decided, was to be the one to casually ask 'Fancy a beer you two?'

He slept in till midday that Saturday and they weren't sure he'd ever get up at all. But ten minutes before the match he came down the stairs on unsteady legs, hair sticking up in every direction, his body and breath all funky and warm.

He took his place on the couch beside Howie, of course, lying down while the pre-match chat started on the TV, and digging his toes under the flesh of Howie's leg. Since he'd returned, he seemed almost unable to part with Howie for a second. And even when sitting no more than a few feet away he needed to feel his nearness, needed to feel his own flesh squashed up against Howie's flesh in some way or another, as if for validation that he was really there.

Before kickoff, and before Tyler even got the chance to deliver his overly rehearsed line about a beer Luke was asleep and snoring lightly.

Luke and Howie turned the television down on the ruined event and exchanged a full-on battle of looks and whispered words. 'Wake him up.' 'Let him sleep you idiot.' 'He's been sleeping half the week.' 'Keep your voice down' "You keep yours down idiot 'Stop calling me an idiot.' 'You are an idiot'. 'So are you.' 'Fuck you.' 'Fuck you too.' 'You're gonna wake him up.' 'Good.'

Then later.

'I'm sorry.' 'I'm sorry too.'

When Luke did wake up, he would wake up screaming.

Howie and Tyler bent over him on the couch, gently trying to urge him back from the dream. They stared down at him with the intensity of two paramedics bending over a hit and run victim in the street.

When Luke was fully awake, albeit still sobbing, they'd asked him what he'd been dreaming about.

From there Luke fell into a regaling of the wild and heightened memory that had been invading his dreams. The story of a time on deployment when they'd searched a ramshackle shed next to a farmhouse and come upon a teenager with a medical condition that left every inch of his face crowded with 'tree bark' as Luke kept calling it (later explaining about Neurofibromatosis).

Apparently, the boy had been chained in the shed, not as a dirty secret, but as bait, for just as Luke and six others from his squad stepped outside insurgents had detonated the explosives hidden within, blowing the shed, the teenager and the other half of their squad into oblivion, leaving a mighty cascade of body parts, wood, stone and blood to rain down upon those who'd been just far enough outside to have survived the catastrophic explosion intact.

"I saw his eye! I saw his eye!" Luke had wailed as Howie held onto him like a drowning man hugging a float and rocked him back and forth.

Apparently in the moments before departing the shack Luke had bent down to the beleaguered young man and searched his tumour clad face for signs of existence. And from that struggling face one eye had opened and looked upon Luke, before glassing over with a tear.

Yes, Tyler Dearlove could quite happily have also gone completely insane.

He mulled over the thought there, on the rocking seats of the Skidaway Island ferry as it swayed with the waves and waited to fill up with passengers. It would not be long before they would be bouncing their way queasily to another world and Tyler would, finally, thankfully, be on his way home.

'I could have gone mad at twenty-eight' the thought kept banging around the walls of Tyler's head, 'being ushered into a cold room full of dead things and given an eyeful of our mother's corpse. Knowing the ridiculous turban they'd stuck over her head was so I wouldn't know she'd just lost half of it under the rim of a juggernaut.'

Tyler ran it over and over in his mind as the last of the passengers clambered on, wishing he could go back ten minutes to the blazing row with Luke on the beach, turn around, ram those home truths down his throat. Adding for good measure. 'I told you not to join the army anyway!'

And he had. Luke had announced it to them when he was eighteen, right after Christmas dinner. He'd already signed up so there was no need for debate. Howie had tried to reason with him and work out if the 'Discharge as of Right' meant there was a get out clause in his contract. Tyler had thrown what was left of the turkey through the kitchen window.

Stubborn little prick. When he made his mind up to do something....

'A drifter, lost, five years after his parents' death. A nomad, looking for a family, looking for home.' Tyler suddenly thought.

He had never seen it that way before.

For years he'd berated Luke for his choice of vocation. It was an ugly time. War was looming. No good would come of it. Then when chaos ensued, and they'd lost him, not to the heavy mass of war's attrition, but to the dark hallways and scars of his own mind, Tyler felt the inevitability and pointlessness of it all with both vindication and furious anger.

What right did the boy have to lose his mind? He'd told him. He'd told him not to go! What did he think he was going to feel, going to see? It wasn't all quick marching, back slapping and banter. He was headed for a world where he would see men with their arms torn off, his buddies with their legs blown off. If you're going to sign up and get your self-invited along to that kind of party for four years, then you had no choice but to dance to the music they played.

'I could have gone mad too! With that stupid turban of periwinkle blue on what remained of her head. When those great arms that had wrapped around me all my life were stripped away what was I? What was left?'

That was when it came to him. Overcame him in fact. They were the same. He and Luke. For years he had thought, as others had thought, that the blood that ran deepest was in Luke and Howie's veins. But in truth, standing back and looking at it in a different light, it was he and Luke who bore no difference at all.

Luke had entered the army at eighteen, in that crazy space between being a boy and being a man, and two huge arms had wrapped themselves around him and hugged him to their chest. In his adult life Luke had never had to book an appointment with a GP, never had to open a utility account, never write a cheque. The Army had taken care of all of that for him.

Then, suddenly and without remorse, at his weakest, his most broken, those two great arms had let him go.

What was he? What would he become?

Tyler's heart filled suddenly with a love for Luke so powerful it felt dangerous.

It drove him forwards like a runner bolting from the block at the sound of a starter pistol. No further thought was needed on the matter. He scrammed through the line of passengers spilling onto the ferry's deck and bolted through the gate, speeding back down onto Skidaway's shores like a man possessed.

The deep woods that flanked the island's great marshes were the kind of place where murderers came to bury their dead. Luke was halfway along the ancient road that wound itself through the wood's midst, still muttering out snatches of his previous argument with Tyler when it happened.

When he saw it, he slammed on the clutch and breaks with both feet, coming to a screaming, tyre burning stop.

The man in the road seemed to hear the shriek of the tyres skidding on the gravel and turned his head towards Luke's car. Luke couldn't see his face as it had been encased in a white plastic bag and taped down at the neck, leaving only the tiniest of holes for air. As the man sucked desperately for oxygen the bag squeezed in to wrap around his features and blew out to form a clumsy balloon on his exhale.

His hands were tied savagely tight behind his back and his dishevelled clothing gave away signs of a recent desperate struggle. Spots of blood, like ink from a broken pen, dotted his white shirt.

He stumbled blindly towards Luke's car, banging heavily into the bonnet with his body, before straightening up and backing away in what appeared to be terror and making his awkward wobbling way through a gap in the trees and disappearing into the woodland.

Luke wound down his window, staring widely; begging his brain to confirm if what he'd just seen was real.

He could still see the white form of the plastic bag, bobbing about in the woods as the man receded blindly into its depths. From the distance of Luke's car it looked like the orb of an incorporeal spirit.

Luke suddenly let go his held breath, screaming after the man in a voice thick and raw with the mingling emotions of hope and dread.

"Howie!!!!!"

Twenty Two

Tyler was bolt upright behind the steering wheel, both hands fervidly gripping the fraying leather coating, his head swiveling wildly in a frantic search for any clue as to where Luke might be.

Fuck those gooks!

He knew they'd rented him the piece of shit twenty-year-old Honda when they had six decent cars standing in the lot.

"It's all we've got English" the six-feet-seven, bald headed fuckwit had told him, intentionally slipping into Albanian with every other word as the smirk spread over the thin-lipped mouth set within the bulbous monster of a head.

Fuck 'em.

Tyler rammed his foot down on the clutch like a man trying to kick through a door, imagining them laughing into their odd shaped cups of foully dark coffee as they imagined him, rattling along on the country roads in the clapped out piece of tin, it breaking apart into pieces, leaving him sailing on his merry way, clutching the steering wheel, sitting atop nothing but a thin metal axel frame with an almighty 'oh shit' plastered on his face like something out of a kid's cartoon.

God dammit Luke. Where are you?

Tyler turned onto the twisting roads that snaked through the marshes. He now faced the glare of the low-lying sun. It speared a blinding light at him, seizing his vision long enough for his hands to shake and the car to jerk and wobble its way crazily from side to side of the ragged rock-strewn bolt of road. An audience of frogs, rats and marsh birds croaked, sneered and squawked. Most amusing. Little man with your silly plight.

Where are you?

Dread clung to Tyler's back like chill wet leaves.

He turned the wipers on full pelt to try and clear the dirt from the windscreen in a bid to improve his vision and shifted his legs as he fought for third gear.

The dark of a shadow slipped out from the marsh reeds way up on the road ahead of him. Tyler tried to write it off as his imagination. But it remained. Robbing the back of his mind like an ancient debt.

The thing was waiting.

Tyler bent forward in his seat, willing the half-ruined Honda to make it up the inclining road.

The shadowy thing shifted, revealing itself to Tyler; rotted broken teeth, hissing with hate. He was right upon it before recognizing it an animal, staring into its ungodly eyes. One yellow like poison, the other blinded by a sarcoma, ghostly white as if it had been puffed full of milk.

His mind already formulated tall tales. Stories for mates on drunken nights. Spilling out of pubs, swilling with beer, en route for kebabs and sex with strangers. 'You should have seen it, it was a wolf, a bear, a pterodactyl.'

But no, this was nothing but a little waggy tail hound dog. The same dog the Hare brothers had set out to shoot for killing the local lambs. That or a pretense for Luke's murder. The same dog who, like Luke, escaped his fate, for now. The same dog who had yapped and howled as it prowled the fringes the beach the night before, its bark a far-off echo, like the feint and distant call of god, the only accompaniment other than the buzz of the frantic fly diving for the light, as Tyler had sat on the edge of his bed and watched his youngest brother sleeping under a moon the colour of sadness.

The dog lifted its bloody muzzle, suddenly snapped viciously at the oncoming car, snarling from its flank as if stung.

Tyler fought with the wheel, spinning it sharply to avoid an impact, hitting something with a dull thud. The dog? No. That was sloping off into the dense foliage, disappearing with a final sway of its mangy tail. A log? A rock? Maybe. Who cares?

The audience of birds, vermin and frogs laughed again in their slippery hearts, most amused by the great cosmic joke and the sudden screech of metal on metal from long worn out breaks, the erratic skid of tread-less tyres.

Tyler thought of his father as he slid across the road. He thought of his father in his prized Saab 9000 turbo convertible hydroplaning across the intersection into the oncoming lights of a lorry ten years earlier. Was this how it felt? The giddying ride, purposeless and pitiful, the knuckles clenched and changed to white, straightened arms rigid as steel, head crammed back into the rest in fearful denial, his mother clawing at his father's skin, screaming for their souls.

As the Honda broke through the marsh's only line of defense, a spiky row of thorn bushes, and catapulted down towards its murky depths, Tyler gave up the useless battle with steering wheels and brakes and instead rammed both hands up against the tatty roof, trying to brace himself but was still thrown mercilessly around like knickers in a tumble dryer. This was no child's ride at a beachfront promenade. The result of this arcade game would not be pixelated orange flames and an animated girl in a pink bikini seductively swaying her hips and blowing a teasing kiss as she purred 'Game Over'.

This was something else. Something real.

I'm sorry Luke.

He closed his eyes.

Twenty Three

The figure with the white bag taped over his head lurched through the thick woods like a drunk. And Luke Dearlove stumbled after him.

A rich smell of wood smoke hung over the world. A world where the white sky was now rolling over grey as the first trace of night crawled across it.

Other than the occasional caw of a crow and the murderous scream of the marsh harriers, returning to their lairs to dismember their prey, the woods were quiet, so quiet Luke could all but hear the pound of his heart.

He broke through the thicket, ignoring the thorns that ripped through his jeans, tore at his calves, gouged his arms. The pain was irrelevant, the chase an exhilaration. He fell, landing with a heavy thud in the carpet of last year's dead leaves, the obstinately protruding stump of a tree branching came close to impaling his eye. He gasped, but shook the thought of what might have happened away, and used the offending branch to lever himself back up, his eyes, mercifully intact, making a frantic search for the hooded man.

He saw the fox first, a monstrous shape in the shadows, peering out from behind a distant tree. It stood at five feet six and wore a dress of white cotton under a leather jacket. Long blond hair seemed to flow from the nape of its neck. A human hand where its paw should have been, curled around the trunk of a tree. When it sensed Luke watching both fox face and human hand retreated from sight.

Luke had no time for his imaginings. He would ignore them. Expel them from his mind as soon as they manifested.

And the man? Could he trust himself to know what he'd seen was real? Or simply what he longed to see. The sudden crack of brittle wood, snapping under heavy foot fall twenty feet away answered this for him.

The man staggered on. He tripped as he fled crazily on his near blind flight. Crashed heavily onto the sodden ground. If he'd hit a branch face first with his hands tied behind his back he'd have broken his nose or his jaw for certain.

'Howie,' Luke whispered breathlessly, and bolted after him.

A lamb made a darting journey between the tree it hid behind and the next, eight feet away, its human body and animal head barely distinguishable in the sudden flash of its movement.

Luke's race through the woods slowed at the sight of the blurred figure between the trees. Tricks of his mind or not, these were the things of horror stories made real. Terror pulsed within him like a set of cold muscles.

Without choice, he pushed on, on towards where the man lay twisting and writhing on the mossy ground, shivering and terrified. The bag encasing his head was sucked savagely in and forced out with each of his laboured frantic attempts to find air through his encasement.

Luke fell to his knees at the man's side, shaking with uncontrollably powerful emotions. He dug desperate fingers in through the offending plastic and ripped it away.

He should have known never to have allowed himself to believe anything on this island would be easy. This island didn't bestow. It took. And here it was, doing it to him again. One more act of pure human fuckery.

The face of the bound man, freed from the plastic bag that imprisoned him, smiled up at Luke, a thick greasy smile, the smile of a viper that had just paralysed its prey. That smile belonged to Tariq Skanderberg.

Luke knew what would follow. And sure enough, dry wood cracked under approaching feet as a shadow fell across him. The shadow of a fox, a fox standing at five feet six in a leather jacket over a white cotton dress, with pretty blonde hair and a rock in her hands.

As he turned she brought the rock crashing across the side of his head. He heard himself letting out a low moaning groan and seemed somehow to see from above, watching his convulsing body fall gracelessly to the ground. His eyes moved rapidly, spasming uncontrollably and darting about inside his head like the quick firing ball in an arcade game. From within his corrupted vision the world dimmed away like the onset of some cold glaucoma.

The fox and the lamb came to stand over him, peering down at the results of their efforts, soon joined by Tariq who clambered up and came to their side.

The fox took off her face and Eva looked down at Luke. She smiled darkly in the gathering gloom.

Luke clung valiantly to consciousness and fought to speak. 'You – fucking – bitch'. The words formed in his brain and clawed in his throat but broke up and died there in a strangled grunt and his record of never having sworn at a woman before remained clean.

Just as his darkening vision faded to deep grey, his final awareness was of the thickly muscled lamb, pulling off its face and bending down to hoist him off the ground, sling him over his shoulder and carry him like a bag of dust back through the tangle of trees.

177

Twenty Four

The island had teeth and had bitten Tyler Dearlove hard.

Even his eyelids hurt as he fought to open them, creaking like old oak doors, warped by time and wind.

The bloodthirsty bite of a mosquito, burrowing into his cheek, was the first evidence he had of being alive. He tried to lift a hand to swat it and hollered in immeasurable pain.

'Dad.' The word came out as an involuntary breathy sigh, so pointless and ridiculous that tears of pain and self-pity stung at the back of his eyes.

A stiff silence had set over the marsh, but it was a brooding silence, punctuated occasionally by the calls of the reed warblers and bitterns demanding their mates return to them with immediate haste.

The orb of the sun had just fallen below the rim of the world and the marsh lay sluggish and steaming in the dwindling light.

Tyler stretched his neck to the right and saw the ruin of the car, lying half submerged in the grassy swampland, its lights disappearing below murky water and setting the surroundings in a hellish red glow, one wiper, broken at an abhorrent angle like a fractured limb, still flailed back and forth in the air in quick rhythmic sways. The first dotted stars of night winked furiously above him; code from the devil, dictating his fate.

Tyler braved himself and looked down to the source of his pain.

Christ, why had he come here?

Mercifully he'd been thrown free of the car. Less merciful was the shard of twisted metal that had been thrown with him and now pierced skin, muscle, nerve and tissue, jutting out of him like a snapped femur.

Slowly, he touched it. Pain screamed through him.

Why the fuck had he come here?

He was not a man of marshes. Of islands, creviced with sin. Of complicity and cover-up. Of courage or concern. He was a man of ordinariness and restraint. Twenty-five thousand a year. It's not much but it'll do. It'll work. It'll work like I do, without question or complaint. 'Say thank you, Tyler.' 'Thank you boss, thank you.'

He looked around to his lonely world, feeling that he might just be the only human left on the planet. Pathetic. Shut up. Too afraid to move, he'd have to scream.

"H-He…" he coughed and stuttered. The word came out in a whisper. "Help." Oh god he sounded a tit. "Help . . . help me". Above a whisper but just as futile. There was no one there to hear it. No one other than a large crane that swooped down and came to rest on the wreck of the car, cocking his head and blinking at Tyler, awaiting the remainder of the evening's entertainment.

"Help me!" Tyler called out, scaring the bird away but feeling as uncomfortable and ludicrous as an untrained actor practicing a part for a play.

"God help me." He breathed to himself. But god sent nothing but a few more scout mosquitos to dance by his ears, dart in for a taste. They'd soon return in their hoards when word reached camp of the easy meal impaled like a stuck pig down in the depths.

He was alone here, with the birds and the slugs and god knows whatever else slithering around his skin. Alone with nothing but the night and the metal thing raping his belly. He'd have to move if he wanted to live.

Thank you boss, thank you. Thank you, thank you, thank you!!!!

He stretched his right leg forward, biting down hard on his bottom lip to fight pain with pain. The ground shifted and gurgled under his weight in a gassy hiss.

The left foot. Move it you prick!

It felt like stepping on pillows, great doughy feather filled things, that held no strength, no substance, no mattress underneath their folds to stop the downward slide.

Through his struggle and his pain Tyler noticed the surface of the marsh was further up around him, now about to touch the twist of metal that invaded his body. Great, now this pissing place is going to swallow me whole.

Panic set in, but with his every wobbling, willful attempt at steps to wade free the ground chewed him more fervently, reached around him like a lover, a lover with no intention of ever letting go.

The crane and a few other marsh birds returned to watch. Maybe this would be entertaining after all. Or maybe they were simply waiting for his arms to lodge so they could dive bomb him in continuous formations, stripping skin from his scalp, leaving him to die with scars sitting across his soul.

They knew the inevitable, as did Tyler, slowly being devoured by a land he'd never wanted, a war that wasn't his own.

Shadows wound themselves languidly around him as he gave up the fight, knowing that soon he would face a lonely death, smothered by mud, drowning in dirt and filth and excrement with only birds to know of it.

Never a man to step out of the ordinary, here he was in the most extraordinary of perils. He cursed his brothers for putting him in this position and immediately his soul ached for them, he missed them, shatteringly. His heart broke for the tragedy that Luke now had a second brother lost to fate. A second story with an ending never to be known. The putrid earth dragged him down another inch as a cruel reply to his lament.

As Tyler awaited his end he thought of his father. Maybe the pain of seeing someone you loved stretched out on a mortician's slab in death's sheer unquestionable certainty wouldn't be as bad as losing someone to the never knowing, to the hell and black corners of nothing but your own answerless imagination.

I'm sorry Howie. I'm sorry Luke . . . my Luke.

Tyler was about to close his eyes on the world one last time when the humming drone of an engine nagged for his attention and a pulsating red light merged with the velvet dark of night.

Tyler looked up to the rim of the ravine, lined by the row of thick thorn bushes, the only break in their rigid uniform being the unsightly gash where the old Honda had smashed through their ranks and catapulted down the bank.

Tyler held his breath, listening to the sound of a truck door opening and closing, footsteps through the mud, picking a cautious pathway towards the edge.

Luke, please god, be Luke.

He would squeeze him into a bear hug with vicelike arms, smother him in grandmother style endless kisses over every inch of his face, gather him up like a baby and carry him off the island whether he wanted it or not, ignore his struggling and squirming until he could place him down on safe shores.

What was he thinking? With his luck it would be Jed Burke and his goons, sneering little laughs at the irony of it all as they cocked rifles and

181

used his head for target practice. Or opened tins of beer and leant against their jeep to watch with mild amusement as the final stand in the great game of Brothers Dearlove vs Skidaway Island was won by the wretched place with sickening aplomb.

But no, of course, it was worse.

He couldn't think of the man's name. But remembered only too well the erratic exchange of insults at the bar the night before. He had remembered it being something biblical. Adam? Caleb? Joseph?

Moses! Of course! That was it. How the hell had he recollected that? He never recalled much of the inconsequential. Despite the surreal quandary which currently held him fast he felt strangely proud.

"Bye then." Tyler croaked out to the receding lights.

Moses had leant on one knee in the scar of thorn bushes, picking out Tyler's shape in the red glow of light that illuminated the murk below.

"Sorry I made fun of you for being a waitress." Tyler had said, only to himself, even the words running across the back of his mind seemed movement enough to encourage the squelching world below to grind him further into its guts.

Tyler was chest deep now as the truck rolled away. Moses had observed him casually for a moment or two before heading back to his vehicle. At least he'd had the decency and good measure not to stand and watch. For some strange reason Tyler wanted to laugh. He'd never been a brave man. Certainly not someone to stare death in the face and smirk. Maybe it was just the mind's merciful slip into insanity in the seconds before water thick with moss and slime and alive with flies and disease was to gag his mouth and stuff his nostrils.

Slowly, slowly, the red lights of the truck grew larger against the dark night.

Tyler remained motionless with the birds and the snakes and the slugs, watching in silent awe as the rear lights of Moses' truck arose above the rim of the ravine like two suns. Moses came quietly out and tied a rope to the back of the truck, now backed up as far as possible to the sloping edge.

Moses nodded down to the man stuck in the hell below. The man whose name he didn't know. The man he'd met once in life and once again in the mid of a half-waking dream where he'd relived their cutting bar room word-brawl. But this time, this time on the version he'd replayed in his dream-sleep, it was altered enough that he'd brought him to his knees, brought him to his knees and watched him weep.

Now, on their second unison, the man was lower than on his knees in front of him. But still he tossed him the rope, which, with accurate aim, landed near enough for the pitiful drowning figure to catch and wind desperately round his fists.

Moses put the truck into first gear and gently pulled away, feeling the sudden strain as the slack rope tightened and the twelve stone slug was heaved out of the mud.

He left his vehicle, engine still running, and came to stand over Tyler, writhing and coughing on the higher ground. With a parting of clouds that released a bolt of bright moonlight Moses saw the violent protrusion of metal jutting from the man's body and sighed.

Christ, what next?

He heaved the man onto the passenger seat, the sudden jolt making him scream with pain and collapse like a heap of rags. Moses wondered about the man. Was he unconscious? Dead? He wasn't sure. He reached for his neck and found a thin pulse.

Soon they were bumping along the uneven road that led away from the marshes and back towards town.

The clouds had receded now, drawn back to the sea as if she'd reached for them, missing her mists. It left the moon a high giant globe of purest light.

"The eye of god is always watching." Thought Moses as he cast his own eye over the sagged heap of a man slumped across the passenger seat beside him.

Great scars of indigo light were clawed across the sky and the air, rushing in through Moses's window, felt as clean and as untainted as it must have been in the long-ago years before man started destroying the world he was born to.

In his year on the island Moses Bogdani had never known such a beautiful night.

He dragged on the gearstick and forced the truck into fourth, the man beside him murmuring with the gentle bump. He turned onto the narrow rocky lane that would lead them, by the light of that luminous moon, to the tiny corner of Skidaway Island Moses Bogdani had come to claim as home.

Twenty Five

"Why the fuck do you keep staring at my tits Dearlove!?"

The screaming bark of a question had come to him courtesy of Corporal James Lily.

Luke liked Corporal Lily. Liked him a lot. He had an overtly no-nonsense attitude to life and a razor-sharp propensity for cutting through bullshit. He could spot the bollocks the human animal descended into as they wobbled their way through life just like an eagle at some lofty height had a way of spotting and swooping in on its prey. And, with the equally eagle-like sharp talons of his acerbic tongue, he could shred the falsity and hollowness of others with decidedly deadly aim.

James Lily joined the army without any aforethought plans. He'd suggested a friend of his, who'd recently lost his job as a car mechanic and slumped into depression, try and join up and Lily had accompanied him to the Army Careers Centre. Out of sheer curiosity he'd taken the entry level exam and aced it; while his friend flunked at the first round. He had no interest in going any further, despite the barrage of calls he received from recruiters trying to convince him to do so. It wasn't a career for him, he had no interest in people barking orders in his face and telling him what to do or where and when to do it. Then, one rainy Thursday afternoon, his boss has galvanized his troops with a twenty-minute lecture on the correct way to colour code a spreadsheet. 'Fuck this,' James Lily had thought. 'I don't want this. I don't want to be you.' And a month later he started basic training and was on track for a career in which he would flourish.

"Dearlove!" He repeated, fighting over the roar of the Apache helicopters that were swooping in to cover them and the screams of a middle-aged Iraqi woman who was sat on the curb twenty feet away from them and wailing her lament over what was left of her husband's half obliterated corpse. "What the fuck is interesting you about my tits quite so much at this particular time?"

Luke shook his head, aware that amid the chaos he had been giving Corporal Lily's right chest consistent glances from under the rim of his helmet. But it wasn't through admiration of the recent work his superior had done buffing up his pectoral muscles, or with any lascivious interest. He was steeling quick occasional glances at the disembodied hairy nipple that was, unbeknown to Corporal Lily, plastered over the body armour of his right breast plate.

Luke had been listening to his superior's unorthodox commands to fire first and ask questions later, but couldn't help but give the torn off nipple of the suicide bomber consistent looks, deciding whether or not, and indeed how, to make Corporate Lily aware of it. He would have behaved the same way had it been a lump of dried mucus hanging unknown from the nostril of a friend during a conversation set against a less surreal backdrop.

Corporal Lily was already agitated, understandably so.

Minutes earlier, his and a second Combat Vehicle Reconnaissance Tract were following a Snatch Land Rover on Route Damage Patrol. The convoy was assessing the integrity of a stretch of land six miles outside Nasiriyah and evaluating where vulnerable or compromised areas might be when a beat up old Chevrolet began trying to slip its way between his CVRT and the Land Rover in front.

Luke could feel Corporate Lily's tension, knew he was in the process of triage; a three-tier assessment and evaluation of their tactical considerations, resources available and associated risk. It was a similar tactic as the one Luke had been trained to apply to his own duty; is this person going to die no matter what I do? If so, move on. Does my treating them put myself, them and others at risk? Are my actions better served treating another who is either more seriously injured, or, stands a better chance of survival?

It was meant to be a routine recce but, as they were about to find out, there was no guarantee of safety from the random hidden rip tides of death and crippling injury when men were at war.

The Chevrolet made repeated efforts to slip itself in between their CVRT and the one behind. Eventually trying to overtake and get between their vehicle and the leading Land Rover. There was no reason for such actions. Locals knew to be wary of the military and had every reason to keep a respectful distance. When it became clear the soldiers were in no way going to allow them to enter their pack they pulled up as close as possible to the Land Rover and detonated their device.

Corporal James Lily and his convoy had just become the first listed target of a vehicular suicide bomber in the war.

For a few hideous seconds Lily and his Gunner were beset with a terrible certainty that they were about to burn alive. Luke, protected from the blast by his position on the rear bench seat, had pulled himself and the other men out. Private Toby Jackson was shrieking and clutching at his head. Corporal Lily pulled off his helmet and quickly realized he'd pulled most of the skin of his forehead off with it. He pursed his lips and put the helmet back on him.

Lily had escaped life threatening injuries. His forehead and arms were terribly burnt. He didn't feel the pain of it then but would later.

"Fuck sake!" Lily barked after looking down to see what Luke was gawping at and swatted the nipple away from his body armour as though it were nothing but a bit of stewed tomato after a meal of over-sauced spaghetti bolognaise. He pointed vehemently for Luke and the other surviving members of the squad to follow him to the Land Rover where the casualties were bound to be writhing on the ground in great numbers. If any had survived the blast at all.

As Luke moved he realized his pants and trousers were saturated with urine; his own. He remembered being in the vehicle's belly behind Corporal Lily, his knees pushed up tight against the vehicle's walls, bone jarring on metal, and the front plate of his body armour digging into his overfull bladder. The bumpy roads of Iraq could churn up your insides like a tumble dryer, and what with his position, bent up like a fetus behind Corporal Lily and the Gunner next to him, the pressure on his insides was unbearable.

The explosion had propelled them sideways. It threw Luke violently into the side of the vehicle where the contents of his bladder burst out of him as if popped and . . . and . . . this time something was different.

He didn't remember damaging his hands. But now they screamed with pain as if dipped in acid. Had he lost them in the explosion? Burnt them horribly in the resulting fire? Had them amputated later at the Field Hospital in Basra? He couldn't be sure. He opened his eyes to look at them.

They were suspended high above him, tied savagely, brutally tight with wire to an overhanging beam. He couldn't see much of them. His eyes were still accustoming to the light. It was minutes before he realized he was now a captive. Held in some darkened room on Skidaway Island.

But his mind was still back in the strange, dribbling dream, laced with memories of the chaotic aftermath of conflict; men dying in a vehicle, men screaming, dying more slowly on the ground. Explosions; tendon, muscle and bone wrenched and pulled beyond the constraints of their malleable strength until they crack, yanking limbs from bodies without mercy. War; proportioned, hysterical, awful, beautiful. And a place Luke would rather have been than where he was right now.

For right now he was laid out flat on a bench. Only his arms were elevated, pulled brutally upright by his manacled hands. Hands that were numb, as if frostbitten, and wet, but whether it was with blood or sweat he could not tell.

To his right an old-fashioned cassette recorder was pumping out an 80's electro-pop Euro trash tune and the huge man who'd been wearing the lamb mask was hunched over a nearby table working intently at something. It was the same posture his father had adopted when working on the build of scale models. But by the acrid smell in the room's musty air Luke knew arts and crafts weren't the man's forte. He was cutting and cooking up drugs.

Further ahead of him sat the woman and her brother. They had the lamb and the fox masks on the backs of their heads, making them look like strange misshapen figures with their faces twisted the wrong way around. The pair giggled like teenagers and huddled together over a laptop.

Luke lifted his head and shoulders off the bench. He fought against the savage pain in his wrists and stretched to get a better look at his bound hands.

The fox woman sensed his movement. She paused the video they were playing on the laptop and twisted hers and her brother's masks so they covered their faces again. As she moved Luke saw they had been watching the video of some barbaric insurgent's filmed propaganda. The disembodied head of a long forgotten soul had been secured onto a railing by his killers.

The fox and lamb bent towards each other and kissed, plastic snout to plastic snout. She got up, turning up the volume on the cassette recorder

189

just as a 1960's pop song came on. With full sass she go-go danced over towards him, stopping only to retrieve a large plastic toy gun, about the size of an AK-47, incorporating it into her routine as she cavorted his way.

Luan got wind of Eva's movement, set down the large knife he'd been using to divide crack cocaine and turned round to look at their captive, now awake and staring at them with beleaguered eyes.

Tariq joined his sister, removing his mask when he saw her do the same. Luke closed his eyes. When the heavy weight flopped down on his stomach, causing his wrists to scream in agony as if sliced into, he opened them again to find Eva sitting squat atop him, peering at his face as if he were a specimen she'd discovered. She sniffed and wiped her nose on the back of her hand with the least lady-like of mannerisms Luke had ever seen.

She nodded to Luan who obligingly went to a nearby disused fireplace, fished inside and returned with a blue towel wrapped around a small object. Luan shook off the towel to reveal a 1940's service pistol. He drew back the hammer and pointed it immediately at the side of Luke's head.

Luke forgot the pain in his wrists and the heavy weight upon him and squeezed his eyes shut, straining against his bindings to lean desperately away from his impending execution.

"Pres!" Eva suddenly cried, getting up from Luke's stomach, making Luan stand down from the assassination. She nodded over to the paused image of the severed head on the screen, staring blindly at the camera with slightly crossed eyes and made the cruel choice to switch from her native Albanian tongue into English. "We need him to die with his eyes open."

Twenty Six

Arifa and Hakem were Moses's most trusted friends on the island. They were civilized men of quiet dignity. Both Moroccan, and both unable to return to their homeland. Neither had been back there for twenty four years. They had been young engineers, focused on their careers, when a rising anti-government extremist group had focused their attention on them.

The men had not known then that their refusal to lend their talents to the design and building of bombs intended to kill whoever got in the fledgling insurgents' way would seal their own fate.

They had fled under fear of death. Decent men forced to abscond like criminals. They and their families had paid everything they had for them to take a precarious journey across the Strait of Gibraltar. Ultimately, they'd been dumped into an offshore detention centre where they were forced to forsake their religion, wash and shave in rivers where all along the bank others were standing and urinating or squatting and defecating, and through it all apologetically hang their heads to the xenophobes.

Finally destiny took them to Skidaway Island where they worked and were respected and found companionship with a grief stricken young widower, a forlorn father who'd lost his newborn son. Friendship grew strongly between them and from there on in the three stood together, taking shared comfort in their sorrows.

As committed friends do, when one asked for help, the others obligingly complied. So when Moses burst through the door heaving a near dead white man with him they rose to the challenge and did everything that he asked.

The three men pulled Tyler across the kitchen floor like a giant slug, the snail trail he left behind him being a long thick line of fresh blood. Arifa and Hakem gave each other wary glances. But trust was the common denominator between them. And Moses was now looking at them, saying with his eyes, 'brothers we must do this' therefore, this is what they would do.

The giant slug suddenly came to life; a surreal form of life, full of absurdities and nonsensical delirium.

"Am I in a cupboard?" He asked them and tried to lean up, oblivious to the horrendous state his body had been left in. They ignored him, propping cushions under his head and ripping open the remainder of the shirt, already practically torn from his body.

"I need a picture with the president." The great slug told them with the most ardent and earnest of expressions on his fevered face. "I can control dogs using only my mind."

They nodded that they understood that he could and examined the great shard of metal protruding from his side like a giant rusty thorn. Arifa reached a nervous hand out and touched it lightly. The slug threw his head back, screaming as if a bear was slowly disemboweling him.

Hakem turned to Arifa and Moses, his face strangely pale under his smoky brown skin, feeling the need to state the utterly obvious. "He's going to die here."

Twenty Seven

The boy Tin-Tin was all that had stood between Luke and death.

That was all there ever was for any man. A perfect storm of occurrences that dictate outcome. A step taken an inch to the left instead of the right and a fourteen year old girl wouldn't have stepped on a mine in a field in Angola and lost both her legs above the knee. Walk the long way home instead of using the shortcut down the back alley the man's not there with a knife to mug you. One more cuddle with his mother, he could have demanded it. Or a row with his father. A spilled drink on their brand-new carpet. Something, anything, that might have had them running ten minutes late, two minutes even, thirty seconds would probably have done it. They would have stopped at a light they had sailed through that night. Been caught up in the evening's traffic. Occurrence upon occurrence, event after event. A different chain reaction that would have kept them away from a juggernaut and instant death.

The blond woman had stared down at him with enough hate in her eyes that could topple the world. 'Pres' she had screamed. Which Luke concluded had meant 'stop'. The lumbering giant pointing the pistol at his head had drawn it away, rewrapped it in the blue towel and stuffed it back up the fireplace. She'd then knowingly switched back to English to ensure Luke heard and knew what was coming, glancing at the severed head stuck on a spike on a railing, staring blankly out at the world like a bug eyed mackerel, before declaring that she needed Luke's death grip affixed the same way. 'Then let's fucking strangle the cunt.' The lumbering giant had countered, ensuring he too verbalized the words in Luke's own language, *mental torture always far more exacting than anything in the physical extreme.*

He'd ordered the other man, Tariq, Luke remembered him and his name from the car rental office, to join his sister and sit down on top of their captive, mumbling something about the fact he was about to start bucking like a woman in labour. With that he took off his belt, used a bit of broken wood to make a tourniquet, and slipped the looped end round Luke's neck.

And buck for his life Luke did, thrashed and kicked and writhed for it, knocking Tariq and Eva Skanderberg around on top of him like they were children surfing waves. Just as the brink of unconsciousness came Luan released the stranglehold. Luke wheezed violently and tore air back into his lungs. His body slumped and the Skanderbergs steadied to a stop. Tariq wrapped his arms round Eva just under her breasts and kissed her neck, she reached back and ran a hand through his thick curly hair with a sickly near-incestuous smile.

Luan began the ritual again. Eva leant in, feasting on Luke's torment, cruel eyes studying him, skating thirstily over his features.

Luan stopped at the point of blackout once again, performing the same near murderous act three, maybe four, times. Maybe a hundred. Luke could no longer tell. He'd been brought to the precipice of death and released from it, like the on-off of a tap, so many times that everything swam crazily around his head and nothing seemed real. He could make out nothing other than the swarm of purple black spots that flew across his vision like a psychedelic dream. Nothing other than them and the shadowy little shape that was crossing the room towards them.

That shape was Tin-Tin. He'd been hovering in the doorway, watching cautiously. His nervous face betraying the man he had invented himself to be and revealing the child he still was. Eva sensed him first and beckoned him over like a mother beckoning her youngest son to join the family by a fire.

She took the boy's hand and led him to sit down with her and Tariq, across Luke's chest, nestled him in with them, hugging him in front of her, excited smiles on their assembled faces, as though they were about to rattle off on a rollercoaster ride.

By now Luke was ruined. Too exhausted and broken to fight. With this tightening of the leather belt death would surely come.

That was when the boy reached up with his Polaroid camera and took Luke's picture like a fledging serial killer, suddenly wanting a trophy of the first of his wrongs.

Eva stood up in the accompanying flash so forcefully she nearly knocked Tariq off Luke's legs behind her. She screamed in Albanian for them to stop yet again. The men all turned to her with quizzical looks.

Her eyes were fixed on the Polaroid camera in Tin-Tin's hands. Slowly she turned them to the impaled, disembodied head on the computer screen.

Luan and Tariq watched her silently, exchanging small baffled looks. Finally she turned back to Tin-Tin to ask. "Does your cousin still have that video camera?"

With that, they understood.

Twenty Eight

Moses nodded weakly as if he were a doctor confirming that 'yes, indeed' the man would most probably die here on their kitchen floor. Then swiftly a look of determination came to him as if someone had suddenly pulled a mask down over his face. He bent down at Tyler's side with a tea-towel, seized hold of the twist of metal and yanked it quickly and efficiently from Tyler's body like a father pulling a plaster from his child's knee without giving him the time to know what was happening.

Blood shot out like ink from a squid, cutting off Arifa and Hakem just below the knees, staining their tan trousers with a thick splattering of blackish crimson, making them both cry out in disgust.

Tyler fell backwards. It was beyond pain. In some strange crease of his unravelling brain he was dimly aware of the three men standing over him, one cramming a tea-towel into his gaping wound.

He was grateful for the merciful wave of near insanity that had come to him. It made the hell tolerable, the agony unreal. He felt like laughing at the irony of it all but all he managed was a hoarse gargle as if his throat had been closed up by the hands of someone throttling him. Maybe it was a blessing that he was rendered speechless. The three men hovering around him wouldn't have known what he meant if he'd been able to express his thoughts. '*It sugar coats the poison – this psychosis thing*'. In his desperate hour he wanted to laugh.

Over the rushing in his ears and the hum of the old fridge he laid next to he was sure he could hear his mother's voice. He wondered if it was his turn now. Now on a stranger's chill ceramic flooring. Was he about to stare up into the folds of heaven itself? Was he about to experience the bliss of reunion with his lost parents? Would it take longer than twenty minutes for his father to start nagging him and driving him up the wall?

In the sickness of his sudden madness, with his mind switched off from itself and no longer able to hold conscious thought, the dreams that came to him were more vivid than life, more unknowable than death.

He dreamt of Luke the night he was born. A different birth. This time his hands hadn't been there to catch him. He'd shot from their mother's flesh like a bullet, slippery with afterbirth, and as unholdable as a greased pig. He'd slipped right through Tyler's grasp and landed head first on the hardness of the kitchen tiles. A surface so tough his brain was dented in like the bonnet of a crashed convertible Saab Turbo 9000. So smashed to pieces he was snatched up and spirited away from them there and then by men who 'knew'.

And decades later Tyler went to war.

He went to war and saw his brother again. He saw him tethered to a cement block in a small shack at the side of a farmhouse, his face bloodied and crusty with ruin, his head still wrecked with the dented smash that left him a lifelong drooling, dribbling mess. A twenty year old as helpless as a great baby, beset with a mind that couldn't think and a heart that couldn't feel. No use to his existence, other than to bear lashings and beatings. A rape toy for his captors. The recipient of any acts of savagery those who *could* delivered to those who had no power to stop them.

"He's going to die here." Hakem repeated.

Tyler heard the man's words, clear and succinct, even through his delirium dreams, as though god had suddenly cleaned out his ears of swamp filth.

The second man said something in a language he didn't know. Through the mingling words around him he now heard his father's voice. *'This way home now little man. You've had a busy day'.*

He sank in a heap of muscles that would not move, blood that would not pump, a mind that would not think, and waited for death to accept his surrender.

But deep inside him a small flame danced against the fiercest of winds. And somewhere distant and untouchable he sensed the presence of an ancient god who seemed to smile knowingly. *No little man, not today.*

And a voice called out from the core of his bones. A voice he knew. The voice of himself, and his two brothers, speaking as one.

And the voice said . . . . *soldier on.*

Twenty Nine

Luke knew he was somewhere inside the holiday complex. He could smell the stench of the shanty town coming in through the small broken window. You never forget the odour once you'd been through your first; the foul unforgettable reek of human filth and ruin, people subsisting beside rivers of their own decay.

It gave Luke hope.

If he could capitalise on this, his one slim chance to escape, and find his way to the catacombs' entrance he could make it back to the south side shores and hide under the cover of darkness till dawn. The islanders there wouldn't rush to protect him. But if he could find the policeman, Detective Ackerly Standing, the one man he'd encountered on the island so far with any resemblance of virtue, he'd stand a chance. He wouldn't need a corpse to prove his point this time. The evidence was now sitting as a row of savage bruises round his wrists, a ring of black ones around his neck. He could lead him back here and they could pull the place apart till they found Howie, or whatever of him remained.

The idea rebooted him with courage as he continued to twist the metal that manacled his hands to the overhead beam. He'd already weakened it. He'd twisted his hands at the wrists, turning them quickly in juxtaposing positions and pushing them apart as much as the pain would allow. He'd worked it to his thinnest point but had had to lift his entire body weight off the bench and remain suspended for an agonising second to increase the strain on the wire to try and make it break apart.

His effort was futile. He needed more leverage, more weight.

He fought through his suffering and pushed his hips off the bench, and anchored his feet underneath it. He heaved himself up bringing the bench with him. He cried out in pain. His body weight and the weight of the bench were now hanging from his wrists. The wire began cutting into them like cheese and he felt as though his arms were about to dislocate at both shoulders. The wire weakened further but didn't break.

Luke crashed heavily back down and bounced on the bench, his body shaking. His closed his eyes tight and leant his head back, moaning.

The boy would return soon with his cousin's video camera and they would finish what they had begun, filming it for whatever purpose they had in mind. He could hear them just outside somewhere on the upper floor. The bulging muscled man-mountain was deep in a drug induced sleep. Even through the blare of another electropop Euro trash song on in the room next to him he slept like a baby and snored with the force of a truck revving its engine. The other two were in the bathroom. He could hear them laughing and a bath being run. God knows why one wanted a bath right now. Perhaps it was a ritual at this time of the evening. She'd give her brother a bath and no doubt a soapy wet tit wank to boot.

Luke kept his eyes shut and thought of his impending death. If indeed that's what she had in mind. She was a clever little vixen; the blonde. It was either his military badge or his Company one that had made him a symbol of her hate-lust.

Luke was still mulling over which when he opened his eyes and saw her.

She'd been standing over him for god knows how long, a small smile on her face. Even in his predicament, his fear and pain, Luke couldn't ignore her beauty.

Then she did the strange, the unexpected, *even for her*. She pulled off her leggings and underpants and climbed back on top of him. Her loose cotton shirt was undone at the top three buttons and as she leant forward to slide down over him Luke could see the rounds of her large, gravity defying breasts.

He was tired, cold, his body was broken and spent. He needed comfort, and the nearness of something warm. However surreal, however wrong, the nearness of the murderous she-bitch brought him the relief he craved.

He began to tremble under the press of her body.

"Shhhh" she whispered, like a prostitute about to score with a virgin, and walked her hand up his chest, slipping it under his shirt and running it over his skin.

"It's a shame we didn't meet in another world you and I." She told him, laying her head flat on his chest. "I think it would be quite something to know you in private life."

"What are you?" Luke asked in a weak, frail voice.

In truth he knew the answer. She was his Dalil Basheer. And he was her Farhan Khan.

Farhan Khan had accompanied him through training and ended up in his squad in Iraq. Unbeknown to any of them an al-Qaeda cell led by Basheer had hatched a plot to kidnap and behead a British Muslim soldier in order to undermine the morale of the army and show the world that despite the battering they were currently taking they still had a few tricks up their sleeve.

Unfortunately for Basheer so did the British Army, who, acting on a leak, dropped in 12 SAS soldiers who managed to penetrate their cave and decapitate the insurgents with a few dozen rounds courtesy of their C8 Carbines before any of them had the chance to do the same to Farhan Khan with a rusty blade.

After the debriefing Luke asked his friend how he was feeling.

Farhan's eyes scanned some inner horizon, no doubt imagining what might have been, unaware he was tightening the neck of his T-shirt around his throat.

'I'm not going to take it personally.' He had said. 'They don't hate me. They hate what I represent. They hate the history behind me. They hate the hypocrisy. Me, they don't even know.'

Luke's thoughts turned to Howie's letter '*before something goes wrong one of these nights*'. Something had gone wrong. Blackly wrong. He knew it. It was his Company badge, not his military one, that marked him out, made him her target. Inducing her hate-lust. Hate of what he represented. Hate of the history behind him. Company history. Company hate.

Eva pressed her face deeper into his skin, finally answering his question as to what exactly she was. "I'm just a little girl in a big bad world, trying to find someone to love."

She had said it with such sadness that for the briefest of seconds Luke felt empathy and yearned to fold his arms around her. It was reminder enough that, because of her, his arms were lacerated, imprisoned, throbbing with pain and bleeding in the air above him. Without further thought for her pain or his own he lifted his legs and tightened them across her back, heaving the two of them up. The wires cut deeper into his skin and blood streamed from them. For a sickening, dreadful moment Luke thought the effort had been pointless. Eva was looking around bemused. Any second she'd wriggle and squirrel her way out of his hold. But, finally, finally, the added weight of her body was enough to break the loop of metal and both she and Luke came crashing heavily back down to the world below.

Still bewildered, she leant one hand on Luan's drug cutting table and began to pull herself up. Luke had to act quickly, and ruthlessly. He ignored the pain in his torn wrists, grabbed the knife Luan had been using and speared it through the tender flesh of her hand so forcefully the tip stuck in the tabletop. It would not hold her for long. Before she had a chance to scream he whipped up a heavy metal tray and held it aloft, the remnants of hashish and cocaine scattering about him. He brought the tray down with brute force on top of the knife and drove it into the tabletop like a tent peg.

Eva threw her head back and let out a guttural scream of shock and agony.

Luan slept on, his snoring never breaking tempo, but Tariq soon appeared in the rectangle of light in the doorway, beaded with bathwater, a toothbrush in his mouth and a white towel tied loosely around his waist.

Tariq Skanderberg was a weedy wiry little thing. Even in his weakened state Luke could take him.

Before Tariq had a chance to protest Luke grabbed a handful of his curly wet hair and pulled him violently into the room.

Eva was screaming in Albanian, no doubt for Luan. But the hulking man's snores could still be heard, along with the throbbing beat of the electropop song which now choreographed Luke and Tariq's brawl.

Luke already knew what he would do and the execution of his plan was proving easy. He would pummel the man with punches until he'd knocked him into a coma. Then find a similar way to subdue and silence his wild cat of a sister. A right hook to the jaw should do it. If his damaged wrists didn't allow it he'd take the tray again and smash her face to oblivion.

Tariq was wobbling around as if drunk. Knocked about easily by Luke's blows. Unable or unknowing of how to defend himself. But Luke sensed danger. The woman was ruthlessly tenacious and, he could guess, her panting breaths and squeals were a byproduct of her efforts to prize the knife back out of the tabletop and her hand.

Sure enough that's exactly what she was doing, wriggling the knife a centimeter to each side, fighting through the pain and ignoring the blood which gushed from her hand with each movement. She screamed a maddened prayer to her god and heaved the knife out along with a thick jet of blood that hit her face and the wall behind her.

She sprang up with cat like agility and tore across the room towards the men, screaming crazily, knife brandished out in front of her like a bayonet.

Tariq staggered on his wobbling legs, punch drunk and clueless about which way to turn. The direction he chose was fatefully wrong. A step taken an inch to the right and you won't step on a mine. Turn right instead of left and the man won't be there to mug you. One more cuddle with your mother, a spilt drink on their carpet . . .

Tariq had wobbled right. Right. Right into the path of his sister's onslaught and the outstretched knife. It slid into his neck as easily as butter. Eva and Luke both gasped and froze. Such was the shock of it. Tariq looked at his sister with something that resembled a small smirk, the hilt of the knife still protruding from his neck and her hands still wrapped around the handle. He swayed against it, began to totter, made a doomed effort to keep his balance, then fell heavily down to his back, the knife remaining in Eva's hands. A spray of arterial blood burst forth from his jugular in a bright crimson arch.

Eva screamed. A sickly wretched unbearable scream, a scream beyond grief. She flopped down to her brother's side and clung to him as he died within a pool of his spreading blood.

Instinct was within Luke; a byproduct of months of intensive medical training. For an instant he was compelled to drop down alongside her

205

and do whatever was necessary to tend to the wound. But another instinct overrode it, one stronger and more primordial. The instinct to survive.

To the sounds of Eva screaming in a strange mix of Albanian and English that 'he' had killed Tariq and barking commands to 'get him', her voice, savage, and shrill enough to wake Luan from his drug dreams and arouse whoever else may be in that house, Luke stole from the room and fled for his very life.

Thirty

Luke had lain against the wet hill of dead things within Hell's Mouth
Curve for three minutes before they'd arrived. It had been Eva who
snatched back the white plastic sheet, barely flinching against the coarse
train of redolence that would have without doubt punched her senses.

What was the woman? Made of metal?

Tin-Tin stood beside her and together they scanned the small hill with
hate in their eyes.

Luke's bid for escape had been a cunning but effective one. Running
blindly from the house within the holiday complex where they'd held
him, he soon reached the stony rigid feet of the bluff where he made a
panting exhausted attempt at recovery. Water slapping in and out of the
mouth of the north entrance to the catacomb, nagged for his attention.

His savaged wrists screamed alive with pain as he yanked back the heavy
iron grate and clambered inside. Adrenaline threw him forward. He'd
made it halfway through the sewage strewn hollows, blindly navigating
the system of tunnels when he heard them enter behind him; yapping
dogs, pounding footsteps, catcalls and hysteria as they followed his smell.

The south side entrance to the tunnel had already been standing
mercifully ajar. With one quick double footed shove he'd have it open
and could flee down onto the beach. But then what? There was only
one way in and one way out of this section. The lynching mob would
have been on him before he'd made it to the relative safety of the dunes
and the few options they could offer for a man to hide.

The white tarpaulin rustled in the moving air as if to call him, reminding
him of the spot he thought he'd find Howie. He neared cautiously, as
cautiously as a man with no time could allow himself. The yaps of dogs

and jeers of men growing in intensity, the first of their flicking oncoming shadows dancing up the slippery wet walls.

Luke Dearlove knew death. But not as this. This was not the final resting place of his brother. This was not the death of one, but the death of many. A vast grave full of unspeakable secrets. A hill of beings who once lived, once breathed, once laughed and loved and feared and faltered, but now lay together in a fused heap of adipocerous fluids, long decayed flesh, jutting bones, stringy hair and thirty thousand insects, feasting furiously on whatever they had left.

Who were they? What brought them to their end? Who? How did they end up in this place?

He did not know, but maybe, just maybe, they'd provide his salvation.

Eva knew the half open grate that faced the beach was nothing but a sham. The rest pushed and clambered by her, not a shrewd thought among them. Nothing but the rush of eager excitement in their silly heads. Bounding after him like monkeys high on coffee.

Her sudden turn brought them up cold. Their chatter ceased and they exchanged silent glances, pulling at their dogs to be still as they waited, wondering if she'd really do it.

Tin-Tin knew she would and stepped up to join her.

Luan held her back with a gentle hand. "No one could go in there."

She would leave nothing to chance. Tin-Tin, the only man among them, nodded his support and watched silently as she snatched back the white sheet to stare inside Hell's Mouth Curve.

Only Tin-Tin and Eva remained strong and upright, the others all doubling up, stuffing their hands over their faces and groaning as if suddenly beset with a mass case of dysentery.

Her eyes scanned it coldly, darting with frightening alacrity to every trifling movement, every beetle that scuttled, every worm that crawled.

I will match you stare for stare.

And Luke knew it. Smeared in the dirt of the dead. Half buried among them with twenty different types of diptera and coleopteran larvae nibbling at the wounds on his wrists, amazed and delighted at being suddenly treated to a meal of fresh meat. His held breath burned inside him, aching to be released, but that would seal his fate, as well as allowing the three inch centipede that had found a comfy warm resting place in the groove of his lips to slip down into his mouth; thirty furious limbs scrabbling through his saliva.

Luan touched her arm again. "Come, leave our brothers to their sleep." He and the others pulled back, heading for the far end of the tunnel and a night of angry discussion and impromptu planning. Eva and Tin-Tin remained, eyes still searching, eyes as dead as the corpses they picked through.

They saw it together, not Luke, something else, something missed a year ago when they'd gathered up their grief and entombed those they'd loved and lost in the baleful place. A blue beaded bracelet, still worn on the blackened wrist of a corpse.

Tin-Tin reached for it. It was his mother's bracelet. His clasping fingers missed Luke's face by an inch. It remained strangely clean as if god wanted it untouched for this moment. Tin-Tin brushed away the only speck of dirt, stretched its elastic innards and placed it tenderly over his wrist. With his other hand he held Eva's, mother and child looking down at the grave with somber quiet respect.

Finally . . . . finally . . . they turned reluctant eyes away and walked slowly back through the tunnel's watery depths.

Luke spilled down to the water's edge, still coated in long dead flesh, clinging adipocerous fluids, beetles and ants. He stumbled to the waves, choked lungs barely working, strengthless limbs violently shaking.

He sank to his knees, then fell to his back in a half faint and lay in the surf like a vacationer, looking up at the stars as the waves ran over him, washing him of slime and filth.

Five, four, three, two, one.

The rocket launch mantra inside his head always worked. Overriding defeat, summing up the final reserves of strength and sheer-will determination imbedded in his sinew. The sea shone on in its sagacity and rushed great whispers of encouragement into his ears as Luke pulled his body into action and crawled from the surf to collapse again, three feet away from the water onto the carpet smooth sand.

Lightening flashed on the sea's far off indistinguishable horizon, setting the night in sudden purple. In its flash Luke saw something with slumped shoulders standing on the far side of the beach, something with savage broken teeth, something with one yellow eye and one eye as white as the moon, as if the membrane of an egg had been pasted over the iris, something with primed ears, listening for prey. It wasn't human.

The head bent down and the shoulders hunched as it padded slowly across the beach towards him, the faint hiss of a growl escaping from the depths of its throat, a warning not to attack, a warning to be afraid until it decided what Luke was.

What had the island saved for him now? Some awful thing of demonic power and endless hunger, something bred here, for moments such as this. Something grown from the dead leaves, something that fed on the festering flesh of those left behind in the catacombs to rot, something primed to kill?

Luke watched it with weary eyes, prone and defenseless on the sand, listening to the unpromising crack of dead twigs and jetsam under its feet as it came for him on its hands and knees.

So you're the one been causing all this trouble?

The words danced across the back of Luke's mind as he recognized the shape on the sand a foot from him as the infamous mad dog, murderer of sheep, mastered by no man.

Likewise. It breathed.

He wasn't sure if he'd actually heard the dog hiss the word back. It was probably just the midnight cry of a cat suffering a twisting rape far back in the dunes, or the wind playing tricks with his mind, or the irregular pants from the mad dog's muzzle as it studied him, his great tongue lolling free, spilling over the edges of a broken-toothed bottom jaw that gaped and yawned and set his mouth in a sickly grin.

Luke relaxed, laid back and exposed his neck.

If I give it up for anyone on this island, buddy I'll give it up for you. I'm tired and I want to go home. Happy hunting.

He closed his eyes and waited for the animal to savage him. Felt its sweetly sour breath steaming on his face as it moved in for closer inspection.

Then, in it came, no broken teeth spearing into his jugular. No, clamped jaws, returning with its reward of tatty torn out flesh. Just the sudden warm lick of the animal's tongue.

Luke cocked his head and looked at it. Ignoring Luke, it continued its work, diligently washing him clean of the final strips of foul stinking

211

matter the waves had left behind. Cleaning him as a mother dog would clean her pups of afterbirth.

Luke reached a trembling hand for the beast, touching the side of its fur tangled face. The dog yelped, maybe from the pain in its infected eye, maybe from the strange sensation of human tenderness, a hand that showed mercy, a man touching him for the first time with kindness.

The invitation was enough. The dog turned in small circles three times on the sand, kicking himself up a pillow, then wrapped itself into a firm tight ball, pressed up against Luke's side, as content as a treasured pet in front of a roaring fire on a winter afternoon.

Luke watched him silently for a moment, barely daring to breathe, then draped himself around the animal as a child might cling in the cot to an outsized toy. Luke nestled into its wet warmth and the deep beat from its heart. Man and beast lay together on the cold sand and soon slept, safe in their nearness, two beings who meant each other no harm. Safe in everything, bar their tomorrows.

Thirty One

Tyler opened his eyes.

He'd made it through the stifling hallucinatory night, skulking around the edges of madness.

As obscene as it had looked, his wound had been controllable, non-life threatening. His wild fever and dance with lunacy was more likely down to the bash to the head when he hit the marshes, the helping of their filth-water he'd inadvertently chowed down on, or good old fashioned hyperoxia as his erratic breathing flooding his system with an overdose of oxygen.

After the impromptu removal of the twist of metal in his belly, they'd cleaned and dressed the wound well. Stitched up the offending hole with whatever materials and means they could find. Still Tyler winced and wobbled as he climbed off the couch, holding his side as though he'd just had his appendix removed.

He could see the three of them sitting at a breakfast table in the adjoining kitchen, *last night's theatre*, sharing coffee, food, stories. They'd clearly had little more sleep than he'd managed but they were in good spirits and easy dispositions. These were good men. Quiet men with gentle natures. Men who understood other men's faults and frailty. Men who forgave easily . . . most things.

Tyler could see that level of benevolence and compassion in Moses Bogdani's face. Still he approached him with the same cautious trepidation and discomfiture as a man who'd got drunk to epically paralytic proportions the night before and couldn't remember whether he'd either emptied the man's fridge or fucked his daughter.

Tyler coughed quietly in the doorway of the kitchen in an awkward but obvious attempt to catch their attention.

Moses looked over at Tyler, put down the coffee he was pouring for his friends, rested his chin in his hand and waited for whatever it was Tyler was about to say.

"I think . . . I think I . . . ," Tyler stuttered, conscious of the embarrassment and shame he felt in the man's presence. "I think I need to find my brother."

Thirty Two

Luke had never been this cold, this tired or this hungry. Never at training. Never in service. Never at war.

His whole body throbbed with an aching exhaustion like a man who had escaped a mangled car wreck and spent the night crawling along a country lane in search of rescue; dripping out steady spots of blood and the last of his life-force all along his route.

But right now it was thirst that disrupted his body more than any other malady. So much so he dispensed with the need for a glass and bent his head into the stranger's kitchen sink and lapped fervently from their gushing tap like a dog. *The dog*. It must have been just as cold, hungry and thirsty as he was.

He had tried to sneak away from it at dawn. Cross the beach without waking it. But the animal sensed his movement with all the wolf-like instincts inherent to it, and soon it raised its head, staring at Luke with questioning eyes, demanding to know why he was off somewhere without him.

Luke sighed, the dejection in the animal's face sending pity through his every agonised muscle. He raised his hands, imploring the dog to stay where it was, but instead it rose to its haunches and with devout loyalty followed Luke's pathway across the sand until it was right by his heels where it sat and waited patiently for his master's next move.

The pattern continued all the way up the hill. Luke insisting the dog go about his business, ushering it away with gently insisting commands 'Off you go. Go on now'. The dog, waiting patiently, wondering if it was a game, watching until Luke got ten paces ahead and then trotting to catch up to his side. Even when Luke hurled a small broken branch into the depths of the woods that flanked the lane, the dog would bound after the stick and soon return with it in its broken toothed jaws, wagging what remained of its mangy tail and offering it triumphantly back to his new master.

When Luke reached the first house, a medium sized cottage that sat in a recess a small way back from the lane, he held a hand up to the dog who dutifully sat and waited while he knocked at the small oak door.

After several attempts to rouse the inhabitants Luke tried the door's handle and found it unlocked.

The dog had waited obediently as Luke had taken his first cautious steps inside, leaning and tilting its head to gain maximum view of his master as the oak door closed and separated him from view.

Luke called out several times once through the door. But the house returned nothing but silence, silence other than the quiet tick of a wall clock and the hum of a fridge in the neighbouring kitchen. The fridge's low droning whine reminded Luke of his thirst.

He'd rushed into the adjoining kitchen; any concern about the house's owners finding him suddenly vanished. The primal instincts for his body to be satiated and cared for and cleaned had overtaken any of his underlying concern.

The water did more than satisfy his thirst. It gave strength back to his limp, tired being. He felt it reach the outer parts of himself, his bowels, his bloodstream, the muscles of his legs, the skin of his feet. He blossomed with it like a shrub.

He thought of the dog.

The second thing they both needed was food. He yanked open the fridge door, ripped a leg from a cold turkey and devoured it greedily. Pulling off one of the turkey's breasts for his new companion and a second leg for himself, he went back to the oak door with it as a grand surprise.

The dog was gone.

Luke was stunned by the level of sadness he felt. Since leaving the army there had never been anyone or anything, other than Howie, he relied upon to never leave his side. But he'd felt a certain kinship with the animal. Maybe the dog had scratched at the oak door for him, then, when receiving no response, began patrolling the borders of the house, looking for his buddy, hunting out the smell of him. Luke couldn't be sure. He tossed the turkey breast onto the path and closed the door, baffled by his increasing gloom.

Now satiated, his attention turned to his wounds. Like a doctor, who never thinks he can fall ill, a well-trained Army Combat Medic is forever reluctant to believe any part of his structure can be damaged. But Luke's hands had grown increasingly numb, feeling more and more like useless appendages, cuts of meat from an animal sewn to his wrists. He had tried valiantly, and failed miserably, to use the house's landline to phone Detective Ackerly Standing. The phone's receiver had slipped through his fingers as though it were smeared with butter and he was left with no choice but to accept the inevitable and prioritise the need to treat his wounded wrists.

Rollovers kill soldiers. Bullets batter battalions. But it was the common germ Army Medics knew they must fear the most. Gunfire wounds and bomb blasts sucked in with them the filth of the environment. Clothing, shrapnel, batteries, other men's bones, parts of cars, faecal matter was often blasted about the human body to lodge and take residence in the most bizarre and vulnerable of places.

Many a combatant across warfare's history would have survived their injuries were it not for the insidious presence of the bacteria of the clostridia family and their cousins; tetanus, gangrene and botulism.

Luke knew the deep dirty gashes in his wrists had left him susceptible. Soon the flesh around them would die. Each dead cell in turn killing his neighbour in a brutal chain reaction until his skin changed colour and began to swell and stink of its own collapse.

Luke needed to act.

A quick hunt through the kitchen yielded no medical supplies at all, not a plaster, not an aspirin. So cautiously he climbed the worn wooden staircase at the back of the living room.

The house was quiet. But that didn't rule out the likelihood that someone was home. Luke's footsteps creaked across the warped wooden floorboards. It was always possible the owners were still sleeping, aged, and deaf to their intruder. One of them could emerge at any moment with a golf club or a rifle.

Luke called out at the top of the stairs. When again, he received no answer, he pushed open the top landing's doors until he found the bathroom where he rummaged through make up, lace underwear draped over every surface, perfume and jewellery until mercifully he found peroxide and a small roll of bandage.

Luke had known he had taken a serious chance, stealing in to a stranger's house like this. Anyone on the island, in any of the houses, could be in allegiance with Jed Burke, or Eva Skanderberg, or the Company, or worse. He'd half collapsed after plunging his savaged hands into the sink bowl, now filled with the recently procured peroxide. It was so much easier to administer treatment than it ever was to receive it. But receive it he must. After using his mouth and each free hand in turn to dress his wounds with the bandages he slumped, breathless on the sink's edge, his wrists screaming alive with pain. It was from this position he was able to peer behind a pink lacy bra and see the picture of Kai Burke and his girlfriend Shelley set in a diamanté frame.

It was also when he heard them, climbing out of a taxi outside, Kai nearly skidding on the turkey breast and calling Shelley every ungodly name men have for women as though she had intentionally left it in his path. Shelley, in return, admonished him for not locking up when they'd left the night before, as they bustled through the door together.

Luke held his breath. The muted sounds of a television came on from below. Then Shelley, speaking to Kai "Do you want to come with me to my cousins? I've got to get my pubes waxed?"

"Fuck off." Kai's courteous response.

Luke crept back to the landing, leaning over the old wooden railing. Kai's shoes were kicked off and discarded in the middle of the room and he was sprawled across the couch. Shelley was tidying her hair in the mirror, reclipping her extensions back into place. "Make sure you lock the door if you leave before I'm back." She ordered.

Kai only remained sprawled on the couch, either asleep or ignoring her. She shook her head. "I'll lock it." She snapped. "You'll have to go out the kitchen door if you want to leave." She turned on her high heels, sashayed through the door, slamming it behind her and double locking it in exaggerated angry movements.

Luke quietly let go his held breath, came cautiously down the first few stairs and stared down into the living room.

He couldn't see Kai's face, only his feet sticking over one end of the couch and the top of his head at the other. Both the feet and the head moved slightly, as if in time to music, and yet all the television played was a 90's action movie.

Luke took tentative steps down the rest of the stairs and into the space of the living room behind him. If he needed to, he could fight Kai Burke and easily win. Despite his weakened condition he would have the upper hand; Kai Burke looked like the type who'd never had to or needed to fight any man for anything. But what the little idiot could do was scream for his father, and god knows how near he might have been. Any time Kai Burke moved Jed Burke seemed to be there keeping a wary eye on his safe being, as though the twenty four year old had never progressed from being an infant. And Luke was certain Jed Burke knew Skidaway Island as well as he knew the cracked map of worn skin on the backs of his own weather ruined hands. There would be no nook or cranny he could find to hide that Burke couldn't have spotted from a mile away and swooped down with outstretched talons to pluck him out.

Luke crept behind the couch, breath held, muscles constricted, unaware of the three spherical ornaments that began to roll as the side table upon which they sat came up an inch as he passed it and pushed up against its side.

The largest rolled and hit its brother, which sent that one crawling across the table like a giant marble to tap into the smallest of the set which, in turn, rolled and spilled over the table's edge. Luke gasped, seeing the cascade at the final second. He darted forward and caught the sphere with one hand in an awkward downwards stoop.

Luke turned slow eyes onto the couch. Kai's socked feet still beat out the same strange rhythm. Luke let go his held breath and turned quickly for the door into the kitchen. This time his sudden action knocked a shelf sending a large vase filled with lilies sailing down to crash into a mishmash of glass, water, petals and stems by the side of Kai's head.

Luke span towards him, tensing his muscles, readying himself to overpower him if needs be. But Kai only remained in his outstretched position; feet visible at one end of the couch, tapping out a beat, head at the other, nodding slightly, like a magician's assistant laid within a box proving to the audience she was very much alive before great squares of steel blades were slammed into her midst.

Luke gave it no further thought, or hesitance, and scrambled through the door and into the kitchen towards his escape.

An escape which was thwarted the moment he got inside.

With his hand pressing down on the kitchen door handle and the beat of his heart so loud and fast he could feel it in the glands of his neck, he saw them. Outside in the lane that wrapped around the back of the cottage were Mason Burke and his extended brood. Luke stopped short, feeling nothing in his stomach but the dryness of fear.

Mason was leaning against the jeep's passenger door, frowning as he checked messages on his mobile phone. Damien and Calum were at the back of the jeep, examining hunting rifles, loading and demonstrating them to two friends. Luke's eyes darted about the group frantically. Jed Burke was absent. A small mercy. A very small mercy. Luke could tell by the bond and familiarly with which Damien and Calum joked and interacted with the two other young men that they were cousins, or the closest of friends. Their ease with each other was enough for Luke to know that they would have acted on their two cohorts' command and asked questions later.

Luke would only have had to open the kitchen door an inch for their assembled attention to crash in upon him. And these were men who would beat and kick him until he broke in half.

Luke turned frantically back and retreated into the kitchen. He would storm passed Kai Burke, send an elbow into his cheekbone if he needed quietening down at all. The door may have been locked but the window wasn't as far as he knew. And if it was he'd smash his way through it.

221

As soon as the plan formulated in his racing brain he immediately had to improvise it.

Kai Burke had entered the kitchen and was standing in his socked feet at the fridge. Upon sight of Kai Luke understood the reason for his bobbing head and tapping feet and his deafness to Luke's crashing passage behind the couch. His phone was stuffed in his pocket and the earphones set deep in his ears. The volume blasted so loud that even from the other side of the kitchen Luke could make out the soft rock song he was listening to.

Still blissfully unaware that he wasn't alone Kai took a glass bottle of milk from the fridge and lifted it towards his mouth.

The slight shift in his position was enough for him to finally catch hold of Luke's presence. Kai dropped the bottle which smashed to shards around his feet and left a white puddle to spread about him. He gawped at Luke as if trying to work out if this was something he was dreaming. Then his face lit up. He could see his uncle and cousins just outside the back kitchen door. He lifted his head to call them but before his cries for them to come could leave his mouth Luke was on top him, forcing his hands over his face and ramming the words back down his throat. The two crashed heavily to the floor together. Kai's back impaling on several of the upturned jagged shards from the milk bottle. Kai let out a muffled scream from under Luke's hands. Luke twisted his body and stretched up to check none of the Hares or their companions were approaching. Kai seized the opportunity, grabbed a large lump of the broken bottle and tore it unceremoniously through the skin of Luke's arm. A line of fresh blood shot out like ink from a busted pen. Luke lost his hold on Kai, instinctively gripping his bleeding arm.

Kai smelt his escape and scrambled up but his socked feet slipped and slid through the blood and the milk and he crashed violently forward right into the kitchen's iron range, the tender exposed bulge of his neck bearing the brunt of the brutal fall as flesh and bone met metal, snapping his larynx with a sickening crack.

Luke took another glance to make sure the Hares were still busy with their own affairs and lurched towards the door which lead back into the living room.

He stopped at the door in the cold silence. A silence punctuated occasionally by small sucking and hissing noises coming from the floor behind him. For the briefest of seconds he tried to pretend the noise away, but the inevitability of it all lingered.

He heard the Hares' footsteps on the gravel outside and terror ripped through him. Beyond him, in the living room, sunlight streamed across the window, sending dazzling spectrums of light to dance on the walls. It beckoned him like an ache. Beckoned him to safety.

He turned his head fractionally back towards the kitchen floor, enough to see the shape of Kai Burke twitching and juddering in small little jumps as if being continuously electrocuted.

Corporate James Lily's distinctly strong voice bounced around in his head; 'Is this person going to die no matter what I do? If so, move on. Does my treating them put myself, them and others at risk? Are my actions better severed treating another who is either more seriously injured, or, stands a better chance of survival?'

Luke shook his head, sighed angrily and tore back across the kitchen, falling down at Kai's side.

"You'll be ok." Luke told him, examining his face. It had become the deathly colour of a silver winter moon, his eyes rolled violently in his head as if he'd been turned suddenly blind and was fighting for the sight of something, anything, in the abrupt darkness. He gurgled like a kitchen drain, his muscles flinching, about to convulse, his fingers clawing the air beside his thighs, clawing at nothing.

"Keep clam." Luke told him with great assurance. He clambered back up, grabbed a knife from a stand on the counter and fished through drawers until he found a plastic pen.

He fell back to Kai's side. "Breathe." He instructed. "You'll be ok." He speared the tip of the knife into the tender skin above Kai's windpipe and air escaped with a gassy hiss. Luke pushed his finger inside the wound; blood ran down either side of his neck in thin streams. Luke nodded reassuringly. "You'll be ok." He bit off the back of the pen with his teeth and spat it across the room. Switched sides and pulled out the nib and adjoining ink cartridge, leaving nothing but a four inch straw of plastic behind.

He positioned it over the wound he'd created to allow Kai to breathe and was just about to complete the final part of the tracheotomy which would have saved the young man's life when he heard the kitchen door open and Mason Hare's startled voice cry out. "Oh my god! Kai!"

Luke put one hand up to protest, shaking his head. If he'd been allowed the chance he would have explained that for Mason to stop him now would mean his nephew's certain death.

But Mason was in no mood for explanations. All he saw was red. A red the same colour as Kai's blood which now pulsed violently from the wound in his neck and dripped from the tip of the knife at Luke's side, mixing with the puddle of milk and turning it garish pink.

The ferocity of Kai's sudden blood loss, Luke knew, was down to the fact that his carotid artery had just ruptured; a fatal result of the blow to his neck from his fall.

To Luke's dismay he saw that Mason was, for a reason he had no time to try to understand, carrying one of the rifles. He pointed it vehemently at Luke and checked his finger's position on the trigger. Luke fell onto his backside and scrambled under the kitchen table.

Mason pulled on the trigger repeatedly but the gun refused to fire. Either through his emotion, his shock or his inexperience, he hadn't worked out how to remove the safety catch.

Luke seized the opportunity. He scrambled out from under the table and began to get up and charge away with the speed of a runner bolting at the sound of a starter pistol.

Mason Hare changed tactic. He spun the gun around and brought it crashing down over Luke's back. Luke cried out and fell unceremoniously forward into an ungainly sprawl.

A hideous, repulsive sound stole their attention and thwarted Mason's follow up blow. It was Kai Burke dying. His blood had pooled and filled the wound in his neck and was coagulating and clogging in his throat. He let out another ungodly groan and his body broke into a series of spasms, blood and froth bubbling from both mouth and wound.

Luke and Mason both seemed frozen. As if neither could move until they'd made the ultimate decision what now they should do. *Is this person going to die no matter what I do? If so, move on. - Do I bend down and hold my nephew's hand while he dies or get my hands on the cunt who's just killed him.* Ultimately each man made the obvious choice.

Mason sank to his knees by Kai, awkwardly clutching his hand and holding the side of his face barely noticing as Luke tore out through the kitchen door.

"Get him! He's killed your fucking cousin!"

Mason's words rang out like a war cry.

Luke had bolted for the obvious door, the nearest door, *the kitchen door*, just a few feet in front of him. Adrenalin had been pumping wildly, thrusting him on, his nerve cells firing on all cylinders. If he'd had time for protracted thought he could have weighed up his options and ultimately chosen to hurdle over Mason and Kai on the floor and smash through the living room window as previously planned. But right-thought had abandoned him in his desperate flight for life and he'd bombed it out the back and into the small group comprised of Damien and Calum Hare and their two cohorts.

They surrounded him now, staring at him with blank perplexed faces.

Stupidly . . . *stupidly* . . . he'd slowed to a stop and was staring back. He should have let the momentum and his adrenaline carry him forwards, charged threw them, sent them colliding into each other like skittles.

Damien looked over Luke's shoulder at his father, squinting as he tried to make sense of what he was telling them. His eyes dropped down to Mason's hands, honed in on the blood dripping from his fingers. He looked beyond him, through to the kitchen of Shelley Morgan's family home where he saw his youngest cousin lying slain on the floor.

His quizzical squint contorted suddenly onto a wretched, ugly grimace of rage. In one fluid motion he lifted the rifle, chambered a round and pointed it at Luke's face, looking down the sights.

Luke knew Damien Hare's handling of a rifle was bound to be more precise and more deadly than that of his father. Without further thought he rushed them, dodging the bullet Hare had fired by merely an inch and knocking Calum onto his back.

Luke fought for oxygen and for his life as he bolted down the hill. He could sense them coming after him. Hear their shouts, the clambering of their feet, the clashing of their rifles. One wrong step, one trip and they'd be on him. On him with either a bullet in the head, or the back, or a frantic, nauseating, merciless death with the savage butts of their rifles and furious stomps of their feet; as ugly and one-sided as a bullfight.

Luke was gaining speed. The wind, or a newfound energy within him, or years of imbedded training and service pumping back into his muscles when he needed it most, giving him the edge. He was moving down and away from them; a long distance runner making a last minute dash for the finish line, leaving his competitors in the dust like a yapping clan of hyenas.

The world span in crazy circles around him.

Luke wasn't sure how he'd fallen; a log across his path, a weakened ankle, a pothole, the overconfidence of feeling he was winning, the tangle of his own two feet, or just the evermore twisted tangle of fate. The force of it threw him forwards, his collision with the ground ripping his trousers and tearing up the skin on his hands and knees.

He could hear one of them, right behind him, so much closer than he'd believed any of them to be. He turned breathlessly onto his back and put one pathetic arm up in defence as Damien Hare slowed to a clumsy stop. He twirled his rifle as though it were a cane and ambled over to Luke.

Behind him the stretch of sky was a hazy scarlet as the sun continued its long slow climb to rise above the rim of the world, making the entire island seem soaked in blood. The moment felt more and more like some nightmare dreamt up in the mind of the devil.

Damien came closer, his brother and their cohorts still far back, catching up slowly. A sense of the inevitable swept through Luke, his breathing becoming loud and erratic.

Damien lifted a warning forefinger to his mouth and ordered Luke to shush, then offered him a cruel smile. "You ain't never gonna tell nobody but god." He lifted the rifle and looked back down its sights, pointing it intently. Luke closed his eyes.

But it was Damien who would be the one to scream as if shot.

Luke's eyes flew open to see his saviour sink savage canine teeth into Damien's arm and wrestle him to the ground.

The dog had bolted from the undergrowth, leaped two feet into the air and seized Damien's limb before he'd had the chance to get a shot off.

The dog shook its head with shark-like savagery, defiant jaws clamped immovably onto Damien's flesh, needle sharp teeth spearing into his skin. Damien screamed like a little girl. Luke clambered breathlessly back up, for an instant enjoying seeing his assailant being made such a mess of in every possible way. But like so many of his moments of joy on Skidaway Island this was to be short lived.

Calum and his two pals arrived. They turned their rifles and their feet on the dog as they would surely also have done on Luke. Battering, kicking, punching at any inch of fur they could reach, Calum screaming hysterically for the dog to 'Get off my brother you fucking animal!!'

Soon Calum decided, spurred on by either his brother's shrieks, or the dog's snarls, that more critical action must be taken. Luke was just taking an urgent step towards them when Calum turned his rifle on the dog and fired.

Luke's scream rang out nearly as loud as the gun shot. "No!!"

The dog let out a piteous high pitched yowl, making it sound more like a puppy than a full grown animal. A low suffering moan followed the yowl and it slumped like a bag of earth. The Hares and their friends shoved the dog's carcass unceremoniously away with a few final insulting kicks and turned their savage eyes back to Luke.

Luke couldn't run again. He couldn't. There was nothing left in him. No energy. And no fight.

He made the token effort of turning and stumbling back down the hill. He heard the sounds of Damien wincing and cursing as he clambered back up.

It wasn't an animal this time, but a car, that crossed the path between would be murderers and their potential victim. It screeched to a lumbering stop ahead of Luke, who fell clumsily across the bonnet. He gawped in at the driver, Rory Benson, who in turn, looked back out at him as if neither knew quite what to say or do at this point.

Finally, Rory nodded and with that permission was given out. Luke stumbled frantically to the passenger side, seized open the door, flung himself in and spun round to pull the door shut.

Calum had got a touch on the handle from the outside and was struggling to yank the door back open.

Rory pulled away, dragging Calum momentarily along with them till he lost his hold and crashed to the earth. Damien leaped over his brother, leaving him moaning on the ground. He smashed his elbow into the passenger window, cracking it into a spider web pattern. He glared through the window at Luke, pointing viciously and screaming hate-filled indecipherable words at him. Words that no doubt carried promises of the violence and torture that would follow should he ever get his hands on him again.

Rory floored the gas and the car lurched away. He glanced into the rear-view mirror, seeing Damien, a lone figure in the dust, hideously battle scarred from the dog attack, bloody, shaking and incandescent with rage.

He was relieved. Damien Hare would have recognised his face on any other day, his neurofibromatosis making him one of the most easily identifiable of men on the island. But he was too charged up with fury to have noticed him. He wouldn't have known his car either. The tumour pressing against Rory's right eye made his eyesight limited. He only drove when necessary, and this had been the first time in years. He could safely get himself and the soldier back to his home in the wilds of Skidaway's countryside and the Hares wouldn't have a clue where he was or who had helped him.

Finally, he turned his eyes cautiously towards Luke.

Luke laid slumped back in the seat as if half conscious, his hands shook violently and his whole body trembled as he fought to recover. He turned breathlessly towards Rory and tried to speak, but all that emerged from his throat was a wordless cracked whisper.

Rory nodded.

The soldier didn't need to do anything to thank him. Not just yet.

Thirty Three

Moses had been to the Skidaway Island Theme Land just once before. And in the space of the year that had passed since his first and only visit the place had changed in its entirety. In its heyday the park had bustled with a frenetic energy; alive with the excitable screams of children, the laughter of all, young and old, music blearing from the rides, beckoning the crowds their way, the dizzyingly sweet smells of cooked fairground treats and a cacophony of clatter-clash discord from the array of one-arm bandits and slot machines plus the rattling charge of the Big Dipper that hurtled repeatedly around the track, blasting through the park like a rush of hot air.

Now the crowds had vanished. The screaming laughter was gone. Its insistent voice silenced. The only music was a tired, limp version of 'Three Blind Mice' emanating from one of the empty rides in a gratingly out of tune rendition as if every third note was played wrong. The paint on the once blue and yellow Big Dipper had weathered to the dull matt of primer and the thing lumbered around the wooden track like a clunky timeworn relic of the past; an old workhorse that seemed increasingly unlikely to be able to make it up the climb of its hills. But make it it did, every time, and continued its pointless loop, ridden by its only passenger, the theme park's manager, thirty two year old Arben Rexha; safety bar raised in the air and his feet nonchalantly up on the carriage in front of him, his greasy black hair pulled back from his pimply forehead then thrust forward as the train crashed to a clumsy stop.

Arben Rexha's job managing the park was initially offered to Moses a month after he'd arrived on the island. But the screams and laughter of young children, the joy of families, was too cruel a joke to be turned on him in his period of initial raw, soul-stinging grief. He declined and the

231

Company soon pulled Rexha out of the Turkey Cage as their man, much to the chagrin of the Lawlor family who, for two generations, had been in charge. Either their departure, or Rexha's management skills which included mainlining and huffing paint thinner under the bleachers, soon saw the place fall into its current state - gutted and useless, saved for no profitable or discernible reason. Other than, perhaps, to piss off the locals.

Moses stood there now trying desperately to wedge a protective hand between the two puffed up chests of Tyler Dearlove and Luan Palacki who were butted up together like a pair of clashing bison.

"That's a fucking lie!" Tyler was protesting, his words sizzled with hate as he threw them at Palacki.

"Is it English?" Palacki spat back and the two men crowded into each other further still until their foreheads were forced together in a turgid standoff.

While imploring for calm Moses was, in addition, trying valiantly to listen to the jabbering story thirteen year old Josef Boci was babbling into his ear as he wrestled for his attention.

The teenager looked closer to a prepubescent eleven year old. Clearly malnourished and sickeningly thin, he wore an old second hand T-shirt that swamped him over his tiny, too small shorts, and made it look like he was wearing a dress.

Despite the predicament, and the sense of impending violence coming off the two men like steam, Moses couldn't help but be taken back to memories of his homeland while looking down at the child.

Street kids like him had flooded the towns there, pumped up to the eyeballs with scorpion, or hash or any other drug that left them impervious to fear.

When his wife had first told him of the baby she was carrying for them the joy that burst through his core was soon replaced with a fear-laced sadness. If his child were born a boy, could that life, or that world, envelope him at some stage? Surely these ragged crooked boned boys had fathers at some stage too. Fathers who'd loved and cared and dreamed of their future. A future other than this.

Moses wondered if that was when the decision that he and his wife should leave their country had kicked inside him with the first sparks of life.

From there on in everything seemed to enforce his decision, as if god's every angel were whispering in his ear 'this way . . . this way'.

His second cousin Saul had fallen into the hands of the local gang most feared and revered in those parts, the 'Head Choppers' as they chose to be known. Not as victim, but as abettor; a renegade recruit.

Saul had pulled him aside the same night as his sister's wedding, proudly showing him his mobile phone. This was nothing new. He'd been showing the phone off to anyone who was or wasn't interested for a month now, the first gift from the group who wanted him forever in their debt.

Moses had nodded politely, before realising that it was the shaky image on the phone's small screen that Saul was insisting he take note of; a sickly smile cutting into his face so deeply and so wide it looked like the gashed wound from a machete strike.

The grotesque performance was that of a smooth skinned boy of no more than twenty, his hands tied savagely tight behind his back. Saul, bending over him, began to cut his throat, the arterial blood soon hitting him in the face. Saul, never faltered; sawing, hacking, slicing, digging, turning the convulsing young man's head this way and that as he searched for sinews and muscles to sever. Finally, he held a aloft the dripping severed head in a grand theatrical gesture, grinning, like a child seeking praise from its parents.

Saul turned to Moses then, as if expecting his praise too for doing what other men would only talk about.

Moses nodded politely, left the wedding and made it home and into his bathroom before vomiting violently.

The video footage was, for him, a bomb, ticking beside him. A creeping barrage, encroaching his existence, as present and near as the explosive nature of war.

'Flee now or you may never escape.' It was his own voice repeating the mantra time after time, in the innards of his brain, crowding out the voices of the angels.

But he could not chance the life of his wife and unborn baby. He *would not.*

The stories of the English Company offering safe passage to Europe to work as labourers on an offshore build which paid five times their average wage were hard to believe. And yet school friends, relatives, businessmen from the area, had made the crossings safely and reported back that it was all true. No dark deceptions, no months held in camps suffering torture and abuse, no extortions to be paid for safe passage, no kidnappings along the route and ransom demands to be met, no being tied hand and foot to poles while eleven men raped your wives and daughters, no hell on high seas in overcrowded boats, no capsizing, no death by drowning or by shark. Yes, the words they were telling him were true.

Moses laid a hand on his wife's still flat belly as he pondered it. Yes, he could believe it to be true. But he would go first. He would go first and then call for her. Just to be sure. Just to be sure.

"Is it English!!" Luan was bellowing again, tearing Moses savagely back from his memories.

Thirteen year old Josef was finishing the story, telling Moses all he knew as the two men went for each other. Moses had managed to get a handful of Tyler's shirt and yanked him back, dragging him yards away from Luan and the toxic tit for tat violence that was boiling up like a kettle.

"It's a fucking lie!" Tyler yelled over at Luan. Then turned to Moses. "It's a lie!" He implored like a teenager demanding his father take his side after a sibling spat. Moses nodded, barely listening, still pulling Tyler further back.

Three of Luan's friend's grouped around him, all sneering over at Tyler, spitting occasionally at the ground and performing any other acts of the grotesque that could reinforce their contempt.

Tyler turned earnestly to Moses. "His whole life my brother has never done anything to hurt anyone."

Moses nodded distractedly, still fending off Josef who was making an attempt to repeat his story all over again. The combined jeers of Luan and has friends rose over the top of the Big Dipper as it made another screaming pass.

"Things are worse." Moses told him, edging him further back from both Josef and Luan and his circle, who looked ready to charge them any second.

Tyler turned his beleaguered face towards Moses.

"Kai Burke was killed in his girlfriend's house this morning." Moses said.

Josef grinned triumphantly and scampered away, no doubt to report back to whoever had sent him with the story that it had been successfully delivered to 'The English'.

Tyler shook his head. Within the last ten minutes he'd heard tales of Luke having sliced open the neck of one of the Albanians and now they were asking him to believe he'd made equally short work of the repugnantly spoiled son of the head honcho of the original islanders.

Tyler was about to contend the insanity of such imaginings when Moses cut off his words before they began with cold words of his own, said in the severest of tones. "I fear your brother is in the gravest of dangers on this island Mr Dearlove. Now, from whichever side may get to him first."

Tyler turned away, kicking a discarded seat from one of the defunct rides.

Moses kept wary eyes on Luan, watching him edging forwards with his friends like a pack of wolves readying themselves for a kill. He kept one hand on Tyler's shoulder, preparing himself should they need to run.

"There must be one man here we can turn to."

It was Tyler, whining up at him.

Reluctantly Moses turned his full attention back to Tyler. Over his shoulder he saw them; four monks standing in silhouette against the first shades of sunset, their movements as smooth and elegant as the gently rolling waves of the surrounding sea as they bowed and swayed in a combination of meditative prayer and ritualistic dance.

"There must be." Tyler repeated.

The eternal sun symbols stitched to the golden gowns the monks wore with such pride tugged at Moses's gaze.

"There may be" Moses countered, "one."

236

Thirty Four

Luke Dearlove had slept the deep and dreamless sleep of the dead there on the scruffy couch in the small corner of the world Rory Benson called home. So far gone from life and all its realities he may as well have been on the moon.

There had been no need for an inventory of the various savages of war he had witnessed in his young life, no mental listing of the victims of sectarian suicides, the tortured, the executed, or their body parts, to calm his beleaguered mind enough for the stillness of sleep to reach him.

This night had been different. This night, Luke had been toxically tired. He slipped under the thinning sheets on Rory Benson's couch as though it were a bed as warm as summer. The noise of a slow cold rain tapping on the nearby windows became as familiar and as comforting as the sounds of his parent's voices seeping up from the floor below in that long ago time when life made sense. The time before he'd come to this island of broken shapes, fallen into its bowels; its blackened heart.

Luke was yanked back to consciousness as if by some invisible force and bolted upright, breathless and damp with sweat.

Once the certainty of where he was and how he'd come to be there returned to his swimming brain he pushed back the thinning sheets, climbed off the couch and scanned his environment.

A large image on the far wall seized his attention and without realising what he was doing he found himself walking towards it.

It was a picture, projected onto the wall. The main focal point being a man, turning away from camera, his long black hair tied casually at the back of his head, with those strands which had broken free of their binding floating out on the breeze.

238

The tattooed etching of an eternal sun symbol sat on the back of his neck, its ink sunk into his skin for time without end. In front of him the hands of scores of his monks reached for him and the tall sunflowers beyond them bowed their heads as if all life gravitated his way. All the world drawn to him as nature to the sun.

A click sounded from the space behind him and the picture suddenly changed. Luke jumped with the unexpected noise as if someone had pulled back the catch on a rifle.

The picture of the man was gone and what replaced his image was that of a group of six, sitting together in tall grass, their faces beset with the savage cruelties of leprosy.

"The Johar family; residents of a leprosy colony in south Kolkata." It was Rory's voice. Luke turned to him in the room's darkness.

He sat in the shadows behind an old style projector, calmly still and full of scrutiny. Taking everything in. Giving nothing away. He clicked to the next slide. Luke glanced back at further pictures of residents of the colony presented by Rory for his perusal, finally settling on the image of a middle-aged man, his afflictions from the disease seeming to mirror Rory's own defacements from neurofibromatosis. "Their faces a ruin, their bodies a joke." Rory continued. "But able to father children, to consider their fate, to give love and receive it as any man. More perhaps. Souls that have known cruelty expanded, often further, than those who know life as a smooth plane ride."

Rory clicked on to the next slide. It bore the picture of a young man burned by fire, the next a woman whose face had been drastically changed by the surgery that would help her survive cancer, the next, a soldier missing limbs and looking at the camera with immeasurable dignity and pride.

Luke tore his attention from Rory's slideshow, scanned the room for his clothes, spotted them at the foot of the bed and hurried to dress. "I appreciate your help. I really do." Luke muttered while pulling up his trousers and hastily buttoning them. "But I have to get back to town."

Rory clicked on to another slide in a motion that seemed to carry anger, making Luke stop suddenly and look back at him.

"There are people looking for you on this island who will kill you without thought." Rory told him.

"Let them." Luke responded in an unemotional tone.

"Is that a soldier's stoic courage?" Rory asked briskly. "Or a young man inviting death through his door?"

Luke shook his head, pulling on his shirt. "I'll do what I must to find my brother and then-"

"I don't want to know about the brother you've come here to follow." Rory cut Luke off sharply. "I want to know about the brother who came here following you."

Luke's buzz of energy left him at the mere mention of Tyler and his every tightened muscle slackened like suddenly deflated balloons.

Rory stood up, knocking the projector slightly, its displayed image casting its colours across Luke's face with the jolt.

Rory walked slowly towards Luke and examined him intently; studying his face as though at any minute his soul would betray his secrets and let them rise like welts to sit under his skin.

Luke tried to turn away, concealing himself in the shadows.

Rory gripped Luke's face, fighting to draw him out of the darkness. "If you don't share your pain, you don't give those who love you, the chance to love you enough."

Rory suddenly put his hands across Luke's eyes, pressing them firmly shut. He brought Luke out into the light and began turning him in slow steady circles. "Even the broken soul yearns to feel," Rory whispered, "the mangled heart to beat. Throw away your exit strategy. So when the day comes you can sing your death song, like a hero going home."

Rory suddenly withdrew his hands and let Luke go. He stumbled backwards and opened his eyes, the light blinding him, as though all stars of the cosmos were dancing across his vision.

He thought of Tyler.

Tyler.

He thought of Tyler, ursine and bombastic. Always saying the wrong thing. He thought of Tyler, the ordinary man, who wanted no part of this war he had begun here on Skidaway Island. He thought of the way he simply could not forgive Tyler the unpardonable sin of being a simple, everyday, decent man. Tyler Dearlove, who liked his job, liked his friends, liked his beer and loved his . . . . loved his brothers.

He thought of his own immeasurable cruelty. Of how he had casually dumped on him the colossal hurt of his own sad, soul-sick journey. Of telling him of his plans to leave this world and all its hell behind and expecting him to respond as though he were rattling off something as inconsequential as the results of a reality TV show. Telling him of his intended suicide with the same casual nonchalance as the way, years earlier, he had told him he was off to join the army.

He thought of Tyler, always standing a few paces behind him. He thought of him, for all his witlessness and his mistakes, being the one who finally found the right thing to say. He thought of the words written on the fridge in magnetized letters for him to find the morning after his Passing Out Parade. The message those brightly coloured plastic letters formed being one he'd automatically assumed Howie had

241

left for him. And how despite his heartfelt thanks to Howie, and Howie's bemused reaction and subsequent claim that he hadn't been the author, it still hadn't occurred to him that Tyler could have put together six simple words that came to touch him so deeply; '*YOU WERE A SIGHT TO SEE*'.

He thought of Tyler, always a few paces behind him, always watching, always there. Always ready to be the one to comfort him, to carry him, to reach for him . . . to catch his fall.

He ached for him, suddenly and profoundly.

He wanted to be beside him, urgently, immediately.

He looked at Rory with huge eyes, like a new-born, seeing the world for the first time.

"I . . . I w-wonder . . ." he stammered. "I wonder can you help me off this island?"

Rory smiled.

Thirty Five

In the air above City Market, just left of the harbour, against the black impenetrable night, a firework display raged in battle, signalling the height of the Annual Festival and lighting up the sky in violent bouts of coloured elegance.

Across City Market's crowded square various fractions of the world's populates spilled onto the streets; Skidaway's jumble of mishmash denizens. The maddening warble-whine of firecrackers and whistles being blasted from, and in, all directions, shot through the air, accompanied by the sizzle and aroma of street food, pungent and spicy, stimulating the senses of the swelling crowd.

Despite an atmosphere to rival New Year's Eve in Rio and a heaving, laughing, dancing, crowd swirling around him like a sea, Tyler Dearlove felt strangely alone.

He tried to force a smile as the three men sitting with Moses Bogdani glanced at him from the table within the tavern. But it was not a smile, just an awkward contraction of his facial muscles as he tried to appease them in his ridiculous way.

He had been gawping through the tavern window at them for ten minutes; *the child left outside while the grownups talked.* Moses had waited alone at the table for a prior ten while the men were summoned; sighing and lifting a signalling hand for Tyler to *wait there and be patient* every time he tapped at the glass and peered in at him with questioning eyes.

Finally the men, all in their sixties, joined Moses; 'the elders' of the Albanian migrant elite, although in truth they were still bordering on the outskirts of middle-age. When your community is made up only of those strong enough to cross a violent sea in the black of night, the eldering fraction of your community are generally sparse, as are the young.

Moses had asked the three men for their help calmly, patiently, at first. They'd glanced over at Tyler and he'd offered back the first of his idiot smiles. Tyler hadn't heard the words but could read all the quiet dignity of Moses's body language. The man had gravitas on the Mandela-scale and Tyler remembered with shame the way he had spoken to him the first day they'd met. If anyone could convince the elders to give up their secrets it would be this man.

But soon Tyler sensed Moses was losing his case. His measured beckoning pleas for help ceased and he began gesticulating more avidly.

A stocky female bartender bent over them, blocking Tyler's vision, her heaving bosoms ready to burst out of her white blouse. 'Move lady.' Tyler willed her silently.

Once she had obeyed his wordless command and retreated back to the bar Moses was seated alone. He looked up at Tyler with a resignation of defeat on his face.

Moses pushed slowly through the tavern's patrons, pulled back the door and soon appeared in the street in front of Tyler.

He shook his head.

Tyler slumped.

"They feel it . . . *wrong* . . . that you should meet." Moses said trying to sound convincing.

"Go back, persuade them." Tyler implored.

Moses shook his head. "They may be right. It would perhaps have been . . . a mistake."

Tyler's head dropped, he buried it against his chest.

"They don't know where he is." Moses added quickly.

"They're lying." Tyler bleated.

"They feel it wrong." Moses repeated.

"They're protecting him." Tyler countered, anger rising in his stomach like bile. He looked suddenly up at Moses with a quizzical stare. "Or you are."

The words caught Moses off guard. He looked at Tyler but couldn't answer. Finally he turned and began edging through the crowd which swallowed him up immediately. Tyler fought through their midst and caught Moses's shoulder. "You know who he is, don't you?"

Moses looked back at Tyler as the jostling crowd pushed and pulled him about on the spot.

"What is the hold this man has on you all?" Tyler demanded to know.

"Mr Dearlove, if you should meet . . . things . . . things can never be the same."

Moses turned and fought back through the crowd. Once more Tyler followed; soon finding him and pulling him gently back out, drawing him away from the noise and the masses and finding a quiet corner against a nearby restaurant's stone walls.

Tyler peered earnestly in Moses's face, gripping his shoulder. "I will face this man, no matter his circumstances, no matter his . . . crime."

Moses sighed.

Tyler sensed a chink in Moses's armour. "Please, I've gotta find Luke. I'm supposed to protect him. Do you know what it means that I can't?"

Moses sighed more deeply, the pain of the great trauma of his own life crowding his brain. "Yes."

"Then if this man can help take me to him." Tyler beseeched. "Please . . . please . . . I'm begging. Please."

Moses's typically even-tempered face seemed to be contorting into a grimace. What he knew to be a bad idea he found himself reluctantly agreeing to. He pulled his truck keys out of his pocket, the action alone letting Tyler know he was begrudgingly acquiescent and began heading away from the crowd back to where they had parked.

Tyler began trotting after him, then slowed to a stop.

Moses turned back with questioning eyes.

Tyler had slumped against the wall. He had won this round and got his way, and yet more and more he was feeling like the man who'd spend months chasing the girl of his dreams only to find, after the first kiss, that he wasn't sure he particularly wanted her after all.

The truth was nearly tangible, hovering just out of grasp but there was something about the idea of the truth, the truth that Skidaway Island had buried and was about to bring up from its dank guts that left Tyler clammy with dread.

"This man?" What did he do?" He asked Moses in a weak voice. "What was his crime?"

Tyler had known the answer to this question before Moses answered it. He groped for strength in the pit of his mustered being but found none. He looked up and awaited Moses's response.

"A year ago," Moses told him. "He killed a security guard."

Thirty Six

At about the same time Moses Bogdani was signalling through a tavern window for the oldest of the Dearlove clan to wait and be calm while he tried to find a solution for his predicament, Rory Benson was doing the same to the youngest, not more than fifty yards away, one street on from the north side of City Market Square.

But the window he motioned through was that of his own truck as he stood on the doorstop of Detective Ackerly Standing's house waiting for him to answer.

He had told Luke to keep down in the passenger seat and remain out of sight. But the moment he had crossed the street towards the small row of terrace houses he'd glanced back only to see him pressed up against the glass, eager and hopeful like a cocker spaniel awaiting its master's return. Rory had never known anyone so tenacious, apart from himself that was.

He knew Ackerly Standing was home. He could hear noises coming from within the house as he stood outside in the cool crisp air; a television replaying a football match; the sound muting soon after Rory first rang the doorbell. The clatter and clash of large things being moved out of the way, the rustle of great rolls of plastic. What Ackerly was doing in there and why he'd seemingly barricaded himself in his own living room Rory couldn't be sure. But he could hear him coming. He would get to him, eventually.

Rory saw Luke fidgeting within the car and feared that any second he'd be striding across the road to join him. He pulled the hood back off his head and tried his best to give him a mother-like 'sit still and be quiet glare' but as Rory knew, the bulge of skin and the tumour within it that half covered his one good eye didn't allow for the most communicative of facial expressions. And he could do without attracting the attention of those people still shuffling their way down to City Market right now.

Even without the added dilemma of having a soldier on the run in tow Rory would have kept his hood drawn down over his face on this part of the island. It hadn't always been the case. Rory carried no sense of shame over his affliction. But what he did have was utter intolerance of the ignorance of strangers. His face was the most distinguishable, and memorable, among all of Skidaway's residents. As much a part of the island as were the chalky white bluffs and the steaming swamps. In the erstwhile time before the Company had arrived people seldom gave him a second look or a second thought. But with the sudden influx of outsiders came the obligatory looks and comments and cruelties, and the indignity he hated most, the pity.

On this same stretch of road, approximately six months after the corporate element of the Company had moved in to oversee planning and construction, a young lady, who, he later discovered, was personal assistant to the CEO, had stopped the small group she was with, walked over to him and proudly placed a ten pound note into his hand.

"What's this for?" Rory had pushed back the tumour pressing against his vocal cords to ask.

She hadn't been prepared for the question, the grand look of worthiness soon disappearing from her pretty face. "Well I thought, I- I thought . . . " she had stammered. With her generous act not quite going to plan, and Rory refusing to nod his overwhelmed thanks and shuffle humbly down the street in awe of her magnanimousness, she had no choice but to come up with an answer to his question. She looked at him, her face paling, glancing back at her group of companions as if for help. They,

248

however, remained rooted to the spot, leaving her in the midst of the situation she had created. "Well it must be hard being a . . . " her voice faltered.

"Being a what?" Rory questioned.

She found her eyes examining him properly; the outer layer of his face and the physical manifestations of his disorder. She seemed almost to become hypnotised by the man behind the condition. Tears crowded her eyes and she broke away, not stopping to re-join her baffled group as she ran back to her hotel.

Three months later Rory saw the young woman again. For reasons best known only to her she had started dating Damien Hare and he and his ridiculous brother were with her at their uncle's bar at the hotel where they'd taken to drunkenly insulting a young migrant couple who'd just arrived on the island. Rory had walked up to Damien, and, in front of the girl, placed a ten pound note into his hand.

"What's this for?" Damien had asked as the girl's eyes fell ashamedly to the table top. Rory had shrugged. "Must be hard being an arsehole."

Further clanging and clanking from inside the Standing house stole Rory back from his thoughts and finally the door was unlocked from the inside and opened. Rory immediately understood what all the clatter-clash from within had been about. Ackerly was dressed in workman's overalls, splattered with blue paint, and still had a glistening brush in his hand.

Luke sat in the silence, feeling at the stillness.

Rory had told him to keep down and out of sight but a force as strong as gravity had continually pulled him up. He wasn't used to being a bystander and an eagerness to take action and play his part fizzled in his bloodstream. In the same way he'd decided he wanted to come to Skidaway Island and find his brother and die alongside him and that need had compelled his every action and dominated his every thought. Now that he'd decided to give life one more try, getting off the wretched place and finding a way back home to Tyler had become the new obsession.

Just as Luke's hand was on the car door handle and about to yank it down, the front door behind Rory opened and Detective Standing stood illuminated in a rectangle of light. Luke watched from the car as Ackerly gripped Rory's shoulder warmly and beckoned him inside.

Rory managed one small glance back at Luke as Detective Standing closed the door behind them.

Luke slid back in the seat.

Suddenly a man in a carnival mask slammed himself against the car's window and pointed in at Luke. Luke's muscles constricted and he readied himself to fight for his life if needs be. But it was only one of the revellers, drunkenly making his way down to the red flickering glow of City Market and all its buzz and excitement. His girlfriend soon pulled him away and they wobbled down the cobbled street.

Luke breathed deeply, his exhalation steaming up the car's windows. He wiped a hand through the condensation and settled back to study the house for the next sign of movement. Patiently now, he would watch and wait.

The thick plastic sheet underneath Rory crackled and scrunched with his slightest movements as he sat quietly observing Detective Standing on the opposite couch; his brow wrinkling into a mask of deep concentration as he silently mulled over the matter which had just been presented to him.

Rory was glad Luke had suggested Detective Standing as their first choice 'go to' man. Initially he had thought of Moses Bogdani. He lived close by and would never say no to anyone in genuine need. He'd passed Moses's truck the day before, with Luke still shaking and distraught at his side after his near murder at the hands of the Hare brothers. Rory had thought of flagging him down then but had chosen to get the young soldier to his home and out of sight as a priority.

Their combined instinct was right. If there was one man on the island they could trust it would be Ackerly. Luke had praised his virtue, having encountered him once before in the Company's boardroom, gently trying to do the right thing while Francis Grayson systematically tore him apart. But Rory hadn't needed much convincing. He too held the detective in uncommonly high regard.

Moses would no doubt have had the heart to try to help Luke off the island. But not the clout. Ackerly was a policeman after all. He'd have all the ethical responsibility Moses would have shown but also the double whammy of a professional duty.

There would be no way Rory could have got him onto the ferry. His face, recognisable as it was, wouldn't have allowed him the necessary anonymity and discretion to have bought Luke a ticket and got him safely away. Not if, as he was certain they would be, following Kai Burke's death as Luke had described it, Jed Burke and his minions were blood lusting for the soldier. Placing blame for his *'murder'* unjustly on Luke's shoulders and keeping their eyes on the ferry port to thwart his escape; vengeance in mind.

No, they needed someone. Moses would have been good. But Ackerly, Ackerly was perfect.

"You did the right thing in coming to me." Ackerly said finally and Rory let out a long protracted sigh, the thick plastic under him creaking and crunching.

"Give me a hand with this will you." Ackerly asked, seemingly still deep in an internal thought process.

Rory got up and helped Ackerly position a large plastic sheet over the top of a thick white rug.

"There'll be murder in this house if I get paint on her carpet." Ackerly said, nodding his thanks.

"Can you get him off the island?" Rory asked earnestly.

Ackerly smiled. "Let me make a few calls."

He got up, pushed his way back passed the stepladder and other workman's tools with another clatter-clash cacophony of noise and headed out to the hall.

Rory heard the beep of his mobile phone and his voice, diminishing as he receded down the hall. "It's me. We got worries here . . ."

Alone in the living room amid the dust sheets, paint trays, protective plastic and half-finished decoration Rory's eyes meandered about the place, taking in the various signs of family life. Ackerly adored his family, that was evident. Rory walked over to a shelving unit and pulled back one of the sheets for further vantage to see the many pictures of he and his wife and children.

They were gone now, no doubt down at City Market enjoying the festivities while dad stayed home and finished the decorating and enjoyed a few beers and a rerun football match on the TV plus some precious time alone.

'You deserve so much more than this.' Rory thought as he scrutinised Ackerly's small modest home. So much more than the moral bankruptcy

252

of Skidaway Island ever afforded a decent man. He hated himself immediately. Was there any difference in his own piteous thoughts than those of the girl who'd proudly handed him a ten pound note or any of the passers-by so keen to drop a coin into his cup. Ackerly Standing didn't warrant sympathy for living the simple life of an ordinary man. He loved his family and they loved him back. He was one of the luckiest men on Skidaway. Even if he wasn't the richest.

It was Ackerly who'd given Rory the old style slide projector. Rory had mentioned in passing that he was planning his next photography trip away and would this time be visiting and mingling with the poor of Jakarta in Southern Indonesia. Ackerly had presented him with the gift and told him of his recent studies in human rights law and his intention to move towards such matters as a career and asked if he could bring his two children round to view the pictures on his return.

They'd made a grand night of it.

Helen Standing had sent her husband and children to Rory's house with a hot steaming dish of homemade goulash and sherry trifle for afters. The children had watched the slide show in a mix of quiet respect and bug eyed wonder, a sensitivity to both of them beyond their years, clearly the results of devoted parenting. After the slide show he and Ackerly had talked for hours. The children soon drifted off on the couch. Rory had found blankets for them and he and Ackerly had chatted till two in the morning, Ackerly imploring him to tell stories of the things he'd seen on his travels around the world and how it all affected him. Inevitably the conversation turned to Rory's own struggles, not just the physical effects of his neurofibromatosis but the emotional and psychological; the human. Rory appreciated this; this genuine interest. It was so refreshing, especially in comparison to the stone faced nerves of the frightened, the sighs of the pitying and the cruelty of the ignorant.

Ackerly had explained how he wanted his children to have more and know more than the world as Skidaway Island alone presented it. And Rory believed him. A month earlier he'd seen Ackerly drinking with friends at the hotel bar and assumed him to be cut from the same rough, self-serving cloth as Jed Burke, Mason Hare and others. But how wrong about a person could you be?

How wrong indeed.

His heart seemed to stop.

It was as if an ice had set through it, freezing all its living parts and bringing its every mechanism to a jolting halt.

With slow cautious hands he parted the framed photographs of Ackerly's wife and children and reached for the one that had caught his attention. The one that had changed everything.

The picture was placed in a thin wooden frame. And set back from the family photos and holiday snaps as if it was just as much a treasured memento but not one that should be readily seen. The picture was of Ackerly, Jed Burke, Mason Hare and, bizarrely Francis Grayson and two other officials from the Company, one being the Chairman and the other a tall blonde woman with her hair up in a high French twist. Rory had seen her before, only ever on the island for the most significant of meetings, at about the same time as the Company discovered the shifting sands of Skidaway Island had ultimately proved themselves *'too shifty'* to build their prized castle upon. There was every possibility Ackerly, a native islander, could have known Jed and Mason enough to have spent an evening with them. But Mason and Jed and the three most senior members of the Company? There was no way. And no possible explanation. Especially with the added factors of the small groups' arms being wrapped around each other, any free hands lifting glasses of bubbling champagne to their photographer, and the smiles on their faces

254

bordering on being euphoric. It reminded him of pictures the papers would display of families or syndicates who'd won the lottery. And something had been won here. In this moment Ackerly had wanted memorialised in a photograph. Something had been attained. Or, some deal had been done. This was a life changing moment, encapsulated for ever.

"And where is he now?" it was Ackerly leaning through the door, asking the question casually. Almost too casually, *desperately casually*, his mobile phone still against his ear.

Rory quickly reset the photograph but didn't turn around.

He could just hear the muted conversation of the person on the other end of the line. Ackerly placed his free hand over the speaker. "Rory, where is he now?"

Rory pushed back the tumour in his throat that hindered his airway, but found it was the most difficult it had ever been to do so. Finally, when he was able to speak, he muttered quietly; "He's out at the lock-ups by Lake Woebegon. He's hiding there."

"Very good." Ackerly replied and ended the call.

Rory felt Ackerly enter the room, just as he felt his own strength fading.

"I feel really bad." Ackerly told him when he was no more than a foot away. "That I don't feel worse about this."

Rory turned slowly round and bravely faced Ackerly just as he picked up a large hammer from beside the paint tray, lifted it to shoulder height and swung it at his head.

Thirty Seven

Luke cursed himself for having slept.

He woke with a jump and the startled cry of "Fuck!"

This was as unforgivable as a guard sleeping on his centurion post.

He wiped his sleeve through the condensation on the car's window to peer at the house, glanced at his watch before remembering it was broken, no doubt through one of his various battles on Skidaway's shores. Rory's truck was too old and battered to have any kind of clock in its dashboard. He could only guess at how long he'd been sleeping.

He climbed out of the car and looked toward the east for any light. There was none.

To his right City Market still thumped with the pulsating beat of music and jubilation. A grey shroud of mist seemed to be rising from it and hanging in the sky above like an overweight storm cloud. But whether that was from the barrel fires and pyrotechnics or nature's own elements Luke couldn't be sure. Either way the streets were dark with something more than night.

Luke turned his collar up, glanced up and down the empty cobbled road and crossed it, heading for Ackerly Standing's front door.

His knocking had been light at first in the expectant hope that Ackerly and Rory would open the door a crack, check it was him, then usher him quickly inside.

When that particular outcome didn't materialise Luke's knocking grew louder and more insistent until he was finally pounding at the door.

Still no one came.

Nervous and perplexed, Luke turned back to the street and checked the line of vehicles. There had been a five year old Volkswagen Passat parked right outside when Rory had gone in. He'd seen it at the Company Headquarters too; Ackerly Standing's car. But why would they have left together without him? Luke was pondering the question when it occurred to him that they wouldn't.

He didn't know the man, *Rory*, all that well. But he'd proved himself to be as blindly loyal as the dog had been. As if amid all the demons that Skidaway Island had saved up for him, they'd also sent him an angel or two. An angel or two who'd never leave his side, fight for him, if necessary . . . *die for him.*

Luke swallowed back the thought.

He went to the ground floor windows and tried desperately to peer through the sliver of opening in the curtains to gain view of the space inside. The classic yellow-orange glow of lamps filled the room, punctuated by the flicker of a muted TV. All signs of a living room. No signs of life.

Luke tried one of the windows. It held momentarily, its brittle wooden frame clinging to its flimsy lock. After a small struggle it gave and slid upwards in Luke's hands with a creaking groan.

Luke took another quick glance up and down the street, all quiet, still alone, *good.* He put one foot on the window ledge and heaved himself up and through.

He landed clumsily in the living room but kept upright.

The acrid chemical smell of paint fumes hit him. He forced a hand over his nose and mouth as his eyes danced about the place, scanning the shrouded couches and rugs, the half-finished walls, the stepladders and paint trays lying here and there.

257

Luke froze. Soon his hand fell away from his face and clutched at his throat. His heart began revving like a motorbike.

He fell to the floor beside the large thing rolled up in the thick plastic sheeting, sat directly atop the thick white rug.

He looked along its length from bottom to top. Hovering above it he pressed down. What was encased inside was revealed to him; Rory's face.

Luke let out a hoarse gasp.

People had gasped at the sight of Rory's face many times before now. But this was not a reaction of the unthinking or they who were taken off guard by his defacement. This was a startled cry of outrage, a breathy lamentation of the sheer injustice of it all.

Luke grasped the nearby sofa and threw it aside; spilling into the space beside Rory's encased head and pulling free the plastic.

Rory's face was the colour of a drying sea-washed pebble. A hole the size of a golf ball was just under his hairline, black blood oozing from it like a spill of melting ice-cream. Luke touched it uselessly with the tip of his finger. Rory let out a pathetic, strengthless sigh. Luke gasped again, this time with thin hope. He bent into his face and searched for further signs of fragile life.

Rory was glad the soldier had found him. He'd struggled and managed to cling valiantly to his last few shards of energy. For years he'd looked forward to this moment. To the end of the suffering experienced across forty four years of cruel existence. But there, encased in the plastic, body temperature rapidly dropping and every laboured breath harder to draw from the tiny opening at the top of the plastic's roll, he had feared to die. Feared to die alone.

He, Rory Benson, the miserable, the abandoned, the abortion to be spurned, kicked at, trampled on. He, Rory Benson, with his extraordinary soul, strangely found that he didn't want to leave the wicked world behind.

Both men wanted to speak, but neither could, tears formed in their eyes. Luke sensed Rory trying to move. He tore back more of the plastic wrapped around his body. Rory lifted a frail arm and reached for his hand. Their fingers entwined firmly, wrapping around each other, palms pressed determinedly together like a handshake as strong as that of world leaders.

Luke frantically, desperately, wanted to find words for him. Wanted to say something human, something real. *I'm sorry for a world you may not have always wanted. A life you probably could not always understand. May you find serenity and peace and love in all that is coming next. May you sing your death song like a hero going home.*

But the only sounds Luke could articulate were the croaked, half-strangled echoes of despair, they poured forth from him, pitiable and weak, and did no justice to the brave man dying in his arms. Luke Dearlove had seen his share of death. But this, this was a horror torn from the underside of night, this was the worst. The most tragic and terrible.

As the old world dimmed around the young soldier, Rory managed a smile. He wanted to leave the young man a small reassurance of the glory that was suddenly filling the space between them. Whatever it was it was supremely, violently beautiful. Rory stretched up, now he wanted to be there, with every fibre of his very being, he wanted to join it. He lifted himself towards the dawn of a future where perhaps the light would always be this astounding and the tranquillity always feel this pure, and where maybe, *maybe*, the passers-by would drop a coin into his cup.

Luke hung his head. Rory Benson's last battle was over. His next one was about to begin. He looked down at the dead man's fingers, still wrapped tightly around his own trembling hand.

He raised his head to the ceiling and screamed.

Thirty Eight

"Wassa matter Mister? Someone got your brother? Someone gonna hang him from a tree around here?"

It was that staid and stone faced boy. That piss stinking, shit smeared rodent of a child. The one from the hotel bar that Luke had pinned against a table top while twisting his arm behind his back until urine gushed down his leg. The one with the purple lips and the eyes so black it made Tyler stop and wonder, even in the midst of his rage, how the little urchin actually managed to see through them.

He certainly knew how to pick his moments. And the moment he'd picked now was a winner by a mile. This was the moment Tyler was slumped against a rough stone wall contemplating the deaths of the last two members of his family. What better time for the little rat-child-scumbag to push through the crowd with a greasy grin and goad him.

"What the fuck d'you say to me?" Tyler demanded, despite the fact he'd heard perfectly well.

Moses had only just delivered the news that this mystery man, this *Martyr* they all revered, this dude who had all the answers and was gonna make all the wrongs feel right, was nothing but a lowlife common criminal. And that everything Luke had feared, and tried so hard to make him believe, was true; that Howie had befallen a terrible fate on the island one year earlier and was buried somewhere in its midst, rotting in a silent grave.

And while Tyler had that to think about, he also had to think about this, that Luke, his youngest brother, the family baby, was about to, or may have already, befallen just as tragic a fate. Either at the hands of the Burkes and Hares, blaming him for Kai's demise, beating him senseless until their grief was spent and then putting a final silencing bullet through his brain. Or, if a bullet didn't feel punitive enough, choking the life out of him with their bare hands, Jed Burke's rough and ruthless hands most likely, so he could stare Luke right in the eye as he died.

Or the Albanians, holding Luke just as responsible for the death of one of their own. But somehow he doubted they'd show the same mercy. They'd make his murder an art. Tie him to the back of a pick-up truck and drag him up and down the street till they'd skinned him like a fish. Or chain him to a chair, naked and cowering, slowly row him out to the middle of Lake Woebegone so he had an hour to think about it under the moonlight, before dropping him down like an anchor to a wretched drowning death and lonely watery grave.

Tin-Tin Borishi could smell the pink-arse's fear. He could practically feel it multiplying at epic speed like germs in a petri dish. This was most favourable, most favourable indeed. He smiled at him with a certain gruesome relish.

The smile was enough to make Tyler snap. The rat-boy's thick roughly chapped lips contorting across his face into a sickly grin, their skin cracking with the stretch of it. It was like having someone smirk at you when you've just been told you have cancer. Or are standing at a funeral looking down at your parents' double grave.

Before Moses had time to protest Tyler was charging through the crowd at full bore. He grabbed the boy by the throat and threw him up against the side of a vendor's hot dog cart yelling into his face, "I'll have you, you slimy wank stain!"

The near murderous onslaught only served to induce Tin-Tin's grating laughter. It came out in loud bubbles of noise, between wheezes, as he fought to prize Tyler's tightening fingers from his throat.

"Should have let my brother break your fucking arm when he had the chance." Tyler spat into his reddening face.

Moses reached them and yanked Tyler's arms from the boy.

Tin-Tin rasped, rubbing his throat. When recovered enough he threw another smile back at Tyler, a smile as dirty and ugly as he could force it to be.

Tyler took an irate step towards him, throwing more promises of violence his way. Moses grabbed Tyler angrily and forced him to look his way. "No!"

Tyler pushed Moses's hands away, still glaring at the boy.

"No Mr Dearlove. No." Moses demanded his attention. "You must be careful what you teach the children. War won't always be confined to these distant shores. "

Tyler turned to answer but what he saw over Moses's shoulder froze his heart.

He stormed passed Moses, knocking him madly, and stampeded into the midst of the dense crowd until he could get no further, his eyes wild with a dizzying mix of utter gratitude and sheer panic. He pushed vehemently at the crowd, but they were as thick as a wall. Finally they broke apart and Tyler spilled through them, crashing to the ground, where he looked back up and screamed. "Luke!!!"

Luke had entered City Market from the north-side passageway. Ackerly Standing's cobbled street merged with it and brought him in at the central point. Charged up like a machine gun and just as ready to spit out endless crucifying bullets, Luke had stormed across the cobbles, Rory's blood still drying on his hands. He'd pushed passed the first of the revellers. They'd swayed against his shoves, some turning to look

263

drunkenly at him. Others shouting expletives at his back in a mix of various languages.

It was only when he recognised, or thought he recognised, a small group from the migrant population as being those who'd hounded him and pursued him through the catacombs the night before that his pushing became more targeted and robust. He threw a heavy-duty whack into the back of the nearest man who then collided into his neighbour. The small group knocked about against each other like skittles but managed to stay upright. Muttering curses of indignation, they turned to their assailant.

"Here I am!!" Luke screamed at them opening out his arms, calling them on as though he were calling on the thunder.

Other men crowded nearer, the strangeness of the situation rendering them suddenly sober. They whispered to each other and nodded Luke's way.

"Here I am!!" Luke bellowed at them, rage coursing through him like poison from a snake bite. He charged towards them, opening his arms wider, bearing his chest as if defying them to put a knife in his heart.

Tyler scrambled up as Moses reached him, both men clung to each other, staring Luke's way. Tyler screamed his name again but Luke heard nothing other than the wave-like roar of the crowd and the pulsating thump of his own fury pounding against his brain.

Moses lifted one arm and pointed in a direction beyond the crowd. Tyler reluctantly looked away from Luke to see what was concerning Moses and his breath stopped in a harsh gasp. His eyes grew wide, and he realised that the sheer panic he'd been feeling was now about to morph into terror.

Emerging from a nearby fish and chip shop were Calum and Damien Hare and two of their thickly set muscle-heavy friends, their recent grief over the loss of a cousin seemingly put aside. They strode down the street all cocks, balls and grimaces, carrying, as they always did, the putrid tangy odour of cheap cologne and car grease.

Tyler wanted to sink to his knees. He wanted to beg god. He wanted to wake and find the entire nightmare he'd experienced on the island had been nothing but an epic dream. But all he could do was stand and stare, dart his head through the gaps in the swaying crowd as the Hare brothers' spotted Luke and his manic display. They dropped the hot parcels of food they were carrying, slapped at each for attention then charged like stallions towards Luke.

Coming at him from behind, they hit Luke like a train. The first of the men knocking him almost into the air and catching him again under the armpits. Another sent an uppercut jab so forcefully into Luke's guts that Tyler wretched, feeling it from where he stood, yards away.

Two more of them grabbed Luke's legs, hoisting him off the ground where the four of them carried him shoulder high back through crowd towards the roadside.

Tyler couldn't tell whether Luke was fighting, or was too taken by surprise and winded to even realise what had happened just yet. Or whether this final assault was just too much. Whether his spirit had been robbed of its last ounce of fight.

They carried him away. The surrounding crowd laughed mightily at Luke's predicament, perhaps assuming it to be his stag do and, however perilous this situation looked, the hands that seized and pulled and held him were those of the men who loved him most.

"Luke!!" Tyler screamed again, still clinging desperately to Moses in the street.

But his voice was lost in the music and madness and all he could do was watch as four men stole his brother away into the night, throwing him into the boot of their car and slamming the lid down tight as that of a coffin.

Trembling in Moses's arms Tyler felt his strength fade until finally it was only his companion's grasp that stopped him spilling to the ground.

As the car sped away he lifted his heavy head and one last time screamed his brother's name out at the encircling night.

PART FOUR

'There is no honourable way to kill, no gentle way to destroy.

There is nothing good in war – except its ending.'

Abraham Lincoln

Thirty Nine

The furniture, carpets and walls of Jed Burke's hotel bar always stank of something in the early mornings. Usually the odour of beer and old cigarette smoke. On this particular morning however, the air was heavy with something else. It was heavy with the smell of recent death.

Not the putrid stench of fusty corpses, but the sour flat smell of grief. Grief that was freshly cut and as open as a yawning wound. A wound so deep and raw its pain wasn't even being felt as yet. It affected all the senses of those present, beyond simply the smell of it. Calum and Damien were near blinded by it. Trying to look at their Uncle Jed, seated at the table opposite them, was like trying to snatch quick glimpses of the sun. The taste of it coated their tongues, filthy and unpleasant. Their skin crawled and itched with it and the silence between them was deafening enough to burst eardrums.

Only Mason Hare seemed immune to the overwhelming hellish awkwardness of it all. He managed to keep his eyes on Jed while his sons could only take quick glimpses before returning theirs abruptly to the table top. Perhaps because he was already a member of that least coveted of clubs Jed had now joined. The club for they who'd lost a child.

He and the late Madeline Hare had lost their firstborn, a girl, to cot death when she was six months old. In those first raw agonising weeks few knew how to look at or talk to them either. When they did it was always with the most erroneous, most imprudent of things to say. *'You're young enough to have more'*. As if it was as simple as replacing one car with another. *'You wouldn't have wanted her to live if there'd been something wrong with her.'* If our child had had something wrong with her we'd have given her twice the love to make up for it thank you. *'I know how you feel, I lost my dog last month.'* And you've just lost two friends this month with that statement you stupid, stupid cow.

"Where is he now?" They were all taken aback by the calmness in Jed Burke's tone. This was the man who had drop kicked a kitten and killed it in the process when the poor thing had inadvertently nearly scratched the two year old Kai Burke's eye. And now he was asking where his son's murderer was with a stillness that shook the room.

Damien tripped over his words nervously, talking to his uncle like a teenager asking a girl out for the first time. "The McGregor's have got him. Out at Trencher's Farm."

Jed nodded, but before either he or Mason or the Hare boys could broach next steps, what they all knew was due to happen, and all dreaded with equal measure, began with a rattle of the front doors opening and the sounds of several shopping bags being dumped angrily in the hall. Mason closed his eyes.

"I hope karma's a real thing I really do!!" It was Janice Burke, her voice shrill and rattled with irritation. "Once a year I go over to the mainland to go shopping. Once a year I ask my son to pick me up!"

Without waiting for them to respond she pulled out her mobile phone and began scrolling through her recent numbers for Kai's name. Mason got up quickly and gently tried to take the phone from her. She pushed him angrily away.

"Had to get a ride back with a pair of gooks. Had to ask them for a lift. A favour! Me!" She went on irately. "I'll swing for that boy I really will."

After pressing Kai's name on her list of contacts she finally noticed the oppressed mood in the room. "Who died?" She asked sharply.

269

Kai's phone began to ring from within Calum's pocket. He scrambled to turn it off quickly.

The various pennies began to drop and fit into their horrifying places in Janice's mind. She looked at her husband. He seemed as he always did, measured, unruffled, near silent, but his eyes, there was something wrong with his eyes.

Her brother Mason gripped her arms, looking in her face, trying to draw her back out of the bar, away from the tables in case she collapsed. She stared at him questioningly, but already knowing the questions in her eyes were ones she didn't want answers to. She knew he was looking at her in the same terrible way she had looked at him thirty five years earlier when she'd found out he and his wife had lost their baby.

She turned stiff with the realisation of it as if her every bone had fused suddenly together. She gasped for air, wide-eyed as if startled, digging her nails into her brother's arms as he tried to hold her. Finally she let out a sickening scream, no words, just a high intensity combined cry of fear and hysteria, so loud it tore at her throat.

Jed Burke got up and went to the bar as Mason Hare pulled Janice out to their living quarters, her continuing screams still sounding through the walls. Jed closed his eyes, but he couldn't close his ears to them. Whisky wouldn't help. But it would do. For now. He reached behind the bar, grabbed a bottle, pushed the cap off with his thumb and drank straight from its neck.

"Uncle Jed I'm so sorry . . . I". It was that repugnant little prick of a nephew of his, Calum, hovering beside him and putting a hand on his shoulder. *Why the fuck was he touching him? Why the fuck was he alive and breathing when his beautiful boy was dead?* Jed smashed the whisky bottle down on the bar, turning it into a weapon, grabbed Calum by the shirt, forcing him up against the bar wall and drove the bottle under his neck.

Damien bolted from the table, knocking chairs flying and screaming for their father. He tried valiantly to get between his uncle and his brother, begging Jed, shaking his head.

Mason ran into the bar and quickly got a handle on the situation. He pulled Jed back and away from his boys and stood protectively in front of them. Calum sobbed and touched the nicks on his neck, looking at the spots of blood on his fingers.

"For fuck sake Jed." Mason sighed.

Jed glared at them then finally threw the bottle aside. "Get the jeep." He demanded and marched towards the stairs.

Jed Burke yanked back the draw to his desk, pulled out his Taurus 44, Raging Bull revolver, loaded it and unlocked the safety catch. He wanted an execution and he wanted it now. He would smash the butt of it into the cunt's face. He'd do it again and again till he stopped hearing the splinter of bones, till he'd ground his face to pulp. Then and only then would he slam the final offending bullet into his brain.

He turned quickly, eager to be on his way, no man was going to stop him now. Indeed, no man would stop him. But a woman managed to do so.

Blinded by rage, he hadn't spotted her when he'd come in the office. She knew what she was doing. Women like her always did. She'd sat herself on a chair by the door, waiting quietly as he burst in and got his gun, then positioned herself for maximum effect for when he did turn round.

One long leg was pointed his way in its impossibly high heeled shoe. The other was at a right angle, blocking the doorway, its foot resting on the edge of a filing cabinet. Her shirt was dishevelled and hanging free, exposing a round shoulder that practically glowed with its golden tan, a

271

mountain of loose blonde hair tumbled over it in waves. She played with one long strand of it, tightening it round her finger and sucking on the fraying ends.

When Jed Burke had first been told of his son's death he thought that would be it for him. He'd never want to smile, or eat or sleep or fuck again. Yet the very next morning he was staring down at what was seemingly an open invitation and feeling sparks firing up from his cock, nagging at him with their repetitive little messages *'come on' 'we've got time' 'right here on the desk' 'you can have your other fun later' 'look her – she'll suck your cock till your eyes pop out'.*

Those impulses were about to win him over when he caught sight of a framed photograph of Kai on the corner of his desk. He found himself pointing the revolver at the woman in lieu of an erection.

Eva glanced at the gun in Jed's hand unfazed. "A bullet to the head. How kind."

"Woman you picked the wrong day to be in my way." Jed told her bluntly.

Ignoring him, she used her raised leg to kick the door shut, got up and strolled casually towards him.

There was a smile on her face that Jed couldn't read. The gook women had often approached him like this. Especially when the company first put him in charge of divvying up the restaurants, bars and businesses along Skidaway's mile long stretch of prime location and throwing them at the wetbacks, *drippings for the poor.* There'd been many a night he'd been in the front seats of the jeep with one of them while Mason was in the back with another. And like a pair of teenagers they'd enjoyed numerous hand jobs and blow jobs and a host of other European *delicacies* neither of them had ever even imagined before. *Get the goods while the getting's good.* But the mission was mostly done now. They were down to the last few original islanders fervently clinging to the mile that still needed a little more *friendly persuasion* before they sold up and moved off and the exile was complete. Leaving the Company to finally get on with the real work and start mining the electric gold they'd promised him a stake in. It'd been ages since one of the Euro trash sows had shown up like this still thinking they needed to curry his favour. But no, she had something else in mind.

"Exsanguination." She said to him and lightly stroked the gun.

Jed said nothing. He had no idea what the word meant.

As if she could read his mind she volunteered; "Or 'bleeding out'. It's the same way we used to slaughter cattle on the farm at home. Ugly way to die. I heard it took your son ten minutes to drown in his own blood." She let her finger trail from the gun to his forearm. "You're obviously a man of great mercy."

Jed lowered the gun. She smiled, this seeming to please her. But the gun hadn't frightened her. No, this bitch sensed she was winning.

Jed stood, silently listening.

Striding around him in long slow circles, she told him more; "I had an idea when I woke this morning. A thought dazzling in its purity. I wanted to make a gift of it to you and your wife. So you can both weep a sweet dream when the long night's over."

She stretched up to him and began whispering her plans into his ear.

Jed listened, calmly, patiently, as she spilled her secrets and spoke of her intent.

Finally he did one more thing that he had thought, following the news of his son's death, he would never have done again. He smiled.

Forty

Luke winced and crammed himself as deeply as possible into the recess of the boot as the lid was opened and the light came crashing in on him like an avalanche.

He'd been in there all night and was thirsting to the point of madness. He'd urinated twice in the night, the second time managing to pee into an empty can he found discarded alongside him and consuming as much of it as his nauseated system would allow. It was ironic how he had wanted to throw his own life away only a day or two earlier but now, now that he wanted to live, he was prepared to go to any level of degradation to preserve it.

Not long after he'd quenched his thirst on his own salty urine, the boot had been opened the Hare brothers and their two hulking friends had pulled him out and bound his hands behind his back. The quartet were obviously acting on their elders' orders. Damien had been the only one of the four to have behaved '*personally*' towards the kidnap victim, striking him hard across the face, then spitting in it for good measure, he was obviously still riled, either by his cousin's death or the subsequent dog attack.

Calum had sniggered at him from behind his brother's back. A double charge of kidnapping and actual assault carried twenty years plus, but their crime was obviously some great game to the idiot. He'd seen sniggering looks like that on the faces of juvenile radicals who'd kidnapped, beaten or shot at soldiers in Fallujah, or associates of the Taliban in Kamdesh, only over there the penalty was either their hands, or their heads; a consequence which soon managed to wipe the smug smiles from their faces. Their two lumbering friends looked at him warily, almost apologetically. Clearly, they were getting increasingly concerned about what they were finding themselves involved in.

When Luke managed to open his eyes and focus against the blinding glare of the early morning sun, he struggling to understand if what he was seeing was real, a dream, or another twisted joke of his mind.

He'd expected Jed Burke and his brother in law, with his boys, seizing him from the boot's depths to drag him around on a dirty floor, play football with his head, either while it was attached to his body pre-death or detached from it after they'd slain him.

But the faces that peered in at him now, half silhouetted against the early morning sunlight were that of a rabbit, a fox, a wolf, a lamb, a cow and a pig.

They reached in and seized him from the depths of the boot, pulling him unceremoniously out and leaving him down on his knees in the chill morning air.

And the barnyard participants weren't alone. A generation had come. Their faces shielded by whatever means they could find. When the animal masks had been allotted they'd clearly delved into the backs of closets for the jumble left over by long ago Halloweens. Many masked their faces behind plastic pumpkins, rubbery witch heads, werewolves with dripping plastic fangs, white cloth ghost masks. Others had simply tied scarves over their noses and mouths, or resorted to stockings, manipulating their features until they looked like strange squashed fruits.

This was no dream.

Luke looked to the five-foot six inch pig, long wisps of blond hair hanging down from under her chin and laying against her black leather jacket. Next to her the rabbit loomed six foot seven. Luke knew these two immediately.

275

The blond pig turned on a video camera and pointed it his way. Meanwhile her neighbour, the six foot seven rabbit placed a hand written note on the ground in front of him.

Luke scanned the first few lines and a drowsy terror stole through him.

"I'm not reading that." He said as defiantly as his weakened being would allow.

"I say you will." The blonde pig retorted immediately. "I say you must."

Luke shook his head.

The rabbit kicked him, knocking him savagely backwards. Before he had a chance to recover one of them was hosting him back to a kneeling position, back to his spot for the camera to leer in his face again.

Luke spat a mouthful of blood out onto the ground in front of them.

The rabbit shoved the note defiantly under Luke's face with his foot.

Luke looked from it to them with a look in his eyes of utter defiance.

The rabbit struck him again, this time with the flat of his hand.

Luke fell face down in the dirt. He rolled and tried desperately to struggle back up, a feat near impossible without the use of his hands. That was when he saw it.

The Company 'Keep Out' sign nailed across a large plank rooted to the ground was silhouetted up on the hill against the climbing rise of the sun. A sun which cascaded ribbons of light around it making it look uncannily like the blessed cross of Calvary.

It was when Luke saw the club hammer and set of nails the rabbit was retrieving from the boot of a car that he finally realised what they had in mind.

"God." He whispered.

Forty One

Ashen daylight was congealing over the land by the time they arrived at the hotel.

The baseball bat was all they could find for a weapon.

Moses had kept it in his truck after two attempted robberies. Both the attempts had been made by kids so he kept it there mostly just to scare them. Mostly. As Moses knew only too well there is always a tipping point where the metier of children turns to the deadly intent of men. He let Tyler take it, while he picked up a brick from the street.

They were debating whether, and when, to storm the hotel when the small red car passed them and two women with frantic looks on their faces parked it haphazardly and rushed inside.

Soon after, Mason Hare and his two sons barrelled out of the front doors and sped away in the jeep.

Jed Burke wasn't with them. This gave Tyler hope. He'd been clinging uselessly to his fragile hope all morning and throughout the previous night that Luke was still alive, and that they had the possibility of rescuing him.

Getting the measure of Jed Burke as he had during his time on the island, the one thing that gave him the flimsy hope he now clung to was that the bastard would want to drag his revenge out over hours, days even. This would give them the chance to find Luke. He wasn't a fighter, a warrior, but he would fight for him. A fight he wasn't prepared to lose. He'd then help him to recover from whatever he'd been through. He'd get it right. This time.

If Mason Hare and his sons were on their way to carry out Luke's murder then Jed Burke would have been with them. His son was dead

278

and the revenge he no doubt would have craved would have warranted him playing the major part, or taking a ring side seat at the very least.

With the baseball bat and his useless hope Tyler waited till the hunting jeep was out of sight then he and Moses crossed the drive towards the hotel.

Tyler used the bat to push open the door to Jed's office.

They'd passed the living quarters where Janice Burke was wailing and screaming and tearing out her own hair in great bloody handfuls as the two women who'd arrived minutes earlier tried valiantly to both restrain and comfort her.

Moses had pointed Tyler in the direction of the office. He knew its exact location within the hotel having visited it once before, ten months earlier in what you could loosely call an interview for the job in the bar. In truth it had been nothing more than a series of grunts from Jed Burke and a few blunt threats about what he'd do should Moses ever steal from the till.

Inside the office Burke was crowded around the screen of his laptop, staring ardently at it like a teenager viewing porn for the very first time.

After a few silent gesticulations between Tyler and Moses, Tyler tightened his grip on the baseball bat and the two men crossed the room and stepped up behind him.

Tyler lifted the bat aloft and brought it crashing down on the corner of the desk, sending the framed picture of Kai up in the air only for it to land dramatically back down on the wood where the glass cracked.

Jed looked calmly around, as if he'd been distracted by nothing more than a cool breeze.

Tyler raised the bat above him, with a promise in his eyes that meant the next time he brought it back down it would be over the man's head.

"I'll ask this just once." Tyler informed him. "Where the fuck is my brother?"

Jed looked at the photograph of Kai behind the cracked glass and swallowed hard, as though he were drinking absinthe.

"I'll show you." He replied and leant back so that Tyler could have full view of what he was watching so intently on the laptop's screen.

Luke lifted his bowed head. It was swelling with the signs of recent bruises, sickly yellow lumps that spread out to a more beauteous damson. Clearly marks of the recent influence which had persuaded him to relent and read the roughly scrawled note; now held to the side of the camera.

Luke spoke in as flat and unemotional a tone as he could manage, ensuring no future audience of the film he was being forced to star in, would believe a word that left his lips was actually his own.

My name is Luke Dearlove, my father's name was Howard, my mother's name was Mary. I am the youngest of two brothers who are, like me, dogs of your Company.

Furthermore I am a soldier.

You, Company pigs, wanted me for your prize. For your posters. You wanted to parade me as your hero to trick the world into thinking of you as men of honour.

But now I am paying the price for your vanity with my life.

The people you brought to this island now ask you this:

How, Company pigs, do you sleep in your beds at night, knowing that because of your greed, thirty innocent people now sleep in their graves?

Their blood, like this soldier's, is on your hands.

In time, god may forgive you. We will not.

With that Luke bowed his head again and the camera fell clumsily away.

Tyler took an urgent step towards Jed's laptop, heart pounding, no weight in his stomach, desperate and terrified of what he needed and simultaneously dreaded to see.

Soon the shaking image returned and the full adhesive nature of its horror took over Tyler's mind and scorched itself in.

They were carrying Luke now, hoisting him high in the air above their shoulders and taking him on a giddying ride up the hill.

Many of them danced, laughed, clapped. Some jabbed at Luke when they could, each wanting to be an intrinsic part of this momentous event. Each wanting a story for their children.

Eva was careful to keep the camera right on Luke when they reached the top of the hill. She pulled off the pig mask, just as Tin-Tin took the scarf from his face. This was something they both wanted to see with clear vision. The camera would relive it for them. But this original scene could only be feasted on the once.

Luan carried Luke up the ladder at the bottom of the 'Keep Out' sign.

Soon others were around him, pulling him taut against it from all directions. They wrapped rope around his outstretched arms and bound him to it first. It was only when he was strapped to it, pinned in place like a frog awaiting vivisection, that Luan held the first of the nails against the tender exposed flesh of his palm.

Luke looked down the length of his arm, tied to the impromptu cross. His eyes grew wide as Luan drew back the club hammer.

Luke had closed his eyes and turned his face away as Luan sent the club hammer sailing down onto the nail's head, driving it through skin, flesh, and ligaments and sinking it deep into the wood behind.

Tyler had not.

The image on Jed's laptop flickered and died. Tyler gasped at the loss of it, for one surreal moment reminding himself of his father and his panicked gulps whenever the wind knocked the TV Arial out of place and cost them their signal in the middle of a match.

Jed looked up at Tyler and his lips peeled back to a thick ugly smile.

For the first time in his life Tyler wanted to kill someone. He wanted to end the life of another human being. The weight of normalcy had slipped and the pure bred pulsing madness of hate was within him.

He wanted to punch his fist into Burke's chest, rip out his murderous heart, show it to him still beating in his hand while the man looked at it aghast and crumpled to the floor.

But Tyler was Tyler. An ordinary man. No killer, even in this white brain roar of fury. He brought the baseball bat smashing down, so hard it made Moses flinch. But his target was not Jed's head, it was his laptop, his desk, his things, his picture of Kai.

Moses grabbed Tyler, pulling him back mid rage. "I know where this place is. Come. We don't have much time."

As the two men turned for the door Burke rose, the Taurus 44 revolver in his hand pointed their way. "Dearlove!!!!!" Jed bellowed.

They turned and looked back at him, saw the gun, flinched, grabbed at each other, expecting the worst.

Jed's eyes flicked onto the image of Kai's face amid the broken glass.

"Go to your god like a soldier." He told Tyler before placing the revolver in his mouth and firing. The bullet and explosion of gas that accompanied it blasted violently through blood, brain, bone and skull leaving what remained of his head looking like half a smashed apart pomegranate. He balanced precariously on his feet for a millisecond then wobbled like a drunk before hitting the carpet with a heavy squelching thud.

Forty Two

By the time the Martyr found her in the bathroom she was lying up to her neck in a tub of water. He sat beside her and she lowered her eyes away from him. He dipped his finger into the water, swirled it, causing a mini whirlpool. The water was cold. The only warmth available to her was from the endless stream of tears that poured silently down her cheeks. She must have been lying here like this at least an hour. All her savage and darkly compelling magic seemed to have drained from her and was now stagnating in the water along with her until such time as she finally chose to rise and let it all drain away.

Whether she was crying for herself, or her brother, or her shame, the Martyr did not know. He'd just been shown her handiwork. All the residents of the Turkey Cage were watching and re-watching the footage with a communal delight not seen since Partizani Tirana beat Celtic Glasgow 1-0 in the first round of the 1979 European Cup. Outside in the shanty town a party had started that would no doubt rage on for the rest of that afternoon and through the night till dawn.

Normally when she felt his presence, the worship of his eyes, especially cast over her naked body as they now were, her own eyes would turn to him immediately, drink him in. Yet now, sad and still, she gazed beyond him as though she were gazing out to sea.

He swirled the water again. The faint noise of the gently moving water broke the silence between them.

Finally, she looked at him with huge sorrowful eyes. Like those of a wayward child hoping sad eyes and tears would induce her father's forgiveness.

284

He took off his belt, wrapped it around the back of her neck and used the wide end where the eternal sun symbol sat to daub at her tears and dry her face.

"Eva, Eva, Eva," he said softly, "what did you do?"

More tears silently fell before she answered him. "Something they can't ignore."

From where Luke was, the acres of sky above Skidaway island were nothing short of breath-taking.

It was amazing how quickly boredom had set in. Luke didn't know what they'd been expecting. The nails they'd used had been thin, picture hanging nails most likely, not the inch-thick barbaric iron spikes that had skewered the tender flesh of the Christians twenty thousand years previous.

They'd gawped up at him from the ground once the nail in his other hand had been battered into place, staring at him like a theatre audience waiting for a play to start.

After several minutes they'd begun whispering to each other and nudging one another in the crowd.

What the fuck did they want? Him to scream like an animal for their own sick amusement? Or burst into flames as the dramatic climax to their unearthly actions? All the powers of darkness to rise up from below and claim him for their own?

After a while the first of them began to trail away. The blonde woman had cursed them zealously. Clearly she wanted the world there to share in his suffering, right till the very last moment of it.

'Your fuck-up she-bitch.' Luke thought with a certain irony. Even if they had got it right and driven decent nails through his wrists instead of his hands, it still could have taken him several hours, even a day to die.

285

Were it not for the ropes that fettered his arms he could have torn his hands free from the slender nails that pinned him to their impromptu cross. And mercifully a public notice order nailed to the bottom of the Keep Out sign's pole provided a rest for Luke to position his feet and stop the full weight of his body from hanging from his arms. Luke understood enough to know that that would have eventually separated his shoulders from their sockets and suffocated him when his chest sagged and he could no longer lift his ribcage to breathe. If she was waiting for his death, it was going to be a long wait.

What would be more likely to finish him off here would be thirst, or exposure, or, in time, just a voluntary surrender of his life. Right now he was surviving, barely. His body was damaged but held together as if by glue; weak glue. The parts were wearing but they hadn't broken yet. At some point soon all strength would snap.

Luke couldn't be sure how long it had been. Minutes? Hours? From such a predicament the mind simply has no grasp on such matters, but at some point the once braying crowd had dispersed leaving only the woman and the boy staring up at him. Even her camera had given up, running out of battery or tape. Or perhaps the weight of it was just getting too much in her arms. If the weight of anything ever became too much for this woman.

She had glared up at him and he had looked calmly back. *I will match you stare for stare.*

Finally, only after the boy had begun nagging at her incessantly, did she throw him a final black look, take the child's hand and leave.

Soon after the rain came, cooling his face like a blessing. He'd begun to weaken then. The wounds from the pins in his hands wouldn't have been lethal, but the others he'd sustained on the island might have been, especially now he was left strung up in a position as vulnerable as this. A blood clot could be climbing slowly through his veins like an animal and lumbering along on its way to his heart. Or his body could have lost so much blood and fluid that soon his heart would fail to beat, and he'd be dead with hypovolemic shock in minutes.

There was also the possibility of cardiac rupture, acidosis, sepsis, arrhythmia, pulmonary embolism; a myriad of options on the smorgasbord of fate. Religious artists had toned down the most graphic details of this barbarism over the centuries. Crucifixions of contemporary culture had become far too pretty.

Luke wanted to laugh at the ridiculousness of it all. A warmth came to him in the high breeze. A warmth he thought at first was something spiritual but soon realised was nothing but his urine running down his leg inside his trousers. Something he could ill afford to do given the propensity for dehydration. He'd have to disallow any tears too and forced their onset back down his throat.

He would not cry, he would not piss, he would not pray, he would not moan. He would stay here and be quiet, nailed to his cross, stinking of his own slow cold death.

But that military resolve did not last long. Sometimes the wrongness of the world is enough to make even soldiers fall apart. Vital organs were being eaten up. He felt the pain of his body's impending collapse. He was becoming more and more a living cadaver. A rat skewered to a stick at the cruel hands of vicious children. The whirling vortex of death's quiet call was sucking him slowly, irresistibly, inescapably into its depths. *How else would death call you?*

"Howie," he called out in a soft piteous tone. "Howie."

He wasn't sure why he had called Howie's name. Maybe the diaphanous folds of the clouds in the sky in front of him, parting as they were to let the light cascade out to him like a path that must be followed, felt so much like a call to another world that he wanted to ensure his murdered brother would be standing on the other side of it, quietly waiting to carry him home.

Or perhaps he was, in his own small way, screaming one last prayer to the universe, in the hope that the person who loved him most might just still be alive and would hear, however quiet his call. However far away.

Luke's head fell forward, his shoulders screamed in pain and despite his resolve the tears came and splashed down into the puddled collection of rain and blood in the muddy earth below. He was more wounded and closer to god than ever he realised himself to be.

'Try again,'

It was nothing but the wind, speaking to him. Speaking to him as only a mother does who still believes in her child when the rest of the world has turned away.

The beauty of the heavens beyond him beckoned like an ache. *But even the broken soul yearns to heal, the wounded heart to beat.* Rory's words came back to him.

He would, he would try again, despite the agonised pain even lifting his head now caused. *On your feet soldier. That's an order. Do it now. Call to the person who loves you the most. Who'll hear you. No matter how quiet your call. No matter how far away.*

Luke lifted his head and spoke through his tears, through his pain, *"Tyler"* he said.

As Luke's head fell forward like a stone and the light of the world began to dim away, his final vision was that of the man approaching from the east. His thick dark hair was tied in a loose ponytail at the middle of his head and he wore a golden robe with emblems stitched onto it.

He was surrounded by several other men, all in similar robes, *although none as grand as this first man*, all with heads shaven free of hair and smooth as sand.

'They're carrying ladders' thought Luke as he fought to keep cognizant long enough to ensure they reached him. *'They're carrying hope.'*

With that all thoughts ceased and his suffering carried him down to the black dreamless world of unconsciousness.

Forty Three

"*Do something!!*" *Howie screamed it from the side of the gangly wrecked thing lying amid the conifer plants. The gangly wrecked thing that once had been their little brother.*

Tyler shook his head, staring breathlessly at them, still struggling to recover after their mad dash through the woodland.

Howie prized the scissors from Luke's shaking hands, his eyes skating forlornly over the hacked off hair, the network of gashed wounds criss-crossing his prone naked body.

Luke struggled to speak, but all that emanated from his throat was a series of broken groans as he fought to articulate the words he was trying so desperately to say. Howie reassuringly held the side of his face, nodding that it would be alright, before glowering up at Tyler.

"*Do something!!*" *he said again fiercely.*

What the fuck did he expect him to do? Find a brick and put the dribbling drooling thing out of its misery? Call Belleview back and tell them they'd made an epic fail? Call another, less fancy nuthouse, tell them to come and cart it off and lock it away in some unknown place where families hid their secrets?

Of course none of these thoughts were scenarios Tyler was actually contemplating. They were merely the smash and grab ramblings of a mind that couldn't yet deal with the tragedy on the ground in front of him.

"*Come here.*" *Howie said in a low authoritative voice and nodded to Luke's side.*

Tyler staggered on the spot as if some unseen force was holding him back.

"*I can't,*" *Tyler finally said to Howie. "I can't look at him like that.*"

290

And two years on Tyler Dearlove stood on Skidaway Island staggering in the same ridiculous fashion and saying the exact same words. Only this time the words were to Moses Bogdani and the state he feared to see his brother in now was the sight of him crucified on the Company's 'Keep Out' sign.

Moses raised his hands incredulously. He'd driven as recklessly as a drunk through the residential area and torn through the marshes to get them to the hillside in breakneck speed. Then, when they had to leave the truck and bolt across the grassland and were no more than a few yards away from the last turn that would bring them to Luke, Tyler had dried up and turned to stone.

If he wasn't able to face it, then Moses would have to, alone. He'd already faced the worst thing life would ever present to him, anything else, even something as unimaginable as this would be something he could cope with.

He turned the corner around a rocky bend and stood at the foothills looking up to whatever fate was going to present him with.

He rubbed his eyes and squinted against the light.

Finally he turned back to Tyler. "Please come Mr Dearlove."

"I . . . I can't." Tyler responded, resorting to his stock answer. "I can't look at him like that."

"I fear you must." Moses said. And there was something in his tone that compelled Tyler. He swallowed back his fear and came slowly to his side.

They looked together at the same scene they had viewed on Jed's laptop. Only instead of finding Luke's hanging corpse, still pinned by the hands, or him writhing in agony and clinging to life, all that presented itself was the Company's 'Keep Out' sign, as austere and threatening as it had

291

always been; the only mark of Luke's presence being the remnants of blood pooling on the ground in front of it.

Slowly, the final pieces of the puzzle dropped into their respective places.

Tyler turned deliberately round to Moses. "I think it's about time you told me where my brother is."

Forty Four

"I kill you!!!" Tin-Tin screamed and pointed a plastic gun at Sokol, shooting him while emanating a violent 'pow-bang' noise that reinforced the chaos of his bullet sprayed death.

Sokol died triumphantly, with all thumbs up for pantomime effect. Isni pulled Sokol's limp body back behind a couch, while shooting back at Tin-Tin and 'powing' with his own toy gun.

Tin-Tin had taken a 'hit' to the shoulder and span in crazy dramatic circles with the force of it, plastering himself up against the window like a squashed bug. Through his smooched eyes he saw him, *the English*, walking casually up the path.

Tin-Tin withdrew from the window, his demeanour alone making the other boys lower their guns and end their game to come to his side. They pulled themselves back and hid behind the couches, peeking through gaps in cushions to watch The English making a visor with his hands and peer in through the window.

The boys nodded warily to each other and retreated further back behind the couches to keep out of sight.

Tyler shouldered the door to the house. It bounced against its fragile lock but remained on its hinges.

He looked back to Moses at the far end of the lane, waiting at the side of his truck.

They'd argued valiantly, Moses insisting he come with Tyler. But Tyler knew, somewhere primal he knew, that this part of it may risk life, and Moses had done enough. The most he should ask of him now was to wait at the far end of the road and provide getaway should Tyler make it back unscathed.

He shouldered the door one more time, feeling the subsequent strain of the wood. He turned back and signalled to Moses, making sure he remained safely outside the Turkey Cage and surrounding shanty town in the open ground where he could, at any point, jump in the truck and flee.

Tyler turned back to the door, sent a kick into its middle and watched as it bounced on its hinges and flew open.

Tin-Tin, Sokol and Isni remained in their clandestine spots, watching through the gaps in their cushions as the English searched the living room, the kitchen, closets and finally climbed the rickety staircase to the upper floors.

When they were sure they were alone they crept out, stealthy as little elves before Christmas. Tin-Tin looked to the two members of his gang. Games with toy guns were over. "Get your brothers, get your cousins." He ordered. "Get everyone."

Tyler regretted not having taken Moses's baseball bat. He was more than vulnerable and dangerously alone as he searched the upper floors of the main house in the Turkey Cage.

After pushing open the doors of each bedroom he was about to give up and go back and ask Moses if he'd been sure this was the right place. That was when he saw the staircase that led to an attic room.

It was an attic room that stank of its secrets. Tyler's footsteps across it were slow and cautious but purposeful. The wearing wooden floor groaned and creaked with his every step.

294

As he crossed it his eyes skated about, making a quick inventory of what he saw. The bench laying skewwhiff on one side of the room, an overhanging beam with a large loop of wire around it as if it had at some time held a giant Christmas decoration. The table covered with a litter of leftover drug remnants, the desk with a laptop freeze-framed on the shot of a disembodied head staring aghast at the world from its impaling spike. And the bed.

Tyler froze.

He knew the shape under the white sheet was that of a body; the round of a head at one end, the two valleyed hills created by the feet at the other. He'd come to find Luke, in whatever condition. He'd come to bring him home. Even if only to give him a decent burial.

He couldn't bear to look. Not like that. But there was no one here to bemoan to this time. He had to face it, and face it alone.

He gripped one corner of the sheet and, keeping his back to the body, slowly walked away. His measured pace made the sheet slip gradually from its place and glide behind Tyler like a bride's train.

Tyler saw the reflection of the body first, in an old mirror on the other side of the room; the shock of blonde hair startling him and making him spin urgently back.

Even deceased Eva Skanderberg was a beautiful woman.

She had avoided the chaotic tumble of death's graceless sprawl. Her naked breasts were still soft and becoming, her skin still golden, other than the increasing prominence of her veins, clogging with her pooling blood. Her long legs, albeit purplish blue at the lowest part, with gravity forcing the haemoglobin to settle there, were still striking. She lay as if she were positioned for an artist to paint her.

The only signs of a murder victim's aspect were her puffed tongue poking through her teeth and her reddened eyes, bulging from her face and staring madly, mirroring the expression of the disembodied head on the laptop screen adjacent to her. But that beautiful head was still attached to its golden shoulders. Her face's contorted death chill was no doubt down to the scarf with the eternal sun symbol emblazed upon it which wrapped three savage times around her neck and still bit callously into it.

And suddenly, with one of death's cruellest indignities, the cessation of the brain began shutting down the regulation of all bodily functions. Eva's sphincter opened with a sudden gaping yawn and a flood of shit and filth came cascading out.

Tyler cried out at what appeared to be a dead body seemingly returning to life. Once over the shock of it he reeled from the stench of it, putting his hand under his nose, standing back. He threw the cotton sheet back over the bed to enshroud her once more and stumbled to the window, forcing it open and breathing in air from the outside world.

That was when he looked into the central gardens that sat like a lush green oasis in the middle of the Turkey Cage. It was also when he saw Luke.

Forty Five

Tyler's shadow fell across Luke. He was lying on a sun lounger at the edge of the garden's immaculate lawn. Someone had dressed his wounds, someone had bathed him, fed him, given him clean clothes. Someone had loved him.

Now he slept and was as calm and peaceful as Tyler had ever known him to be. It was almost a shame to wake him.

He bent down to his brother and when Luke did stir and groggily opened his eyes Tyler quickly laid one hand gently over his mouth. With the other he put an index finger up against his own lips and beckoned Luke not to make a sound.

Obligingly Luke silently watched as Tyler got back up and turned towards the Martyr.

He was standing at the edge of the flower bed, watering and tending to his alcea plants, cosseting and whispering to the tall headed flowers as though each had its own personality and required his love. Meanwhile, beyond him on the other side of the grass, another set of his 'beloveds', his monks, bowed and chanted in some form of meditative prayer.

His golden cloak was flowing freely in the warm breeze, exposing his lean back and high definition abs. *'You can spend a lot of time working out when you've not got much else to do.'* Tyler thought while glancing down to the empty belt loops in his robe. The missing belt, no doubt, still wrapped three times round the neck of his most recent murder victim in the attic room of the adjoining house.

Tyler wished more than ever that he still had Moses's bat and could get the man's attention via a sudden blow to the back of the head. Instead

297

he internalised various guesses at how to address him 'Hey Floaty Hindu Guy, hey Jesus Dude, hey knock-down Buddha on a Saturday night, hey Christ wannabe.'

None seemed right.

"Turn around." Tyler said to him.

The Martyr turned his head not more than a fraction of an inch, still pampering his plants and leaving Tyler nothing more than the back of his head and his exceedingly oiled ponytail to talk to.

"Turn around." Tyler said again.

The Martyr remained quietly defiant. Tyler resorted to having to use his Christian name.

"Howie. Turn around."

With that the Martyr turned and smiled at his oldest brother. "Hello Tyler, we've been waiting for you."

Tyler pursed his lips, studied him in his glory, *his golden light*. "Still getting away without a scratch?"

Howie smiled. A smile which riled Tyler more than Tin-Tin's had in City Market the night before, more than Jed Burke's had earlier that day. He grabbed him by two handfuls of his pathetic golden robes and forced him bellicosely up against a tree.

The monks broke off their prayer and tried to gently weave themselves between the outsider and their Martyr. Tyler ignored them, roughly elbowing the nearest few away.

It was only when Luke squirrelled his way between them, pale and desperately weak, and begged with his eyes for his brothers to stop that Tyler let go his stranglehold on Howie.

From there Luke half collapsed. They both instinctively darted down to catch him. Howie was there first. He picked Luke up and carried him back to the sun lounger, laid him back down and pulled a blanket back under his chin.

The Martyr, Before

"Bring your torch. It's a dirty night."

It was advice, given to Howie Dearlove in the last eighteen minutes of his life, he would come to regret having taken.

The human mind holds fast to its surroundings when death is near. Clings to quick snatches of experience as a drowning man clings to whatever he can grasp. For Howie Dearlove there would be no exception to this trick of the psyche. *The wind whipping about him, rain sheeting across the tarmac and cutting into his skin, the father holding his dead baby son hard against his cheek, the half-naked blonde woman screaming at the moon, the boy spitting at his feet with a look in his eyes that meant more than murder.* The tangled chaos of these moments raced and repeated across Howie Dearlove's brain as if played and replayed at double speed.

Howie couldn't be sure when the point of cessation had actually occurred. Maybe with the opening of the third lorry. Maybe earlier than that, when they'd told him the real reason for his placement on the island and offered him the alluringly enticing salary and other accompanying bonuses that would go with it. The way out of debt. *The way into ruin.* And he'd negotiated his price.

Maybe it was when the boy Tin-Tin found his dead mother lying on the ground and wept for her with a heartbreak that seemed to rise above the thunder.

Maybe when the tall man with the gentle face and the dead infant boy in his hands climbed off the truck and blessed him under the moon.

Maybe when his colleague, fellow company security guard, Alan Watson, so terrified of the encircling mob that he lashed out anywhere and at anyone, caught the young boy Tin-Tin across the side of the face. He'd spat at them, called them a word in his native tongue he'd later learned meant 'murderers'.

Watson had swung at him then. The boy flew backwards. His tiny body catapulted into the crowd, knocking them wildly. So wildly they threw Moses Bogdani off balance and his dead baby son fell between their legs to be trampled and kicked about like a piece of rubbish.

'I'll bring my torch. Mind if I use it to smash your clumsy face in?'

Maybe it was when Watson raised that ungodly metal hook of his again, threatening to take further swipes at them. Maybe it was when he'd decided that he would not allow the man the chance and lifted the torch he'd so thoughtfully instructed he bring. Maybe it was when he brought it crashing down over his cranium and murdered for the first time.

Maybe it was when their rage had stilled and they came to look at him as an ally. Or when he helped them move the dead carcasses of their families into the depths of Hell's Mouth Curve so that he could hide evermore in their midst. Maybe when they helped him move Alan Watson's body to the lockups at Lake Woebegone so he could hide, evermore, his crime.

Maybe, maybe, maybe . . . a perfect storm of occurrences that dictate outcome. A step taken an inch to the left instead of the right and a fourteen year old girl wouldn't have stepped on a mine in a field in Angola and lost both her legs above the knee. Walk the long way home instead of using the shortcut down the back alley the man's not there with a knife to mug you. One more cuddle with your mother and she won't lose half her head under a ten tonne truck.

Maybe, maybe, maybe. A thousand of them, each enough to lay lesions on your brain.

On that dense black and unearthly night, Howie Dearlove died and another man was born. And on his dying breath three words left his lips.

I'm sorry Luke.

He slipped away.

Forty Six

They'd been brothers once. He and Howie.

They'd sat like this before, side by side on a park bench, several times in fact. Not looking at each other, looking ahead, at their laps, at geese, or a pond, or the sunset, as men often do to detract from any real intimacy. Side by side on a bench was the best set up for when they needed to discuss the major issues; messy breakups, a pregnant ex-girlfriend, an arrest after a pub fight, spiralling debt, their parents' death . . . and Luke.

Luke was the distraction they focused on now. He'd soon slept again, calmly, peacefully, lying on the sun lounger like a young man without a care in the world.

Tyler and Howie sat side by side with their eyes trailing the gentle rise and fall of his chest.

Each struggled silently for the appropriate line with which to open this particular conversation. And that opening line would have to be a good one, after all, never in a million years did Tyler expect to find himself in a situation as surreal as this.

"So now you're Yoda?" said Tyler.

That worked well, the tension eased a little. Howie even managed a small silent laugh. He nodded at the monks, practising their rituals on the other side of the grass.

"Have you ever been in exile? It's boring." Howie said.

"Not fucking their wives are ya?" Tyler asked.

Howie let out another quiet laugh. "I started teaching a few of them Taekwondo." He glanced up at the attic window. "And so a people who'd just been through hell learned their religion from a man who deserved a place there."

Tyler nodded at Luke. "You always had a knack for becoming the most undeserving of heroes."

Howie shook his head with great earnest. "No, no brother." He pointed to his own forehead. "The birds scream and the worms crawl and somewhere in my mind it's always raining."

Tyler didn't know what irritated him more. The wankish statement, which Howie, or his new alter-ego, had probably memorised after seeing it in a book. Or the self-pitying way he'd chosen to say it. Tyler got up. "Howie," he said. "You don't half talk a lot of shit."

Tyler began walking away. Howie urgently grabbed his arm. "If late one night the phone rings and a voice you can't quite hear, sounds something like mine. Or from a taxi window you see someone standing in the shadows of a doorway who carries my shape. Promise me this, you'll remember that I was your once brother and that . . . there was love."

Tyler looked down at Howie, sighing deeply. It was another passage full of a mawkish sap that made his skin crawl. But Howie's earnestness and the genuine regret in his voice made it forgivable somehow.

A group of the monks passed, all bowing their shaven heads to their Martyr, adulating his divinity, one of the youngest pausing to take and kiss their deity's hand.

Once they'd moved on Howie let out another small near-silent laugh. "The thing is that it's a joke." He looked up again at the attic window where his second murder victim lay. "I'm no fucking good."

Tyler thought back to the way hate and blood lust had coursed through his own veins when he'd seen what the woman and others on the island had done to Luke. How he'd ached to smash the baseball bat over Jed

Burke's head, rip his heart right out of his chest, slaughter him, as they had attempted to slaughter Luke. As he looked at Howie his memory of it made his brother's murderous reaction forgivable somehow. *Who was the better brother? Howie for having done so, or him, for holding back?* He thought of Howie, and others across history's stretch of centuries who'd been so outraged by the treatment of the weak and the exploited that they'd acted, picked up a sword, *or a torch*, and taken a strike against those accountable. *Who were the better men?* Howie and those others who raged against the oppression of a people, even if it meant getting blood on their hands, or the likes of himself who asked no questions, kept their heads below the precipice, took twenty five thousand a yeah and were quiet. Maybe they were right to call him their Martyr. Maybe Luke was right to call him the air that he breathed. His everything.

Tyler looked from Howie to Luke's sleeping form. He knew then that Skidaway Island was now a permanent home for both of his brothers and this would be the last day of his life to ever have Luke at his side. A yearning part of him wanted to spin back and half beg, half threaten Howie to take care of him and do the right thing by him from here on in. But in another part of himself, a deeper part, he already knew that Howie would do that and more besides.

So instead he simply bent forward, squeezed Howie's shoulder and walked away.

He'd thought of leaving Luke while he slept.

Howie had wrapped him up in a trust so gentle that Tyler feared if he touched him now to say goodbye he'd stain this pure, reborn version of his brother. This version of Luke he'd longed to have back for so many years.

He knew Luke thought of him as a man of ignorance, uncouth manners and insensitive words. While Tyler always got it all wrong, Howie got it so right he'd taken a place in Luke's mind, as he had the refugees of Skidaway Island, as nothing short of a king.

Tyler had tried once before. He'd left the silly note on the fridge in magnetic letters after Luke's Passing Out parade, '*You were a sight to see.*' And he had been. Tyler had been awestruck watching Luke that day. He'd gone along with Howie and two sisters they'd been dating at the time. Howie and the sisters had buzzed with excitement, got dressed up like they were going to the Oscars or something. Tyler had begrudgingly put on a suit and scowled all the way through the ten minute taxi ride from the hotel, determined to have a miserable time; the thought of Luke committing to life in the Army still leaving the worst of tastes in his mouth.

Then Luke came out into the parade square with forty-five other lads. Seeing him for the first time in full military dress, stern faced, but with eyes looking toward the future, stole Tyler's breath from his lungs. All the other lads seemed to disappear. All Tyler saw was his brother, his boy, marching out there in front of him like a young god.

At twenty-eight Tyler had become father to a thirteen year old. A job he hadn't asked for and, at the time, hadn't wanted. But that job had become his world. He'd fathered him, protected him, and watched him grow into a man. *And what a man he was. Look at him down there, shining a light, what a sight to see.*

But Luke hadn't even noticed his attempts to express something meaningful. He hadn't acknowledged it at least. Tyler had been disappointed at first. He'd had a few beers too many that evening and descrambled the letters into a more idiosyncratic 'Fuck you', then panicked in the middle of the night, stumbled drunkenly down at 2.00am to pull the letters off the fridge door and dump the whole set in the bin. They were all grown men now. Time to put away childish things.

He'd tried once more after that. Just after Luke's first breakdown. For him it was like speaking in a half-learned language. But still he trawled the internet looking for an appropriate message to write and leave with Luke in hospital, so he had it to turn to any time he needed reminding that he had a brother who held him in his thoughts.

And, although Luke had never seemed to know it, Tyler's thoughts of him were long, long thoughts.

Despite his lack of extended education something about the few short lines he had found felt right:

'Sometimes

The strongest among us

Are the ones who smile through silent pain

Cry behind closed doors

And fight battles nobody knows about'

Tyler had cried as he'd written it out. *Tsk tsk Tyler Dearlove, that you've come to this.*

But sure enough Howie had had the same, or perhaps even a better, idea and found a poem which he'd had printed and framed for Luke to keep, sitting beside his bed:

Brother, my brother,

How selfish was I

While you seemed to struggle,

I sat idly by

Brother, my brother

Yes, try as I might

I now realize

It was also my fight

Brother, my brother

Now look at your arm

It's cold and immovable

Lost all its charm

Brother, my brother

Now look at your leg

There's so much left missing

Yet not once did you beg

Brother, my brother

Though I lost more in mass

It is you far more haunted

By our mistakes in the past

Brother, dear brother

Listen when I say

I will stick by your side

Until this goes away

Brother, dear brother

Believe when I say

I will be by your side

Until our final day

Tyler thought back to it with a pang of desperate agonised regret.

There was enough space in Luke's heart for them both. There had been nothing stopping him from holding Luke's right hand while Howie had held the left.

There were so many things, on so many occasions, he could have said to have soothed Luke's fractured soul, instead of making him feel his psychological wounds were nothing but an embarrassment, an irritation.

There was one time, years earlier, he'd got it right after all.

The day of their parents' funeral. He and Luke were the only two not to have cried. To have stood, stoic and tall at the edge of their graves and held back their grief and their tears, while all others sobbed with impunity.

And yet the poor traumatised thirteen-year-old Luke had no doubt been dying inside.

Tyler found him later when all the guests had left and there was nothing in the house but a mountain of washing up and a sickly atmosphere of 'what the fuck do we do now' uncertainty and unfathomable grief. Large silent tears were rolling like great stones down that pale and listless face.

Tyler had sat on his bed beside him and held his hand, given him time to be able to speak. And when he did it was with one piteous question; "Now . . . now that they're gone. Will I be ok?"

It was harder at that moment for Tyler to hold back his tears than it had been at his parents' graveside. He squeezed the tiny hand within his own and smiled reassuringly at him. "We will." He had said.

The words had enveloped little Luke Dearlove then. Tyler hadn't imagined it. They'd given the boy a hope that made the pain seem survivable. Made him feel there was a reason for his heart to go on beating. And if he'd managed to find the right words once he could do it again. He fought to get his flow of thoughts together and bent down at Luke's side.

Luke stirred, woken by his nearness, and looked up at Tyler with those same huge doleful eyes.

Tyler spoke quickly and firmly, determined that nothing would stop him now. "To do what you did," he said to Luke. "To look a monster in the eye and call him a monster. That's the courage of a man. That's a soldier who's been to war."

He laid a strong, long kiss on the side of Luke's face, stood, and quickly walked away.

PART FIVE

'War. . . War never changes.

Men do through the roads they walk.'

Ulysses

Forty Seven

The gangly wrecked thing on the ground amid the conifer plants looked up at the two figures looming above him.

"Do something!" One was shouting at the other.

He wasn't sure what the 'something' was the yelling one was ordering his cohort to do but if they were a pair of Terry Lizards then them sinking a round into his guts would come as a great help.

He'd grabbed a pair of scissors as he'd escaped Belleview and fled. After scrambling through the woodland (for a period of time his mind had no hope of being able to measure) he'd collapsed to the mossy ground and begun cutting lumps of flesh from his belly, his torso, his thighs; digging their dull blades into his skin, burrowing for little holes. The relief from it was exquisite. The pressure escaping from the tiny wounds like little jets of steam was bliss. It was a pressure that had been building up within him for so long his whole system felt ready to rupture.

If the two Terry Taliban standing above him were to shoot him through now he'd be sure to explode like the carcass of a gas-filled dead beached whale. Fire up into the sky with the force of a directional charge, and cascade down in a sea of gore to coat the two befuddled snipers.

But why would there be two Terry Towlies outside Belleview anyway?

No, more likely it was two of Belleview's own clinicians. They had seen him escape and were stampeding after him in their white coats with their fucked-up theories and useless ideas and their bottles of pills to stuff down his throat. Instead of setting free that unbearable pressure they would stitch him back up and trap it all inside of him again, let the poison swarm through his blood stream until he was septic to the core.

"Do something!" One was screaming to the other again. And there was something in that urgent voice he recognised.

They moved about him, the dry wood and leaves crunching and cracking under their frantic feet. 'Oh God, it was them. His brothers.'

It hadn't been Belleview he'd escaped from at all. It was their home. He remembered it now. He'd wandered around aimlessly, looking for Howie. He didn't find him. But what he did find was the key to the back door.

The grass was cool and soothing under his feet and the fresh damp air heaven against his face. Suddenly he could no longer stand to be contained. He'd gone to the hole at the back of their garden fence. The one that years back he, and his friends in the neighbourhood, had used to escape from many a monster, a charging gang, a space alien, and the various other imaginings of boyhood.

Even with the sudden weight loss it was too small a hole to squeeze through now. He found the scissors in a toolbox in his father's old shed, widened the hole with them and squeezed himself through. The fence's jagged poking edges tore into his skin like nails. The feel of it was sensational. He wished it had snagged him so roughly that it had torn him free of his entire skin, left it hanging on the fence in one large sheath.

He ran through the woods with the speed of an animal. Desperately trying to outrun his own soul. Everything helped. The Pyracantha firethorns lacerating his legs. The crack willow branches knocking him violently around. The woods would tear out chunks of him, bite him, scratch him, pound him, till there was nothing left. Only a smear of what had once been Luke Dearlove. A dirty stain of him left on stinking wet leaves to fester and rot. A few tatty hanging tendrils of veal coloured flesh caught on tree bark, an easy meal for beetles or worms.

Finally, when his heart could no longer beat with the strain, his lungs could no longer power him on, and his legs collapsed underneath his form he fell to the earth. He took the scissors and tore through his clothes to get to his skin, tore through his skin to get to his core, tore out hair or hacked it free, crawled and shook and squirmed in the damp mud.

That was how they found him.

He knew what they would do. Even in the recesses of a brain as chaotic as his, he knew. They would bend down and work on him, valiantly try to fix him like two teenagers refusing to give up on their first worn out car. They would patch him back together. They would stick back the pieces with glue.

His whole body shook in violent thunderous waves as he tried to beg them not to.

They were bent down either side of him now. Howie had reached him first and prized the scissors from his hand, tossed them out of reach. He'd then bellowed at and berated Tyler until he too sank to his knees along with him. They bent towards him, trying desperately to understand what it was he was trying to say.

Finally, through an agony as cruel as torture, he was able to deliver his words; "Let me die . . . let me die." he begged them and shivered and shook on the cold dank earth as above him, each of his brothers' hearts violently broke in two.

It was different now.

Luke had had the same dream, the same memory of it, so many times. It was patched together from his own reminiscence and from the stories of others, overheard snatches of conversation from relatives in waiting rooms and doctors in corridors. But now it closed with a new ending.

In the years of his reoccurring dream of it, it immortalised itself with subtle changes, the colours of the trees, the depth of his wounds, the smell of the air, the seasons. But full credit always went to Howie for the last heroic act. With arms like steel he'd scooped him out of the earth, effortlessly lifted him up, cradling him against the thump of his heart as he carried him home.

But today Luke saw it differently. Saw it as it was, as it had really been. His dream of it showing him an honest portrayal. His beleaguered mind seemed settled and calm enough now to allow him to see the event in its actuality.

He *had* cut and torn and exhausted himself. He *had* lain down in the dirt to rest and bleed. He *had* shaken and crawled, stripped himself naked, hacked off his hair in great clumps, dug scissors mercilessly into his own skin. And he had tried to speak to his brothers when they found him. After trying and failing several times, he finally found a way to force his words out of his strangled throat and begged them to let him go, let him leave.

But his brothers had not been prepared to entertain such a suggestion. They'd fought back their tears and kept their strength. But the hands that touched him first were Tyler's. As were the arms that lifted him. Not the iron hard arms of his imaginings, *of Howie*. But Tyler's; human, weak, real, shaking with the load they bore. Tyler's was the shoulder he laid his head against. The body that kept his shivering naked form warm. Even when Howie fussed at his side, tried to help, Tyler insisted, '*No, no, I've got him*' and like that, without fuss or complaint, and remaining silent throughout the years when all accolade went Howie's way, Luke finally knew it had been Tyler who had carried him home.

Luke came back from his sleep and his memories, still lying on the sun lounger. He touched his face and found it wet and realised that in the depth of his dreams he had been weeping.

Forty Eight

The boy Tin-Tin threw up when he entered the attic room and found her body under the sheet on the bed. She was lying there like a jelly fish melting on the sand under a blistering sun, an odious substance seeping out from under her and spilling onto the wooden floor.

But it wasn't the smell that caused him to empty out his guts, adding to the heady cocktail of nauseating bodily fluids and post death emanations now pooled at the side of the bed. Life had whittled away and shaped Tin-Tin Borishi so robustly that he may as well have been made of granite. No, it wasn't the smell. Nor was it the memory of his mother, lying sprawled in such a position on a rain drenched tarmac one year previous.

It was the shame he had of his own weakness.

Tin-Tin had put away his humanity that night. He'd grieved for his mother with a strength that shook the mountains. Then a titan arose from the crumbled ruin of that child. The world had carved him up with its cruelty. It was never having the chance to do so much as scratch him again. He would steal, he would lie, he would hate. He would show empathy for no man, and compassion even less. He would shit upon what others cared for and ridicule them in their grief. He would not feel, not with anything other than contempt.

But then she found him.

She had come along, and she had changed him.

She had loved him. And without realising it he had loved her back.

He wanted to vomit again at the thought. At his weakness.

"Kurrë më, kurrë më, kurrë më." Tin-Tin repeated the mantra over and over in his head. *'Never again, never again, never again.'*

As he chanted the words he reached up into the fireplace for Luan's pistol and soon found it. It was the reason he'd come to the room. He'd instructed Isni and Sokol to spread the word through the Turkey Cage that each man should bring a weapon. And he would bring this.

Few men had his strength. If needs be he'd have fired the pistol into the air to kick off the battle. Or perhaps, fired at the English pink-arses' feet, watched them dance.

He looked back at her stiffening corpse wondering which one of them had robbed the Martyr of his belt and used it to strangle the life out of her. It didn't matter which, both were going to pay. *I warned you pink-arse. You come here looking for hell? You gonna find it.*

He stepped carefully through the puddle of bodily fluids and vomit on the floor by the bed, kissed her icy cheek, took his mother's blue beaded bracelet from his own wrist and placed it over her cold dead hand.

Forty Nine

From all around the Turkey Cage and shanty town beyond it they had come.

They stood together behind the thin wire fence that separated the road from the village of corrugated iron, plywood, cardboard and plastic behind it. As with most outcast settlements, commerce, *and the defiance of the human spirit,* had evolved from the squalor. Sausages and grilled fish were being sold from overturned crates and makeshift barbeques; the entrepreneurial among the denizens cashing in on the drunken hunger of those still celebrating the first act of rebellion made against the Company earlier that day.

But for now, sausages were left to blister and pop, fish left to burn. The traders, their patrons and a larger assembled crowd were standing silent as death and staring intently at Tyler Dearlove.

Many still wore their various masks. They held hatchets, pipes, rocks, hammers. One boy, no more than nine, smiled at Tyler, an ugly smile that showed intent. He had one hand on the frail metal fence, his tiny fingers poking through the holes. In his other he held a tyre iron. This mob had come with hastily grabbed improvised weapons. Weapons for murder in its most rudimentary form; dreadful, dirty, and rusting with decay.

Tyler felt the urge to simply sit down on the front steps of the house and laugh. His stamina for the awfulness the island perpetually threw at him had been fully worn out.

He could make out Moses at the far end of the road, hovering by his truck, putting a hand up to his eyes to shield them from the light as he struggled to make out what Tyler was doing. Occasionally he made a desperate beckoning gesture for him to come.

Tyler sensed in the turn of his guts that the slow lonely walk he'd have to take to get to Moses would be his last. He'd seen a natural history programme not long ago about a mob of chimpanzees teaming up to chase, rip apart and devour a solitary red colobus monkey.

He looked at the gauntlet ahead of him and knew what the poor little fucker must have felt like. There was something unpleasantly hungry about the crowd that studied him. The faces of the children were blackened with smoke from the fires they had sat around at night and their clothes were stiff with body grease. While the adults seemed intoxicated and dazed by the numbing rush of whatever alcohol or drugs they'd been consuming since Luke's crucifixion that morning.

If Tyler had experienced this predicament in that long ago life before he ever set foot on Skidaway Island it would have produced a fear that cut deeply, viscerally, through his skin and punctured his organs. What he felt now was little more than a dull ache. He looked up at the paling day and thought about his inevitably hopeless outcome.

One foot in front of the other Dearlove, off you go. Twenty five thousand a year and no questions asked. Say thank you Dearlove.

Thank you boss, thank you!

That was when the door opened behind him and he knew that Luke was there.

Tyler turned to his brother. They wanted to speak but could not. They were both pale and weak; but their tired faces were showing signs of hope; hope for a new future. Of the start of a new life.

Luke looked up at Tyler with the same sad eyes as those of his thirteen year old self, the day of his parents' funeral, asking his oldest brother the piteous question as to whether his life could now ever be liveable.

"Over there," Luke finally said, "on the other side of the water. Wil I . . . will I survive?"

Tyler realised he'd been staring at Luke as though mesmerised by him. After a long moment he smiled and gave him the only answer he could. The same answer he'd given him years earlier sitting on the side of his bed. "*We* will." He said.

With that no more words were needed. They turned together, an army of two. They were men enough to face what was coming. They were renewed by their brotherhood, strengthened by it, by the blood they shared and the bond reborn.

They began the walk together. Treading their path with the steady cautious courage of soldiers traversing a minefield. Tyler kept his brother close to his side, proud and defiant. At first several men from the crowd only spat. When the first of the missiles, a rock, was thrown at them Tyler wrapped an arm urgently round Luke's neck, pulled his face into the safety of his chest.

With the hurling of the rock a permission was given out and more projectiles were thrown in their direction, bottles, bricks, wood, metal. Tyler took the first hit, a milk bottle smashing on his shoulder and cutting his arm.

As they neared the end of the fence the ferocity of the attack increased. The Molotov cocktails came out in full force. Rags were lit, and petrol filled bottles were thrown, exploding alongside them. Tyler and Luke picked up their pace dramatically, running as best they could. Tyler kept a tight hold on Luke, pulling him along while fending off the array of missiles and, now that the unsteady fence collapsed, punches and kicks that were thrown.

They were close enough now to hear Moses's voice above the chaos. He was shouting something and pointing avidly to their left. They saw it at the same time, breathing out an audible 'oh fuck' simultaneously. It was the Hare's hunting jeep tearing up the lane.

Damien parked clumsily on the roadside. He, Calum and four of their friends bolted out and charged towards the Dearlove brothers. Suddenly the attack was from all directions and insanity came with it as it rose to fever pitch. Fists were flung wildly at them and they flung theirs wildly, blindly back.

The riot was choreographed to a soundtrack of women screaming, children laughing, dogs barking and car alarms sounding from different directions, along with the distant dull beat of garage music from those too drunk to move who had chosen to stick with the party in the shanty town's deeper heart.

Now the opportunists made their move, barging into the makeshift stalls of the traders selling fish and sausages, upending their goods, knocking women to the ground, seizing hold of apron purses stuffed with the collection of money that had been made that day. The traders and their families screamed back in outrage, throwing rocks and punches at their assailants.

Through the chaos Tyler could see Moses getting into his truck and charging through the crowd. He pulled Luke urgently in that direction.

Three men had returned with a new batch of Molotov cocktails. They lit them and hurled them vehemently. But their aim was off. The first smashed beside Calum, lighting his trousers on fire. Damien put his attack on hold and kicked dirt at his brother, putting out the flames. The Hare brothers turned wildly towards the tall thin Albanian who'd hurled it their way, their eyes savage with hate. Damien rushed him and headbutted him, knocking him onto his back.

His neighbouring friends assaulted Damien with a pummelling of fists in return. The rage spread like wildfire. The crowd on the right turning their aggression towards the Hares and their cohorts, who, in turn, seemed to have forgotten that the Dearloves were the only reason they had come, and soon commenced battle with the encircling mob.

Luke and Tyler seized their opportunity. They fought their way through the clan violence, the price on their heads seemingly elapsed. Each side of the island's war forgot their rift with the two brothers and came at each other, loaded up with ire and blood lust. Tyler and Luke clambered out of the anarchy, spilled clumsily into Moses's truck and left them behind to their war.

No one seemed to notice.

Except the boy with the gun.

Tin-Tin broke free from the battle just as Moses sped the Dearloves away and out of sight. His eyes were alive with the madness of those who kill for the killing's sake. Luke had come across his kind many times before, unpredictable, untamed, capricious, deadly. *'I got me all fussied up fellas and I greased my gun. Come on cowboys, fuck with me! Gonna shoot me up this town before sundown.'*

Societies in conflict always have their volatile limits and always one lone wolf who thirsts for violence while others partake of it. The psychopath, who puts on a uniform, grabs a weapon and is only too happy to take on the whole world single handed. The components required for the making of such an animal are complex as a gun and just as deadly.

Tin-Tin watched the Dearloves being carried away to safety and let out a shriek as thin and sharp as a shard of glass and stood in the street shaking with hate as behind him, the battle raged so high it seemed almost able to blot out the sun and half the very sky.

Fifty

Luke and Tyler Dearlove took their one way tickets from the man who should have been their brother.

Luke looked up at Moses with a small nod of gratitude and retreated to the harbour's rocky wall. He sensed that Tyler had been through an experience with this man as intense and life changing as his own had been on the island and wanted to give them their space for a private goodbye. He also wanted to keep his eye on the harbour for the approach of the ferry.

Skidaway Island had already thrown the most nefarious twists of fate their way and he didn't trust it not to send a tidal wave out, just for jokes, to knock the ferry off course, hurtling it east towards Norway, or a megalodon, to rise from the depth of extinction to swallow it whole. But soon enough the white boat sounded its horn and made its appearance, negotiating its clumsy turn over the waves and into the inlet where a line of families were once again giving up their lives and their worlds for distant shores. Luke thought of shouting over the harbour wall at them, imploring them to go back and reclaim what was rightfully theirs, their houses and businesses, and the well of 21st century oil that none of them knew they had been sitting on all these years.

But he knew Tyler couldn't cope with any more acts of half mad heroics, so he would let things be as they were. Fate would have the final say for these people and the only salvation he would worry about now was their own. The ferrymen were throwing the hawser out to the dockers and heaving the boat into port.

They were as good as home.

"You should come with us." Tyler said to Moses. He'd only just thought of it, with no more than a few steps to go before they were finally free of Skidaway Island and could leave it and its stinking secrets behind them.

He thought Moses's eyes would light up with the idea but instead he smiled and shook his head. Tyler could scarcely believe it, his incredulous face betraying his emotions.

"Someone always stays." Moses said, answering his thoughts. "Someone still has to tend to the land."

Tyler sighed, shaking his head. Initially it had been a spur of the moment idea that felt immediately right. Rapidly turning into something Tyler deeply wanted. Despite their beginning the man had become someone he trusted and cared for. He could have shared their home for as long as he needed it. He could have been a lifelong friend.

Tyler kicked at a clump of overgrown plants spilling out of the cracks in the stones beside them. "It's more than I'd ever give to this stinking rock." Tyler said morosely.

Moses immediately put a hand on his chest, ushering him back, as if even his aggression towards the weeds was offensive. "No, no Mr Dearlove," he said with that graceful dignified voice. "Tread softly on this earth. My son lies here."

The words stopped Tyler cold and he understood. He accepted Moses's choice without further question. He nodded once and extended his hand to him.

Moses took the outstretched hand firmly in his own, pulling Tyler into him, whispering into his ear. "Kama vita vinaweza kuanza kwa uongo zinaweza kusimamishwa na ukwelij"

325

Those words, beyond the grasp of Tyler's understanding, when translated from Swahili meant 'If wars can be started by lies. They can be stopped by the truth.'

Tyler cocked his head, bemused. No clue as to the word's translation. He took a wild guess. "Safe journey home?" he asked Moses.

Moses smiled. "Close enough."

With that he turned and walked back to his truck, pausing briefly to shake Luke's hand and bid him farewell.

Tyler watched as he gently touched the side of Luke's face, before getting into his truck and pulling away, kicking up a cloud of earth and dry sand as he left their lives forever.

Below them in the dock the ferry was sounding its horn. This was the smaller of the two ferries that served Skidaway island, this one ran a shuttle service. The passengers were beginning to board now, it wouldn't be long before the small boat would be ready to leave. Luke was standing, waiting for Tyler to join him and head to the port. Tyler looked at him a long moment then turned the other way.

There was somewhere else he wanted to go first.

Fifty One

"The ferry's leaving soon." Luke said to his brother's back.

Tyler had been standing, staring quietly at the sea for ten minutes now. Luke had watched him from the harbour wall. When the queue of those boarding the ferry was down by half Luke clambered down and crossed the beach to him.

Tyler turned his head a mere fraction of an inch and nodded that he'd heard.

"Never took you for someone who stood and stared at the sea." Luke said.

"Who knew?" Tyler replied and kept his eyes on the far off horizon.

When he'd made his way down to the beach the sky had been an aching blue. But now the sea had turned the colour of lead, the sky that of smoke, and between them in the brooding gloom a storm flickered out its 'on-off' promise of arrival like a faulty light.

Luke was surprised Tyler hadn't been yanking at his yoke to leave the island behind.

Now Luke was the one eager to get away from Skidaway's shores. The place had chewed him up and spat him out and with that he'd experienced a rebirth, a promise of a different tomorrow. He had a new life now and was eager to begin it.

"Really," he said to Tyler. "We should go."

"Okay," Tyler said sombrely without turning round. "Just . . . just give me five."

Luke bit his bottom lip to control a smile, dared himself. "You have three." He said sheepishly.

Tyler turned immediately back to him.

Luke lost control of the smirk he was trying keep from his face and it broke into a wide grin.

It was the first time in years Tyler had seen Luke smile. That huge mischievous irrepressible beam he had so loved seeing and had missed so dreadfully.

Tyler smiled back, his melancholic mood suddenly forgotten. Soon the two were smiling together, then giggling, then laughing as though the world was their own. As though never a pain or a problem had passed between them. As though their time on Skidaway Island had been nothing but a stag weekend that had gotten a little crazy, or a camping trip under the sun that had left them the meal of choice for mosquitos, irritating and somewhat painful, but forgotten within hours of returning home.

Tyler shook his head when the laughter finally subsided, his face turning suddenly serious. "How many was it Luke?" He asked. "When you were over there. How many men did you save?"

The smile stayed on Luke's face but there was a sadness in his eyes that was palpable. "Not nearly enough brother." He said softly. "Not nearly enough."

Tyler looked down at Luke, his heart swelling with pride over him. Over all he had done. The paths he had trodden, both there and here. The battles he'd won, and those he'd simply survived.

Suddenly Luke looked vaguely troubled. He scanned the beach ahead with a frown of puzzlement. Something he was seeing over Tyler's shoulder seemed to make no sense. Then, with a sad slow resignation it made perfect, dreadful, sense. It was coming and he knew it.

Some minutes earlier he and his brother had been given an endless stretch of time to walk a new path together. Now, again, fate was robbing them of what it once had promised. Luke looked quickly around the vast expanse of open space about them and realised that the stretch of time they had together had just closed in to a bleak narrow shard. Without time, without hope, he did the only thing he could, gave Tyler the one message he wanted to leave him with the most. "Tyler," he said urgently. "I'll carry you home."

And it was in that same moment that Luke Dearlove died, in much the same way he had been born, suddenly, shockingly, and in his brother's arms.

The mounting growls of thunder had been getting closer with every minute. So when Tin-Tin fired the pistol Tyler had written it off as the boom of the approaching storm. It was only when Luke's head flew fiercely backwards and his whole body jolted so hard that Tyler had to catch him by the shoulders that he realised something was so very wrong.

He looked instinctively behind him as Luke sank to his knees. Tin-Tin's two friends were holding his bike between them up by the opened grated entrance to the catacombs at the foot of the bluff. Meanwhile Tin-Tin was marching vehemently across the sand, the recently fired pistol still smoking in his hand.

Others around them were noticing now, staring in disbelief, finally reacting. Fishermen dropped their rods in the sea and took urgent wading steps their way. Passengers queuing for the ferry stretched up to see over the gate at what was happening on the beach. Drivers clumsily stopped their cars, got out and looked down at the shoreline from the harbour wall.

Tyler turned back to Luke. He still had no idea what had just happened. Then the realisation of it hit him like a train. He felt a crazy urge to laugh. Fate did pick its jokes with impunity. *A step taken an inch to the left instead of the right and a fourteen year old girl wouldn't have stepped on a mine in a field in Angola and lost both her legs above the knee. Walk the long way home instead of using the shortcut down the back alley and the man's not there with a knife to mug you. One more cuddle with your mother.* Give up one self-pitying moment to stand and stare at the sea and the twelve year old boy with the festering wounds in his soul and blood flooded with hate wouldn't be there in time to slam a bullet into your brother's head.

For a moment every thought in his mind disappeared. His skin turned to ice and his throat closed and he began shaking uncontrollably with powerfully overbearing emotions. When he finally did find a way to speak it was only to scream Luke's name.

He shook Luke, trying desperately to rouse him back from death.

"It's ok! You're ok!" He bellowed, shouting above the roar of the waves and the pound of his heart as he tried to reassure himself Luke was only fainted, collapsed.

But how long could he ignore the fact his brother's face had swollen and was now fluid filled and yellow as though he'd been repeatedly punched. Or the carpet of blood that was seeping sluggishly onto the sand. Or the fact that he was holding Luke's brains in his hands as they pulsed out through the gunshot exit wound and accompanying broken section of skull at the back of his head.

"Oh god!" Tyler raged and pulled Luke's limp form tight against his chest. He'd had him back, not five minutes earlier, he'd had him. The boy stuck back together from all his broken parts. He was smiling again. They were on their way home.

Tyler screamed at the injustice, at the utter savagery. He screamed at fate's cruel joke, at death's terrible irreversibility. He screamed for every time he'd misunderstood how war could have left his brother in such ruins. And how many times he'd ignored Luke's explanation of his own unravelling brain, *'You'll never know till you have a man die in your arms.'* Now he knew it. My god. How he knew it now.

Tin-Tin had made it across the beach and was up behind them, pointing the pistol at Tyler. He squeezed the trigger, but the aged mechanisms jammed. He fought with the bolt, trying and failing to send a second bullet into the older one so he could finish off the pair of them.

Tyler rose. He punched Tin-Tin savagely in the face, breaking his nose immediately and knocking him into the surf. He pounced upon him like a dog, pushing down on Tin-Tin's chest as the waves folded over him, blood and screams rising up to the water's surface. "What did you do?" Tyler roared at him. "What did you do?"

Isni and Sokol watched as Tin-Tin lost the upper hand and was now being slowly drowned. They dropped his bike and raced towards to the shoreline, Sokol pulling out his pocketknife.

"What did you do?" Tyler bellowed at Tin-Tin again before realising the boy was near death. He pulled him suddenly out of the waves and cradled him against his chest, rocking him. "It's ok, you're ok."

Dipping in and out of madness he realised it was his brother's murderer he held to his heart. He shook the boy, growled words that made little sense at him, tossed him away, got up onto legs that felt hopelessly drunk on a world that's surface seemed no longer solid and stumbled back to where Luke's body was now gently rolling in the surf.

He held Luke hard against him and barely felt it as Sokol gripped a handful of his hair and began slicing through his hairline with his pocketknife.

Three of the fishermen reached them just as Sokol half scalped Tyler and let off a sickly scream of triumph. They pulled Sokol kicking and screaming back and seized hold of Isni and Tin-Tin, now soaked with sea water and blood.

All Tyler had left of Luke was his death.

He held Luke's lifeless body against him with the same strength as he had held him as a new-born years earlier, and the same vehement desire to never let him go. Half his scalp flapped back and forth in the wind like the broken visor of a baseball cap and blood stained his face red like war paint.

Finally, the brewing storm released its power and rain tore down, violently, uncontrollably, as if the entire island were weeping with shame for everything it had done to them.

Tyler, After

The air that July Thursday was heavy and hot, despite such an overcast, unforgiving sky. It was a monsoon summer day rising against a morning of winter-white.

Tyler sat on the edge of the table in the security control room staff area in a T-shirt and boxer shorts, staring at his Security Guard uniform hanging on the door in front of him.

His reluctance to get dressed into it wasn't down to the sticky oppressive heat. In the months since Luke's death the uniform itself was becoming more and more difficult to wear. A heavy cumbersome weight, like a suit of iron, or sodden clothes you've had on in a swimming pool. Not to mention the itch and scratch of it rubbing against his skin. No matter how many times he washed it, it felt infested, alive with biting fleas.

In the months since Luke's death.

Luke's death.

Those words, and the thought of it still felt insane, illusory, imagined. Too absurd to be real. Even inside his own mind. Strangers, invaders in this life of his, now so brutally reshaped.

He had witnessed it. He had seen Luke's head burst as violently as an exploding sun. Felt his brains in his hands, slippery wet and washed out grey like sea smoothed pebbles.

He had buried him. The papers had reported it, loosely, briefly. 'Former Soldier and War Hero Murdered by Child Migrant'. The country had gasped then yawned. Death gets our attention but not our long-term regret. The forgetful world hurries on.

His friends had offered him beers, nights out, weekends away. He wanted none of it. All he wanted was a listening, understanding ear.

The company had offered him time off, then counselling, as well as plastic surgery for the four-inch scar that ran along his hairline. There was something obscene and ugly about that. That he should take professional help from the organisation he blamed for his brother's murder, almost as much as he blamed the twelve-year-old who'd fired the bullet that had slain him.

He wanted neither them, nor his friends, nor anyone else to persuade him out of his grief. It was all he had left of Luke. Mourning him kept him close. Kept his memory, his life, alive, something that had been real, despite its savage end.

Luke's death had damaged him. Damaged him as war had damaged Luke. The parts were wearing but they hadn't broken yet. He regularly felt the discordant call of what may have been madness reverberating around his brain. The full and total collapse of his mind seemed only ever a heartbeat away. He was like an epileptic, teetering on the edge of a fit, always balancing, always near tumbling.

The internal arguments tormented him through the endless days. Then crept up on him again, night after every night. *Why didn't you get straight on the ferry? Why did you go down to the beach? Why didn't you leave when he said you should? Why didn't you understand, forgive him his pain? Why didn't you set up a camp bed beside him at Belleview, hold his hand through the nights of sickness and insanity? Why the fuck did you ask him why he couldn't just be normal? Why? Why? Why?* A thousand of them punched at the inside of his skull. The same nagging questions to which no answers could ever be produced.

Maybe there are some things we were put on this earth not to know.

It takes a mere second for the life you have to change, to end suddenly, abruptly and leave you with nothing but the shards of what remains, creating a ruined tainted version of yourself to walk among a world that looks at you now and wonders *'Why can't you just be normal?'*

Because I can't Luke, I can't, not now.

Tyler closed his eyes, months on still reeling from the pain of Luke's unending absence. His grief, savage in its persistence, like a biting dog with its jaws locked and teeth sunk into your flesh, was felt over everything. The force of it was as strong as the moon's pull on the tides. As inexplicable and pitiful as was the pain of war's limbless maimed whose nerves still yank and pulse as they search for missing legs and arms and send the agony of what could not be found back to the brain. So Tyler's every nerve and sinew searched hopelessly for a missing brother, and returned only the unyielding pain of what was missing, what was lost.

He knew that he could no longer reach him. Not even the smell of him on his bedroom sheets. No ferry could be taken, no stretch of water could be crossed. No battle, however brutal, however bloody, could be fought and endured in order that he might get the chance to bring his brother back home. As the months went on he feared even the memory of his face might vanish. Pass into nothingness. Become lost somewhere at sea.

But all that was lost was already out at sea. Lost with the other things. The parts of Tyler himself that were decomposed and drifted away. Floating along the tide with Luke's blood and leaving him brotherless, alone. A veteran, savaged by war. Shell-shocked and ruined. An amputee.

Tyler opened his eyes again and looked once more at the uniform he was to wear, perhaps for the rest of his life. The same uniform Howie had once worn. As had Luke. The uniform that, had Luke lived, the only way he'd have worn it now would have been if they'd nailed it to his back.

Had Luke lived.

Tyler wanted to close his eyes again, collapse under the weight of his own shame. But he couldn't. He was Tyler Dearlove, a hard worker, an ordinary man. He did as he was told and wore what they provided and kept his head down for twenty five thousand a year and no questions asked. Say thank you Tyler.

'Thank you boss, thank you.'

He was about to slip off the edge of the table and get reluctantly dressed when his colleague, Mark Neville, came bustling in through the door carrying a uniform of a different kind.

Fifty Two

Tyler fidgeted in the tuxedo as the limo brought him up outside the Monument Hotel.

He'd forgotten that the 7th was the date of the Awards Ceremony and that, in the raw agonising days after he'd come home with Luke's body, the Company had suggested he collect the 'Champions of Britain' hero award posthumously for his brother.

He vaguely remembered agreeing, possibly just to make Mark Neville from HR stop talking and go away.

Why they had to have a full dress rehearsal breakfast for it that norming he had no idea. Although he did know enough about his Company to know they left nothing to chance.

The hotel concierge opened the limo door for him and he climbed awkwardly out, fussing with the shirt's stiff collar.

He noticed the homeless man before anything else. Before the Monument Hotel's stunning architecture, before the strange spectacle of others there for the rehearsal striding around a London street in full evening dress at nine in the morning.

The vagrant was no more than sixty, sitting amid his meagre camp with a wiry little terrier-mix dog for a friend, their home was an alleyway at the side of the hotel. His thick curly hair and full beard was still a younger man's jet black. His eyes, just as dark, were soul boringly penetrative, as though they'd lived a thousand years. Just as Luke always recognised another military man in the few short years after he left service, so now Tyler recognised the vagabond as a man who'd been a soldier once. He remembered Luke telling him how every soldier knew another when he saw one. He knew he didn't belong in their company – those men of

337

whom our nation is so proud. Maybe he'd simply picked up his brother's mantle.

They regarded each other in the sultry morning air. Their faces expressionless, their bodies still, and yet some strange unspoken message seemed to be passing between them.

He thought of the words Moses had left him with. Words spoken in a language not of his own. A message he could never pick apart, unravel, understand. And yet that unknown message, those words, had stayed with him since.

The concierge ushered Tyler towards the building's grand front entrance doors and the homeless man sniffed back the air, pulled at the fraying camouflage jacket he wore despite the heat, and swallowed his breakfast from a dented can of beer.

"I was certain you would come."

Chelsey Muldowney said and bent towards Tyler, planting firm cold kisses on each of his cheeks.

For a moment he wondered if she'd mistaken him for someone else. However she soon followed up with; "Francis kept telling me you'd chosen not to. But as I said to him if there's one thing we can always rely on Tyler Dearlove for it's devotion and loyalty."

"That's two things." said Tyler.

Chelsey laughed a strange humourless laugh. "We'll take loyalty."

She loomed above him in her stilettoes, her heavily made up face hanging in the air like a mask. The blonde French twist that rose prominently into a pile of curls pinned atop her head, gave her another inch of height.

Tyler felt small and pathetic in front of her. As he had the only other time she'd ever looked his way. It was at the previous year's Christmas party. Several of his workmates had convinced him she'd been telling a few of the P.A.s that she'd spotted him around the building and taken a liking to what she'd seen. Charged up with confidence on a belly full of beer and a few whisky shots, plus his friends enthused encouragement, he'd drunkenly stumbled over to the scorching hot blonde and offered to buy her a drink. She'd looked him up and down with a derisive sneer before telling him to save his money and pointing out that the company had laid on a free bar for the masses that night. She'd then abruptly turned her back on him and continued her conversation with the group of big wigs around her.

Now she was looking at Tyler as though he were the only man left on earth.

She cast her eye over the scar on Tyler's forehead, tidied his hair to help cover it. "It's healing nicely."

She stood back and admired his tuxedo, smoothing down the sleeves and brushing away specks of dust like a teenager readying her date before prom. Her eyes went to his collar and registered disapproval.

"I couldn't wear the bowtie." Tyler immediately offered. "The clasp was broken."

Chelsey frowned with a *'this will never do'* expression and beckoned a nearby cocktail waiter over with her finger and without explanation or justification began loosening his bowtie until she could unknot it and pulled it from his neck.

The waiter, who was probably no more than nineteen, and terrified of losing his first ever job, blushed as he spoke to her. "Miss Muldowney, our manager told us to be in full dress this morning."

"Who's your manager? Frank? Eddie?" Chelsey asked with the raised tone and confidence of a stage actress.

"Peter." The young man replied.

"Peter!" Chelsey acquiesced "Well, now you tell Peter that Chelsey said it would be okay."

She pulled a fifty pound note out of her purse and tucked it in his top pocket.

The young waiter looked down at her actions, his face aghast.

"Oh don't look so shocked." Chelsey said. "We all need a little corruption. Just to grease the wheels."

Chelsey took Tyler's arm and lead him across the lobby towards a spot where posters advertising the Awards Ceremony were being placed.

"There's an opening in Executive Services that's come up and we thought of you." She said. "It's twice the responsibility and three times the salary. There is some red tape - what with the confidential information that crosses that desk but it shouldn't be a problem. As Francis and I both told the Board, there aren't many people we trust to keep our secrets as much as you." She let go his arm and looked at him. "What do you say?"

"I don't know what to say." Tyler replied.

She smoothed out the shoulders of his jacket. "Your brother would be so proud of you."

Tyler eyed her suspiciously. "Would he?" He finally replied.

She reached up and pulled his hair further over his forehead to help cover the scar. "There. Now no one will ever know."

A colleague beckoned for her attention. Chelsey motioned for Tyler to wait one moment and sauntered off to speak to him.

Alone, Tyler's eyes meandered around the hotel's lobby. The place was clearly built just after the First World War and its interiors designed as a tribute to those who had fallen.

On this day however, what had been created to honour the war dead was being temporarily obliterated by the Company's overpowering efforts to showcase the Awards Ceremony for the planned filming that evening.

Tyler pushed aside one of their hanging posters and revealed a set of sepia toned photographs of young soldiers of that era, set within a glass display case. Other than the picture of a Colonel in full dress, sporting a large moustache that curled up mischievously at each of its ends, the soldiers were all lads, Luke's age and much younger.

Their faces were strangely familiar to Tyler. Maybe because they all looked as bright, as shining with pride, and as hopeful as Luke had been on the day of his Passing Out Parade. Maybe because all soldiers share a common experience. These millions of the mouthless dead. Off to find an honourable end in the boot sucking mud. To unknowingly, obediently, innocently, slay other boys from other countries of their own age. To react with human emotion and fear and be labelled *'a coward with thy tail between thy legs'*. To cower and shake on a floor and spurn a new term 'shell-shock'. A term that even when, a century later would be renamed 'post-traumatic stress disorder', would still be derided and misunderstood.

To become the muse of poets and the shame of a generation.

Tyler's eyes skated down to the lines engraved on a bronze plaque beneath them:

I am hurt but I'm not broken

I am sore wounded but I'm not slain

341

I will lay me down and bleed a while

And then rise and fight with you again

Tyler looked back to the face of the smiling Colonel with the twisting moustache. His smile seemed to be just for Tyler. He gazed knowingly out at the hotel lobby as though for the past hundred years he had sat there, silently observing the absurdities of human life. Tyler bent in and could almost hear him breathing.

He looked back to the rows of young boys seated below him.

'Don't look for me to be a hero.' He begged them in the privacy of his mind. 'I'm just an ordinary man. I'm just a brother with grief inside his bones.'

Tyler sighed, and the words grew louder inside his own head. 'I'm Tyler Dearlove, an ordinary man, I like my friends, I like my beer and I like my job. I do as I'm told and wear what I'm told and keep my head down for twenty five thousand a year. It's not much but it'll work. It'll work like I do. Say thank you Tyler.'

The young soldiers looked at him from their sepia hued photographs. Quietly waiting.

'Say thank you Tyler'

Tyler breathed deeply.

'Fuck you boss. Fuck you!'

Fifty Three

Chelsey flew from the hotel doors, nearly tripping on her heels as she rushed down the hotel's entrance steps and stopped short on the pavement. Ignoring the bemused glances from pedestrians, wondering why an irate looking woman was wearing a full evening gown at 9.15 on a Thursday morning. Her eyes scanned the street for any sign of Tyler.

"Where is he?" She demanded of the concierge who shook his head numbly.

She'd expected to find him right where she left him, obediently waiting like a basset hound. Irritation mounting, she'd gone back to that glass display case he'd been so fascinated by. But he was neither there, nor anywhere else in the hotel lobby. She began gathering a host of bemused looks, her subordinates weren't used to seeing her ruffled, they stole quick peeks at her while carrying out their duties, whispered about her to each other behind cupped hands.

One more person looked her way and she'd knock them into next week. That was when she caught sight of the Colonel, peering at her and smirking, smirking in a sepia photograph within the display case on the wall, his grin barely hidden by the ridiculous curling moustache. She glared at his image, picked up the length of her dress and hurried for the doors.

The useless doorman was just as infuriating. What the hell did he have to do that prevented him answering one simple question? She was about to again demand he tell her where Tyler had gone to when she noticed his tuxedo jacket. It was being worn with pride by some stinking tramp with dark curly hair, an unkempt dark curly beard and an equally unkempt dark curly rat-like dog at his side. He smoothed down the lapels of the tuxedo with monumental pride, spotted Chelsey watching him, clapped his hands together, pointed her way then performed a little jig with much satisfaction.

She glowered at him and turned on the spot, searching for any sign of Tyler among the early morning tourists ambling about and the office workers, pushing passed her to start their day.

343

Fifty Four

Tyler drew a deep breath and listened to the thump of his heart as he thundered down the high street. Suddenly he felt like a man who deserved the salute of the nation.

He tore the bowtie from his neck, breaking the clasp and threw it into the gutter in the side of the street.

It felt like the rescue of his sanity to be able to rise and gaze out at the world again. This was the beginning of the gradual renewal of a man, his passing from one world to another, the start of a new story that's ending was not known.

He was sure he could feel Luke willing him on from the side lines. Certain that if he looked up into the huge white summer sky, he would see him placing large coloured letters up there as a message just for him, 'You are a sight to see.'

He would take them on. He would tackle the darkness. He would call them thieves, murderers and liars. And if he had to fall, he would fall like a thunderbolt.

They were closing the heavy iron gates across the nearest tube station just as he reached it. *Fuck that too.* That wasn't going to stop him. Not now. He would walk all the way if he had to. Or get on a bus. He hadn't been on one in years. He'd feel like a schoolboy again. Giddy and free. He'd ride the top deck. As well as a brain flooded with adrenaline, he had the youthful energy and vigour of a child within him.

He passed the small crowd, gathering round the firmly shut gates to the underground station, berating their contempt to each other and the tube worker who'd had the misfortune of being the one to lock them out and prevent them their journeys.

'*Miss work,*' thought Tyler. '*Who gives a crap? Count yourselves lucky for once.*' The line at the bus stop stretched around the corner and into the next street. But luck was with him now, the trade wind in his sails. A number 30 rattled up and most of the queue piled on. As it pulled away Tyler saw a second number 30 approach. He picked up his step, marching to it with a hunger for life gnawing inside him.

As he neared the bus stop, he pulled out his wallet. His Company security pass was next to his travel pass. He tossed it into the bus stop's rubbish bin and followed the other passengers on board.

He rode the top deck like a man who owned the world. As the bus jogged bumpily along its way Tyler revelled in the sense of freedom. It was like the first day of a school summer holiday. Exams were over, and an endless stretch of adventure awaited.

The bus made a turn and ground to a sudden stop. Tyler glanced out of the window. The traffic was bad, even for a London rush hour. No matter, he would get there, eventually.

He pulled out his wallet, fished in the tenants until he found the picture of Luke at the harbour on Skidaway Island, turned it over, reached for his mobile and dialled the number on the back.

"We'll send a car for you." Detective Kier O'Bannon said on the other end of the line.

"That's ok, I'm halfway there." Tyler replied, struggling to see out of the bus windows at the insanely unusual build-up of traffic, more tube stations were being closed and locking passengers out. This was going to be one of those crazy London days.

"You're doing the right thing." O'Bannon reassured him.

Tyler smiled a small quiet smile to himself, turning over the picture and staring at Luke's winsome face.

"Are you sure we can't send you a car?" O'Bannon asked again.

The bus jerked and bumped slowly forwards like a lumbering animal. "That's ok" Tyler said, "I'm on a bus just coming into Tavistock Square. I'm as good as there."

"We'll see you soon." O'Bannon said before hanging up.

Tyler put his wallet and phone back in his pocket and glanced round at his fellow passengers. While he'd been on the phone the bus driver had come to the upper deck, explaining about a power surge causing havoc to the transport network and advising passengers they may prefer to alight here and walk.

Half remained, as did Tyler.

Ah well, he'd get there soon enough.

The newspaper discarded on the seat next to him caught his attention, David Beckham and Kelly Holmes beaming excitedly under the headline 'London to Host the 2012 Olympics in 7 years'. Tyler's face broke into a smile. "We did it." He said. "We won." He nodded to the paper and a passenger getting up to move downstairs.

"Where've you been?" the passenger asked. "That's yesterday's news."

"Good news always is." Tyler said quietly in reply with a sad smile.

The bus jerked clumsily along on its slow journey.

Why, why, why? A thousand of them. They'd banged around his head for so long now that Tyler felt empowered, enlivened, to finally be able to let a few go. The world wasn't always kind. It didn't always bestow, it often took. It bit the good and the honest, just as Skidaway Island had bitten him and Luke. Asking the world to treat you fairly because you're a good person was like asking a shark not to eat you because you're a vegetarian. The word 'why' had to be closed to the last chapter of his life now. It would destroy him, slowly drive him insane if he let it. There were some things in life it was just better not to know.

He had no idea why one of them hadn't asked for one more cuddle with their mother and taken back the thirty seconds that would have saved both their parents' lives. He had no idea why he'd so needed time alone staring at the sea rather than getting on the ferry straight away with Luke and saving them from the murderous onslaught that changed the course of their existence. Turn right instead of left and the guy's not waiting in the alley with a knife to mug you. One inch to left and the girl in a field in Angola doesn't step on a land mine and lose both her legs.

If he'd got there earlier, later, walked, taken a different bus, gotten off this one when the driver suggested it, fate wouldn't have placed him in the seat directly opposite the suicide bomber who, unbeknown to Tyler, had tried and failed to detonate the bomb in his rucksack on the underground twenty minutes earlier. Equally unbeknown to him was that fifty two lives would be claimed that morning, in what was to become the worst act of atrocity and largest loss of British life through terrorist activity since the September 11th attacks four years previous.

Tyler looked at the young man sitting in the seat opposite him, hugging the large black rucksack to his chest as though his life depended on it.

Suddenly the man seemed to know someone was watching him and turned his large brown eyes Tyler's way.

They faced each other and something seemed to be understood on both sides.

How else would death call you?

Tyler felt a sense of calm. A knowing. Suddenly things were clear and accepted. That ancient god who'd told him he would make it through the night on Moses Bogdani's kitchen floor was now saying to him 'today.'

Slowly, Tyler Dearlove closed his eyes, knowing when he opened them again his brother would be standing there, quietly waiting to carry him home.

For those who lived

Those we lost

And those they left behind

Printed in Great Britain
by Amazon